Take a Bow

The Perfect Plans Series

C.J. Wells

Take a Bow (The Perfect Plans Series #2)
By C.J. Wells

Warning: MATURE CONTENT
Content contains sexually explicit material and is intended for mature individuals over the age of eighteen. By downloading this book, you are stating that you are of legal age to access and view this work of fiction.

Cover Illustration Copyright 2014 Jill Syed Photography
Cover Model: Colin Herder

PUBLISHING HISTORY
C.J. Wells Paperback Edition / December 2014
C.J. Wells Publishing 2014
Take a Bow / C.J. Wells
The Canadian ISBN Service System (CISS)
ISBN: 978-0-9937485-7-8

Fiction – Contemporary Erotic Romance
www.cjwells.org / info@cjwells.org

PRAISE FOR
The Perfect Plans Series

"A pure fairytale fantasy for grown ups that's heavy on the hot-as-sin celebrity who falls in obsession, possession, and lust for-ever-after with our lucky heroine."

- Smokin' Hot Book Blog

"Alexander Tate. That could actually be a verb. He *Alexander-Tated* me."

- For the Love of Books & Alcohol Blog

"C.J. Wells wove this story seamlessly with great characters and fantastic writing."

- Andrea Joan, Author

"Beautiful, creative writing...written in a style that is a mixture of romantic prose and contemporary work."

- KL Shandwick, Author

"C.J. Wells brings us a story of make-believe, but makes it feel so real, it could happen to any one of us."

- Tracey Podger, Author

"This is a well-written, addictive romance."

Salem Archer, Author

"Simply Brilliant...Drama, humor, romance, lust, and ultimately love. Fabulously written...full of twists and turns."

- Imy Santiago, Author

"Will thoroughly captivate you...offers romance at its best

and a very sexy, erotic, and capitivating story line."

"An outstanding romance that tugs at your heart strings and never lets go!"

"C.J. Wells hits it out of the park with a home run...Witty, humorous and boldy written. The sex scenes are even HOTTER! You'll need a tall drink to cool you off...BRAVO!"

"I enjoyed it from the very start and was totally hooked and swooning over Alex and all his hotness. He tugged at your heart-strings and left you waiting for more."

"Funny, witty, charming, HOT, I mean REALLY HOT (you may need more than a few cold showers while reading), and emotional. The way the Authors describe the emotions, the expressions of each character, made me feel like I was there in person witnessing it."

Also by the author

Perfect Plans (The Perfect Plans Series Book #1)

This is dedicated to perfect love...
Just two imperfect people who refuse to give up
on each other.

CHAPTER One

"**Y**OU LEFT ME bound to the life you left behind, trying like hell to figure out how to live without you. It seems you still have all of me, Aby," he says with a sad smile. "It's taken a long time, struggling to figure out how to live my life alone. But throughout these months, I've come to realize that even though you were *with* me all that time, I was alone all along anyway. I will learn to let you go. Eventually. But you will always have a part of my heart. Always."

"I'm so sorry, Liam," I whisper, unsure what I can say to extinguish his ever-present hurt, regardless of his stoic admittance. After spending a good portion of your life with someone, gauging happiness and pain becomes second nature. *Unless you're a good actor, of course. Something for which Liam has never been good at*, I note, taking measure of his charming face, tilted down, staring at his lap. I can see his pain masked behind a slight edge of bravado and acceptance. No matter how much you succumb to it, or how right the reasons, I can admit that we've both lost something special.

Liam's gaze darts to mine at my pleading apology and I reel further in my envelope of shame and regret. "No, don't. I don't need your apology. We were both living a lie - both of us wanting, needing, something more. *I* should be apologizing to you. I held you back, I see that now. I think I even did it knowingly out of fear that you'd leave me."

Wow. This is so surreal. The man sitting across from me is not the Liam that I knew so well. He's a man who's clearly grown since the demise of our marriage. He's calmer, more reflective. It's a beautiful thing to watch.

He looks as handsome as ever. His short brown hair casually styled, his bright blue eyes warm despite the pain they reflect. I'm almost tempted to reach out and run my fingers along his slight stubble - a kneejerk reaction after so many years together.

"It's okay, though," he continues, grabbing my hand with a gentle squeeze. "I'm fine, Abs. Great, actually." He offers a small grin. "It took a while, but I've finally started to turn my life around. I even bought a bike."

"That's wonderful, you've always wanted one." I'm elated to see the splash of pain quickly fade from his gaze, replaced with boyish excitement.

"Yeah, it's pretty cool. I'm leaving next week, touring through the States. Might make my way to the west coast and stay awhile. Find someplace nice in L.A."

"Good for you, Liam. I know you've always dreamt of traveling through California. You must be excited to go."

"No kidding," he laughs, looking down at his hands in his lap once more. "I'm excited, and thankful."

"Thankful?"

"Thankful to you," his gaze returns to mine, "...for finally knocking some sense into me. For pushing me to live out my *own* dreams as well."

I lower my head shyly, not quite sure what to say as I sit across from my now ex-husband, the signed divorce papers like a beacon on the table in front of us. I feel completely overcome, overwhelmed that the man who was once my *everything*, whom I left brokenhearted in my search for more, is now thanking me for giving him *his* freedom. Who knew that such a tragic story could turn out so fulfilling?

Yet the irony is lashing. I'm back in my hometown, having walked away from my freedom, *my* dreams - discarded back in England - while Liam is now off to fulfill his. My penance perhaps?

"Say something," he pushes.

"I'm not sure what to say," I look up to him. "I'm happy for you. It makes me happy to know you're happy. I truly never meant to hurt you."

"I know, Abs. And I'm not going to lie and say that you didn't. You did. But I realize now that everything is the way it should be. We can both fight for the life we're meant to have," he pauses, offering a gentle smile, seemingly filled with thought. "I see you've snagged yourself a hot-shot boyfriend," he jokes halfheartedly.

Ugh... the media gossip. Of course he's seen the images of Alex and I by now. I wince at the reminder of Alexander Tate, the incredible, sexy actor - the man of so many women's fantasies. The wonderful man I left behind in London without a word.

"Ummm...not quite. The jury's still out on that one," I attempt to act casual, though I'm trembling a little. The remembrance of Julia's warning that inevitably Liam would be pulled into that media bullshit...I can't even think about it again. Not right now. "Things are a little up in the air," I offer at Liam's questioning gaze. "It's...difficult," I add, a cold shiver running down my spine, Alex's own words blasting through me like an arctic wind, *'It can be...difficult'*.

"Oh," he nods, his hands clasped, dangling between his wide spread legs. "Well, don't give up too easily, Abs. You need to fight for what you want. You taught me that," he adds, apparently seeing through my act of bravado, if not pretending to. I really can't be sure if I can fool anyone anymore, Liam included.

Oh, Liam, if you only knew...what I walked away from, and why. I can't even believe I'm here, back in Toronto, having this conversation with him. Never in a million years did I expect us to be so cordial to each other after all that's transpired. Talking of dreams, boyfriends, and freedom. Especially after sitting together in comfortable silence, signing our divorce papers. What a shock to my system.

"I should go," he stands from the sofa.

I'm unable to form a reply as I watch him pick up a copy of the papers and fold them in his hands. I simply follow suit as he makes his way to the door.

At this moment I realize, *this is it*. All of our wonderful times, meaningful moments together come crashing back to me in a flurry. A whirlwind of emotion rushes over me as I begrudgingly follow him, mentally preparing myself to say goodbye. In this brief instant, our life together flashes before my eyes - Liam and I in Mexico, sunbathing under the warmth of the heated sun; smiling at him on our wedding day as his huge smile beams at me from his place at the altar; our day-to-day normalcy of a seemingly happy existence. I'm struck completely speechless, my eyes filling with unshed tears.

I know deep down that my inner turmoil is heightened all the more by what I've left behind in London. Alex. My dream world. Although, in the end, it wasn't much of a dream world was it? The grass may appear greener, but it's full of fertilizer. Full of shit that I couldn't trudge through.

Reaching the door, Liam turns to look down at me, a melancholy expression donning his face. "I love you, Aby. I will always love you," he says, pulling me into his arms.

"I love you too," I whisper against his chest, a tear finally slipping down my cheek as I absorb his familiar scent. This is the closure we've both needed - the final stamp for us to move forward towards our freedom, our dreams. I can't help but feel a weight lifting off my shoulders. It's comforting to know that my walking away didn't cause irreparable damage to a friendship I hope to maintain for the rest of my life.

Releasing me, he reaches for the door. "Good luck, Abs. I hope every one of your dreams come true," he offers with a sweet, yet morose, smile.

"You too. Good luck on your road trip. Stay safe," I add - our long used term whenever we'd leave each other.

"Always," he smiles sweetly in remembrance of our favorite parting words, opening the door to exit Stacey's apartment. His one final look speaks a thousand words - our final goodbye.

Grabbing my arm to pull me onto the front stoop, he takes me in a final lingering embrace as though reluctant to leave so quickly. His blue eyes sparkle with kind love above his handsome smile when he finally lets me go.

I smile in return - a smile filled with love, thankfulness, and hope, though my heart aches a little. I watch him step onto the landing before suddenly stopping dead in his tracks.

Shielding my eyes from the bright morning sun, I look past him to see what's halted his departure, losing my breath at the sight of Alex, looking ashen standing at the bottom of the stairs.

Oh my God. What is he doing here? I stare shocked, my lips parted in the sudden strangling awe, taking in Alex's real-life form as he regards Liam and I with curiosity. His clothes are a wrinkled mess, his hair in disarray above his beautifully sculpted face covered in seemingly day's old stubble, if not older. He looks tired and more than a little annoyed, yet still has the ability to take my breath away.

My heartbeat lodges in my throat. I never would have imagined he would show up here. Certainly not after I so abruptly left London without a word. No note of good-bye, no explanation. Though I have no idea what he's thinking as he stares up at us, I can only assume he's imagining the worst, watching me bid farewell to another man.

In the stunned silence, I note Liam's body tense and stammer slightly - a testimony to his ongoing struggles with jealousy, regardless of whether we're divorced or not. I'm suddenly in the eye of a hurricane and a flying fucking cow just hit me in the gut. What are the odds of this shit? As my jumbled head ricochets between both men, I'm unable to formulate a coherent thought. How exactly does one handle this? Should I introduce them? *"Man I discarded, allow me to introduce you to other man I discarded..."*

"You want me to stay, Abs?" Liam asks, looking back to me briefly before locking his firm gaze back on Alex.

I note Alex's eyebrow quirk at the question, his head tilting mechanically, betraying his gentlemanly composure.

"No, I'm okay," I manage, pulling my gaze from Alex. "Thank you for stopping by. Thank you for...everything." I attempt to smile reassuringly when Liam finally looks back towards me.

He offers a small resigned pull of his lips before he turns from me to amble down the stairs, taking slow measured steps making his way towards Alex, still standing unmoving.

Can you say AWKWARD?

Reaching the bottom, he stops abruptly, turning to face Alex dead on. *Oh shit, what is he going to do?*

Their tall, strong frames are locked and cocked in an alpha-aura of male dominance like some He-Man showdown in the ready. "Don't hurt her," I hear Liam warn, brushing past Alex to continue on. I exhale a breath of relief as he walks away, not naïve that under normal circumstances, the Liam I know would have said and done more.

Looking back to Alex, I note his clenched jaw, quickly averting my gaze to watch Liam drive away. I purposely delay the inevitable confrontation, my eyes peeled to Liam's Chevy truck as he maneuvers out of the parking lot, before succumbing to look back down the stairs into the eyes of the man I've fallen in love with. I'm torn between wanting to rush into his arms to wrap myself tightly around him, and blinking to make sure he's really here in front of me. My shattered heart isn't braced for the impact his unexpected presence is pummeling into my system. I wasn't prepared to see him yet. My broken body isn't strong enough. I can't speak.

I'm not sure what to read in his eyes as he walks slowly up the steps towards me, but he looks pissed - his gaze unwavering, holding me hostage. Reaching the landing, his sparkling blue eyes bore into mine as he brushes past me, walking into the apartment.

I feel like a child about to be spanked. A week ago, such a notion involving Alex might have been excitingly delicious. Right now? Not so much. Taking a deep breath of composure, I follow him inside and close the door, resting my forehead momentarily against the wood before turning to face the obvious wrath he came to bestow. I summon the courage to lift my head and face him with confidence, only to lose my breath once more at the sight of him, his incredible body tightened below the clenched jaw of his gorgeous face.

"I'm sensing a trend here, Aby," he begins, the venomous rasp of his voice both staggering and foreign, "…it seems that whenever I get off of a plane to come to you, I find you with another man."

Oh shit. He brought the big guns.

I bite my tongue despite his sarcastic venom hitting all of my defensive buttons. I deserve his anger, though I'm breaking inside at the sight of it. His presence at this moment is sucking up all the air in the room. I'm struggling to breathe.

"Maybe I should learn to fucking call first," he adds with additional bite.

Yeah, that would actually be really good. I would absolutely be much more prepared right now to deal with this adolescent-like scolding. However, I think it best I opt to keep that thought to myself. No need to add fuel to his ever-raging fire.

Taking another deep breath, I aim for deflection - the mind-boggling question behind his shocking arrival - while I attempt to portray a shield of strength to cover my somewhat trembling façade, "Why did you come here, Alex?"

"Brilliant question," he replies sharply before a flicker of pain flashes through his stonewall exterior. "I'm not exactly sure myself, right now," he begins a slow pace, running his fingers through his mane of brown curls.

Oh God, don't do that! Hell, what difference does it make? *Everything* he does brings me to my knees. "Did you come all this way just to vent? If that's the case, I'll take it."

Stopping dead in his tracks, he turns his malevolent gaze to me in frustration. "Vent? You think I came all this way to vent? Chase you down even though you left me without a fucking word? Which, I might add, was fucking great news to receive from your *neighbor boy*."

I close my eyes in shame, unable to imagine how awful that must have been. Knowing how Alex feels about my London neighbor, Andrew, I cringe at the thought that he had to find out about me leaving that way.

Andrew had been a breath of fresh air for me, someone I'd grown to consider a friend in the short time since I'd moved into my flat. But Alex's opinion of him varied, to say the least. How sour it must have tasted for Alex, knowing I'd told Andrew I was leaving, yet kept him in the dark.

Shivering, I recall the many awkward occasions between Alex and Andrew over the last month. Regardless of how innocent my interactions with Andrew may have been, I'm not naïve to the fact that, at that moment, Alex must have felt even more betrayed.

"No, *Aby*, you have Stacey to thank for my being here," he adds, the way my name spits from his beautiful lips sending shivers down my spine.

Sucking in a breath, I stare perplexed. "What? What are you talking about?"

His quick, lashing snicker burns my flesh, "It seems your friend was under the impression that you'd made a mistake, but clearly she's confused. You obviously have yet to share that you're reuniting with Liam."

"No, Alex," I shake my head. "You've misunderstood. Liam was here to sign the divorce papers. I'm not getting back together with him." Though I sense a possible flicker of relief in his eyes, his countenance remains unchanged as he harshly takes a seat on the sofa, his angry eyes avoiding my direct gaze. "I'm sorry you thought…I'm sorry, Alex."

"You're sorry?" he looks up towards me, his glare blasting my already shattered heart. "What are you sorry for? For leaving me when you promised you wouldn't? Or for saying nothing before you left?"

His words are like a punch to my gut and I struggle to find a reply. "I'm just sorry…for everything," I offer, knowing my response is inadequate. I'm not sure what else to say as he continues to stare at me, an angry, yet baffled, expression donning his face. Time stands still, akin to an eerie break in the storm, a fleeting calm in the midst of the hurricane allowing you to run for cover or brace yourself for the impending destruction. I attempt to formulate my thoughts as he pulls his gaze from mine to look down into his lap once more. "Alex, when I left a week ago…"

His head darts up towards me, crazed pain etched in his eyes and tone, "A week ago? It's been nine fucking days!"

"I..." *Shit.* I don't even know what to say. When I left, the only thing I knew was that I had to get away...to sort through everything that was happening. I hadn't stopped to think about how long that would take.

"When I realized you were gone, my world crumbled, Aby."

I have to turn away from the penetration of his pain-filled eyes, looking down at my fumbling hands, my fingers intertwining. The momentary break of his gaze gives me the strength I need to hold it together, though my defensive tendencies are poisoning my composure. "How do you expect me to believe that, when you just admitted you're only here because of Stacey?" As the question leaves my lips, I shudder at the selfishness of it at the hands of my own insecurities.

"Believe? Aby, I've *never* lied to you." He stands and walks towards me. "For once, can *you* be honest with me and tell me why you left? I need to know."

Looking up towards him once more, his piercing baby-blues locked searchingly onto mine tests every ounce of my composure, my guilt. "Alex, I left...the way I left. I tried to tell you, that night..."

"The night I made love to you?" his interruption jars me momentarily, the words stabbing me in the chest. I flinch and he closes his eyes as though sensing his impact on me before he opens them quickly, once again veiled in angry hurt.

"What I was trying to tell you was that I needed time...time to figure everything out."

His eyebrow quirks in disgust, "No, Aby. You told me you thought you should go. And I recall my pathetic attempts at begging you to explain why."

"Yes! And you weren't hearing me when I attempted to tell you!" I blurt in desperation. "Why do you think I gave in? Stayed that night only to leave once you were gone in the morning?" Frozen in his fury, he's either waiting for me to continue or unable to fathom an answer to my seemingly ridiculous question. "I couldn't even allow myself to try to leave a note...that..."

"That what? Would have meant being honest if only on paper, at least?"

"You're putting words in my mouth. I don't expect you to understand why I left the way I did, but I thought you'd somehow understand what I was trying to deal with…"

"*Deal* with? Is life with me something you have to try to deal with, Aby?"

"No-yes. You're twisting my words."

"Am I? It doesn't even hold a candle to how you reached into my chest and twisted my fucking heart out."

Silence. Painful, torturing silence. Fleeting glances - pain, regret…hope.

"I know I was wrong to leave without a word. I was so very wrong. I tried to tell you, but," I close my eyes, opening them quickly to continue before he interrupts me again, "…if I sat down to write you a note, I wouldn't have been able to go through with it."

"It?" he spits.

"Leaving," the word escapes on a cowering shiver. "I know I would have broken down again and stayed. But why I left…the reasons, I thought you would at least understand where they were coming from. You said…"

"I know what I said," the bite in his words matches his glare. "I also know what *you* said. You said that you would never run. Fuck, Aby. What I feel for you is burning me alive, and you fucking walked away. You fucking *ran* away! Because of the media… my public life? Maybe even because of Ben," he winces, recovering quickly in his anger. "Hell, maybe you ran from Julia's backlash."

He runs his fingers through his curls and I shiver at his unknowing accuracy - Julia's attempt to run me off. The image of her smiling at the idea that *she* was the reason I left, burns through me like lava. I guess I handed that to her on a silver platter. But I left for *me*, not just for Alex. As if I believed for one second that her use of Alex as her reasoning for wanting me gone was ever genuine.

"Answer me. Is that why you left?"

"Yes…No…" I shake my head, trying to find the right

words.

"Yes *and* no? Jesus Christ. Do you even know the answer? Maybe you just left without a word because you were too much of a coward to tell me it was over."

"I'm not a coward!"

"No? What would you call it? Enlighten me, Miss Ryan. Tell me you didn't leave because you were too much of a coward to tell me I wasn't what you needed. Wanted."

Oh, God. "Is that what you think? Alex, I left *for* you…and, for…me." I reach for him and he flinches from my touch. My heart drops beneath my stolen breath and I swallow the lump in my throat, my hand falling back to my side. "When I met you, I walked into a fantasy. You…*you* are my fantasy. But it comes with a reality I wasn't prepared for, as much as I thought I could be…for you. I wanted to be strong for you, but when things turned so quickly, I-I needed to take the time to figure everything out. Everything was happening so fast. I just needed to…"

"*Figure everything out*?" His sarcastic tone is cutting.

"Yes."

"For me…*and* for you?" he tilts his head in his condescending stance.

"Yes."

"And yet, I have to stand here and spell out for you how one sided that is? 'Me' and 'you' - that's *us*, Aby! I will not be what Liam was to you."

"What the hell does that mean?" I snap.

"You spent your entire relationship hiding your feelings from him. I guess I should be thankful that you chose an alternate escape for me, should I?"

"Alex…I just needed time…" I rein in my defenses against his earned vengeance.

"And have you had enough? Time?" Again, the bite behind his words is lethal.

"I-I don't know."

"You don't know? Well let me tell you what *I* know. I'm sure as hell not going to let you do to us what you did to your relationship with Liam. You don't get to run away and make decisions about *us* without including me, Goddammit." He grabs my arms, forcing me to take his penetrating, dominating gaze. "*Mine*," he spews as though the word is pathetic. "Did you lie about that too?"

At my inability to reply, my lips parted in the shock of his accusation, he leans down to take me in a desperate, forceful kiss, its edges serrated, cutting with an overflow of hurt and pain - his...mine.

"I never lied to you!" I pull my lips away, tearing myself from his grip, the emotions he's stirred in me with his reference to my relationship with Liam fuelling the breaking of my defensive dam; a strong and equally ugly alternative to the building sobs I'm holding at bay.

He looks stunned at my abrupt withdrawal, and I'm dying inside, losing the internal war between my heart and my mind. He's right. It is exactly what I went through with Liam. My actions a flipped version, but the bottom-line is exactly the same. I don't know what I want or need. And, right now, I don't know what to say. My defensive anger, however, is shielding my broken heart from giving in to him. "I tried to tell you what I *didn't* tell Liam. *You* didn't want to hear it!" I spew at him, my harshness, along with his slapped reaction, suddenly reverberating my actions. I'm lashing back at him, hurting him more, just to protect my own pain. "What more do you want me to say, Alex?"

"I want you to say that you made a mistake! Tell me that you wish you didn't leave! Jesus, Aby. Just when I was falling in love with you..." he stops suddenly, as though realizing he's shared a sacred secret with the devil.

I take an unconscious step back from him at his words. *Oh my God. He was falling in love with me...*

The alarm in his gaze at the hands of my unintentional retreat signals his clear misinterpretation of my reaction. I watch a myriad of emotion pass across his stunning face, from hurt to defeat to anger in a matter of seconds. The shock to my system paralyzes me. I want to correct his perception, but my mouth isn't moving.

"You needed time? You got it. But you don't get to decide

for *me* how long that window is open. I'll be at the Ritz Carlton, Suite 515, until tomorrow evening," he turns to leave.

"What are you saying?" I question as though he's speaking a foreign language, finding my voice in a blast of panic. I know exactly what he's saying, yet I can't help but offer myself up for further clarification of the clear warning.

He faces me from the open doorway. "Consider that window closed when I get on my flight. You're not the only one who has a heart to protect," he adds before walking down the stairs.

My mouth hangs open at his final words, my chest heaving from the loss of air. I stare at the absence of my dream-man before finally closing the door on him. And my dreams.

Perfect plans are not so perfect. I've just watched two of the men in my polar opposite lives both walk out the door.

CHAPTER
Two

SEATED CROSS-LEGGED ON the sofa, I stare at my new cell phone, vibrating against the glass-top of the coffee table with each ring, my mother's picture indicating the caller's ID. It's her third time calling today, making me regret finally replacing the one left broken in pieces on the floor of my flat in London over a week ago. *Nine days ago to be exact* - Alex's harsh reminder echoes through my head along with each ring from my mother's call.

"Aren't you going to answer that?"

Looking up, I find Stacey setting her oversized purse down atop her suitcase, closing the front door.

"Stacey!" I jump up to run into her arms, nearly taking her off her feet. "I'm so glad you're home!" I'm unable to hold back my looming tears any longer in the arms of my best friend.

"Oh, babe, I'm glad to see you too," she returns my tight hug, running her hand lovingly along my back. Releasing me with a gentle push, she looks harshly into my eyes, "Now sit your ass down, you have some explaining to do."

A little taken aback at her firm order, I turn to walk at my own pace back to the sofa, wiping my tear-stained cheeks. "I've already told you what happened," I take my former seat before looking towards her in defensive mode, ready to take whatever my feisty friend has to offer. "I didn't realize I would have to *explain* myself further, especially to my best friend."

"Abigail Ryan, don't you dare try that defensive shit with me - *especially* me. I know you better than anyone, doll face," she joins me on the sofa.

Ain't that the truth, I sigh. I can't get any bullshit past Stacey. She's known me much too long, too well. She's seen me through everything, been my biggest support, from the time we met in high school, through my marriage and it's subsequent demise - my desires for *more*.

"So, have you spoken to your mom yet?" she continues in my silent sulking.

I say nothing, simply shrugging my shoulders in reply.

"Well, at least you managed to replace your damn phone, finally. Does she even know you're home?"

I roll my eyes, and finally shake my head.

"So, you're avoiding *everyone* now? That's a change, isn't it? You go from years of pretending nothing is wrong in your world to running from it?"

I don't miss the sternness in her voice, and I'd be lying if I said it wasn't hitting me in the stomach like a wrecking ball. Deciding to just get it over with, I remain mum. I'm emotionally drained, and really don't have the energy to fight back right now.

"Let's cut straight to the point, shall we, my little peach?"

I grimace a little, though its unintentional sarcastic lacing is obvious. I don't think I've ever heard Stacey this pissed - at me, personally, anyway. It's definitely pushing my defensive buttons.

"This is one of those times when one needs to be reminded that communication via email can lack...how does one put it? Emotion? Tone? Don't get me wrong, Abs, I was sincere in my open door policy for my bestie - you can crash at my pad anytime. Mi casa es su casa, sweetie. You know how much I love you, right?"

I nod my head, fighting back a renewed well of tears. I do know how much she loves me. As much as I love her.

"Good, because I do. And now that the mushy love shit is out of the way, we can skip the bullshit brigade. Let me begin by correcting any of that lost emotion or mixed signals in my reply," she pauses to lock our gaze dramatically. "What. The. Fuck.

Were. You. Thinking?"

It's a question. That's very clear. An answer, however, she is not waiting for.

"Aby, I will always, *always*, have your back. Whatever makes you happy makes me happy. But you spent twelve years, *twelve years*, fighting your own gut instincts to keep *others* happy. And I listened, supported, consoled, without opinion or judgment because I. Love. You. But this? This I will not support. Or console. And I most certainly will not withhold my opinion or judgment. You fucked up. Royally, babe."

"You weren't there, Stace! You don't understand..."

"Wait. Hold up," she raises her palm towards me, spanning the room around us dramatically in search of something or someone that isn't there, before looking back at me sarcastically. "I'm sorry, were you expecting the pity train? Sorry, sweet tits, it derailed at the corner of Suck It Up and Butter Cup."

Ouch. That hurt. My mouth drops open, my jaw locking beneath my scrunched brows in shocked awe.

"Now, what was it you were going to say?" She offers a closed lip smile, suggestively warning me that her zero-tolerance bullshit policy is now in effect.

"I just needed some time. I didn't mean to run, Stace. I just didn't know what else to do."

"I get that, babe. I really do. And that's exactly why I called Alex. He's coming after you, Aby..."

I close my eyes at the mention of his name, the memory of his visit like salt in the oozing wounds from the lashing of his wrath.

"Aby?" she asks, craning her neck towards me. "Please tell me he hasn't already been here. *Aby*?" Flailing her arms in the air, she bolts from her seat, circling the room in a bizarre, inaudible, ritual type chant.

"Yes," I manage in a whisper. She doesn't answer. I'm not even sure she heard me. "He was here. I-I think I've lost him..." the event replays torturously in my mind. "I didn't handle it very well."

She stops suddenly, "I'm sorry, what? I couldn't hear you, I must have rolled my eyes out loud."

Her glare isn't helping me find my words.

Clasping her palms together at her lips, she inhales a breath of composure before sitting back down beside me. "Okay," she nods calmly, yet slightly craze-laced, "…just tell me everything that happened."

SILENCE IS GOLDEN. Unless it's at the hands of Stacey Stevenson. In which case it means shit's about to hit the fan. She hasn't said a word since I spewed every little detail of Alex's visit - several moments of it repeatedly at her crazed and demanding request. I'm not sure how much longer she plans to sit here staring at me - her internal struggle of judgment versus quest for composure obvious in her gaze, and bleeding into my already crumbling demeanor - but I'm sure that if she doesn't say something soon, I'm going to explode, myself. I need help right now. Not a scolding. Whether I deserve one or not.

"So, let's recap, shall we? Just so I'm clear. He flew all the way here, and you sent him away?"

"No…I…not exactly," I sigh, feeling the numbing walls that I've been hiding behind begin to crumble at the hand of her battering.

"Oh, did I use the wrong words? Let me rephrase. He flew all the way here, and you *let* him walk out the door? *After* you left him without a word in London, and he chased you anyway. Better?" She certainly isn't holding any punches, her honest, in your face harangue effectively silencing me, pushing me deeper into my pit of self-loathing.

Wrapping an arm around my waist I cup my chin in my palm, my eyes pleading with her to understand what I don't even understand myself.

Her glare doesn't reflect what I'm looking for. "Do you realize that he must have jumped on the first flight out of London last night after I spoke with him, Aby? Jumped. On. The first flight! Can you believe that?" She's no longer looking directly at me, her agitated gaze roaming the air around us as though she's speaking to an imaginary jury ready to convict me with the manslaughter of Alex's heart. "*And, she let him walk out the damn door?* Un-fucking-believable," she shakes her head, capturing me in the manic madness behind her eyes. "Well? What the *fuck*, Aby?"

"Stop yelling at me!" I finally scream, lashing out at her prosecution, desperate to feel anything other than this pain. "You do realize that you could have helped the situation, don't you?" I ignore the bitchy shock she displays. "A heads up about your *little* chat with Alex would have been great."

"Seriously?" Her stare blasts my desperate attempt to pull her down with me into my pathetic pit of despair.

I'm a mess. Alex is a mess. And now, I'm trying to add Stacey to the mix. *What the hell is wrong with me?* I bury my face in my hands.

"Okay, let's try going back to the beginning, why *did* you leave London?" she questions in frustration, forcing a calming breath at my wince of her continued harsh tone.

I don't even know the answer anymore. "I already told you," I whisper, swallowing back looming tears. I feel like a criminal holed up in the interrogation room, emotionally exhausted and breaking.

"Tell me again. Was it Ben? Julia? The paparazzi? Or, what the bitch told you about how it would affect Liam? *Why*, Aby?"

"Yes...all of it, I guess..."

"You guess? That's bullshit. You ran because you're scared!"

"Yes! Yes, I'm scared shitless! Is that what you need to hear? That I'm weak, and pathetic? That I finally had the courage to chase after the life I've always imagined, only to turn around and run away from it? Run away from the one man that fills me with so much love and desire..." my words fall away, stolen by the swell of emotion threatening to drown me.

"You're in love with him," Stacey's tone is softened, her gaze alight with sudden understanding, mixed with a glimmer of acclamation for finally breaking through to me.

I close my eyes, the lashes freeing the build of tears to roll down my cheek. "I'm *madly* in love with him," I correct her on a whisper.

"And that scares you?"

"Yes," I sniff, wiping my cheeks, looking into her eyes. "But he scares me more."

Pained confusion sweeps across her face, "I don't understand, Aby."

"It's so much more than *who* Alex is, and what comes with that," I shake my head, my vision blurring as the tidal wave of emotion washes over me. "The way I feel with him, it...consumes me. *He* consumes me. Everything he is, everything he does, it's as though I've conjured him to life from fantasy." My teary gaze finds hers, the loving concern I see there giving me the strength to admit my biggest fear, "I'm so afraid of waking up from the fantasy. I don't think I'm strong enough to survive waking up to find out it isn't real."

"Aby," she exhales my name on a breath of compassion, wrapping me in her arms. "Oh, sweet pea, it's not about fantasies and perfect plans."

Oh, God, I cling to her, sobbing into her shoulder. Why did I let him walk out the door? "I'm such a fool," I whisper as she pulls back to look at me.

"You spent twelve years denying your feelings, don't let fear force you to deny them altogether now."

My eyes bulge at the instant reminder of Andrew's similar words that day at the café. The memory of my slight defensive snap-reaction to his advice merely adds to my pile-high shit-storm of mistakes and remorse.

"What is it?" Stacey cocks her head in question.

"It's just that Andrew once said something very similar..." I trail off, reliving the conversation in my mind.

"Did he?" she purses her lips, seemingly impressed, nodding her head. "Smart fella," she adds with a shrug.

"He was wrong about one thing though."

"Yeah? What's that," she questions, pulling her leg up to lean on it.

"I'm not wearing rose-colored glasses. But I kinda wish I

was," I pout through a lingering cry-fest hiccup.

"No you don't, buttercup. All they would have done is delay the inevitable. The fear would have surfaced at some point, in some form of doubt along the way. Mind you, you might have been less of an impulsively neurotic spaz about it," she winks.

The glimmer of a grin sneaks a quirk of my lips before fading quickly into fool's shame. "He called me a coward." I have to turn away from the flash of sympathetic pity that floats across Stacey's face. "And now I've lost him. Pushed him away because I *am* a coward."

"If you stay here and do nothing about it, then yes, I'll agree with both of you," she smiles, her eyes widening sarcastically, reaching to wipe a lingering tear. "And what makes you so sure you've lost him? I mean, other than crushing his heart twice… but I digress. *What*?" she flinches at my evil eye. "My point is, if you'll let me finish, he left an invitation for you to talk to him. He's not looking for perfect, pumpkin, he's looking for honest. So?"

"So, what?"

"So, why are you still sitting here with me?"

"I-I don't know…" I sit up in awe, my hands darting to my head, my fingers brushing through my hair as I realize the simplicity of her question in stark contrast to my ludicrous response. "I have to go…" I jump up, frantically tidying myself as though I have a coherent thought as to my next step. I need to do something! I need to fight for him. So why do I feel like a fish out of water with no clue how to get myself back into the bowl, when I'm the dumbass that jumped out?

"Take my car…and your phone," she grabs it, ushering me to the door. "For gawd's sake, call your equally neurotic mother on the way. I'd hate to think what she'll do if she doesn't hear from you soon. Go get him, girl!"

ONE HUNDRED YARDS. The short distance stretches out before me, yet I'm frozen in place, staring at the Ritz Carlton from

Stacey's parked car. I feel sick, replaying different scenarios with Alex over and over in my head. *What should I say? What will* he *say? Oh God.* My *future* - a future for which I seemingly could have ruined indefinitely due to my stupidity - is waiting just across the street. And what am I doing? Sweating. Sitting. Staring. And sweating.

Brushing the back of my sweater sleeve across my forehead, I jump at the shrill ring of my cell phone to see my mother's caller ID flashing across the screen once more. *Dammit.* I need to answer, if only to ensure that she doesn't call incessantly while I'm trying my damnedest to beg Alex's forgiveness. I should have just called her as Stacey suggested. But my head isn't exactly on straight. Not to mention, my mother may just twist it a little more.

"Hi, Mom," I reluctantly answer, stretching my neck in preparation.

"Abigail Ryan! For the love of all that's holy, why are you avoiding my calls? And why didn't you tell me you were home? Your father is having a fit! This isn't right, Aby. We've been worried sick!" she yells, making me cringe.

"I know...I'm sorry, Mom. Something came up and I had to come home quickly. I meant to call, but..." I stop mid-sentence, unsure how to phrase it. I can't very well admit that I've been in such a distraught place that the mere thought of seeing my family made me physically ill. No, that wouldn't be good at all.

"Aby, I just don't understand you. I had to find out from Liam. *Liam!* My *ex*-son-in-law had to tell me that my own daughter was home!"

"What? *Liam* told you?" I question, bewildered and suddenly sidetracked from my obvious scolding.

"Yes, sweetie. I do speak with Liam from time to time. He called to say goodbye, given he's leaving for his trip. Funny how *he* calls and not my own daughter. Imagine my surprise when he expressed that he'd just said goodbye to *you*! In person!"

Hold up...My mom talks to Liam? *WTF?* Do I tell her that I find it completely inappropriate that she still speaks to him? Remind her that he's *no longer* an intricate part of my life? Sure, he's my friend, but my mom still acts as though he's a part of the family. Once again, I feel the sinking sensation of 'failure' running through my head - my mother's constant meanderings that I'd ruined a perfectly good marriage, and her inability to acknowledge my choices, without judgment. Why the hell can't she just accept that I'm a grown woman, capable of making my own decisions, for *me*! *Ugh!*

"Mom, I get that you think I messed up, that I should still be with Liam, but I'm not. And no matter what you think, that's a good thing. I need you to support my decision, and...stop talking to Liam!" my voice raises slightly.

"Aby, I *do* support your decision. Not initially, but I do now. I don't understand it, but that's not for me to say. I'm just worried about you, honey. You don't seem yourself."

I *was* myself, finally. *At least I was beginning to be* - my thoughts instantly return to Alex, my gaze darting fleetingly to the hotel, perusing each window as though in question of which room he's occupying right at this moment. "I know exactly who I am, Mom," I finally reply, knowing this is my moment to fight. To fight for Alex, and the person I spent so many years denying - me. "I'm a girl who decided to go for it." *And that's exactly what I plan to do.* "I'll come see you tomorrow," I add, not giving her a chance to reply. "I need to take care of something important."

"O-okay..."

"You'll see me tomorrow, I promise," I reassure her quickly.

"I love you, Aby..."

"I love you too, Mom," I end the call with a sigh of guilt. But I will make it up to her. Right now, I have to make it up to Alex. Taking another enormous breath, I smile at my reflection in the rearview mirror, fully prepared to win back the man that I love.

YOU CAN DO this, Aby. Everything you want - no, NEED - is waiting for you behind this door.

Dammit this is tough. I'm standing here like a fool, staring at the door of Alex's hotel room, nerves twisted and knotted once more. Does he even *want* to see me? *Yes, he does.* He left the window open himself. But, will he like what I have to say? I have to tell him the real reason I left. Admit that I fucked up. My God, if it wasn't for Stacey, I wouldn't even be standing here right now ready to fight for the man I love, fully understanding that I left him for all the wrong reasons, ashamed that I allowed the lines of my fantasy dream-come-true to blur against the reality of… reality itself.

My typical self-doubt always seems to take over at moments like this. With Alex laying his heart on the line for me earlier, I should feel confident that he'd open his arms to me now. But knowing and actually believing are two very different things.

Gripping my sweaty forehead in angst, I begin a defeated pace of the hallway. I simply need a few more minutes to wrap my head around what I'm going to say. Delay the inevitable groveling Alex so surely deserves. I'm certainly not opposed to begging. God knows I deserve it. I've made so many mistakes.

"God, I'm an idiot", I mutter to myself, absently walking back and forth, shaking my head at my stupidity. *Okay, enough pussyfoot dilly-dallying…*

Marching to his door, I knock twice, my nervous breaths slightly accelerated. I purse my lips at the lack of response, waiting a few minutes before knocking again, a little harder this time. With each passing second going unanswered, my heart rate rockets, my initial doubt taking root. *Oh, God…he's gone. I've lost him.* My chest constricts, my breaths coming in anguished pants, hyperventilation setting in with each frantic knock of my knuckles against the door.

"Alex? Are you in there?" I plead, to no avail.

My world starts to spin, crumble, and panic sets in. Swallowing a sob in forfeit, I begrudgingly turn to leave, tears welling in my eyes. I'm shattered, torn apart at the seams.

Grabbing my cell, I frantically dial Stacey's number, needing guidance as to what I should do. Do I rush to the airport? Do I follow him to London?

"Aby?" she answers on the first ring.

"Stacey, he's not here. I don't know what to do..." I manage, my tone defeated as the threatening tears spill down my cheeks, blurring my vision.

"What? What do you mean he's not there?"

"He's g-gone," my voice cracks at the lashing reality of it.

"Babe, calm down. What do you mean he's gone?"

"I me-e-an he's really gone. *Literally*! There's no answer at his room," I reach the bank of elevators, looking back down the empty hallway in regret.

"Honey, maybe he's just gone out," she tries to plead rationally, but my head full of frantic thoughts isn't registering.

"No, Stace. He's gone. I'm too late!"

"Aby! Calm the fuck down and breathe! I need you to be strong right now! You *will* get him back. Listen to me...come back to my place, we'll figure out a plan. You'll just have to talk to him in London, babe. Don't worry. Come home, we'll figure this out together."

Her lucidity calms me marginally, my breathing evening out as I push the elevator button. She's right. I'll just follow him to London. I'll do whatever necessary to win him back. "Okay, I'm coming home. But I'm afraid, Stace. What if I've lost him?"

"Impossible, sugar plum. Everything will work out, I promise."

"I'm just such a fucking idiot. Why did I run?" I mutter, a renewed well of tears threatening.

"I know, sweetie. We all make mistakes. It's how you deal with them that matter. And, you will fix this."

A ding signals the elevator's arrival, and I absently swipe at my cheeks, wiping away the residual tears in hopes of exiting without looking like a blubbering idiot. The doors slide open, and I'm stopped dead in my tracks.

Alex.

CHAPTER *Three*

ALEX STANDS ALONE, unmoving in the elevator cab, staring blankly at me. He looks amazing, as always. And even more so with his muscles bulging, overemphasized beneath the damp, clinging black workout shirt he's wearing. Clearly, he's just returned from the gym. He's sweaty, and breathless - though the latter is very plausibly at the hands of my sudden appearance. And judging by the pulse of his clenching jaw, it's also possibly not a pleasant revelation. Regardless, I can't help but devour him with my gaze, my eyes dropping to the loose fitting gym pants hanging sexily from his lean hips, before working their way back up. His brown curls slightly damp and in disarray, hang partially over his forehead, framing his incredible blue eyes - eyes fixated on me.

My mouth is watering at the image and all I can manage to do is gawk at him, my cell phone held to my ear, Stacey's repeated calls for my attention a muffled distraction.

"Aby? Can you hear me? Are you still there?" she repeats, finally jarring me from my stupor.

"I'll call you back," I mumble, disengaging the call, unable to tear my gaze from Alex moving to stand before me.

"What are you doing here?" his tone is flat, though I sense a hint of light in his eyes - my hopeful imagination perhaps?

"I came to see you," I manage, my voice broken and raspy.

He searches my eyes for a moment before turning, without

a word, to walk down the hallway, leaving me standing in place. The cold gesture tears me apart.

Closing my eyes on a deep intake of breath, I wipe my cheeks in hopes of erasing any signs of my meltdown, following dutifully behind him, stopping to stand by his side as we reach his room. "Can I come in?" I ask as he inserts the key card, his lack of acknowledgement or words confirming my fears - *This isn't going to be easy.*

His expression is completely unreadable. Although it doesn't help that he avoids my gaze before opening the door, forfeiting his typical gentlemanly gesture to hold it open as he makes his way into the living area of the suite, tossing his gym bag to the floor.

With another breath of composure, I adjust my shirt at the waist and steel myself for the inevitable conversation ahead, following him in. *This is it.* Time to start begging...*if that's what it takes.*

The twinkling lights and flashing billboards of the Toronto city-skyline frame his stunning form as he stands staring out at the night sky. My breath hitches at the sight of him; the beautifully decorated suite and incredible view from the large window paling in comparison to this beautiful man. The man I ran away from. The man I love.

"Well, you're here," he begins without turning, his tone almost void of emotion. "Perhaps now would be a good time to elaborate on the purpose of your visit," he adds, his arms folded as he turns to face me.

"I'm here because...I love you," I barely manage the words, swallowing the lump in my throat, fighting my lingering tears.

Flinching at my statement, awed emotion flashes across his face as he bites the corner of his mouth, his eyes gleaming slightly at the return of his clenching jaw. "You *love* me?" he spits the sentiment back in my face, his mouth parted through angered breaths.

"Yes," I whisper, taken aback by his vehemence; a fresh stabbing ache in my chest making it suddenly harder to breathe.

The smirk of disgust he flashes sends a shudder down my

spine. "Love doesn't mean anything without trust. *Not to me*," the latter comes out on a slight snarl before he turns away once more. "Words are cheap, and yet the cost of believing yours seems rather high," he adds, staring out the window.

"Alex, I'm sorry I hurt you. And I'm so sorry that I've made you doubt me…"

"*Doubt* you?" he spins around. "Lying tends to have that affect, *sweetheart*," his harsh use of the word renews a shiver, a deliciously cold, yet delicious, current flooding through my trembling fear.

I've learned to both expect and draw from the unavoidable sexually explosive cocktail that this man creates within me with his every emotion. It fuels me. Gives me strength to fight. Fight for him. "I haven't lied to you, Alex."

"No?" he cocks his head in mocking indignation. "You lied to me about Ben."

"Omitted, not lied, remember?"

Dropping his folded arms to his sides, he strides towards me with gaited self-assurance, stopping directly before me.

I gasp at the sudden proximity.

"I'm pretty sure we've already ascertained they are mutually exclusive." His jaw clenches as he stares down into my eyes. "But most importantly, Aby, you lied to me when you said you wouldn't leave. You lied right to my face, even when I begged you to stay. Why? Why did you leave? Just tell me the truth!" he grabs my arms to force my gaze.

The hurt I can finally see in his eyes is my undoing. My tears well, threatening to fall as I take in the anguish written all over his face. "I was scared," I begin, visibly trembling. "I *never* meant to hurt you. I realize, now, that I allowed myself to hurt you in the worst way. Exactly as you had feared…"

Releasing me, his arms drop to his sides once more, his eyes closing on a defeated breath. "Life with me…" he laughs half-heartedly, turning away, running his fingers through his hair.

"It can be…difficult," I finish for him, repeating his own warning. I summon the courage to hold his gaze when he turns to face me, knowing what I'm about to say will only hurt him more. "The paparazzi, endless invasion of privacy…the price of fame," I walk towards him, praying for strength as I witness his face twist in pain. "Yes, Alex, it scared me, more than I wanted to admit. Even to myself."

He looks away as I reach him.

"All of that scared me, just as you feared. But you didn't let me finish," I cup his face in my trembling hands to force his gaze. "Something else scares me even more." I close my eyes, my hands falling from his face to slide down his chest. The feel of him beneath my palms is incredible. I *need* to feel him. To know he's really here. "I'm so afraid that if I let myself believe, for just one moment, that everything I've dreamt of is right here in front of me," I look up into his eyes, "…I'll realize that it isn't real. That you're not real."

"I *am* real, Aby," he takes my hands in his at his chest, squeezing them. "*This* is real."

"I want so much to believe that," I smile through the tears streaming down my face. "You are everything I've ever dreamed of…my ultimate fantasy come true. But fantasies don't exist in reality, do they?" the doubt surfaces on a whisper. "And even if they possibly could," I look down in shame, "…can I live in yours?"

"Fuck, Aby. What are you saying?" He tries to search my averted gaze before releasing my hands and taking a step back. "Did you come here to tell me that you're just giving up?"

"No," I shake my head, trying to express every ounce of remorse in my tear-filled eyes. "I'm saying I'm scared…for more reasons than you feared. And I came in hopes to make you understand those reasons." I bravely take a step towards him. "I'm asking you to forgive me for *almost* giving up on us. I've fallen madly in love with you, Alex. And as much as that scares me, losing you frightens me more," I pause, swallowing, trying to remain audible against my sobs. "I choose us. I think I'm making a healthy choice," I attempt to smile. "I can't seem to breathe without you."

The look in his eyes steals my breath anyway. Taking a step to close the small distance between us, he cups my face in his hands, taking me in a ravishing kiss that swallows my gasp for air. The feel of his lips crushing mine is overwhelming, a feeling I thought I'd never have again. And I'm unable to contain the sudden squeaky cry-moan that escapes me.

"Shhh," he whispers between nips and kisses. "Jesus, I thought I'd lost you. I can't lose you, Aby. I can't," he mumbles inaudibly through his kisses.

Wrapping my arms firmly around his waist, I try my best to reassure him, to ease his hurt. I realize now that his steely demeanor from a moment ago was simply his hardened shell - a defensive mechanism against his pain, his fear, and his own hurt. A reaction I'm all too familiar with. "You won't lose me, Alex. I'm here. I'm not going anywhere. I'm so sorry. I'm so very sorry."

"God, baby…"

"Make love to me, Alex. Please…" I beg, the words so easily falling off my lips. I need to feel his touch. I need to feel his skin on mine, to wrap my arms tightly around him, to feel him consume me. I need to feel that he's *real*.

Groaning into our kiss, he scoops me up in his arms, carrying me to the bedroom, setting me down on my feet beside the bed. He takes my face in his hands, his beautiful blue eyes penetrating deep into my soul.

I moan into the return of his feverish kiss, my core pulsing from the onslaught, my hands taking him in thankful ownership, working their way around his waist, up the sculpted form of his back and shoulders.

His fingers slide into the hair at my nape and pull tight, cocking my head back roughly to force my gaze. "Fuck, I've missed you," he pauses, his eyes searching mine. "Don't. Ever. Fucking. Lie to me again. Do you understand?"

"Yes. I'm sorry. Please…"

His mouth crashes back to mine, desperate orders spewed into our kiss…"Don't ever leave me again…You're *mine*, Aby." His large body overtakes me, forcing me onto the bed. The sight of him crawling over top of me sends my pulse racing in anticipation, soaking my panties. The feel of his weight is intoxicating as he lowers his lips passionately to mine. I relish in the strength of his body, running my hands along his form, needing to feel all of him, my fingers squeezing and clawing at every perfectly defined muscle.

Our kiss is hectic, intense. We consume each other, reaching to the deepest recesses of our mouths, the need to brand each other mutual, heated, our fingers working in a desperate need to touch. Our clothes come off in a whirlwind of hands, tugging and ripping each other's shirts off, before moving to discard our pants. I gasp as he slowly, teasingly slides his hands along my core, tearing my underwear from my body, eliciting my slight scream.

My eyes dart back to his, and I whimper at the intense heat emanating from his gaze as he slides his muscled form over top of me, resuming his passionate kisses. Kisses that work their way down my trembling body, pausing at my nipple, my belly button, to tantalize with savoring licks of his devouring lips and tongue.

"Alex," I moan against his intentions as he spreads my legs with a firm pull, my pussy clenching in anticipation of his sinful mouth, but desperate for his fill.

"You're so perfect," he whispers, kissing my thigh, teasing my sensitive bud with his tongue, capturing it between his lips.

My body bows to his delicious mercy, his two fingers sliding along my wet folds before pressing inside. Grabbing his hair, I moan with every thrilling thrust of his digits, pulling and urging the return of his lips to mine. What he's doing to me feels out of this world, but I need him inside me.

He groans in response, pulling his fingers from my core to tease my engorged clit. Moving upward to settle between my widespread legs, the brush of his hardened erection along my folds elicits another. "I can't hold back, baby. I need you. Now."

"Then don't," I grab his face, resuming our frenzied kiss.

Reaching down to grasp his cock, he glides it slowly along my wetness, the juices coating its thick head, lining himself up to thrust deep. Our simultaneous moans echo through the tangle of our lips; he feels incredible inside me, filling me.

He slides his cock out with slow precision, its tip tantalizing my quivering sex. His gaze is filled with fire, and I'm mesmerized. "*This*, this is real," his whispers gruffly, his words consuming me before thrusting deeply once more.

"Oh, God… Alex!"

The feel of his erection slipping through my folds, pushing deeper and deeper inside me, feels completely brand new. The intensity is incredible, his hardness awakening every nerve inside me, my womb contracting in desperate need, clutching and gripping his cock. I buck uncontrollably, bowing in helpless abandon as his thickness plunges again. Seated fully, he stills, lifting his head to stare into my eyes, his blue gaze searching mine, leaving me speechless. Breathless. The pure emotion reflected in his stare has me sucking in air.

"I love you," I whisper through my gasping breaths.

His eyes close as though he's savoring the words. Brushing his fingers along my forehead, he pushes the strands of hair away. "Do you know what those words mean to me? *Do to me?*"

"I love you," I repeat them, suddenly eliciting a powerful force within me, realizing how much my use of them - laced with such absolute, undeniable truth - affects him so profoundly.

"Jesus, baby…" he groans. "Don't ever leave me again."

I'm completely overcome with emotion, pulling his lips back to mine to resume our kiss, putting every ounce of my happiness, honesty, and faithfulness into it. I pray that I can show him exactly what mere words could never fully relay.

He pulls his cock marginally from my core, plunging back inside as I mewl into his kiss. My hips meet his thrusts measure for measure, needing him so deep inside me that I'll never survive otherwise. Our coupling frenetic in our need for each other.

Pulling his lips from mine, he places suckling kisses along my jaw, my collarbone. His hand slides beneath my back, pulling me upwards to arch my body towards him, my head falling back in abandon, offering my breasts to his wanting mouth. With succulent brushes of his lips along my chest, he swipes his tongue along my nipple, sucking it between his perfect lips.

I release a crazed whimper at the sensation, my pussy throbbing around his hardness, my climax imminent.

"Mmmm…yes, baby. You're so close. I want to feel you

come around my cock. Fall for me."

His words are my undoing. The sexy timber of his voice, combined with the steady tempo of his thrusts sends me plummeting over the precipice. Screaming his name in release, I slide my hands in his hair, gripping hard, riding the overwhelming waves of pleasure, convulsing uncontrollably.

His thrusts pound relentlessly as I ride the waves, in and out, deeper and deeper into my clutching depths, before he finally stills above me. The sensation as he spills his desire inside my pulsing core is as thrilling as the delicious groan he releases into my neck.

Harsh breaths amid the grasp of each other's arms, we await the slowing of our rapid heartbeats in euphoric silence.

Sliding his still semi-erect cock out of me, he chuckles at my elicited whimper, turning to his side on the mattress, pulling me with him. "I'm not done with you yet, sweetheart," he warns playfully, running his fingers gently along my sweat-slickened back.

"I hope you'll never be," I bite my lip through a small smile.

"Good," he wraps me in his arms, lifting me up with ease, moving to stand. "Time for a shower," he smirks, carrying me to the bathroom, holding me in one strong arm, leaning in to turn it on.

Steam slowly fills the room as he places me down inside, pulling me against him under the warmth of the cascading water. Lovingly brushing his hand along my jaw, my satiated body flutters to life with delicious shivers of returned desire. His own unwavering arousal is equally evident, sinfully tantalizing against my stomach in his tight hold.

Our insatiable need is intoxicating, but in this moment, I can sense his longing to move slowly this time. He's savoring me. And I want nothing more than to just give in to his loving embrace.

"Thank you," I whisper.

"For?" he questions, running his fingers gently along my back.

"For your forgiveness," I look deeply into his eyes. I could lose myself in the beauty of them. "I'm so grateful to you. You came for me. You believed in me…in us, even when I couldn't. I truly never meant to hurt you," I look down, feeling a build of shameful tears. "The way you left this morning…I thought I'd lost you."

"No, never. Don't ever think that," he lifts my chin to meet his gaze. "I would have done whatever it took to make you see reason. To make you understand just how much I…" flinching, he stops, closing his eyes.

Oh God. He can't say it. How can I blame him? I've hurt him so much, its bite so recent, still lingering despite his forgiveness. I have to understand that. I have to be strong for him to get past it. "You don't have to say it, Alex."

Opening his eyes to look at me, I avert my gaze, battling my insecurities against my strength just a moment ago. He tilts my head, pulling my gaze once more, his eyes saying more than any words could convey, without question. I don't need to hear the words aloud, not until he is ready to give them freely. And I know that trust will play a large roll in when that time comes.

"It's okay," I reassure him, wrapping my arms around him to pull him closer, resting my head against his chest, the water raining over us. "I have to earn your trust. And I will. But…" I pause, searching for the right words, turning my head to kiss his slickened flesh. "I can't promise that my fears will be gone when we wake in the morning," I add cautiously, my lips lingering against him.

He bends into my hold, leaning down onto my shoulder, his breaths warm against my skin in his silence. I wish I could see his eyes, desperate to try to read what he's thinking, but I give him the moment he seems to need.

"I just want to be honest with you," my words slip out without thought. "There's only one thing I'm sure of in this moment," I pull away from him, needing him to see the truth in my eyes. I'm a little taken aback at the somber tone reflected in his. He's scared too. If he wasn't before I left, he is now. And, at my hand. I *will* gain his trust back, but until then I can only reassure him what I know is true, *real*…over and over…"I love you, Alex."

His eyes close again at my words, and I lose my breath when he opens them to me, electric blue in color, oozing desire. Gently, he glides his lips along mine, taking me in a sensual kiss. I can feel his love for me in every slide of his tongue along mine, every sashay of his fingers along my body. It's overwhelming and utterly enthralling. I feel at home here in his arms. I am home. Alex is my absolute dream come true. My *perfect plan* come to fruition. He's everything that I've ever wanted and so very much more.

Releasing me slowly from our kiss, he whispers against my lips, "Honesty is incredibly sexy."

"Is it?" I question playfully.

"Mmhmm," he mumbles, kissing my neck.

"Well, allow me to elaborate my candor," I manage through his onslaught, pulling every ounce of strength to cement my words. "I will fight those pesky fears to the bitter end. I'll never run again. I promise you that," I add, leaning my lips against his chest, waiting in hopes that he heard my truth.

He pulls back, the corners of his mouth curling up into one of his heart stopping smiles. "Well, Miss Ryan," he brushes his fingers along my tummy, eliciting electric shivers, "…you realize that means you are stuck with me now."

I can't help but laugh at his boyish charm, now thankfully returned. *God, how I've missed it.* "Likewise, Mr. Tate."

Placing a quick kiss to my forehead, he pulls me tighter, sighing contentedly into my neck. The feel of his smile against my flesh is indescribable. "Stay the night?"

"I'm not going anywhere."

CHAPTER *four*

"OKAY," I POSITION myself between Alex and the front door of my parent's home, looking up into his beautiful blue eyes with weary caution, "…once you step inside this door, you may never see me the same way again. Are you prepared for that?"

His lips curl into that sexy smirk that immediately scorches down my core. I have to bite my lip against the thought of just jumping in the car and taking him back to bed.

"Sweetheart, I'm prepared for anything and everything that is you," he wraps his strong arms around my waist, his words as charming as his smile. "And I'm more than willing to turn around and take you right back to the hotel to prove that a few more times, if you wish," he adds, pulling at my bitten lip with his thumb.

"Don't tempt me." I can't resist trailing my palm along his chest beneath the opening of his tweed jacket, my fingers begging me to reconsider his offer. "Let's just get this over with," I sigh, reluctantly turning in his hold to open the door. "So, remember, my dad's not much of a talker, but he has a heart of gold, and Mom," I pause, turning to look at him, "…well, let's just say that at the end of the day, I think she means well."

"Got it," he nods, lips pursed before that crooked grin curls back into place.

God help me, I'm insatiable for him. And he knows it. "Are you going to tease me all day with that wicked, sexy smirk, Mr. Tate?"

"I won't be teasing," he whispers in my ear, his hand trailing down my back to caress my behind.

"No? What would you call it?" I challenge, playfully.

"An extended warning."

Oh, gawd…

"Mom, I'm here," I call out as we enter. *Let the fun and games begin.*

"Aby?" she calls from the kitchen. "Well, thank heavens you finally decided to grace us with your…" she stops abruptly, finally having us in view. "Oh," she smiles, smoothing down her perfectly wrinkle-free clothing.

"Hi, Mom. I'd like you to meet Alexander Tate. Alex this is my mother, Dianne."

"It's a pleasure to meet you, Mrs. Ryan," he shakes her hand gently, offering his incredible smile. "May I call you Dianne?"

"Oh, yes, of course," she giggles, caught in that familiar 'Alexander Tate' awkward trance as she stares at the man I've fallen in love with. "Abigail, you should have warned me you were bringing a guest," she fiddles with her perfectly styled hair. "I would have done something with myself." I roll my eyes - it's not like she can see me, she's fixated on the Adonis of a man at my side. "It's wonderful to meet you, Alexander," she gushes.

"Please, call me Alex."

"Yes, of course." Her giant, frozen smile seems to swallow the moment of silence. It's hard to look away from her awestruck gaze before she opens her mouth again to speak, "Reggie! Aby is home, and she's brought a friend. Come, come inside you two," she grabs Alex's arm, entwining it in her own to pull him along.

I follow behind, shaking my head slightly. This is more than comical.

We enter the kitchen to find my dad sitting at the table, his reading glasses perched on his nose, his face twisted tightly in concentration as he tries to decipher, what I can only assume, is the day's crossword puzzle.

"Reggie! Did you not hear me calling? Abigail is here, and

she's brought a friend."

Begrudgingly pulling his gaze from the newspaper at the shrill, yet undoubtedly partially tuned-out voice of my mom, instant warmth flashes in his eyes when they land on me. "Aby, honey, come here," he stands, walking towards me, his crossword forgotten.

I immediately fold into his arms, hugging him tight in return. "Hi, Dad," I smile against his chest, savoring the familiar scent that is my dad.

Pulling back to hold me at arms length, he flashes me his smile. "It's good to see you. Have you been eating?"

"Ugh, yes I've been eating," I chuckle. "Dad, I want you to meet my boyfriend," I gesture towards Alex, standing idly by. "Alex, this is my dad, Reggie."

"It's a pleasure, Mr. Ryan," Alex smiles, reaching to shake my dad's hand.

There's no question I can see the wheels turning behind my father's gaze - part 'who the hell is this guy' and equal part 'you're not good enough for my daughter'. So damn adorable.

"Likewise, Alex," he replies. *Yup, the man of few words.* I can clearly see the strength in the grip of his handshake, the motion of the gesture continuing a little longer than necessary.

"Now, Alex, what can I get you to drink?" Mom saves the day, the men pulling their hands apart. "Lemonade?"

"*Lemonade...that cool refreshing drink,*" I sing the little ditty from Eddie Murphy's *Delirious*.

"I hope you're hungry. I've got brunch coming up shortly," Mom continues with a smile, ignoring me, my joke lost.

Humph, I thought it was funny. Taking in Alex's tweaked brow, I shrug playfully. *What? Can you smell it?* I giggle to myself. *I love Eddie Murphy.*

Masking a chuckle, Alex turns his gaze to Mom, "Lemonade would be perfect, Dianne, thank you. And brunch sounds lovely."

Gushing from his sweet gentlemanly words, Mom readies his lemonade, not bothering to offer me any. I guess I don't count as a guest anymore, despite having not lived at home for years.

"Thank you," Alex takes the glass with a smile, eliciting my mother's giddy shrug. I cringe at her ridiculous display. *I need to get this shit under control. Alex gets enough of this outside of his comfort zones.*

"Why don't you go on into the living room? I'll be there in a second," I smile, gesturing in the direction.

Alex merely grins, turning to make his way out.

Out of earshot, I zoom in - the best defense is a good offence. "Mom, *really*? You're acting like a crazy person. I warned you Alex was a celebrity," I shake my head. "This is hilarious."

"What kind of celebrity?" Dad pipes up. "I thought I recognized him."

"Oh, Reggie, I told you that already. He's a famous *actor*. You just don't listen to me."

"Dianne, you did not tell me that."

"I absolutely did tell you! Ages ago. Remember? When Aby confessed to being shacked up with an actor. So you listened, you just don't *hear* me. Maybe you need to get your ears checked, darling."

"I would have remembered that," he mumbles under his breath. "And, maybe I'd hear you if you didn't nag at me every single second of every day."

Oh sweet baby Jesus. My family's fucked. "Okay, okay," I pipe in, interrupting their sidetracked tirade. "Yes, Alex is an actor. Yes, I *stayed* with him for a week. But he's my boyfriend, and moreover just a regular guy. Let's not make his career a big deal, okay? *Please*? I'm begging you not to embarrass me." I'm pleading now. I don't want Alex to think my family is any more certifiable than necessary.

"Of course, Abigail. We would never embarrass you," Mom states, her hand held to her chest as though it's a ludicrous notion.

"Okay, I just needed to make sure we're all on the same page."

"Are you happy, Aby?" Dad asks suddenly, sincerity in his gaze.

"Very," I smile.

Clearing his throat - his typical swallow of emotion - he turns his attention back to his discarded crossword. "Well, you don't need to worry about your mother, Aby, honey. I'll keep her in line," he chuckles, and I turn, shaking my head as I make my way out of the kitchen. *That woman couldn't walk a straight line sober.*

I find Alex standing at the console table full of portraits of my sister and her family. "This is what I call the 'shrine'," I whisper with a halfhearted laugh, taking in the large framed portraits above the numerous ones spread on the table.

He offers me a questioning glance, eyebrow raised.

"I think the evidence speaks for itself, no?" I roll my eyes. His sudden amused gaze makes me feel silly for allowing my petty jealously to show, and I purse my lips. "Sorry."

"Don't be," he smiles, wrapping his arm around me, pulling me against him. "I'm not particularly a fan of *your* shrine, myself." He kisses my forehead.

Huh? Now I'm the one confused. I follow the direction of his nod towards the wall behind me. *Oh, my ever loving GOD! You have got to be shitting me!*

Framed beautifully, a giant wedding portrait of Liam and I hangs between two smaller framed images - one of me graduating from University and one of Beth and I. Needless to say, there would be no faded paint around these recently hung portraits, and I love the added touch of my sister in *my* seemingly new mini-shrine. But, the giant wedding picture? *What. The. Hell?*

Mortified, I turn to face Alex. He's staring at the portrait of Liam and I, the pulse in his jaw unmistakable, though it feels as though he's trying to hide any signs of a reaction. He's failing. Miserably. *Shit.*

"Alex, I…"

"Show of hands for coffee with brunch," Mom peeks around the corner.

Dad always told me that if looks could kill, I'd be a jail-bird, and that dagger-shooting eye talent of mine is currently set to max. Number one target? My mother. "Interesting new photo collage, *Mom*," I spew, trying very hard to control my pending explosive outburst in front of Alex. The last thing I want to do is add to his discomfort.

"Oh," she replies in high-pitched nonchalance. "I found that in your belongings, and had the perfect frame for it. They say to display items in threes, and I think the smaller frames really make it pop, don't you?" she questions, walking towards them, correcting the tilt of one at the corner.

"Oh, it pops something," I mutter, Alex stopping my motion to step towards her with his gentle hold of my waist. "Mom," I take a breath of composure, "...you wait until I'm divorced to hang a wedding portrait?"

"Sweetie," she turns to face me, confused exasperation behind a smile-for-show. "Technically, you were divorced just yesterday. Your father hung these for me at least two months ago."

"Don't hang *me* out to dry," Dad joins us, taking his usual seat in the recliner in front of the TV. "I didn't know what your mother was planning to hang, I just do what I'm told," he shrugs. "I warned you that Aby wouldn't like it," he adds, glancing at my mother.

"Well, I'm sorry," she huffs, her gaze flickering between my father and I. "I thought it was a shame to have such a beautiful picture of my little girl sitting in a box in the basement." She reaches for the large wooden frame, struggling with its weight, attempting to lift it from its hook.

"Allow me," Alex steps forward with a smile.

I can't help the purse of my lips to avoid grinning at the underling-amused sarcasm in his gentlemanly offer, knowing full well it's completely missed by my mother's self-absorbed oblivion. Sensing my father's gaze, I glance towards him to catch his own amused wink at me, it speaks volumes and I smile. The man of so few words can tell me so much in just one action. He's very happy for me. *And* Alex.

"We're here," I hear Beth call from the foyer. My niece and nephew race to the entrance of the living room before Beth calls after them, "Your shoes! Come back here and take off your shoes!"

"Yes," Mom's hand darts to her throat in controlled panic. "Take your shoes off, little ones," she continues, making her way to greet them.

Dad slowly gets up to follow her, flashing me a roll of his eyes, and a wink.

Shaking my head on a smile, I turn to find Alex straightening from leaning the portrait on the floor against the wall. I note his pause of consideration as he eyes the image of Liam and I, our wedding smiles taunting him. Biting at the corner of my mouth, I watch him retrieve the discarded portrait, turning it to face inward, completely out of view.

Ugh, I cringe. I can't believe he just had to do that. "I'm so sorry," I whisper as he takes me in his arms. "My mom…"

"Don't apologize," he smiles, cupping my face in his hands for a chaste kiss. "Remember," he continues, his thumb lovingly brushing my cheek, "…she means well."

"What she means is to hit every nerve in my body with her metaphorical Taser."

"Perception is everything, sweetheart." He leans down to kiss me once more, his hands still in place at my jaw. The brief, teasing entry of his tongue before he pulls his lips away is delicious…and merciless.

"You don't play fair," I bite my lip.

His sexy smile thrills me to the bone.

"OH, NOW THIS seems more like a shrine," Alex teases as I pull him up the staircase. "I have to say, the braces were a good look on you."

"Stop it!" I giggle, trying to pull him away from the wall of embarrassing childhood photos. "This isn't a shrine, it's the walk of shame. For Beth too."

"Oh, and that hair…" he continues, pointing to another image as we pass; my tug more forceful to drag him towards my former bedroom. "You were pretty hot," he flashes a sinful smile as we enter.

Clearly, he's just trying to make me feel better, and I love him for it. "Oh, I don't know about that," I argue playfully, closing the door behind us. "Cute maybe. But hot?"

"Oh yes," his husky tone whispers down my core as he backs me up. "Hot."

"You're incorrigible," I utter breathlessly, loving every minute of his sexy display, pinning me against the closed door.

"For you, absolutely," he bends to take me in a kiss. "Insatiably so," he mumbles through our joined lips, swallowing my gasp as his fingers curl behind me, cupping my ass.

His kiss is slow. Tantalizing. My body is suddenly floating on air from the magic touch of his fingers trailing up my sides, his other hand cradling my jaw, his magician tongue filling me with the fluttering of butterflies right down to my clenching core.

Pulling marginally from my lips, he takes a deep breath. "What you do to me, Aby Ryan," he shakes his head a little, releasing me.

I giggle as he adjusts his loose, perfectly fitted jeans at the crotch. His returned smile is breathtaking. *My God, I love this man.*

"Wow," he takes a look around my bedroom. "This is your old room?" he asks, seemingly dubious. "It looks as though you never left it," he adds, obviously referring to its perfect order and pristine cleanliness care of my mother.

"I know," I smile, taking it all in myself. The girly pink walls are cringingly accented with a pastel pink wallpaper border, a single white bed - its pretty little canopy shaky atop flimsy finials, screws desperately needing tightening after years of wear and tear. The epitome of a little girl's haven. *My* haven. The peaceful memories of my escape from the cray-cray in this house still intact, as though I never left. "Dad would never let my mother throw any of it away, even if she wanted to."

Walking over to the matching white desk, he runs his hand along the stack of books, his smile curling into a devilish smirk. "It seems your reading taste has changed a little."

"Ummm, yeah, a little," I smile, taking in the titles in the pile...*Charlotte's Web, Little Women, Lord of the Flies,* and a few Judy Bloom's mixed in between. "I enjoyed reading fairytales too," I point to more books lining the bookshelf in the corner. "I just like them a little dirtier now," I add with a flirtatious gaze his way.

"Be careful, Miss Ryan, I'm not sure that darling little canopy can survive what I'll do to you if you continue to flirt with me. Not to mention, you may struggle stifling your moans."

"Idle threats, Mr. Tate?"

"You have no idea," he shakes his head again, adjusting his pants with a defeated sigh.

I couldn't wipe the smile off my face if I tried. I feel like a little girl playing naughty tease with her boyfriend in her bedroom, her parents unknowing downstairs. *Hell, that's exactly what I'm doing.* I may not be a little girl anymore, but I sure feel as though time has turned back, transporting me to that innocence of youth. Head over heals in love with prince charming, wanting him to sweep me off my feet. I'm giddy. Elated. In love.

"You and Stacey?" he asks, picking up a frame from the desk.

"Uh-huh," I move closer to take a look.

"Interesting costumes."

I laugh at his humorous grin. "We thought it would be fun to theme-style our Halloween costumes. She was adamant that we switch up our personalities, though her version of an angel is little more risqué than most."

"And you make quite the sexy devil," he adds with a sinful gleam in his eye.

"I can role-play," I wink.

"Now there's an idea," he teases, the thought filling me with a burning fire I can feel tainting my cheeks.

He stares at me for a moment, pausing at my mouth as I take my bottom lip between my teeth, before flashing that core clenching smirk of his. Turning away, he places the frame back down, looking up to the bulletin board hanging over the desk. "What's all this?"

"Things I liked, was interested in…dreamed of," I explain, scanning the pinned images from a lifetime ago.

"And this one?" he gestures to a picture of a beautiful outdoor path ensconced and magically illuminated by twinkling lights. "Where is it?"

"I have no idea. I just thought it was beautiful," I reply, lost in the vision I loved so much. "Magical," I add, leaving his side in a giddy bounce to quickly turn out the light before reaching for a switch hanging over the headboard. The semi-darkened room is softly lit along one wall by hanging strands of twinkling lights.

"Romantic," his eyebrow shifts in that sexy quirk. "In a Christmas kind of way," he smiles, teasing me.

"It's not Christmasy - is that even a word?" I laugh, moving towards him to caress his glorious chest through his shirt. "I was going for *dreamy*, but right now I would certainly call it romantic." I step on my tiptoes to reach his lips for a kiss.

"Romantic is good," he replies through the lingering touch of our lips.

"It is," I agree, feeling the delicious pull of his building desire, the quickening of our breaths.

I give in to him, his tongue teasing for entry, melting against his chest as he pulls me close. I'm not sure if it's the soft slowness of our kiss that makes my heart beat faster, or maybe it just feels that way - like I'm floating as I lose myself in the taste of him. He cups my cheeks in his hands to deepen it, the sensual lure enough that I could drift away. A shiver runs down my spine at the thought that just yesterday, I could have lost him, and I pull firmly at his nape, desperate to hold him to me. I never want to let him go again.

Our euphoric spell is quickly broken at the pitter patter of little feet outside in the hallway followed by my sister's muffled order, "Give Aunt Aby and Mr. Tate some privacy, honey." We laugh against each other's lips at little Jessica's cute reply, "Why, Mommy? What's piracy?"

"Romance can wait," he caresses my cheek, brushing his thumb across my lip. "I actually have something I want to ask you," he adds, taking my hand to sit us down on the bed, its aged creaking giving me momentary pause for concern.

"If this is an offer to take me to Prom, I'm sorry to say, you're too late."

"Oh, you already have a date?" he asks, playing along.

"Yeah, I do." I pull my leg up, turning to face him with a

playful shrug.

"Then I guess I'll just have to wait until it's over to whisk you away with me to L.A."

"What?"

Alex chuckles at my confused expression. "Filming begins in two weeks, and could last for up to four months. I have a place on the coast, and I want you to come with me."

"For like…a visit?"

"No, Aby, I want you with me *for like* the entire stay," he teases, taking my hand in his. "I want you to move to L.A. with me."

I'm speechless, fairly certain my eyes are bugging from the sockets, mentally standing to do a giant jumping jack on my bed.

"Well, I was thinking, since you're working on a freelance basis with Ashley Fines, work won't be an issue." He bends to look more closely in my eyes, "Aby, say something."

"No…" the word comes out as an afterthought as I finally begin processing his words.

"No?"

"Yes…I mean, no, work won't be an issue," I scramble for my words to catch up to my thoughts. "But there is the issue of Amira's flat - although, I guess she won't mind that I'm not actually *in* it, as long as I continue to pay my rent."

"You don't have to worry about that," he bends to nibble at my neck.

"Alex, I signed the sublease for a six month term, I have to fulfill my obligation. Wait…what do you mean?"

"I just don't think it's something you need to worry about," he mutters through the delicate brushes of his lips against my skin.

Nothing I need to worry about…"You've done something," I push his shoulders to draw the attention of his gaze. "What did you do?"

His delicious mouth pulls up at the corner before he gently grabs my nape to kiss me. It's an obvious attempt at distraction, and despite how easily I could give in to it, I brush him off. "Spill it, Tate," I order with a playful glare.

"Spill what?" he questions coyly, aiming for my neck again. "I haven't done anything...recently." He ups the game of his nibbling lips with his caressing fingers down my spine.

"Recently?" I pull away once more, biting the corner of my mouth to avoid giving in to the adorable pout he offers. "Please tell me you didn't do something crazy like pay my lease out?" I laugh - I *was* joking. His expression, however, is spoiling the humor. "Alex? What did...?" I trail off, suddenly remembering the day we met with Amira - the way she looked to Alex momentarily when I asked what the rent would be. "What exactly did you and Amira discuss before I came to the flat that day?"

"We discussed you, of course."

"And...?"

He lets out a defeated sigh with an awkward smile. "Let's just say, Amira and I came to an understanding about the rent."

"What kind of *understanding*?"

"A mutually exclusive agreement."

"Alex Tate, I swear, if you don't..."

"I offered to pay her rent for the six months she is away, if she agreed to sublet her flat to..."

"*What?*"

Smiling, he shrugs.

"Well, that certainly explains the low rent I pay," I shake my head, unsure if I should be appalled or flattered. "And what exactly would you have done if I hadn't agreed to go out with you after all that?"

"The thought never entered my mind." His devilish smile is ridiculous. The man could melt butter.

"Oh, really...cocky much?"

"Not at all, I actually wasn't thinking that far ahead." He takes my hand to kiss it. "I just knew I had to make it happen." The sincerity in his gaze is my undoing, akin to an injection of a mind-numbing drug into my veins. My body reacts to the familiar rush that only he can give me. "The rent you have been paying has been going to a charity that Amira and I agreed upon."

"You're incredible," I shake my head.

"It's a charity near and dear to my heart," he begins to explain as though he should, "...however, you can choose your own, now that you know."

"You really are a wonderful man, Alexander Tate," I take his face in my hands to kiss his beautiful lips.

"I don't know about that," he replies, shyly. "I do, however, know that I would have done whatever I had to, to make you mine."

*And I almost gave you up...*my breath hitches at the thought.

"So, back to what we were discussing," he pulls my lip from its bite with his thumb, caressing my jaw. "Will you move to L.A. with me?"

"Oh, that. I just don't know..." I play indifference, pretending to fiddle with my hair.

"Aby, I can't go without..."

"Yes! Of course I'll move to L.A. with you!" I wrap my arms around his neck, a little too tightly.

"Aby, I...can't breath," he mutters playfully.

"We're going to L.A.!" I jump up on the bed to pull my imagined leap into reality, landing on my side, pulling him into my arms; the bedframe swaying from the impact, its creaks akin to an eerie horror movie sound effect.

"You're excited about this," he notes, wrapping me in his arms.

"I'm excited about you...just being with you," I correct him, melting into his kiss.

"I think you will be excited about Necker too," he says, pulling away to rain kisses down my neck.

"Necker?" I question, giggling. "Are you suggesting you want to brand me, Mr. Tate? Hickey's are highly frowned upon."

"I'm suggesting four days to ourselves on Necker Island," his lips twist into a smile against my neck.

"What?" I pull back, pushing him away at the shoulders. "What's Necker Island?"

"You mean, *where* is Necker Island?" he corrects me with a jovial smirk.

"Stop it," I give him the stink eye. "You know what I mean."

"It's in the British Virgin Islands," he pauses as though that will clear it all up for me. His devilish grin suggests he's playing with me, stretching it out to tease. "It's Sir Richard Branson's private island." My slight head shake and neck crane urge him to elaborate. "I took the liberty of hiring the island exclusively," he finally adds.

"Get out!" I shove his shoulders in awe. "Are you serious?"

"Yes," he chuckles. "Does this mean you want to go?"

"Are you serious?" I repeat in a high-pitched squeal, jumping up from the bed. "When? When are we going?"

"If we fly back to London tonight, we can pack tomorrow and depart for the island the following day. If that works for you?" His charming smile is ridiculous.

"Are you kidding me? Yes, that works for me!"

"Well, you're not just packing for the island, you have to pack for L.A. as well. We will fly directly there from Necker..."

I jump into his lap, cutting him off with my lips against his.

"So, that's a yes?" he laughs through my onslaught.

"It's a *hell* yes," I push him down on the bed. *Screw the flimsy canopy...*

CHAPTER *five*

"WOW. THIS IS just…beautiful," I spin around in place in awe of our stunning guesthouse, nestled in the center of the private island. Decorated impeccably in Bali style, the dark, rich wood accents along the high peaked ceiling is carried through in the dark wood of the furniture, upholstered in off-white linens with added turquoise accent pillows. The open concept exterior walls of retractable glass doors are framed with matching white draperies, allowing the warm breeze to waft through uninhibited. The teal blue ocean beyond goes on forever. "And this view," I continue, spellbound by it. "It's breathtaking."

"Oh, I would have to agree," his tone is sinfully inviting.

Turning towards him, I'm assailed with the equally sinful, sexy grin he's flashing me as he bends to prop a suitcase in the stand.

I'd be lying if I said those smirks weren't getting to me after the very many he's sent my way since boarding the very first plane to get here - two torturously tempting flights by his delectable side, followed by an incredible ride to Necker Island on a luxury catamaran. To say he looked sinfully heavenly against the backdrop of an ocean that matched his perfect blue eyes, yet paled in comparison to the Adonis of a man, is a serious understatement. And the man can fill out a pair of khakis like no other. Top that with his light blue dress shirt, his hair wind blown and disheveled, the temptation was jarring. It took everything in my being to keep from pulling him below deck to do the things those deliciously curled lips of his were inviting me to. But I've lasted this long, and the idea of playing with him - dragging it out a little longer - is turning me on even more.

"Honestly, though," I pretend to ignore his suggestive demeanor, "...I'm not sure what takes my breath away more, the villa, or the view," I walk towards the wall of open glass doors.

"There's no question," he comes up behind me, wrapping his arms around my waist, brushing my hair over my shoulder to kiss my neck. "*You* take my breath away," he whispers.

Closing my eyes, I lean back into his hold, wrapping my arms atop his at my waist, our fingers intertwining. Nothing could feel better than being in the arms of this man...*Except that*, my eyes dart open, the feel of his erection at my behind eliciting delicious quivers down my core.

Lust threatens my playful composure as he rains delicious nips and kisses down my neck, the teasing licks of his seductive tongue on my flesh too much for my body to ignore. Uncontrollably, I arch back, desperate to brush against him. I couldn't fight the desire he evokes in me no matter how hard I try. I'm his for the taking. *Always his*.

The feel of his smile against my skin pulls my lips into a defeated grin. He knows the affect he has on me, and I give in to my body's captive longing to grind against his arousal in needy affirmation.

His breathless growl brushes my ear before he turns me swiftly to face him, his hands caressing my behind. The longing in his gaze is my final undoing. I belong to this man. Mind. Body. Soul.

"I love you," I whisper, lost in the beautiful blue eyes staring down at me.

"You know what those words do to me," he whispers on a groan.

His kiss is forceful and sensually erotic as he claims me, wrenching me against him to take the onslaught of his evident desire against my core. I moan through the assault of his perfect lips, wrapping my arms around his neck, my fingers lacing in his curls, pulling at his nape for more.

His fingers work sensually up my back beneath my shirt, lifting it in their wake. "I need you, Aby," he groans with husky desire, the acclamation echoed in the workings of his strong hands and their electrifying glides across my skin.

Reaching my arms beneath my loose blouse, he guides them from my hold of his neck, inciting me to raise them in assistance as he pulls it off over my head. My skin perks in excitement as his fingers glide back down my bare arms, pinning them in his one hand behind my back, bending to devour my décolletage. *God, I love when he takes control.*

The sensual swipe of his free palm across my breast hitches my breath, releasing my gasp as he aggressively frees my breast from the cup of my bra to the attack of his magical tongue.

"You're so beautiful," he whispers, pulling back to look into my eyes. "So fucking beautiful," he grabs my nape, pulling me to his lips.

Frantically, I pull at the buttons of his shirt, desperate in my need to touch him, to feel him bare against me. Every perfect part of him.

The sudden loss of his lips against mine shifts from a flicker of pain to thrilling excitement as he moves to finish what I started, jerking the tucked hem from inside his pants to release the final buttons before peeling it back over his shoulders. It falls to the floor and I reach for him instantly, greedily devouring his perfect form, my fingers hungrily trailing their way down his sculpted chest and abs, and back up again.

He watches me - my gaze torn between his and the delicious path of my touch on his perfect flesh. Touching him is like touching heaven, and I don't ever want to stop. I couldn't if I tried. My hands have a mind of their own, and I'm enraptured by their trail of desire. Electric currents squeeze through my core as my palm snakes down his happy trail, gliding over his belt to brush down along his khakis. Reaching his groin I steal a sensual swipe back up along his covered erection, captivated by the effect I have on him, his eyes closing, his head leaning back on a groan.

The return of his lustful gaze catapults my pulse; the desire emanating from his stare so intense, my body jolts from their sinful blaze. His breathy parted lips pull my attention, and I whimper in longing as he grabs my ass, wrenching me roughly against him, lifting me to my toes, his pant-covered cock ramming against my needy sex.

"Jesus, Aby," he moans through an assault of my neck, his squeezing hold of my ass rocking me against him in a sensual lure that leaves me panting with desire.

His lips and tongue scorch a trail of heat along my shoulder, his hands gliding up my back, making quick measure of unclasping my bra before reaching between us to grab it, swiftly tugging it off. Tossing it aside, he takes possession of one nipple with his lips and tongue, the other with his hand, both teasing and devouring, my head falling back from the pleasure.

He drops leisurely to his knees, pulling me from my euphoric trance, his perfect lips and tongue leaving a quivering trail of puckered flesh down my stomach along the way. I watch through bated breaths as he slowly and sensually glides my skirt down my legs, the onslaught of his tantalizing mouth below my belly button luring my fingers in his tousled curls.

Leaving my skirt in a pool at my feet, his hands glide up the back of my legs, his fingers massaging the cheeks of my behind before gripping my thong. "Fuck, I want to taste you," he whispers huskily, his lips lingering at the small patch of material shielding my pulsing mound.

"Oh God, Alex," I moan as he jerks my thong down my legs, his tongue taking teasing ownership of my wet folds, his hands back on my ass, squeezing, spreading me for his pleasure from behind. It's incredibly sexy to witness his loss of control, on his knees before me, his hand sliding around to work alongside his sinful tongue.

I gasp as he plunges two fingers inside me, sucking my clit into his mouth. I can't take my eyes off what he's doing to me, and as his eyes find mine, I loose my breath completely. His beautiful baby-blues mesmerize me with their sparkling desire, his tongue teasing my engorged bud, his lips curled sinfully up at the corners as he watches me.

"Do you like that, baby?" he whispers, the warmth of his breath like fire on my throbbing sex.

I bite my lip, barely managing a nod through my moans, my frantic agreement inaudible in my lust filled haze, glued to his sinful stare.

He closes his eyes on a groan of his own, the break of his gaze sending my head falling back in abandon as his lips recapture my bud, his tongue lapping in perfect rhythm with his fingers, driving me wild with a slow sensual thrusting.

I grind into his onslaught, riding his delicious mouth and the quickened thrusting of his digits as my orgasm builds. The loss of his lips pulls my gaze once more, and I watch as he licks the finger of his free hand, returning it to my behind, to tease the opening there. My body relaxes, welcoming the temptation of his wickedly delicious assault. The combination of his double penetration, the workings of his lips and tongue, sends me plummeting over the edge, screaming his name as I grip and pull at his hair, desperate to hang on for dear life.

"Fuck, Aby," he whispers, his hands working ravenously up my body, capturing me firmly in his hold as my legs give out beneath me.

I reply with a string of indecipherable breathless moans, curling into his embrace, his sexy chuckle drawing me back to earth. "That…" I gasp a few extra breaths, "…was incredible."

"*You* are incredible," he strokes my back lovingly, allowing me to come down from my high. "And beautiful…" he whispers, his lips brushing a soft kiss across my forehead.

"I feel beautiful…in your arms," I mutter through a trembling grin. I've never felt more alive, more myself, than when I'm in Alex's arms. It's incredibly rewarding and frightening at the same time. He consumes me in every way. And that still scares me.

Finding the strength to lift my head to look up into his eyes, the hunger I find there fuels the quick return of my own. My body is like kindling to his desire, a simple glance holding the power to set me ablaze.

"If you only knew how beautiful you really are," he shakes his head, his stare burning through my system like wildfire. Consuming me.

Grabbing his face in my hands, I pull his lips to mine, teeth crashing, tongues tasting in desperate longing through his deep sexy growl. My pussy clenches in longing anticipation of his fill, and I reach down, frantically maneuvering the removal of his pants, struggling with the belt buckle in my wanton craze.

"Hold on, baby," he warns through our kiss, lifting me to stand, my arms and legs wrapping around him instinctively as he carries me to the bed. Its height is inviting as he lays me gently down on my back, my legs spread at his sides as he stands before me, the bed's high platform aligning my core perfectly for his taking.

Leaning up, I bite my lip in eager yearning, watching him unfasten his belt and pants before bending to discard them with his boxers, his hungry eyes never leaving me. The sight of his ready cock as he stands upright, its tip glistening with pre cum, makes me lick my lips in anticipation, followed by my needy whimper at his sensual stroke of his shaft. My eyes dart to his, sapphire passion staring back at me atop his breathtakingly parted lips.

"You're fucking perfect," he reaches out to stroke my check, brushing his thumb along my lips, staring into my eyes.

I'm insatiable for this man, as he is for me. Yet every time feels like the first. The best. Our undeniable chemical connection too strong to ever fade.

I swallow hard, trying to remember to breathe, watching his gaze leave mine to follow the teasing touch of his fingers down my quivering tummy, his cock still gripped in his hand amid slow, sensuous pumps. My pussy clenches at the sight, begging for his fill. His hand pauses at my pelvis, his thumb finding my sensitive bud, rubbing in perfect teasing circles that rocket the burning heat in my core.

My body arches into his touch, pleading, enticing, desperate for him. Sensual arousal consumes me as I move to massage my breasts for his perusal. Taunting him as he taunted me. "Take me," I bite my lip, staring into his eyes before glancing down to his held cock.

His chest rises and falls in his breathless, silent stare, his tongue lingering at his perfect bottom lip. "God, what you do to me," he groans, brushing his hardness along my wet folds, lining up, teasing my entrance with the tip of his glorious cock.

Oh, God. My core pulses around the engorged head, our gazes locked in the delicious moment. I'm on fire for him, his tantalizing measured pace driving me wild. "Fuck me," the words fall off my tongue, the order laced with a sensual craving echoed in my body's bucking for urgency.

He plunges inside, our gasps swallowed in the silence as my body settles around his deep girth. Reaching up, he brushes his thumb along my lip, gently pulling it down and I take it in my mouth, sucking greedily as he pulls his cock back for another forceful thrust.

My lips part on a gasp, his thumb, dampened from my suckling, moving to tantalize my clit amid his incredible pounding thrusts. Over and over, I meet him measure for measure, gripping the bed linen at my sides for momentum, my body tensing from the impending eruption. "Alex," I scream his name, closing my eyes to euphoric white light as I explode around him.

Grabbing my legs, he holds them wider, his perfect cock pumping into me with abandon, his breaths ragged amid his grunts of desire. "Look at me, baby," he orders breathlessly, pounding through the wildest orgasm of my life.

Our eyes lock, his face twisting in his passionate completion, stilling as my pussy milks the delicious pulsing ridges of his explosion.

"Fuck," he mutters, flopping down on top of me, our chests heaving, gasping for breaths. "You will be the death of me, Aby Ryan," he whispers roughly, his parted lips smiling against my breast as he struggles for air. "Every perfect part of you."

MMMM, I MOAN in contentment, stretching in peaceful wakening before opening my eyes to the most beautiful man staring back at me. "What are you doing?" I whisper sleepily, not ready to lose the serenity of the moment.

"I'm enjoying you. Appreciating you." The slow, perfect pull of his lips into a smile is breathtaking.

"You're watching me sleep," I laugh lightly, reaching to touch his perfect face. "How long *did* I sleep?" I jolt up, looking around for signs of dusk, panicked at the idea of sleeping our first afternoon away.

"Just an hour. You needed it, baby."

"What I need is to spend every waking moment of this amazing vacation appreciating *you*. And, perhaps, a shower," I grimace playfully, lying back down on my side to face him. "We need this time together. I don't want to sleep it away."

"No rest for the wicked," he winks, the gleam in his eyes hitting me straight between the legs.

"Do you plan on keeping me in this bed for the duration of our stay, Mr. Tate?"

"Don't tempt me," he traces his finger down my arm, across my bare chest, his eyes devouring the trail of goose bumps in their wake. "I actually plan on doing many things with you while we're here. And, no," he looks into my eyes, "…a bed is not a necessary requirement."

"Warning heeded," I smile devilishly. "So, what's on the agenda first?"

"I believe *you* were on the agenda first," he teases with a sinful simper, my core clenching at the memory of his touch. "How would you like a romantic dinner on the beach?"

"Sounds perfect."

"It does, doesn't it? I thought we could investigate the island first." The grin of excitement plastered across his face is a joy to witness. His love of adventure and the outdoors is one of the very many things I've come to admire about him.

"That sounds perfect too," I smile. "Everything with you sounds perfect."

"Everything?" his brow skyrockets, and I just want to lean up and lick the damn thing. "I'm not sure the flashing cameras and invasive microphones thrust in our faces at the airport could be classified as perfect," he adds somberly, averting my gaze, his eyes tracing his finger down my arm.

"Au contraire, my love," I attempt to ease his obvious worry about my fears - though, at the time, I absolutely was a bundle of nerves and sweat at the hands of the vultures. "Your brilliant answers to their asinine questions were perfectly perfect."

He doesn't look up, his lips pulling into a bashful, crooked grin, "You handled them perfectly, yourself."

"I *ignored* them," I laugh. "And gladly faded into your background."

His gaze darts to mine. "You could never fade into the background. And it was wonderful to have you by my side," he adds softly, cupping my cheek in his hand, his thumb brushing lovingly along my jaw.

I swallow hard, reeling from the sincerity in his eyes. The man the world fantasizes about, the man the paparazzi hunt shamelessly, is so much more than the beautiful British heartthrob actor they see. I know him for who he truly is. The real Alexander Tate. For that, I feel truly blessed. I owe it to him to draw from his strength - the poise he's demonstrated so many times at the hands of the prying eyes of the world. "I'll always be by your side," I kiss his lips. "Or hiding behind you," I add playfully with a shrug. "They're like bloody vultures," I scrunch my nose dramatically.

"Bloody vultures?" his thick British drawl makes me laugh out loud, and he laughs with me. "I don't particularly like the idea of you hiding behind me, Miss Ryan. I want to show you off to the world. I want everyone to know you're *mine*," he annunciates the word, staring into my eyes, stealing my breath away. "Besides," he adds, his lips curling devilishly, "...I much prefer the idea of you on *top* of me, or under me," his eyebrow quirks as turns me on my back, his rock hard, delectable body coming over me.

I giggle through the motion, my pulse picking up pace. "Mr. Tate, we will never make it out of this bed at this rate," I manage, my breaths fluttering in a pant of stirred arousal.

"You want that romantic dinner on the beach," he sighs playfully in defeat, his inner struggle for control pinching his lips into an undecided pout of his own.

Nibbling my lip at the tempting idea of never leaving this guesthouse, I nod, eyes bright with the equally inviting thought of romance.

"I want it too," he smiles sincerely, moving to stand in his deliciously naked glory, his jaw dropping erection pulling my gaze. "I'm looking forward to wining and dining my beautiful lady. Right after we take that shower you suggested," he adds with a wickedly suggestive grin, offering me his hand.

Oh dear God.

"I'M SORRY, I'VE been going on and on," Alex pulls his napkin from his lap, wiping the corners of his mouth.

"Don't be. I love hearing stories about your childhood and your family. Your parents sound like such well-rounded, wonderful people. The apple doesn't fall far from the tree," I add with a smile, taking a sip of my wine.

"They are great. I'm blessed to have them, but every family has their moments," he shrugs, grinning.

"Ummm, I think mine has more than it's fair share. *We're all a little crazy*," I add dramatically on a whisper.

Laughing, he shakes his head, looking into my eyes with a sweet smile. "Call it what you will, it's one of the many things I love about you."

Uncontrollably, my eyes widen at his use of the word and I immediately note the shift of his brow and cock of his head at my reaction. "You know what *I* would love?" I quickly aim for a detour of distraction. "A walk on the beach. It's so beautiful and quiet out here," I look up and down the strip of isolated sand before looking back to him. "The staff really do leave the guests in peace, don't they?"

"Yes, they do. And since we're the only guests here," he stands, taking my hand to pull me up against him, "...a private stroll by the water sounds very inviting."

"You want me naked and wet, don't you?" The thought elicits an eruption through my core.

"Oh, absolutely," he simpers. "But I'm still delivering the romance portion." He cups my jaw to hold my gaze, his thumb brushing along my lip. "Let's talk a little more," he adds, kissing me softly before bending down to remove my sandals, a soft hold of my calves through the motions. Laying them to the side, he looks up at me, his eyes filled with longing as his hands run up the span of my legs. "Did I tell you how beautiful you look this evening?" His touch glides up with my short sundress as he stands. "You really are beautiful, Aby," he whispers, bending to kiss my neck.

Closing my eyes, I bite my lip against the shrill of ecstasy coursing through me. His words are my euphoria. They hypnotize me, leave me breathless. Speechless.

"Come," he offers me his hand, looking into my eyes, flashing that amazing combination smile - the sweet, though sinfully sexy, knowing one that drives me wild. "Let's go for that stroll." Kicking off his sandals, he leads me toward the water's edge.

The ocean breeze blends with the warmth of the evening as we walk hand in hand in silence, just out of reach of the slow, soft waves. We've been here less than a day, and it feels like a peaceful forever. A world away from all of our troubles. All of my fears. The quiet moment is perfect. Safe.

"It's all about perception, you know," he says out of nowhere, and I look to him in confusion - clearly he's not riding the thoughtless wave with me. "The issues you have with your family. Or, rather, I should say, your *Mum*," he continues, his eyebrow doing its sexy shift.

"Nail on the head," I tap my nose at his accurate summation of issues with my mother. "Do go on, Dr. Tate. I welcome your psychoanalysis with an open mind," I tease with a smile, before looking ahead. I'm not sure why he's thinking about this right now, but I'm intrigued as to what he has to say.

"Perception is everything. In my world," he pauses, pulling my gaze before continuing. "*That* world we agree can be difficult," he purses his lips and I laugh. "My every word, every step is perceived by everyone, rightfully or wrongfully. It's particularly eye opening to be on the constant receiving end of those presumptions and assumptions. However, the positive side is that it reminds me to try to look past what appears on the surface. I try to see what is *real* beneath, before allowing my own perception to come into play. We can never predict the reactions of others to our own actions, Aby. Anymore than they can truly perceive them in light of our honest intent."

"Wow. That's deep." I try to hide my smile. He's being sincere, and I feel bad for making a joke.

"I'm just suggesting that perhaps you should try that with your Mum." He offers a closed lip smile with a small shrug, before his lips curl into a playful grin.

He's the sweetest man I've ever met. His boyish charm is ridiculous.

"So, essentially," I smile at him genially in return, "…you're suggesting I'm projecting my own self doubts onto the actions of my well-meaning mother."

"Essentially, yes." He squeezes my hand, and I bump into him playfully as we walk. "Your Mum adores you and your sister equally, Aby. I can see that. Why can't you?"

"I know she does," I sigh. "And I know you're right. I do look for things in everything she does, and take them the wrong way. But," I put my finger up with a laugh, "…she still drives me crazy regardless."

"Because she loves you, worries about you, and wants the best for her daughter. I'm sure Anna would agree with everything you're feeling, Aby. I do see how my Mum treats her daughter differently than she does her son."

"Ahhh, the proverbial son," I tease and he laughs, pursing his lips.

"I wouldn't say I'm *spoiled*. My father would never allow his son to ride the easy road. That being said, yes, Mum does dote on me," he flashes that boyish smile that pulls at my heartstrings. "So have you ever spoken to Beth about how you feel? Perhaps she feels the same way, and you're simply unaware."

"I seriously doubt that," I mutter, suddenly realizing I'm doing it again. Perception…Assumptions and presumptions. Yeah, it's definitely a bad habit. "Communication is not exactly my family's strong suit," I add, grimacing at my part in the lack there of.

"So, I'm *assuming*," he nudges me teasingly, "…you haven't spoken to your Mum about it before either."

"Now that, Dr. Tate, is a very good assumption. See, they're not all bad," I laugh. "Mom would never be open to such a conversation. She'd take it completely offside as a negative attack and associate the entire ordeal as me blaming her, instead of trying to tell her how I fell. Translation, *I'm* assuming that *she* will assume wrongly. And I'm probably right."

"The apple doesn't fall far from the tree," he squeezes my hand again, and I turn to take in his mocking smile.

"No, I guess it doesn't," I laugh.

We fall back into peaceful silence, our gait having moved into the oceans waves. This feels right. Being open with Alex. Sharing my demons and talking through them. I'm a work in progress. We're a work in progress. And it feels wonderful. He feels wonderful.

"Thank you," I look towards him, captivated, grateful, for everything he is to me. "For the talk and the advice. For all of this," I span the air around us. "For just being you," I look into his eyes as we walk, the warm water rolling in over my sinking steps in the soft gooey sand.

"You're welcome," he smiles bashfully. His humility melts my heart. "I would like to talk about what happened earlier as well," he adds, his eyes on the stretch of beach ahead.

"I'm open to talk about anything, but you'll have to be a little more specific. Which part would you like to discuss? The one where you swept me off my feet, or the one where you swept me off my feet?"

"Well, *specifically*," he glances towards me, "…the part when you bugged out a little when I mentioned the love word."

"I didn't *bug out*." I scrunch my nose in mock defiance. "You're really picking up the North American slang, aren't you?

Maybe I'm a bad influence."

"Aby, I'm serious."

"Alex," I stop abruptly, turning to face him. "I love you," I reach up to touch his cheek. "I can say that because I'm ready to. It doesn't mean I expect you to reciprocate something *you're* not ready to." My hand slides down along his chest; it's a purposeful motion to avert my gaze. I'm not lying to him, but I would be lying to myself if I ignored the pang in my heart that longs to hear him say those three words. "Love comes with trust for you," I bravely smile up at him. "And despite that I've tested that lately, I do know how you feel about me."

"Do you?"

"Yes. I do. And until you're ready to tell me," I nip at my lip seductively, desire oozing from my gaze, "…just show me."

His eyes burn sapphire in the moonlight, his mouth parted on a husky breath as he cups my face to take me in a fierce kiss.

Trembles of need burst through every nerve as his tongue claims me, his hands devouring their way down my neck and spine. I reach for him, moaning as he grabs my waist, squeezing me tight against him. Every touch, every brush of his lips and tongue speak more than any words possibly could. I feel his need for me, his pull to me, as strongly as the air I breathe.

Reaching for the hem of my dress, he tears it up and over my raised arms, tossing it to the side before I witness his surprise. He devours my nudity, looking into my eyes with carnal hunger - a hunger that tells me we wouldn't have made it this far into the evening if he had known what was missing beneath my pretty little sundress.

Grabbing my nape, he pulls me in for another assault of the senses at the realm of his perfect lips and tongue, my hands feverishly tugging at the closure of his shorts.

I moan from the loss of his kiss as he reaches to pull off his shirt, bending to discard his bottoms to the sand. The sight of his erection, bobbing eagerly against his sculpted abs is the end of me. Pouncing, I wrap my arms around his neck, reclaiming his lips as he cups my ass to lift me, my legs securing around his waist as he carries me out into the warm ocean waves.

CHAPTER Six

"MMM… WHAT WAS that for?" I mumble against Alex's lingering lips.

He brushes my cheek, straightening to sit down on the porcelain edge of the claw foot tub, "I woke up wanting to kiss you." His eyes, raking over my submerged body, leave a trail of goose bumps in their wake. "As delicious as this visual is, it wasn't nice to find you weren't lying next to me."

"I'm sorry," I pout dramatically. "My body was begging for a bath. I swear I have sand in every crevice."

"Not possible." His heated gaze repeats its consumption of my naked form before his lips curl up in slow, soul burning grin. "I devoured every crevice of your perfect body in the shower last night." He dips his hand in the water, lathering me with lust at the touch of his fingers up my thigh and tummy, a breathtaking, teasing caress of my sex in their journey.

"Well, perhaps you weren't *thorough* enough," I bite my lip devilishly.

His smirk widens, and I take advantage of the attention of his eyes returning to mine to display my overwhelming need for him in my gaze. Insatiable doesn't describe what this man does to me. Being naked and wet under the captivating pull of him merely adds to his effect on me. Not to mention the euphoric romance of our locale. I only wish we could stay here on our little fantasy island, hidden from the realm of reality forever. For now, I'll settle for the warmth of his beautiful body wrapped around mine in this tub. "Off with thy pants, Alexander the Great."

"Not just yet," he replies on a whisper, tracing a path through the beads of water leading to my belly button, his eyes lost in the motion.

I'm lost, myself, to the feel of him, my body reacting to the explosive current of his electrifying touch and the heat of his gaze. In his hands, under the spell of his eyes, I'm transported to another world. His world. And he has this way of making me feel like I'm the only one in it.

Mine, his profession zings through my psyche as his touch tantalizes along my core. *Yours*, I reply silently, moaning, closing my eyes in the pleasure of his fleeting graze. *Always*.

Opening them to his stare, I note the sudden melancholy floating across his face. "Alex?"

He says nothing as he stands, turning to dry his hands in the terry robe hung nearby. Although he offers a warm grin at my questioning frown, I can't help but shiver at what lies beneath it. Leaning against the wall, he bites the corner of his mouth as though preparing to break bad news. *Damn*. Please don't be bad news.

"I received a message from the producers," he begins, looking down momentarily in regret. I'm sure it has something to do with the disappointment that unconsciously, though, undoubtedly flashed across my face. "They need to push the shooting forward," he looks back to me, crossing his arms over his chest, relaxing into his lean against the wall.

"What does that mean for you?" I attempt to lace my question with an odd mixture of nonchalance and understanding; an added forced smile in hopes of passing. I'm sure I failed.

"We shall see. I have to call them."

"Okay," I smile sincerely, trying to make him feel better. He's obviously worried this may affect our little escape, and more so how I will react. The least I can do is lesson his guilt. It's not his fault that reality is calling. "Why don't you go make the call, I'll get cleaned up for breakfast by the..."

"No," he shakes his head, the return of his devilishly, delicious smile reheating my skin despite the cooling water. "I'll go make the call, *you* stay right where you are. I have to scour every inch of you for lingering sand," he adds, bending his legs to hover at the side of the tub. Brushing an escaped strand of my pinned hair behind my ear, he leans in to whisper a soft kiss across my lips, his tongue teasing a lick that I feel right between my legs. "Don't go anywhere."

I watch him walk away, leaning my chin on the side of the tub, devouring his incredible physique. My eyes linger on his perfect ass beneath his white pajama bottoms before moving up to his broad back, my nails aching to scratch down every delicious muscle as I scream his name. I stay that way, involuntarily staring towards his long retreated form, until I shiver from the chill of the water, and the loss of his touch. The chill of reality lurking.

It's not like we can hide from it. Alone on an island or not. Sighing, I lean back into the mould of the tub. *Maybe I can hold him hostage here*, I purse my lips at my inner dreamers fanatical contribution to a solution. *Arg, pirate Aby*, I mime the title, giggling to myself. I've officially flown the coop. Less than two days in the sun on a tropical island certainly has its way of easing up my defensive wall. As well as being a willing prisoner of love to one *Alexander the Great*, of course. The combination has worked wonders. It feels good to let go. Being back in Alex's arms is all I need to face the lingering fears of reality - *his* reality. *Thank God for second chances*, I smile, sitting up to unplug the drain and turn on the hot water.

Settling back into place, I dip my toes in the cascading stream, running my hands through the water to pull the renewed warmth upwards to surround me. My flesh is perked from the chill, my nipples even more so at the thought of Alex's return. The slow reheat of the water titillates every aroused pore, and I close my eyes, basking in the anticipation of his touch.

"You're stunning."

My eyes dart open in surprise, a delicious flutter running through me at the sexy sight of him leaned against the doorframe watching me. "You're not so bad yourself," I reply breathlessly.

His sweet smile doesn't reach his eyes, and I take a deep breath in preparation for the pending news. Folding his arms, he leans into the frame further, his jaw clenching. It's clear he's gauging his words - and my reaction.

I hate that I've created this hesitation in him at the hands of my history of bad reactions. *Pathetically* bad reactions. Well, not anymore. I need to be as strong for him as he has been for me. "Whether we have to leave today, tomorrow, or the next," I begin with a comforting smile, "…it doesn't matter, Alex."

His gaze drops to the floor for a moment before he looks back up to me, a small closed-lip pull of the corners of his mouth.

I feel the pang of disappointment in my gut at his silent affirmation of the early end of our island excursion, but I don't want him to feel it too. At least not because he feels guilty about how *I* feel about it. "As amazing as this escape has been, as long as I'm with you, it doesn't matter where we are," I pour every ounce of love and strength into my tone and smile. "So, when do we leave?"

"Tomorrow afternoon," are his only words of reply.

"Well, in that case, Mr. Incredibly Sexy and Romantic," I cup my chin seductively in my palm, leaning against the side of the tub, "…what are you waiting for?"

Desire curls in around the melancholy glimmer of his irises, effectively transforming his gaze and demeanor with burning returned want. Reaching for the waist of his pajama bottoms, he pulls them down to the delight of my watchful eyes.

A devilish smile escapes me as I lean back and watch the man of my dreams, in all his glorious nudity, walk towards me, anticipation soaring through my clenching core.

THE BRIGHT SUN glitters across the pool, its warm rays dancing with the cool water beading on my slickened flesh as I float weightlessly in Alex's arms, lost in the erotic euphoria of his hold.

"This is amaze-balls," I close my eyes, relishing in the feel of his strong hands beneath me, gliding my body along the water.

"I'm glad you approve," he chuckles, adjusting his grip of me to keep me afloat with one hand, cupping water in his free palm, playfully pouring it over my stomach. "If only we could stay longer. I'd keep you here forever, if I could."

Opening my eyes, I use my hand as a shield, taking in his darkened silhouette from the brightness of the sun. His wet curls slicked back, water droplets sluicing down his cheeks, neck and wide shoulders from his recent dip, send my heart rate soaring.

"You *can* keep me forever," I smile, reaching up to touch the perfection of his chest. "It doesn't matter where we are, as long as I'm with you," I remind him. "It's *you* that's amazing." I need him to know that it's not the expensive locale that has me in awe. It's him. It's everything about him.

"I could say the same, baby." His shy smile makes me love him even more.

"Do you realize how hooked you have me?" I question with a playful evil eye, maneuvering from his hold. Wading the water to stand before him, I place my hands on the heated skin of his tan shoulders, desperate to feel him beneath my palms.

He welcomes the shift with a sinful smile, reaching for my waist to hold me in place, looking into my eyes with adoration.

I could stare at him forever, this man I love. Held in the engulfing dominance of his large hands, I feel precious. Protected. Loved. I don't need to hear him say it to know how he feels. His actions speak so much louder than any words. And though I hope mine do as well, I can't help but want to tell him over and over. But…not right now. This moment is perfect, and I don't want to ruin it with a reminder that what I feel for him is bigger than the both of us.

To be honest, I'm still trying to wrap my head around the enormity of the love I already feel for him. Isn't that, after all, the real reason I ran away? I've faced that epiphany. Shared it with him even. But we never really delved into the underlying question behind my fear - Are we moving too fast?

"Can I ask you something?" I search his gaze, running my fingers leisurely along his chest, my palms luxuriating in the heat of his skin.

"Of course, sweetheart, you can ask me anything," the squeeze of his fingers at my hips confirms his words, the sensual pressure sending a delicious current down my core.

"Do you think this is crazy? How quickly we found each other…how quickly our relationship has developed?"

His contemplative gaze flickers in turn between my eyes. "Do you?" he questions, his bright baby-blues eying me uncertainly.

I open my mouth to respond, though no words come as my shoulders sag, heavy with guilt. I'm left gawking at him like a guppy, regretting bringing it up. Possibly spoiling a perfect moment after all.

"You're adorable," he reaches up to brush his fingers along my jaw, the chills of the wet touch no match to the warmth it surfaces in my cheek. "Talk to me, baby."

His warm reminder that he isn't giving up on me - that he *never* gave up on us - both swells and deflates my self-reproach at the same time. The latter winning out as I remember my vow…*I promised no more lies*.

Feigning a small smile through a breath of strength, I look into his eyes. "I can't say it hasn't crossed my mind more than once," I begin, pausing to gauge any reaction in his loving stare. The only thing I see is silent encouragement to continue. "There's no question we've had a connection from the very beginning. A connection I never thought possible outside of dreams and romance novels - an unbelievable happenstance, so much so that I ran away from it." I look down, shuddering at the memory.

He pulls me closer, instantly reminding me how right this feels. In his arms is where I belong.

"But I keep trying to remind myself that sometimes when you know, you just know," I add, snuggling into his hold, my cheek against his chest. "And the one thing I know…the one thing I'm absolutely sure of is that you are the one for me. The only one."

He says nothing, though I feel the jump of his heartbeat, the quickening of his breaths.

"This feels right, Alex," I look up into his eyes, sliding my hands up to his face to cup his jaw. "This is where I belong. With you. *Anywhere* with you." Lifting on my tiptoes, I place a chaste kiss on his lips, pulling back to witness lust dance across his eyes.

"Aby, I've wanted you since the first moment I saw you," his husky tone licks down my spine, a gasp released from my parted lips as he bends to cup my ass to lift me, securing my thighs around his waist. His hungry gaze devours me. "It can't possibly come more quickly than that. But do I think it's developed too quickly? I would say, no. I know I want you. And I've known from the start that you were it for me."

The brush of his hardening cock between my legs, separated solely by the thin material of my bikini bottoms, sends my ardor careening in intense need. Everything about this man makes me so responsive. His words. His actions. Everything.

Sliding my fingers through his damp hair, I take him in a searing kiss, trying to relay every ounce of gratitude I have for having found him. Our tongues dual, our breaths coming in heated pants as he walks us towards the pool's edge. The sudden feel of the cold, hard concrete against my back adds a delicious shiver to his assault of my senses; his firm grip of my ass at the mercy of his massaging fingers, the moan I release as he wrenches me against his hardness.

A whimper escapes my lips as he pulls away, cupping my cheeks in his hands to force my gaze. "You may have dreamt of *me* once, but I need you to know…I dreamt of you, too."

"Alex…" I whisper, my breath taken away by his words and the sentiment in his beautiful eyes. "I love you. Madly," I reach up, covering his hands with my own, shaking my head in awe of him.

The world around us seems to disappear as he searches my gaze, his sparkling baby-blues penetrating deep into my soul, searing me with a heat so close to fire that I fear I could combust in his arms.

I melt further into oblivion as he leans forward to place a kiss to my forehead, his lips moving to brush along my cheek, my jaw; a tender nibble on my lobe. "I love you, too," he whispers, his words instantly bringing tears to my eyes.

A gasping sob threatens to release the swell of my emotion, and I have to remind myself to breathe as he pulls back to look at me once more, the pool of tears ready to burst before his witnessing gaze.

"You know that, right? How much I love you, Aby?"

"Yes…" I confess on a breathless whisper, pulling his face to mine. I kiss him savagely in my hunger for him, for everything he means to me. I feel like I've waited my entire life to find him, for him to find *me*. And now he has. We've found each other, and I don't plan on wasting one second of it. I plan on showing him every moment of every day just how much I love him, adore him, worship him…

We can't seem to get enough of each other; our lips colliding, our tongues mimicking what our bodies so desperately crave. Always crave. Our hands explore each other's flesh, sluicing along our slickened skin, our hips gyrating, seeking measure despite our swimsuits.

I moan as his lips glide along my chin, down my neck, his nips and licks leaving me panting as I reach along his muscled back, clawing and pulling to get him closer. I want him inside me. I *need* him inside me. "Alex, I need you, *please*…" I beg as he bites my shoulder, his fingers gripping and squeezing harder on my ass.

Leaning back to look at me, his eyes are filled with fire, the emotions and love we feel for each other heightening our passion to an inferno, our bodies burning and sizzling in its magnificent blaze.

I quiver in the magnitude of his gaze, quaking in absolute need, devouring the love and desire reflected there. It's a moment my heart longs to capture for all time, skipping a beat taking in the beauty of him, stunningly magnified in the gleaming sun.

Squeezing my ass, his fingers move to caress my thighs - thighs that tighten along his hips to hold myself in place, bracing my weight against the pool's edge, desperate not to lose the feeling of him pressed so tightly where I need him the most.

I moan as he grinds against me knowingly, running his hands

slowly along the top of my legs, his fingers teasing between my tight hold of his hips. *Oh, God, yes...touch me*, my arms pull at him in desperation, persuading the return of the supportive hold of my ass, my gripped thighs loosening to the fleeting grazing touch of his free hand. The curl of his fingers around my sex titillates an instant squeezing want.

"Are you ready, baby?" his sinful expression holds me captive, unprepared as he suddenly plunges downwards, submerging underwater before me.

I gasp as he spreads my thighs around his neck, my legs dangling over his shoulders as he buries his face between them to rub his mouth against my core. The eroticism of his suggestive act draws my wanting moan, my fingers finding their way into his hair, tugging and pulling for more.

Expecting him to come up for air, I startle and yelp in surprise as he moves to stand, emerging from the water with my core still at his mercy, his fingers spread on my ass, holding me securely in place around his neck. The strength of his maneuver excites me as much as his face, still buried, between my legs.

Moaning, I absently tighten my grip in his soaked hair to gain measure in my balancing act atop his strong shoulders.

Water sluices off our bodies in the motion; mine held high in the air as he straightens fully, nipping and biting along my bikini bottoms, along the insides of my thighs. His hands glide up my spine, his fingers splaying wide on my back, guiding me, gently laying me down on the side of the pool.

"Alex..." I quake at the sheer magnitude of his power, his ability to hold me, maneuver me as he wants. Mold me any way he wishes.

My legs relax over his shoulders as he leans up, avidly tugging the strings of my bottoms undone, pulling them out of the way to expose my saturated sex to his wanting gaze. His eyes meet mine in a moment of sensual warning.

"Oh, God," I moan with a shriek of pleasure as his tongue plunges inside. My head falls back from the sensual onslaught, the depths of his devouring strokes, the feel of his hot breath on me, inside me.

His returned groan sends a spike of desire up my spine, drawing my returned gaze. My needy hands tug and pull on his wet hair, urging him closer to assuage the desperate ache in my pussy. I can't bring myself to look away, the act so erotic, so incredibly sexy, I can barely breathe through my lust-filled euphoria.

Opening his cerulean eyes to me, he laps at my slick folds, holding my gaze hostage as his tongue circles my clit. His stare is penetrating, searing me with each devouring lick and suck; the incessant sensual motions my undoing.

My core clenches in desperate need to be filled, and, *oh God*, the sexy, knowing smirk he flashes through his sinful assault is enough to make me willing to beg. "Alex…please…" I plead, panting in absolute want.

I gasp in instant release as he thrusts his fingers inside me, curled magically to hit the perfect spot he knows so well. The effect pushes me so quickly over the edge that I scream out loud, my body bowing uncontrollably in his grip, holding my knee in place over his shoulder.

His magician tongue and thrusting fingers don't wane as my orgasm rushes through me. My body is on fire, burning within the grip of his steady rhythm.

Pulling his lips from my pulsing clit, he kisses along the inside of my thighs, slowing removing his fingers from my throbbing core as I shutter and quake, not wanting to let them go. A whimper of defeat escapes me at the loss, and he chuckles, gently removing my legs from his shoulders, laying them to dangle over the pool's edge into the water.

I'm utterly spent. Satiated in euphoric bliss. And since I'm more akin to a floppy noodle, it doesn't surprise me when he reaches for my hands, limp and lifeless at my sides, linking his fingers in mine to assist me in sitting up.

Despite my floating euphoria, however, my body feels as though it weighs a thousand pounds, and I rest my head on his shoulder, wrapping my arms around his neck. "Mmmm, Alex, that was…wow," I mumble incoherently into the warmth of his flesh.

He chuckles again, and I want to playfully smack him for teasing me, but I don't have the strength. Instead, I relish in the glide of his fingers along the abraded skin of my back from the coarse concrete.

"Oh, I'm not done with you yet, sweetheart," he states in rebuttal to my blissful moans, curling me in his arms to carry me through the water.

I melt, taking in his stunning face, the sweet, loving smile that fills it, the heart stopping way he looks into my eyes. And for a moment, as he wades us towards the steps, I'm unable to break his gaze - that is until my attention is caught briefly by my discarded bikini bottoms floating aimlessly in the water. It's an instant delicious reminder that beneath that beautiful, gentlemanly exterior lies a sinfully sexy man that owns me. Naked or otherwise.

Resting me on my feet before the opened glass doors of our suite, he flashes me another deviously delicious grin, slowly pulling the strings of my bikini top, my nipples puckering as it glides from my flesh.

Impatient for him, I nip my lip invitingly, plunging my fingers inside his board shorts to push them down his hips; he steps back to assist, kicking them to the side.

Every nerve ending is alight, burning with my renewed desire; the warm breeze like an aphrodisiac seeping into my pores as we stand, staring into each other's eyes. The intense love and longing I see reflected in Alex's gaze consumes me, my lips parting on a breathless moan from the assault.

"You have no idea how fast my heart races when I look at you," his breathless words steal mine, his perfect eyes penetrating my soul, before he bends to lift me in his arms.

Carrying me to the bed, he lays me down gently on the white linen sheets, crawling over top of me, my hands gliding along his thick, corded muscles, savoring every rippling ridge.

His gaze steals my breath once more, his lips inches from my wanting mouth. "I love you. I love you so fucking much, Aby," he whispers huskily, taking me in an earth-shattering kiss, his tongue insinuating his desperate need. "I can't wait...I need to be inside you," he manages against my lips.

"Yes, Alex. Take me. Now," I beg, moaning in anticipation as he settles his hips between my spread legs. "God…"

Our groans collide in unison as he slides his cock along my wetness, teasing back and forth along my clit, lining up to thrust deep in one long fluid motion. My fingers curl and flex at his back, my head leaned back, eyes closed in absolute abandon. I love the way he feels inside me, the way he makes me feel. He makes me whole. Complete.

His thrusts quicken, pushing us to the edge, plunging inside me over and over, hitting each and every sensitive nerve. Our bodies shake from crazed desire, lust; sweat coating our flesh, my nails scratching down his sinewy back.

Savage in our need, primal in our frenzy, his lips nip and lick along my collarbone, the sensitive skin at the curve of my neck, his hands holding my head in place, gripped tight in my hair.

"You feel so fucking good, baby," he groans. "Mine…"

"God, yes! Alex, I'm coming!" I scream, my feet digging into the mattress, my hips gyrating to meet his thrusts measure for measure.

"Yes, baby, come. Come for me…" he demands, and I fall, plummeting into oblivion; my gaze blackened in the rush that spirals into a white haze of ecstasy.

I scream his name over and over, matching his incessant plunges into my greedy, soaked core, my legs shaky and quivering as I flood him with my orgasm. "I love you…" my screams dwindle into a whisper of euphoria.

His thrusts slow, his body bowing and tightening above me, before he stills, careening through my haze with every bucking ridge of his cock filling me with his come. "I love you more," he replies on a husky whisper.

CHAPTER
Seven

"GOOD MORNING, SLEEPY head."

I open my eyes to find a playful Alex staring down at me. "The only thing good about it is waking up to you," I stretch, turning into his warmth. "Was that the door bell I heard?" I question just as it chimes a second time.

"That it was." He smiles, hopping out of bed in his naked glory, grabbing his pajama bottoms to pull them on. "I ordered an early breakfast. We have to leave for the airport by noon."

I can't help but pout as his glorious manhood disappears beneath the white fabric, then I smirk at his knowing grin. "Don't give me that cheeky smile, it's your fault I'm so sleepy this morning."

"And it's your fault," he bends to lift my chin for a chaste kiss, "...that I'm so in love with you, I can't help but keep you up all night long. What would Stacey, say? Suck it up, buttercup?" His crooked grin is the end of me.

He leaves to answer the door and I decide to freshen up quickly while he's dealing with room service; donning my white boy shorts and matching tank before exiting the washroom. Upon my return, he's sitting up in bed, waiting for me.

"Breakfast is on the veranda, it can wait. Come here," he orders in that tone I can't ignore.

I walk obediently towards him, only to purse my lips at a second showing of his knowing simper. "You're the devil," I turn away, but he grabs my arm, pulling me down into his lap.

"If I'm the devil, Aby, you are the angel that will save me," he tips my head with the touch of his finger, taking me in a sensual kiss.

I'm breathless, spinning in a loving haze, by the time he releases me.

"I wanted to keep you here, hidden away with me for just a little longer," his eyes reflect the truth of his sentiment.

"I wish you could have," I smile. I really do, but at the same time, I need to get back and face reality with Alex. Learn to exist in his world, without ever wanting to run from it again. "Being alone with you was never part of my fears, Alex." I sit up, facing him; he shifts to make room for me at his side. "When I'm alone with you, the rest of the world doesn't exist. And, as it turns out," I shrug, grimacing playfully, though half-heartedly, "…we won't always be alone. I want to face the real world - *yours* - by your side. No more running."

"You don't have to prove anything to me, Aby. I trust in your love. Our love. But this little getaway of ours, it was about more than just romance - though that played a very large role."

"A role you could win an Oscar for pulling off, seamlessly, I might add."

His humble smile always takes my breath away. "I'm glad to hear you think so," he brushes my cheek. "The other part of my plan in whisking you off alone was because I needed you to trust in *my* love for you, too. To make you see that no reality can ever change the way I feel about you."

It takes a moment for my lungs to fill with air. "That was the most romantic thing I think anyone in the entire world has ever said to…anyone," I grasp for words, still awestruck by his.

His eyes search mine, and I realize he's waiting for an answer to a question he never actually asked. But I heard it, and it's lingering now in its continued silence. "I do, Alex. I trust the love you feel for me. I think I trust it even more because you made sure to show me, made sure I actually saw it, felt it, even before you said the words. Thank you for that gift." I reach out to cup his face in my hands, leaning in to kiss him with as much gentle passion as his actions and words speak to me.

Covering my hands with his as we break our beautifully perfect kiss, he holds me in place to look into my eyes. "I love you more than I ever imagined possible, Aby. I'm bound to you, sweetheart. Irrevocably yours."

"As I am to you. I love you."

"I love you more." His playful smile pulls at mine, and I can't help but play back.

"Bound, huh? Like, wrapped around my little finger?" I tease, holding it up, flashing him a smile.

"Oh, absolutely," he nods, his eyebrow shifting in sexy agreement.

My eyes flicker to the ribbon holding the netting canopy to the bedpost, a delicious idea popping into my mind. Reaching for the long, hanging strands on one side, I take his hand, biting my lip as I prepare to tie them around his wrist.

"Bondage, Miss Ryan?" There's a hint of humor mixed with his enticing tone. "Ideas from your latest romance novel?"

"Possibly…" I tease flirtatiously, bowing the ribbon to secure him with a loose knot. "I think it's time for a little pay back."

His brow repeats its devilish shift, his lips curling into that sinful grin as I mount him to make my way to the other side. "Payback?"

For a moment I just stare, lost in his incredibly hot, challenging gaze. It really isn't fair, the effect he has on me. The memory of his lips and tongue devouring my chocolate covered flesh squeezes down my core, and I grind reflexively atop him. *Who knew frozen yogurt could be so much fun?*

Releasing a breathless groan, he reaches for my ass with his free hand, rocking me against him with his firm grip. The effect is thrilling, but I'm not relenting control.

"Hungry?" I ask playfully, grinding a second time, watching the desire twist in his gaze.

His eyes close on an openmouthed release of breath before his lips curl into another slow grin, his hips undulating beneath me.

"I'll take that as a yes," I smile, removing his hand from my thigh to secure it on the other side of the bed.

"You can take anything you want." His eyes watch mine as I sit back down in place atop him. "I'm just not sure your little plan is going to keep me from taking what's *mine* in return," he adds, pulling lightly on his bindings in warning.

"Patience, stallion," I grin wickedly, bending to kiss him, my hips matching the teasing efforts of my tongue as I work my fingers through the tousled curls at his nape. The feel of his arousal beneath me is exhilarating.

His hips buck against me, sending squeezing pulses to my core as he swallows my needy gasp. It's almost enough to make me lose control. Almost.

Pulling from his lips, I trail kisses down his neck, sliding my body down his, my fingers devouring the path of my lips and tongue. I relish every inch of him, every perfectly sculpted ridge before reaching his happy trail, disappearing beneath the band of his white cotton bottoms. Pausing, I catch his mischievous gaze followed by his teasing shrug at my momentary hindrance.

"Cocky, Mr. Tate?" I raise my brows in playful defiance.

He laughs, his beautiful mouth inviting me, pulling me like a doll on a string to surrender and pounce.

It's a test of composure that my body is begging to give in to, but the thrill of anticipation wins back my upper hand. "Allow me to wipe that smug little smile off your face," I add with devilish desire, sensually swiping his covered erection from base to tip.

"Aby," he groans, his arms tugging at their bindings, his smile effectively twisted into needy, breathless lust.

God, I want him. I almost lose myself in the lure of his stare, quickly pulling at the waistband of his pants. The release of his erection jars my restraint further, and I unconsciously lick my lip, biting it to fight for control, as I watch it bob against him enticingly.

"Come here," he orders in husky need, pulling at the bindings once more.

My gaze slits defiantly, his command restoring my desire for control. Stepping off the bottom of the bed, I pull his pants off in the motion, discarding them to the floor. I can't take my eyes off of him. Naked and bound, he takes my breath away.

His muscular legs are spread enticingly, his cock ready and waiting at their apex - a flashing beacon, like a tantalizing runway, inviting me to land on this Adonis of a man. It's so hard to walk away when all I want to do is fly.

But this is *my* game.

"You'll be okay here for a little while?" I ask, resorting to playful teasing to rein in my threatening bashful and impending surrender.

His eyebrow lifts above an amused challenging smirk. "I'll be just fine," he replies as I turn to make my way to the veranda. "When I get my hands on you, however," he continues in a sexy warning, "…you won't be walking so leisurely away by the time I'm done."

His inviting admonition elicits a naughty visual, a smile creeping across my face as I pretend to ignore him and continue on.

Eying the table full of mouthwatering breakfast delicacies, I raise my brow at the dessert options. A lover's breakfast. *Brilliant. This place thinks of everything*, I smile to myself, deciding on the bowl of chocolate covered strawberries and vessel of whipped cream.

Dipping one of the strawberries in the cream, I take a taste as inspiration builds from the onslaught of anticipation. I move into his view, standing in the center of the wall of open glass doors. "You okay?" I question with playful sarcasm, licking the whipped cream before taking the last bite.

His grimacing smile highlights his impatient discomfort, though the underlying desire in his gaze is thrilling.

"I'm thinking about a dip in the pool," I continue, bending to remove my boy shorts, seductively brushing along my core as I reach for the hem of my tank top.

He tugs on the ties a little, shooting me warning glare.

"Oh, I'm sorry," I add, tossing my top to the floor, "I forgot. You're hungry." I pout teasingly.

Clenching his jaw, he moves to speak, but I turn away to grab the bowls, smiling at my effect on him. It's empowering, and incredibly sexy, and I saunter in my gait back towards him.

"Breakfast in bed, my love," I climb up beside him, resting back on my heels, offering him a prepared strawberry.

He eyes it, held in my fingers at his mouth, before glancing into my eyes. "Payback?" he laughs, locking me in his sinful gaze.

I shrug with defiant confidence.

He takes a bite, and my core clenches at the sight of his tongue licking the cream left behind. I can't look away, taking my lip in my teeth as I'm assaulted by the sexual pull of this man. His mouth alone can strike down my control.

The pull of his smirk jars me momentarily before his erection flickers at my side, grabbing my instant attention.

He doesn't play fair. How do *they move it like that?* I turn my knowing glare back to his, the teasing bounce of his brow thrashing me back into gear. "You know," I begin, conspiratorially, "…sometimes you just have to give in and admit that you don't always have control. *Mine*," I add, reaching for him, my grip taking ownership around the underside of his shaft.

His immediate groan elicits the stroke of my hold, a brush over the top and back down the underside once more. It feels incredible to watch him lose himself to my touch.

I massage his length, over and over, my fingers magically mastering his moans as I take ownership of his desire. Desire that threatens to implode through me, building with each undulation of his hips at my will. I'm on fire for him, the feel of his girth in the control of my palm scorching through me. My pussy clenches for him, desperate to have him inside me.

Closing my eyes, I lose myself in the moment, my free hand caressing my breast in time with my strokes of his shaft. Uncontrollably, I lift my ass, mimicking a desire to ride him, my hand gliding down to fill his absence as my massaging fingers continue to devour his length.

"Untie me," he orders in a firm, breathless whisper.

Overtaken by my seduction, I nip at my lip, locking our gaze as I ride my fingers slowly, erotically; rimming his erection with each gentle, squeezing stroke.

"Fuck," he growls, his muscles bulging and rippling, breaking free from his bindings.

A delicious shiver courses through me as he grips my ass, lifting me to straddle him. I gasp as he pushes me back on the bed, my legs spread around him, my wet, clenching pussy splayed for his perusal.

"Oh, God," I moan, as he fills me with his fingers, my body arching in desperation. The building desire threatens to consume me as he fucks me with his masterful digits, working my core the way only he can. I'm his. Always, and only his for the taking.

I whimper at the sudden loss of his fingers, choking into a gasp as he grips my ass. His eyes burn with desire as he bends forward, lifting my core to meet his mouth, his tongue plunging between my slickened folds in ownership.

Moaning, I grab the linen, squeezing it, my body building to explosion at the working of his tongue.

His strong hold secures my core in place at his mouth, his lips gently sucking my clit, as my body lashes from the onslaught of my orgasm. I'm gasping from the quakes of the mind-blowing eruption when he lowers me back down onto the bed.

Flashing me a satisfied smirk, he brushes his fingers along my soaked core, the desire in his gaze sinful as he reaches to slide them between my parted lips.

I suck greedily under his watchful stare.

"Breakfast in bed, sweetheart. Thank you for *that* gift."

OH MY GOD, I shake my head at all of the unread messages from Stacey, one from Mom. *Ugh, why did I turn my phone on?* I decide to go for Stacey's first. I don't want to ruin my mood.

Subject: Yo Ho!

See what I did there? You're like a pirate on an island, AND a fucked-silly whore. You are, right? I hate

you. Hope you're having fun!

Stacey xx

Subject: I'm drunk

And you're a whore on an island. Love you bitch.

Stacey xx

Subject: Missing you

The only thing I've accomplished today is using my boobs to make a waterfall in the shower...and you're probably fucking under one. Love you, but hate you too.

Green-eyed Stacey (no kisses, bitch)

"What's so funny," Alex makes his way into the room. "I could hear you from outside."

"I'm reading Stacey's texts. She's nuts."

"Oh yeah? What is your feisty friend saying to incite such blithesome laughter?" he joins me on the end of the bed, lifting my crossed-legged knee to shift me closer.

"She's insinuating we're having a lot of sex," I purse my lips.

The incredibly slow, devilish pull of his smirk is his only response - no words required, as just how much sex we've actually had catapults through my psyche.

"Wow, we've had a lot sex," I admit, cataloguing our sex-ca-pades.

"We have ten more minutes," he looks playfully at his watch.

Laughing, I shove his shoulder, his boyish smile returning

to take my breath away.

"Aby, I've had you alone on an island, are you so surprised?"

"Well, no, I guess you're right about that. But now that I think about it, we have a lot of sex *all* the time. We're like, super-sexed."

His head tilts back on a delightful chuckle, and I can't help but stare adoringly at the brilliance of it.

"Ummm, were you super-sexed *before* you met me?" I ask, his former fuck buddy, Whore-a-the-Explorer, flashing through my mind.

Laughter roars from deep in his chest, before he turns his amused gaze to me. "So, now that you've ascertained an approximation of how many women I've *been* with, you'd like a frequency report?" he laughs.

I cringe remembering that incredibly uncomfortable conversation that really wasn't meant to come out the way that it did.

"I told you that day, Aby. I'm insatiable for *you*. I've never felt this need, this pull. It's you. It will always be you."

His words touch me, their purity washing away the naughty tainting of our love for each other. "Well, you've certainly put a spell on me, Mr. Tate. This is new for me, too." *Clearly. Like* that *needed to be said out loud.*

Smiling, his brilliant blue eyes sparkling, he swipes my hair behind my ear in a loving gesture. "I'm going to gather the luggage, sweetheart."

"Okay," I manage, still awestruck by his words, watching him walk out of the room.

Grabbing my cell, I reply to Stacey:

Subject: Leaving paradise

Trip cut short. We're heading home. And yes...EPIC SEX. You can hate me later. ;)

Aby xx

HOLY HELL, FLASHES blind me as we exit the arrivals gate. This is it. The ultimate test of composure - the *world-renowned* vultures of LAX.

"Just stay with me, baby," Alex reassures me with a smile.

Comments and questions come at us from every direction as we walk, Alex handling those he can, with gentlemanly finesse. He's amazing. Patient, warm, kind. I, however, feel like a fish out of water. I need a distraction...*cell phone. Brilliant.* Pulling it from my purse, I turn it on, a fake smile plastered across my face despite inwardly cursing at how long it's taking. *Mother fucker, turn on! Jeez, finally.* Scrolling through, I'm desperate to immerse myself in something, *anything*, yet the only thing I find is the unread message from Mom. *Fuck it, I'll take it.*

Subject:

Just wanted you to know that I'm thinking of my beautiful, brave girl. I realize my actions don't always express how much I love you. But I try. And I'm more proud of you than you know.

Love Mom

I'm stunned. *Oh my God, Mom.* I have no idea where that came from, but the heartfelt strength it gives me in this moment is beyond words. Feeling confident, I put my cell away, looking up, head held high.

Alex's gaze catches my eye first, his beaming adoration pulling my questioning smile.

He says nothing, simply smiling in return, taking my hand with a gentle squeeze before looking ahead; another question called from behind a camera, stealing the moment of silence.

"Alexander, what kind of underwear do you wear?" a reporter asks, walking sideways to keep up, dangling a microphone in Alex's face like a carrot to a horse.

I stifle a laugh as I catch the look Alex flashes the reporter's way.

"Not a good question, buddy," Alex replies on a laugh, following it up with a smile.

"Boxers or briefs?" he tries again.

"Dude, seriously," Alex squeezes my hand a little - for his own composure perhaps?

"When does filming start?" the reporter goes for three as we pass him, reaching the car.

"Tomorrow, in fact," Alex turns to offer the nuisance a final smile, ushering me into the backseat of the Black Yukon Denali. "Take care, man," he adds, taking a seat beside me, the driver closing the door behind him.

The incessant camera flashes are insane. *Jesus*, I look around, taking them in from all sides, grateful for the tinted windows inside our semi-private seclusion.

Giving my thigh a squeeze, Alex pulls my gaze, "You handled that beautifully."

"I was feeling suddenly brave," I sidle into his side, looking up with a smile, his quirked brow urging me on. "I received a nice text from Mom," I shrug, trying to pass it off as no big deal, when really I'm still reeling.

He smiles knowingly, leaning down to kiss my forehead. "Are you ready to see the sites of L.A.?"

"Hell, yeah!" I settle into him, excited as we exit the airport, maneuvering onto the I-405.

Wrapping his arm around me, we settle into comfortable silence and I lean into the warmth of his hold. I can't believe we're here. I've never been to L.A. before, and I'm almost unable to contain my schoolgirl excitement - the only thing reining it in at this moment being the spell of Alex.

"As much as I enjoyed our island retreat," Alex jars me from our tranquil moment, "...I'm immensely looking forward to showing you our home."

His words hit deep. *Our home.* The thought sends butterflies through my tummy, anticipation setting in as we exit the freeway, my excitement unleashed.

"Sunset Boulevard," he nods out the window and I lean over him like a giddy child.

Stopping at a set of lights, I watch wide-eyed as a Michael Jackson impersonator puts on a free show from the sidewalk. If I didn't know any better, I'd swear he was the real deal. Passing another block, I spy a scantily clad woman - or man, who knows - lingering at the curb. It's terrible, but I have to ask, "Will we see hookers? Cause, I think I just saw one."

The deep baritone of his laugh sings down my spine.

"*Hello? Pretty Woman*…Hollywood Boulevard?" I explain.

"We're on Sunset Boulevard, sweetheart," he smiles, still laughing.

"So? What? They only congregate on Hollywood Boulevard, not Sunset Boulevard?"

"Do you *really* want to know if I know that answer?"

My mouth hits the floor before his smirk gives him away. "Jerk," I slap his chest playfully. "So not funny."

He laughs and I ignore him to continue perusing out all windows, taking in as much as I can. "There's so much I want to see."

"We have tons of time, baby," he grins, beaming exuberance.

"I want to see Rodeo Drive, that Chinese theatre place with everyone's foot prints, the walk of fame…Malibu, Beverly Hills. Oh! And I *really* want to see that dude walking up the sidewalk chanting, 'What's your dream? Everybody's got a dream'." I catch his peaked brow and shrug, "*Pretty Woman.*"

"You're adorable, Miss Ryan," he laughs. "I'm not sure we'll manage to see *all* of that this evening." His saucy smirk pulls my stink eye.

"Okay, then I only have one request tonight. It's the biggest of all, the most important. *Iconic*, is what it is," I whisper the latter dramatically, nodding with the accuracy of my statement. "The Hollywood Sign."

"That, we can manage, sweetheart," he pulls me in for a chaste kiss.

I'm enthralled with the scenery; images I've seen before, though only in movies. We sit in comfortable silence for a while and I lean back into the warmth of his hold.

"Doug, why don't we take Laurel Canyon to Mulholland Drive for my girl."

CHAPTER *Eight*

"GOOD MORNING, HANDSOME," I manage, pausing for a drool-worthy moment at the entrance to our bedroom. *Our bedroom.* A week in L.A. and it still hasn't set in.

Having found Alex tugging a t-shirt over his head, I'm in a familiar state of rapid-fire adrenaline that instantly kick-starts my kegels at the sight, his glorious chest and rippling abdominal muscles shielded too quickly as he pulls it into place. *Damn.*

I've been awake for a couple of hours, enjoying the sun on the deck while I let Alex sleep. He was so tired last night when he returned home, these long days filming clearly taking its toil, I simply couldn't bring myself to wake him up.

"Did you sleep well?" I ask, folding into his arms for a hug, attempting to hide my pout at the end of the delicious show I'd walked in on.

"I did, thank you," he lifts my chin to his gaze. "However, I would have much preferred waking up with you beside me."

"Oh," I release the word on a breathless whisper. This man never ceases to take my breath away with the way he looks at me. "Well, I've been up for ages, I didn't want to wake you. You needed your beauty sleep, Mr. Hot Stuff."

"Is that right?"

"Uh huh," I reply cheekily. "Sadly, though, it seems I waited too long to check on you - it's such a shame I missed the show,"

I playfully tug at his shirt, pulling out of his light embrace. Walking around him, I teasingly smack his bottom, placing the book I'd been reading down on the dresser.

On a growl, he turns towards me, taking gentle hold of my arms to walk me backwards. "Well, if the lady wants a show," he whispers in my ear, sending goose bumps along my flesh, "...I'm all for a repeat performance."

"Is *that* right?" I ask breathlessly amid backward steps, purposely mimicking his earlier question. I'm already lost in a haze of lust at his words alone, the mere thought of him touching me, coming inside me, has me panting as I curl my fingers around his muscular biceps.

"Yes, that's right. Are you ready, baby? Do you have any idea what I plan on doing to you?"

Oh God. I'm putty in his hands, a complete ball of yearning just waiting to be taken, devoured. I moan as his words invade my psyche, the lascivious thoughts now floating through my mind creating a whirlwind sensation of desire cascading through my system.

I falter slightly as the backs of my knees hit the ottoman, before Alex assists in setting me down into the adjoined chair, running his fingers along my bare legs, spreading them wide.

"Don't move," he whispers huskily. "Stay right where you are."

Wetness pools between my spread legs at the sheer cadence of his voice, his sexy command; my jean shorts feeling slightly constricting in my need to simply get naked and have my wicked way with him.

Sprawled in the seat, my feet flat on the floor on either side, I watch, transfixed as he saunters slowly backwards, his eyes taking me in, consuming me with each step.

His gaze sears me; devouring my eyes, lips, breasts, before landing on the apex of my thighs. My nipples pebble and my sex throbs under his blatant stare, my need overwhelming me.

"Alex..." I plead breathlessly, moving to sit up, wanting him to return.

"I told you not to move, Aby," he reminds me in that authoritative tone I love so much…the alter ego of the gentleman I love so much.

Obediently, I sit back to rest against the cushion, giving in to his dominance not because I have to, but because I want to. I love when he tells me what he wants. When he directs me with his commanding, seductive words, enticing me with a provocative warning of what is to come. My body falls under his sexy spell, hungry for him to take me to orgasmic bliss. Simply knowing that the latter is a foregone conclusion once he unleashes this side of himself is my undoing, and I offer no argument in submitting to his bidding.

"Good girl," he stops, his gape molten, his irises darkened a deep shade of blue. His fingers move to undo the button of his jeans, pausing slightly, taking in my watchful, wanting gaze as he lowers the zipper. My desire is evident as I stare at him in lustful need, and his sinful smirk tells me he's very aware of the effect he has on me. "Do you want me, Aby?" he asks, baring a hint of the sexy trail of hair that cascades down beneath his white boxer briefs, the treasure that lies within making my mouth water.

"Ye-es."

"And, what else do you want?"

I tremble slightly, unable to reply as he removes his jeans, slowly pulling each leg off, discarding them to the side. His manhood tents his boxers, and I whimper with need at the mere sight, the sheer magnitude of this gorgeous specimen.

"Tell me, baby. Do you want me to lick your sweet pussy? Devour your pink flesh with my mouth, my tongue? Do you want me to fill you full with my fingers until you scream?"

"Oh. My. God." The words plummet from my mouth through my sexual haze, my legs shaking with desire at his flagrant inquisition. I've never heard him talk this way. The shock to my system is excitingly delicious.

I can't keep from biting my lip in anticipation as I watch him grab his t-shirt from behind his neck and pull it off in one fluid motion. The man puts every underwear model in history to shame with his incredible physique.

"Do you want this?" he slowly swipes the length of his erection through his boxers.

I lose all vocal ability, an inaudible mumbled gasp escaping my lips as he pulls at the waistband, releasing his clear desire. It flexes and bobs in its freedom against his stomach before he bends to shed the final piece of clothing.

Moaning in need, I inadvertently bring my hands to my breasts, plumping them in my grip to assuage the incredible ache for his touch, the mounds heavy and full in my palms. I shudder at the sensation as my fingers glide along my hardened nipples.

"Tsk, tsk, tsk," he predatorily walks towards me in his naked glory, "…I believe I told you not to move." Resting one knee on the ottoman between my wide spread legs, he grabs my wrists in his hand, holding them above my head. "Do I need to tell you again, sweetheart?" he asks, looking into my eyes. Holding my throat, he leans down to my ear, "Don't. Fucking. Move."

My heart slams in my chest at his forcefulness; his aura of sexy dominance careening through my system. My pulse pounds heavy in my throat, my skin prickling with sweat. I'm so utterly insatiable for him. Always insatiable for him.

He makes quick work of undoing my shorts, pulling them down my hips and legs with my lift of eager assistance; my cotton panties soaked through on display for his avid, unwavering gaze. "Mmmm…Always ready for me, aren't you, baby?" he growls, swiping his finger teasingly, fleetingly, along my core.

My body jolts at the impact, and I whimper at the loss of his touch. "Alex…please," I beg.

"Please what, baby?" His breath on my earlobe sends a spasm of lustful shudders through every inch of my body, his question filled with enough sexual foreboding to elicit the clenching of my core in anticipation.

"Please, take me now. Please…" my plea is desperate.

"Oh, I will, Aby. I'll take you. Every part of you. I'll devour you, cherish you…" his teasing touch mimics his words, his fingers seductively gliding along my curves, his palms swirling against my nipples. He knows that drives me crazy for him. Makes me wild for him.

"Alex, please…fuck me," my demanding request is but a

mere, begging whisper. It's effect, however, is loud and clear - evident in the swift lock of his gaze on mine. It's as though I flipped a switch, turned things up a notch, set off the fire sprinklers. The desire dripping from every inch of him is suddenly soaking me.

"Oh, I'll fuck you, baby. I'll take you so far, fill you so deep, you'll still be feeling it when you wake tomorrow," his confession is as bold as the grip he takes of the end of my flimsy tank top with both hands. Tugging hard, he rips it in half up my torso.

I shriek at the sensation, the sheer enormity of strength in his grasp, before he spreads the cotton material, exposing my bare breasts. His pleasure at the absence of my bra solicits his husky groan as he leans forward, taking a nipple into his mouth.

The bolts of pleasure send instant spikes of need to my clit amid my moaning scream. I want so desperately to run my hands through his hair, along his glorious shoulders, desperate to touch him, feel him. Yet I don't. I stay exactly as he's instructed me, commanded me. His order an imaginary tie, binding me, spiking my desire higher to dangle me over the edge. It's too much. I want to fall..."Ahhh, please!" I beg.

I feel his grin against my breast, his fingers tweaking and pulling at my other nipple, before he leans back on his haunches to stare down at me. Grazing his fingers along my stomach, my muscles rippling and shaking in their wake, he slides teasingly along my inner thighs. "Touch them. Play with your nipples for me."

Though it's his body I'm desperate to feel, I immediately obey, plumping my breasts, palming my nipples in a circular motion as though my touch were his own.

His approving smirk is sinfully delicious, leaving me breathless, panting, as I watch his eyes, mesmerized, devouring me all the way down to my core, his gaze hungry with want.

Tugging my panties to the side, he swipes his thumb along my wetness before slowly pushing it inside me, my body tightening and gripping in welcome yearning.

Yes...I moan, grinding towards his teasing fill, needing more, my body begging without words.

He pulls his thumb out with a devilish snicker, my gaze immediately darting to his knowing simper. "You want me to fuck you, baby?"

"Yes! Please…" I plead, pinching my nipples slightly to assuage the overwhelming ache, closing my eyes against my desperate need. I feel him slide my panties to the side once more, his thrust forceful as he buries himself inside me to the root. "Oh, fuck…Alex!"

"God, Aby", he groans, leaning down to tantalize my nipple with his tongue. "I love fucking you, baby. You feel so good, so tight, squeezing me, clutching me as though you don't want to let me go."

"I don't ever want to let you go!" I manage through a gasp as he pulls back and fills me once more, my legs wrapping securely around his waist.

Primal in our need for each other, we're frantic in our touch - tugging, pulling, scratching, and moaning in each other's arms; the screeching of the seating on the floor beneath us from his deep and heavy thrusts an animalistic auditory aphrodisiac.

He pumps into me repeatedly, deeper and deeper, in long fluid motions. His relentless drives send me careening further and further into sexual abyss, his fingers sliding into the hair at my nape, tugging hard to expose my neck to his devouring lips.

"Fuck, Aby," he growls, gliding his teeth along my flesh. "Come for me, baby…"

"Ye-es!!" I scream as I fall. My core clenches around him like a vise as I ride the waves of my orgasm before feeling him still above me, groaning in my ear as he fills me.

"Fuck, I love you," he manages through labored breaths.

"I love you, too," I reply in my euphoria, momentarily noting that love isn't a strong enough word.

CHAPTER Nine

"FUCKERS!" I CURSE aloud, slamming my laptop closed. *Could the media be any more ridiculous?*

I'm not sure what deep-rooted affliction I suffer from, given my incessant need to peruse the Internet in search of any new drivel the media has written about Alex - or *me*, I should say. Each time I find something I get annoyed, promising myself I'll never look again, only to go searching the next day. *Yup, it's an affliction, alright.*

It's amazing what the gossips come up with. According to the bullshit write-ups to date, I've been pregnant with Alex's baby; am Alex's live-in escort/hooker; and a boat load of other completely ridiculous - and might I say, incredibly uncreative - fabrications of the media's imagination. *Whatever sells magazine I guess.*

I'm not sure why I bother looking. Again, it's an affliction. I simply can't help myself. It's almost addictive. Particularly when I'm bored out of my skull, as I am at the moment. I love my free-lance work with Thomas, but it doesn't take up much of my time - an hour or two a day, maximum. With Alex constantly filming, it leaves me with a *ton* of free time - free time to surf the net and aimlessly pad around the beach house looking for something to entertain myself with.

I'm the type to clean when I'm bored, yet I can't even do that. Alex insists that we have a cleaner. A cleaner! Maria comes every two days and now avoids me like the plague - my absolute boredom resulting in my following her around, chatting, and trying to help, clearly getting to her after the first week. Unless she really can't speak English as she initially pointed out. *Humph.* I honestly thought she was pulling my leg.

It's not like I can hop in my car and go for a jaunt around L.A. - as much as I'd love to. Sadly, I have no car. Not that I necessarily need one. I *could* hop in a cab and boot somewhere for the day, but I'm simply uninspired to take that measure. This beach-like atmosphere day in and day out has me stuck in perpetual vacation mode. It's funny, I always thought that permanently living on a beach, living the life of luxury, not having to work full-time, if at all, would be heaven. Well, the novelty can wear off pretty quick.

My sole solace, despite my incessant boredom, is Alex. I get to look forward to his arrival at the end of every day. Just the thought of his stunning smile lighting his face when he walks through the door has me now grinning from ear to ear as I make my way down the deck stairs towards the beach, the sand sliding between my bare toes. That quickly, my internal pity party evaporates.

Pulling my cell from my pocket I type Alex a quick message.

Subject: Thinking of you

Hi handsome. Missing you today, as always.

I love you

Aby xx

Smiling, I slide my phone back into my pocket just as the vibration alerts a new message. *Wow, that was fast.*

Subject: You never leave my thoughts

Perfect timing, sweetheart. Done for

the day. Be there in five. Meet me out
front...Have a surprise for you. And I
LOVE YOU MORE.

Alex xx

A surprise? I'm giddy just thinking of what Alex has in store, sprinting towards the deck and into the house, wiping my feet off on the mat. Trudging towards the bedroom, I rush into the master bath to brush my teeth and quickly comb my fingers through my wavy hair.

Who knows what his surprise entails. Maybe he's going to take me out? *God knows I* really *need to get out*, I think to myself, quickly applying mascara and lip-gloss. Changing into a silver tank top and white maxi skirt, I rummage through the closet for a matching shawl before making my way downstairs. Glancing at my watch, I figure I made it just in time, opening the front door.

Alex is standing on the front step, a wide smile donning his face. "Hello, beautiful," he pulls me into his arms, placing his luscious full lips on mine, his tongue teasing, begging entry.

I kiss him back with every ounce of joy I feel at his presence, my day's boredom effectively forgotten as I moan into his kiss.

Chuckling, he pulls back, kissing the tip of my nose. "Happy to see me, I take it," he teases, running his hands up and down my bare arms.

"Happy might just be the understatement of the day, Mr. Tate. More like elated," I smile in return, resting my hands against his broad chest, his heat permeating my palms.

"Well, on that note, ready for your surprise?" he asks, eyes twinkling.

"Your presence home early *isn't* the surprise?" I purposely avoid his playfulness, though I'm exciting about whatever he's decided to spring on me. Every day with Alex is full of surprises, yet for some reason this time feels different. He gait alone is telling enough, as he flashes me an excited, and oh-so heart stopping smile.

"Not quite, however I'm overjoyed that you would consider me surprise-worthy. Come this way," he takes my hand, walking us down the path towards the front of the house.

My heart stops in my chest as we round the corner, the gleaming black Land Rover parked in the laneway, peaking my curiosity. *Who owns that?* I don't want to jump to conclusions, but based on Alex's M6 BMW parked alongside it, I can wager a guess. "Alex, what…?"

"It's yours, Aby," he turns to me, a boyish grin plastered across his face. "I know you've been somewhat house-bound these past few weeks, so I thought this might help. A slight relief to your boredom?" he grins. "And now that you have a lay of the land from our drives together, you can manage on your own."

I'm blown away. Not only because Alex has bought me a car - and not just any car, but a freakin' *Land Rover* - but also because he's so attune to my recent boredom. I thought I'd hid it so well, not wanting to come across as juvenile. How easily I forget that Alex can read me like a book.

"Alex, I don't know what to say…you bought me a car? A *Land Rover*? This is crazy," I manage, my words a breathless release.

"Well, Maria did allude to the fact that you appeared quite," he stops as though searching for the right words, "…uninspired, of late," he grins. "It seemed like a good idea."

Oh. Humph. He wasn't attuned to my boredom - the non-English speaking cleaner told him. *'No speaka English'* my ass. *She's a nark. An English speaking nark.*

I'm honestly at a loss. I have a hard enough time with Alex refusing any contributions towards the beach house, our groceries, *anything* - adamant that he has the money - but to buy me a car? I simply can't believe it. Once again I'm faced with the reality of Alex and his career, the fact that I'm in love with an incredibly rich Hollywood actor smacking me in the face. I suppose to him, buying a Land Rover on a whim - for the sole purpose of relieving my boredom - is a regular, every day happenstance.

"Say something," he urges.

"Ummm…I'm sorry, I'm just shocked," I reply, holding my

hand to my chest. Finally shaking off the surprise, I turn to him, "Thank you, Alex. You didn't need to do this, but thank you."

"Don't be silly, of course I did. You know I would do anything for you, baby," he pulls me into his embrace. "I wish you'd told me that you were bored. I would have bought it sooner."

I was trying *to hide that from you.* "It's not your responsibility to entertain me," I pull back to look up into his handsome face. "I've simply struggled with finding things to pass the time," I shrug. "You're been so busy lately with work, which I completely understand, but my days can tend to drag."

"I understand, sweetheart," he leans in for a chaste kiss. "The fourteen-hour days are the toughest, but trust me when I say the few hours I get to spend with you are worth a thousand hours I spend without you," he adds, lingering at my lips before pulling back, the excited gleam returned in his gaze. "So? Good surprise?"

Laughing, I reach up to stroke his cheek, "*Amazing* surprise. But, Alex, simply surprising me with a night out on a date would have sufficed."

"A night out, hmmm? Is that what you were hoping for? A date?"

"Well, not being able to go out on a *regular* date is sometimes a hard pill to swallow," I confess, quickly continuing, not wanting him to assume I'm struggling with this life in the limelight, "...but, I'm not complaining. I understand and accept everything that comes with your career."

Contemplating my words, his eyes search mine. "Paint me a picture of a regular date."

"Ummm, dinner and a movie would qualify as a decent date in my book."

"Then, let's do it."

"Wait, do what?"

"Go on a date. Dinner and a movie," he clarifies as though it's the simplest of tasks and the most brilliant idea ever.

"Alex, you know we can't just go out to dinner and a movie. It would cause pandemonium - the media. I can just hear it now, 'Alex Tate and his live-in escort take in an afternoon flick before a mob of two thousand fans raid the theatre'."

Laughing, he pulls me back into his embrace. "Well, even live-in escorts deserve a night out once and awhile," his cheeky reply pulls my laugh. "Why don't you leave the semantics to me. I'm taking my beautiful girl on a date."

"THIS IS SO nice," I murmur, leaning my head on Alex's shoulder. Such simple pleasures - held in his arms, the darkness of the movie theatre, the indulgent smell of buttery popcorn permeating the air - simplicities often taken for granted in his far from simple world.

So far, our date has been somewhat *normal*. No fan-frenzies. No paparazzi. It's almost hard to believe. Sure it's mid-day, and we're in the middle of butt-fuck nowhere, catching a matinee in this rickety old theatre, but I'm not complaining. A classic flick with this Adonis of a man by my side, the cinema almost to ourselves - it's the perfect date. The solo guy oddly seated behind the couple at the front, however, *is* a little weird. Creepy comes to mind. But who am I to judge? To each their own. I'm with the man that I love, enjoying an afternoon indulgence. Doing the ordinary. Yet with Alexander Tate by my side, it's far from ordinary. More like extraordinary.

"It *is* nice," his gruff voice sends shivers down my spine as he places kisses across my bare shoulder, his thumb idly playing with the spaghetti strap of my tank top. "I'm glad you're happy, Aby. I want nothing more than to make you happy every day," he adds, his tone laced with the smile I imagine is donning is gorgeous face.

Make me happy? Is he kidding? Turning, I look up into his dazzling blue eyes, unshielded by his backward-turned ball cap. "Everything you are, everything you do, makes me happy. I love you, Alex," I whisper, watching as his eyes darken with lust. I know what those three words do to him, yet I said them anyway. Here. Now.

I stare, transfixed, as a familiar desire washes through his features, his lips parting on quickened intakes of breath, mine heightening in equal measure as his sapphire eyes sparkle in the light of the opening credits. The movie has started, yet we don't care.

"Aby," my name falls off his luscious lips, kicking at my pulse with a brewing of butterflies in my tummy.

Despite our locale, he still has the ability to stir my blood, regardless of who may be watching. I'm unable to control my instant arousal as his fingers slide slowly and sinuously up my arm, leaving tingles and goose bumps in their wake.

"I love you too," he whispers, taking me in a soft kiss.

God, those lips. The feel of them caressing mine, his tongue rimming the seam, begging entry, has me moaning into his mouth. I close my eyes in complete surrender, my body lax, as his strong hands circle my jaw, holding me firmly in place.

Whispering his lips delicately along my jaw, he nuzzles into the crook of my neck, placing succulent kisses on the sensitive skin under my lobe. When he kisses my neck that way, I'm a goner. Completely weak in the knees. Breathless. *His.*

His fingers slide along my collarbone, edging towards my aching breasts, leaving a shivering trail of lust in the motion. Cupping my breast in his hand, I whimper as his thumb and forefinger tweak my nipple through the thin layer of my cotton top.

The pleasure of his touch is sinful, eliciting an uncontrollable, libidinous moan that calls me back to reality, my eyes jerking open, my hand darting up to halt his delicious assault. "Alex," I whisper breathlessly, "...we're not alone."

He's unfazed by my interruption, maintaining his sweet kisses on my neck. "Shhh, it's okay, sweetheart."

Oh, god. How can I resist him?

Glancing quickly at the other patrons completely engrossed in the film, I close my eyes in acceptance, giving in to the thrill of his tongue wetting my flesh. The eroticism of our near public display is overwhelming, and incredibly arousing. Whimpering in need, I quake in my seat, pushing into it with tiny gyrations in hopes to assuage the throbbing ache in my core, my sex clenching in absolute want.

He glides his fingers inside the cup of my bra, and I stifle a moan as his thumb brushes across my distended nipple. "Touch yourself, Aby," he whispers, cupping my breast in his palm. "Slide your hand in your skirt, inside your panties. Play with your clit for me."

Holy shit. My gasp is equal parts shock and lustful excitement. I wage the war inside, yet his words evoke the animal within me - desperate to satisfy my body's overwhelming demands for fulfillment, desperate unabashed desire to please him. I'm slave to his request, shivering with need, as he alternates between breasts, tweaking and pulling each nipple.

Sliding my hand inside my skirt, I push my panties to the side, my fingers teasing along my soaked core. It feels reckless. Naughty. A slight moan escapes my lips at the sheer pleasure of my own touch. Hot currents of desire course through me as Alex continues his feverish kisses, singeing along my overheated flesh.

"Are you wet, sweetheart?" he whispers.

"Y-yes..." I manage, trembling as I glide my fingers along my sensitive bud. Once. Twice. "Oh, God...Alex..." I moan on a hushed sigh.

"Yes, baby, play with your clit. Feels good, doesn't it?" his husky breaths float across my flesh amid succulent devouring nips of my neck.

I'm panting, the theatres patrons completely forgotten.

"Slide your finger inside, finger that pretty pussy for me," his whisper at my ear is harsh with lust.

I gasp at his dirty words, yet simper in the need they evoke, my fingers sluicing along my wetness to slip inside my aching sex. It's not enough. My body begs to be filled, pounded into oblivion. It's *his* fingers I need. His cock. Curling my finger inside, I squirm in my seat to gain measure; my lame attempts to fuck myself harder. Deeper.

Sensing my desperation, Alex runs his hand along my thigh, slipping beneath my skirt. I feel the heat from his hand as it cups mine, pinpricks of desire coursing through me at his touch. His finger teases around mine buried deep in my core, rimming the outer edge, and I close my eyes on a moan as he slowly slides his in alongside mine, the motion pushing us deeper inside me.

"Does that feel good? Both of us inside you?"

"Mm-hmm…" I manage in my haze. It's mind-blowing. Even more so as he takes over, guiding our movements. I follow his rhythm, mimicking his thrusts, my core pulsating and soaking our fingers further.

Lifting his head from my neck, I'm ensnared by the heated strength of his gaze as he takes my lips in a ravenous kiss. He swallows my muffled cries, pumping our fingers harder, faster, plunging further into my depths. The eroticism of our joined thrusts, curling along my sensitive nerves, takes my breath away. My orgasm rushes to the forefront as his thumb maneuvers along my clit, the pressure enough to send me plummeting, whimpering into his kiss.

Gasps from the onslaught of my orgasm rushing through me are captured between his sinful lips; he grabs my nape, holding me firmly to steal them. I fall quiet putty in his hands, before he releases my mouth to rein kisses along my cheek, holding me as my breathing slows.

Returning his lips to mine, a quick teasing lick of his tongue, he guides our fingers out of my soaked core, securing my hand tightly in his grip.

That had to be one of the most erotic moments of my life.

"God, Alex…" I mumble incoherently into his chest, breathing in his masculine scent. "You make me do crazy things," I admit, reality of our locale setting in once again - another *holy shit* moment passing through.

Chuckling, he kisses my forehead, releasing my hand to adjust my panties, settling my skirt back in place. "I could say the same, sweetheart," he smiles. "I'm insatiable for you."

Holy crow, are you ever. And apparently so am I. *I can't believe we just did that.*

I'm more than uncomfortable knowing my essence coats our fingers in the middle of a movie theatre. "Ummm…I think I'll visit the ladies room," I move to stand, my gaze darting to his evident erection, straining in the restriction of his khakis. *I don't think he'll be joining me to wash his hands.* "Can I bring you some napkins?" I whisper, grimacing playfully.

He smiles, leaning back in his chair, getting comfortable, his unwavering gaze holding mine. Bringing his fingers to his mouth, I stare, transfixed as he sucks my juices away. "That's not necessary," he secures my wrist with a devilish grin. I tremble as he follows suit, sliding my finger between his warm lips.

Oh sweet lord. I'm speechless, staring at him; his eyes closed in satisfaction of my taste, before giving my finger a gentle kiss.

"Alex…" I manage in hushed awe.

"Hmmm? Yes, baby?" he smirks.

"I'll be right back," I turn to make my way along the aisle, legs wobbly in the aftermath of his overwhelmingly erotic display - not to mention the most naughty orgasm I've ever worked for.

It feels as though all eyes are on me as I make my way down the aisle, despite the few patrons' avid attention on the screen. Breathing a sigh of relief, I push the doors open, stepping into the light of the main lobby.

Whoa, I catch a glimpse of the mass of people waiting near the exit. Clearly we came to the *least* popular show time.

Making my way quickly into the ladies room, I wash my hands, my sex clenching in remembrance of what we just did. I stare awestruck at my reflection in the mirror, still absorbing our theatre escapade. Alex certainly knows how to keep things entertaining. Keep me on edge. Although, maybe I should ask him about his alter ego's climb up the naughty scale. *Not that I'm complaining,* I bite my lip, my inner vixen staring back at me, her cherry very well popped. The entire notion sends an embarrassed flush to my cheeks and I exit the washroom shaking my head. *My God, someone could have seen us.*

"Abigail Ryan!"

I jar hearing my name, my gaze darting in the direction as overlapping voices follow suit.

"Are you here with Alexander Tate?"

"Are you enjoying a movie together?"

"Where is Mr. Tate?"

Unsure what to do, I frantically bolt into the theatre, practically tripping up the steps.

Alex stands immediately seeing my agitation, marching to the aisle, before forcing my gaze. "Aby, what's wrong?" he whispers in alarm.

"Alex, they're here!"

"Who? Who's here?" he questions.

"The paparazzi."

"Are you okay?" he asks.

"Yes, I'm fine. It just took me off guard."

Though concern laces his gaze, he's so calm it's beyond me. "I'm sorry, sweetheart. Would you like to leave?" he asks softly.

"But, how do we get out?" *There's no way I'm going through that lobby.*

"We can leave through the emergency exit," he smiles sweetly, disappointment mixed in his concerned gaze. "Let's go," he takes my hand softly in his, leading us along the aisle towards the opposite side of the theatre. How he's so calm is beyond me. I'm still shaking, the surprise hounding still in my system. *Jesus. This is crazy.*

Pushing through the door, we find ourselves in a back alley, crates and discarded boxes littering the sides. We glance from end to end, gauging our best route of escape, the exit door slamming closed behind us. What had started as a nice, *normal* date has twisted into Alex's reality. *Poor Alex. Poor me.* This is something I simply need to accept. Get used to.

Alex leads me around the corner of one side of the building. *Oh, shit. Wrong way.* "There they are! Mr. Tate!" they yell, making their way towards us a rush.

We quickly turn, heading in the opposite direction.

My pulse is pounding, the uncontrollable urge to escape overwhelming me. I've become somewhat accustomed to the fan-frenzies, the paparazzi, however I realize in this moment that the majority of our interactions have been pre-empted. I've had the luxury of mentally preparing myself for the inevitable rush of crowds. But today? Not so much. Their presence was the last thing I expected in this small, practically deserted town.

Alex gently pulls me along, increasing in speed with each step. "This way, baby," he directs me further up the road.

I follow him obediently, glancing over my shoulder, desperately hoping - no, praying - that we've successfully evaded the mass of photographers and paparazzi.

"You okay?" he asks, squeezing my hand as we reach the car after several unnecessary turns around the adjacent buildings.

"Yes, I'm fine," I smile, sliding into the front seat, my heart rate finally slowing to a steady pace.

"I'm sorry about our date…the movie," he leans against the door, his humbled smile breaking my heart.

"Hey, it's okay. We tried, right? That's all I wanted. I don't care about the stupid movie. What happened in there was *so* much more entertaining."

"That is was," he leans down to kiss my lips, chuckling as he closes the door.

On that note, I need to ask him about his recent dirty mouth…"You know, I'm curious," I ask as he takes his seat beside me, "…your alter ego's naughty libido is up a few pegs. Have you been watching porn in your trailer?"

"Porn?" his boisterous laugh thrills me. "No, Aby, it's you. Just you."

THE LATE AFTERNOON sun warms my face, soft sand tickling my bare toes. There's something incredibly romantic about walking hand in hand with the one you love on a quiet beach. Looking to Alex, I smile brightly at his stunning form as we wet our feet along the waters edge.

"Something on your mind, baby?" he questions with a grin.

"Not really. Just enjoying the view." *I could stare at him for hours.*

"Well, who am I to stop you," he teases knowingly, and I playfully swat his arm with the back of my hand. His chuckle is divine, softening his features into boyish bashful charm.

"You know, it's too bad the water is so cold. I would have

loved to go for a swim."

"You would have, hmmm? Who's to say we still can't?"

"Alex, are you crazy? The water is likely freezing," I reply, noting that he's halted our process with a tug of my hand, the wheels turning in his head, his gaze turning mischievous. "Uh-uh, no way," I shake my head on a nervous smile of aroused intrigue. I know exactly what devilish thoughts are floating through his mind. "I am not getting in that water, Tate."

His eyes squint with challenge, his lips curling into a taunting smile before he lunges.

On a squeal, I pull my hand from his grip, making a run for it along the gooey wet sand, laughing at our playful exuberance, the splashes of the cold water amid his chase a delicious thrill against my bare legs.

Catching me swiftly, he wraps me in his arms, lifting and spinning me in the air, my squeals of laughter echoed in his perfect smile.

"No, Alex! Don't!" I plead as he trudges us through the light surf, my shrills swallowed by the onslaught of the icy water, instant spikes of needles coursing through my calves as he places me on my feet. A second desperate attempt to flee is halted as he secures me in his arms. "Oh my God, it's freezing!" I yelp, wrapping my arms around his waist for warmth in my capture.

"My poor baby," he chuckles, bending to lift me in his arms, walking us slowly towards the beach.

I'm almost sad to reach dry sand, not wanting to give up the warmth of his cradling hold as he sets me back on my feet. Taking a seat, he pats the sand between his legs, and I drop instantly, leaning back into his warm embrace, resting my head on his shoulder.

"You're a devil," I smile into his arm, losing myself in the scent of his shirt, his laughter, his warmth. "It really is too bad the water's so cold. I do love the beach."

"I love having *you* on the beach," his sinful tone throws me back to our time on the island, our private fun in the sand.

"Oh, don't be coy, Tate, what you really mean is you love *sex* on the beach.

"Oh, that goes without saying, sweetheart." I turn to catch his slow crooked grin. "But I'll take this," he squeezes me in his arms, "…any day."

"Me too," I smile, looking back out towards the water.

"We can always find another secluded beach to escape to for a mini vacation, closer to home."

"That sounds incredibly inviting. Definitely something to look forward to when filming wraps," I snuggle into his hold.

"Why wait until then?" he adds, his smile evident in his tone.

"What?" my interest perks dramatically and I turn in his hold to look into his sparkling baby-blues, catching the grin I heard.

"Filming is shutting down next weekend, so you're all mine for three days straight," he searches my shocked and excited gaze.

Given his hectic filming schedule this past month, the allure of three full days having him all to myself is intoxicating - almost too good to be true. "Why are they shutting down for the weekend?" I don't want to get my hopes up. The one thing I've learned about this industry is the fickle scheduling.

"Thanksgiving weekend," he beams, taking in my shake of confusion.

"But, it's October…"

"The director is Canadian. He was quite adamant. Not that I'm complaining, I can't think of a better excuse to spend time with my girl."

"Won't you want to celebrate Thanksgiving with your family?" I ask, slightly surprised - though secretly elated - that he'd want to spend it with me alone.

"We don't celebrate Thanksgiving in England."

"Oh…" *But I do. My first Thanksgiving away from home…*

"What's going on in that beautiful head of yours?" he brushes a strand of hair off my forehead.

Lost in thought, I peer out towards the gleaming ocean water, feeling slightly homesick at the hands of family memories… special occasions. *Is there really a toss up here? Time alone with*

Alex, or a visit with family…

"Aby? What is it?"

"Oh, nothing," I laugh lightly. "I just realized this will be my first Thanksgiving away from home. It's just strange that's all. So much has changed…"

"Are you happy?"

His question makes me pause. Looking back to him, I find a glimmer of concern. *Really? How could this man have any doubt?* "Oh, my goodness, Alex…of course I'm happy!" I smile, running my fingers along his chest. "This is my new life. *You* are my new life," I add, snuggling closer, leaning my head against his warmth. "I was just thinking about all of the wonderful family traditions that come with holidays like this. We may be a crazy bunch, but we do love the holidays," I laugh.

"I know what you mean," he replies, running his hands along my bare arms, his head leaning on mine at his chest. "Family tradition is something I miss terribly on the road."

I can't help but feel a pang in my heart for him. This may be my very first holiday away from home, but for Alex it's a sad reality. "We can always stay home and create new memories and tradition of our own," I nip at the corner of my mouth, waiting for his reaction.

"I do like the sound of that."

"Me too," I pull back to look into his eyes, cupping his face in my hand to lean in for a kiss.

"You're sure?" he questions, securing his hand over mine. "Turkey and trimmings over mini vacation?"

"Absolutely," I beam. "Three whole days alone in Sin City with Alexander Tate…Oh the possibilities are endless."

"That's Vegas, sweetheart," he laughs.

"Oh. Really?" I scrunch my nose, in thought. "The City of Angels!" I add with sudden brilliance.

"Well, it certainly holds *one* angel," he smiles, and I flirt my shoulder towards him playfully.

"You had me at turkey, Mr. Tate, save that charm for the bedroom," I bite my lip, flashing a teasing grin before jumping up to bolt down the beach, giggling in anticipation for my capture.

CHAPTER
Ten

THANKSGIVING IN L.A...From the great start to this weekend, I would have to say it's not nearly as bad as I thought it would be. Thanks to a morning full of Champagne, my thoughts of family, friends and tradition have long since 'left the building', so to speak. What's been building instead - thanks to my dear friend, Mimosa - is a very strong desire to get this gorgeous specimen of a man back home. *And now that we're here, it's time to show him how* thankful *I am today*, I nip at my lip, quickly donning a flirtatious smile as Alex opens my door, offering his hand to assist me out of the car.

"That, Mr. Tate, was a wonderful brunch," I purr, succumbing to the aphorismatic effects of my morning cocktails.

"I'm glad you enjoyed it," he smiles, kissing my forehead. "I think you enjoyed the Champagne as well."

"I did. Along with the breakfast. And the *company*," I turn us around, pinning his large frame against the closed door. "Are you ready for dessert?"

"Perhaps we should have picked you up a little coffee to go with dessert," he laughs, rubbing my back.

"Coffee doesn't really go with what I have in mind," I pull him down by the nape. "I'm *very* thankful this year, sexy man of mine. And I plan on showing you in very many ways," I add, pulling his lips to mine.

"Aby," he moans into my kiss, releasing a small gasp as

I reach to caress him through his dress pants. "Sweetheart," he breaks away, taking my elbows gently to pull my gaze.

Giggling, I jump from his hold, leaving him leaning against the car to back away along the path to the house.

"Please come back here."

He seems a little too serious for the game I'm playing. *Humph.*

"Uh-uh," I shake my head, stopping to reach beneath my skirt. I lock my gaze on his - his sexy brow arched in curiosity as I slowly and seductively remove my panties, flinging them in the air around my finger with a flirty open-mouthed curl of my lips.

Trying not to laugh, he folds his arm across his chest, the other jutting to his jaw, rubbing it as he shakes his head. "Aby, listen to me, I need you to come back here for a min…"

"Shhh," I whisper, my finger at my mouth. "Time for dessert," I throw the panties towards him.

His eyes dart to the pink lace on the stone path, then back to mine before I turn to run for the door.

"Aby, wait," he's suddenly firm, chasing after me.

"Come and get it," I flash him a peek of my bare ass with a quick lift of the back of my skirt.

"Stop…"

"Oh, I'm just getting started, big boy," I open the door, laughing flirtatiously, looking back towards him.

"SURPRISE!"

What the fuck? Frozen in place, I turn my head, taking in the sea of faces peering back at me from inside, my focus blurring between each giant smile. My mother. Dad. Beth and Kevin. Alex's sister, Anne and her husband, Gerard. *Oh my God. Please tell me the other two are not Alex's parents.* My gaze darts back to his.

Walking up behind me with a nervous grin, I note him tuck his hand into his pocket, a flash of pink in its wake. *Surprise*, he mouths, his arm wrapping around my waist to lead me inside.

I'm immediately inundated with hugs all around. My head is spinning, flashes of pink twirling around in my mind screaming *COMMANDO - Oh. My. God.* I try to hide the panic in my gaze as my mother releases me, smoothing down my skirt - heaven forbid I be anything but wrinkle-free above my bare ass. *Oh. My. GAWD.*

"Aby, these are my parents," Alex pulls my attention, "…Miriam and Simon."

"It's so wonderful to meet you, Aby," his mother pulls me in for a hug.

"Isn't she everything we told you, Mum? Beautiful, charming, and just cute as a button," Anna gushes.

"That she is. I can certainly see why my Alex is so taken," she smiles up at her son as she releases me.

"You're embarrassing the poor girl," Mr. Tate chimes in. "It's truly lovely to meet you, young lady," he winks.

Though I know my mouth is open, words escape me. Thoughts, however, are endless - the most prominent being, *I'm. Going. To. Kill. Him.*

"I think she's in shock," Beth laughs.

Shocked - yes. Mixed with the humiliation of a cool breeze up my backside - my inner actress fumbles through the script.

"Say something, Aby," my mother urges with an awkward smile.

"I'm sorry," I finally manage. "This is such an incredible surprise! It's such a pleasure to meet you, Mr. and Mrs. Tate."

"Miriam, sweetheart," she smiles warmly.

"My wife doesn't like being put in the same category as her mother-in-law," Simon whispers playfully, his hand blocking her view of his mouth.

"Sounds like Beth," Kevin chuckles, nudging my sister.

Alex's mom laughs too, squeezing Beth's hand in a sweet gesture before turning back to me. "Ignore my husband, Aby, he fancies himself a bit of a comedian."

"Fancies?" Simon questions, playfully hurt.

"Oh come on, Mum," Alex teases, "…he tries."

"He's had *me* laughing since the day Anna brought me home," Gerard joins in. "Nice to see you again, Aby."

"Okay, everyone, let's take this inside, the poor girl needs to breathe," Simon adds, ushering the crowd.

My smiling gaze scans them as they back away, landing on my father in the corner. He winks before turning to disperse with the rest, all chatting and laughing as though they've known each other for years.

"How did you do all this?" I question Alex, without turning.

"I flew everyone in last night," he brushes my hair over my shoulder, bending to kiss my neck.

"Last night?" I swing around to face him. "But when did you…"

"The plans have been in motion for a little while now." Smiling, he brushes his thumb across my lips, locking me to his beautiful blue eyes. "Everyone is staying at the hotel for the weekend, however, they will be enjoying some time to themselves as well, of course."

"Of course," I smile, in awe of his incredibly sweet, over the top gesture to do all of this. "You're incredible, and I love you." The length this man has gone for me, to prove *his* love, simply blows my mind. "This is just…wow," I look back, watching the interaction of our families. "They're all getting along so…well."

"Does that surprise you?"

"Just a little," I lie before looking back into his eyes. My slight nagging fear of an impending clash of the titans, with my usually standoffish mother at the helm, is instantly banished by his loving gaze. He never had any doubt that they would get along; his heart is too pure. "Thank you."

"Does this mean I can still look forward to you showing me all of the very many ways you're thankful *later*? You did offer," his wickedly sexy smirk sends shivers down my spine.

"I'm not sure," I teasingly purse my lips. "Are you going to hand over my panties so I can cover my hidden indecency?"

"I believe they were a gift to me, were they not?"

"That was a gift offered under your act of nondisclosure, sir. I think in such circumstances, it's highly refutable. You set me up."

"Correction, sweetheart. I look *forward* to setting you up," his brow does its sexy shift, his hand reaching between us to cup my core. "Until then, you'll just have to grin and *bare* it."

"ABY, I JUST can't get over this place. It's breathtaking. Stunning," Beth swoons, staring out at our view of the ocean. "Does the word *jealousy* work as a descriptive?" she laughs, and I can't help but smile. "You know what? I think I'm due for a mid-life crisis, I'm leaving Kevin alone with the kiddies and spending a month here to find myself a delicious playboy actor," she spins around, taking in my stunned gaze, "What?"

I can't believe she just said that.

Concern and regret spill from her eyes, "Oh crap, Abs, I didn't mean anything…"

"I know," I smile on a deep breath. It was an innocent statement - coming from Beth's lips, anyway. Had it been my mother…it would have been a totally different, passive-aggressive, situation. Regardless, the judgmental vibe rubs at my insecurities a little. Something I'm still working on, clearly. "Speaking of my niece and nephew," I brush it off, "…are they staying with Kevin's parents? It would have been so nice to see them."

"Oh, gawd," she rolls her eyes, "…if you had seen the look on Kevin's mom's face when we told her we were coming here for Thanksgiving. Needless to say it was either leave them with their grandparents, or not go. An *adult* vacation? Yes please!"

"You and Kevin deserve a little break," my smile is sincere, but not that Beth would notice. I lost her gaze over my shoulder just as her brow scrunched in response to whatever's caught her attention.

"Ummm…Abs, maybe you should go rein Mom in." I follow her gaze to find our mother fretting around the cook Alex has hired to prepare our feast. "I think she's going to have a lack-of-control coronary."

Ugh, I roll my eyes, walking towards her. "Mom…Stop it," I slap her hand lightly from an attempt to stir the gravy. "You are supposed to be enjoying yourself. Go mingle."

"I brought savory, Aby, sweety," she leans closer to whisper, "…I don't think she even bothered using it," she nods towards the dressing prepared in a bowl, her eyes wide with dramatic appall.

I look to my side for Beth's assistance, only to find she's flown the coop. *Traitor.*

"There you are, Dianne," Miriam saves me from having to talk my neurotic mother down off her ledge - under the fleeting glances of the cook to boot. "I remember the first time Alex hired someone to cater for me," she continues, clearly hip to my torment. "It was a belated Christmas get-together, since he was unable to make it home for the holidays," she smiles at the memory. "He wanted to treat me to a day away from the madness of the kitchen, but they had to all but tie my hands together to keep me from intervening. It's something you will get used to," she adds, leading my oddly silent, though appreciatively smiling, mother towards the living room.

I do note the cook's sigh of relief with a slight inconspicuous rolling of her eyes, but I'm too shocked to enjoy the humor of it. I'm still stuck on the 'something you will get used to' part. *Does Alex's mom believe I will be in his life long enough to warrant getting used to all of this?* That's mighty presumptuous. Assumptions are not good…but, *holy crow…was it Alex that gave her that impression?*

"Knock, knock, we made it!"

Oh my God! "Stacey?" I run for the front door to find Stacey and Thomas being greeted by all.

"Surprise, babe!" she beams, meeting me for a hug.

"Perfect timing, my man," Alex shakes Thomas's hand.

"Yes, we're just about to sit down for dinner," Mom adds, hugging Stacey.

"So he got you, huh?" Stacey's turns to me, her smile ear-to-ear as she takes in my elated shock to yet another surprise.

Did he ever, I look towards him, introducing Thomas to his family.

"Quite the sneaky planner, that man of yours," she nudges me. "Wait until tomorrow night! The four of us are hitting the town…Par-*tay*, baby."

"Best Thanksgiving ever," I can't wipe the smile off my

face, literally scrunching in delight.

"Best ever," she agrees, linking my arm to walk into the dining room.

This is all so amazing. I'm overwhelmed with Alex's thoughtfulness, looking towards him as he laughs with our families.

His eyes catch mine, stealing my breath in the brief moment of our silent loving exchange. *I love you*, he mouths, nearly melting me to the floor.

I watch in awe as he makes his way around the table to my side, pulling out my chair to seat me, before sitting to my left. The sudden squeeze of his hand on my thigh pulls my gaze, a flash of pink lace teasing from between his fingers before disappearing with his hand into his pocket.

My wide eyes dart to his, the vision I find enough to make me combust from the heat...

Sin. Perfect, angelic sin.

"DAMMIT WOMAN, CONTROL your *whore*-mones, slut. You look about ready to get your fuck on. I know Alex is *dreamy* and all, but I've heard exhibitionism is frowned upon in public," Stacey shoves my shoulder, effectively halting my stare of Alex's ass as I trail his journey to the bar.

"You're one to talk Tramp-Express. And I can't help myself," I sigh dramatically on a laugh, turning back to her. "He's just so..."

"Fuckable? Yes, my dear, he is. As is Thomas," she turns back to our men, now leaning against the bar placing our drink orders. "But you need to get a grip, sugarplum. Quiet down your slut just a tad, she's getting loud. Have I not taught you anything? Darlin', learn how to keep those hooker tendencies in check - you're about as cool as a hand job on a honeymoon over here."

I laugh out loud. "Stacey, you kill me."

"Alex's big cock will be *killing* you later, if his glances over here are any indication. He's as bad as you are. He's been eye-fucking the shit out of you all night. At least you're both consistent."

"He has?" I turn to glance back at the bar, slightly intrigued by her statement, catching a glimpse of Alex's gaze locked on mine. Flashing me a flirty smile, he turns back to Thomas.

Oddly, I hadn't noticed his lustful looks. Mind you, I *am* drunk. And that may just be the understatement of the century. More like wasted. Yet, so is Alex. It's been quite entertaining watching his progression throughout the evening; eyes glazing over, his perfectly coiffed curls looking a little more rumpled than usual.

"Oh, *come on*," Stacey jars me from my thoughts. "Don't even act like his little looks aren't giving you butterflies in your vagina. It's probably why you're struggling to keep your inner whore at bay. Not that *I'd* particularly mind you two humping like rabbits on this table, but I would suspect that the paparazzi or his cray-cray fans may have something different to say about it. So, quit it."

"Alright, alright," I drawl dramatically for effect, taking the last swig of my beer. "God, I miss you Stace. I'm so glad you and Thomas came. Talk about a surprise."

"I miss you, too, doll. It's been weird not having you around when I'm in London…I just…Goddammit, don't make me drunk cry! It's like ugly cry on crack. You know I fucking hate that."

"Awe, shnookums, don't drunk cry," I pat her hand on the table, "It's not a good look on you," I tease, laughing at her playful glare. "Seriously, though, I know how you feel. But, this move to L.A. *has* been amazing. *Alex* has been amazing. Living together…it's out of this world. And I can't believe he planned the whole Thanksgiving get together for our families. Blows my mind."

"Yeah, I hear yeah, sister. You're like legit in love."

"I guess we are," I smile, turning back to our men, making their way towards the table.

"Your drinks are served, me ladies," Thomas drawls, laying our drinks down with an eloquent bow.

"Why, thank you kind sir," I play in return, smiling as Alex takes his seat beside me, wrapping his arm around my shoulders.

Leaning into him, I practically melt as he places a quick kiss to my cheek, quickly noting Stacey's stink eye screaming 'CALM THE FUCK DOWN' from across the table. I stick my tongue out at her in defiance.

"Hmmm, do I detect some rivalry, ladies?" Thomas inquires.

"No, no," Stacey interjects, flashing Thomas a sweet and innocent gaze, batting her eye lashes theatrically, "I was simply telepathically reminding Aby to keep her vagina in her pants. Or skirt, I should say."

"Stacey!" I squeal on a laugh, as Alex spews a bit of the beer he just swallowed, pulling his arm from around my shoulders to wipe the dribbles off his chin.

Raucous laughter ensues as Stacey relays her sound advice about the poor form involved in having sex on the table in the middle of a crowded club.

I catch a glimpse of Alex's intrigued brow, his sexy drunken lips parted as he stares at me amid Stacey's rant, "So, I told her that if they don't stop eye-fucking each other across the room, I'll open a can of whoop ass," she explains to Thomas, who chuckles and flashes me a quick wink.

Alex's hand on my bare thigh, inches higher and higher up my leg beneath my skirt, thankfully hidden under the table. My gaze instantly travels to the patrons surrounding us and I breathe a sigh of relief to see that his touches are unbeknownst to prying eyes.

His fingers slide between my thighs, spreading them, leaving a trail of lust-filled goose bumps in their wake. I try like hell to stay focused on Stacey, to control my breathing, but as his teasing touch inches closer and closer to my aching core, my pulse kicks into high gear. It's a dizzying test of constraint through our silent, avid show of attention towards Stacey and Thomas amid their back and forth quibbles; perfectly displayed interest, despite his fingers having met with my soaked thong.

From the corner of my eye, I note Alex's chest heave, expelling a large breath, clearly turned on by my avid wetness. I want to turn to him, kiss him, devour him. But I can't. I don't want to give away what he's doing anymore than I want him to stop. Leaving me struck still, having to pretend that his middle finger didn't just glide beneath the lace shield of my hungry core.

It takes everything in me to hold back my moan as his finger fills me, pushing hard to curl up inside. Inadvertently, I drop my hand to my lap, inconspicuously holding him in place, desperate for him to finish what he's started.

His molten gaze lures my own, his eyes flashing with mischief, heat, longing. Unable to turn away, I'm entranced, numb to the ability of formulating a single word.

"Thomas, let's go for a ciggy," Stacey suggests. "Back in a sec," she adds, presumably departing with Thomas in tow. Whether they actually left or not is neither apparent nor relevant as Alex and I stare, our gazes locked heatedly.

The sudden silence at our table suggests they have, and I release my held breath, closing my eyes in pleasure as Alex adds a second finger inside me, his movements quickening as his fingers fuck into me, hitting every sensitive nerve. The pounding base from the dance track hits me in the dim, quiet euphoric bubble of our booth, echoing his sinful wrath of pleasure at my core.

"Yes, baby," he leans in to whisper at my ear, "…let me feel it," he angles his body slightly to protect our risqué naughtiness from view.

"Oh god," I moan, dropping my head to his shoulder. His scent alone could make me come, and I inhale deeply, relishing in his masculine essence of this man.

"That's it. Fall, sweetheart. I've got you," his inviting whispers course through the tensing of my body as I near the edge.

His words are my undoing. I clench and quiver around his digits, my core tightening, plummeting into release.

Pulling my face into his chest, he shields my moans as my orgasm overtakes me, soaking his fingers.

"Home. Now," his husky growl is like an aftershock as I quiver in his arms.

"INSIDE," ALEX ORDERS, pushing the door open to crash against the wall inside, his aggressive commanding tone sending shivers along my core.

The sexual need ricocheting between us is palpable, our inebriation fueling our need to fuck, and fuck hard. A burning fire looms just under the surface as he stares at me with lust-fueled eyes, the sheer magnitude of his display effectively stunning me in place, unable to move, staring at the beauty of it.

Like an animal, a ferocious beast of sexual yearning, he grabs my arm, roughly pulling me inside. I sway slightly in my alcohol-fueled stupor, completely overcome by his erotic commanding force.

My thong soaks further as his mouth finds mine, his tongue plunging deep. My pussy clenches and pulses in desperate yearning as he pins me against the wall, his hands aggressively sliding up my thighs to cup my sex, harshly palming my ass.

"Mine," he spews against my lips, licking the seam, sucking and nibbling his way along my jaw and neck as he kicks the door shut.

Tilting my head at the pleasure of his onslaught, I moan incoherently, shaking to the core in longing. "Alex. please…" I need him to take me to that place. I'm desperate for him, the aphrodisiac effects of the alcohol fueling my desire further.

Lifting his gaze to mine, his stare is molten, burning with a desire like I've never seen before, searing me deep with its passion. A rush of breath pours from my mouth, a shiver coursing through me at the sight. The effect of the alcohol is permeating through his want, his eyes heavy with lust, hair disheveled, begging to be pulled.

Our dual need to feel, taste, consume, overtakes us; our mouths meeting in a fury, lips devouring in a ravenous kiss, so hot, so pervasive, it could burn us both alive.

He cups my jaw in his hands, holding me securely in place for his ravaging kisses, my body shaking in need. I'm so unbelievably desperate for him, I would give just about anything, say just about anything, for him to take me here, now - to fuck me up against this wall, on the floor, anywhere, it wouldn't matter.

Gripping and squeezing his thick arms, I savor the feel of his corded muscles tightening and flexing beneath my palms, the knowledge that he's about to come undone almost bringing to my knees.

I need him crazed, out of control; my need to spur him on causing me to unleash the dirtiest words I've ever uttered into his kiss, "Fuck me, Alex. I need to feel you inside me...fucking me with your big cock. Take what's yours...my pussy is desperate for you," the words continue, falling from my lust-fueled euphoria.

He's as turned on by the images my dirty pleas evoke as I am by having created them. My words fuel his ever-raging fire sending him growling against my lips, his fingers flexing slightly at my jaw before lowering to grip my shirt in his hands, harshly ripping it open, buttons sent spewing, pinging to the floor.

I yelp in surprise at his dominant display, his hands returning to my face, taking me in another searing kiss that melts me from the inside out.

Tongues dueling, devouring each other's mouths, he frantically slides my shirt off my shoulders, making quick work of my bra before tossing it to the floor. My breasts are heavy and engorged, on fire, desperate for his touch, his mouth.

Swiping his palms along my nipples, my needy whimpers spike his ardor, his hands gliding up, gripping my shoulders, "Take what I want, baby?" his husky words whisper against my lips, before he pulls back, staring into my eyes. "I want you on your knees," his gentle shove sends a delicious pulse down my spine as I drop to the floor before him.

Savagely, I undo his pants, grasping his engorged cock with greedy fingers, massaging up and down his shaft. Desperate to taste, I lick the slit, the salty essence coating my tongue, driving me wild for more. I trail my tongue along every ridge, leaving no glorious inch untouched, before rimming the tip, taking him deep.

I moan at the feel of his thickness, the masculine flavor that is Alex; his raspy groans urging my hungry lust. I feel frenzied, out of control, bobbing up and down on his cock, swirling my tongue along his hot flesh. Cupping his balls, I massage them in my palm amid my devouring; savoring the delicious feel of him in my mouth.

"Fuck," he growls, grabbing my hair firmly to secure me in place, his hips undulating into my rhythm. His sexy, dominant hold is thrilling, and I take advantage of it, reaching around to grab his ass, taking him deeper.

On a guttural groan, he pulls back, the head of his cock teasing my lips, before he pushes back inside, brushing the back of my throat, my eyes closing in abandon as he takes control.

Resting my hands on my knees, I'm at the mercy of his demands, his controlled pace, as he maneuvers me along his length.

"Fuck, baby, you feel so good…" he lures my gaze to his, filled with desire as he watches me swallow him whole.

Closing his eyes above his sexy parted lips, I witness the pleasure twist through him as he fights to remain in control - control that threatens to break before he pulls his cock from my mouth on a growl, swiftly lifting me to stand.

Turning me, he reaches around for a quick teasing swipe of my core before wrapping his hands firmly around my waist, walking us the few feet to the living room. "I'm going to fuck you, Aby. Rest assured, I will most certainly take what's mine," he growls in my ear, passion and lust evident in his warning.

"Yes…" I reach back, sliding my hands up around the nape of his neck, tugging on his curls in desperation, arching my ass to grind against his hardness.

Placing a hand at the small of my back, he forces my shoulder with the other, bending me over the back of the leather chair. My hands instinctively reach forward to gain measure in the incredibly sexy assault, a warm flush spreading across my skin as his fingers skim under the hem of my skirt to tease the round globes of my ass, bare to his touch.

Pushing the hindrance of my skirt up around my waist, he releases an appreciative groan, reaching for my thong, tugging it to the side, my pussy clenching and quivering in anticipation of his fill.

"Fuck, baby. I need you. I need to be inside you", he emits

on a desperate plea, his fingers gliding along the cleft of my ready sex, grasping the lace of my thong to drag them down my hips.

"Yes…do it", I urge, arching back for him, taunting him, my panties sliding down my legs, pooling at my heels.

I whimper as his engorged cock slides against my core, squeezing my eyes shut on a moan as he strokes his shaft in his grip, teasing it along the wetness.

"You're so wet, baby," he groans.

"Oh god," I manage, my head dropping forward, unable to contain my desperation to feel him inside me; my need to feel him fucking me senseless engulfing me like an inferno.

Lining himself up, he plunges deep, thrusting his cock to the hilt. His fevered momentum has me screaming out in abandon with every lashing thrust of his ownership; my pussy squeezing him like a tight vice, gripping him greedily.

Reaching aggressively for my hips, he lifts me to the tips of my toes, driving into me over and over again; the pounding, slapping of skin meeting skin melding into my pleas for more. Unabashed, wild love consumes me. Never have I felt so complete with another person. Never have I loved another as much as I love him.

On a harsh growl, he fucks into me with mindless abandon, pulling my ass into the air as I continue to balance myself, shuddering from the rawness of the pleasure.

"That's it, baby. Come all over my cock," his demand roars above my shrieks of ecstasy, his forceful thrusts unwavering as my pussy trembles near the edge, squeezing his cock, pushing me closer and closer.

"Oh, god, Alex! I'm coming", I scream, falling over the precipice.

"Fuck, yes!" he groans, releasing my hips, his large body looming against my back, stiffening rigidly before his cum jets up inside me.

I relish in the feel of his muscular body tightening, his groans of satisfaction as he fills me; whimpering uncontrollably through the remnants of my orgasm quivering through my body with shudders of release.

"I love you, baby," the sole words I register as I succumb to orgasmic surrender. "I love you so fucking much."

CHAPTER
Eleven

"**D**ONE!" I TRIUMPH aloud, hitting the send button on my email to Thomas, profoundly proud of myself for my contributions to this particular marketing campaign. Closing my computer, I push up from the deck table, unwinding my sore muscles, atrophy setting in from sitting for so many consecutive hours. I stretch my raised arms to the sky, smiling as I close my eyes in delight, the bright afternoon rays licking across my heated skin.

Feeling invigorated, I snatch up my laptop and notes, making my way inside, machinations of preparing a luscious home-cooked meal for Alex lighting my steps. I love nothing more than pampering him when he gets home from a long day filming. When I can, that is. Sometimes he's gone for hours and hours on end, oftentimes slipping in bed beside me well into the evening.

Walking through the open glass doors leading to the kitchen, I discard my work on the table as I pass, heading towards the oversized gourmet island, thoughts of a romantic dinner-for-two floating through my mind. Pulling out my trusty recipe book, I begin flipping through the pages, aimlessly searching for a meal Alex will absolutely love. My thoughts mingle enticingly with the many delicious dessert options we can play with - either before or after we eat.

The interruption of my perusing by the door chime doesn't shake my heated reverie. As a matter of fact, the idea that it could be Alex home earlier than expected is as inviting as my thoughts of having him for an appetizer.

A surprise strip tease at the front door? - my inner dreamer elicits suggestively in delight as I make my way to answer it.

"Oh," I stagger in surprise against my swift opening of the door. "Liam? Oh my God! What a surprise!" I'm shocked, yet slight enthusiasm seeps through at seeing him so unexpectedly. He looks really good, his skin slightly tan, emphasizing his striking blue eyes beneath his almost buzzed-cut hair - his former pretty-boy, perfectly coifed mane gone. I note the biker helmet in his hand, realizing why. His plain white t-shirt, untucked over baggy jeans, adds an attractive rebellion to his new carefree, relaxed style.

"Hey, Abs! A good surprise?" he questions, a slight twinkle in his eyes.

He looks happy, and it's infectious. "Of course a good surprise. Come in, please," I stand back to allow him entry. Closing the door behind him, I smile warmly at his familiar face, watching as he takes in his surroundings. It's amazing what you get used to, I realize, taking in my lavish abode through Liam's eyes, the luxurious furnishings and artwork displayed to perfection. Truly magazine worthy.

We sink into silence, and I feel an odd pang at having him here - a piece of my past amongst the sometimes unbelievable reality of my present, my new world foreign to him. Yet he's a welcome sight to my slight homesickness, and I shake off the alien vibe with a heartfelt smile. "Would you like some coffee?" I offer, pulling his gaze back to mine.

"Absolutely," he follows me into the kitchen. "Nice place." He takes a seat at the island, absentmindedly fingering through my discarded recipe book, "Cooking plans?"

I note the slight smirk on his face, his passive-aggressive insulting of my culinary skills light-heartedly obvious. "Ha, ha. I've improved in the cooking department, I'll have you know," I retort, preparing the coffee. I can't help but chuckle at his easy laughter that follows. He always was good at making me laugh. "I honestly can't believe you're here. I admit it slipped my mind that you were making your way to L.A.."

"Jeez, Aby. I'm wounded that I'm so easily forgettable. Break my heart, why don't 'ya."

My breath catches at his choice of words, and my movements still. *He was joking, let go of the guilt, dumb ass* - my inner actress pops into my psyche as though rubbed from her genie bottle.

Liam's chuckle interrupts my internal tirade, "Abs, I was kidding. And, stop. You've beaten yourself up enough when it comes to me. Clearly, I'm doing fine. All wounds healed," he gestures, arms outstretched, charmingly showcasing his lean body.

His playful pose elicits my laughter; my ever-present guilt over the hurt I've caused him effectively evaporated at his good-natured humor. "Yes, you do look good. Happy even."

"I am. This trip has been unbelievable, baby. I'm..." he freezes.

I freeze.

The moment washes over with Liam's quick shake of his head, as though he snapped his fingers and erased the blip. I'm fairly certain my eyes are still bulging slightly at his slip of the tongue, yet he continues on through his surprisingly unfaltering smile of excitement, "I'm staying at a small cottage up the coast for the next few weeks before I head out again. Riding is addictive. I'm finding it hard to stay in one place for too long before the itch to take off hits."

He's like a kid returning from the state fair, high on his cotton candy, tilt-a-world-riding buzz. "That's wonderful. I'm so happy for you." And I mean it. I feel a sense of utter peace at having Liam here, regaling me with his journey.

"And speaking of happy, you look pretty happy yourself. You always did look amazing with a tan," he flashes his winning smile.

Laughing, I pour our coffees, adding his preferred additives from memory before passing him the cup. "Thanks, it's hard to avoid a tan when the deck constitutes as my office. Freelance work has its perks," I shrug.

"What a change, eh? Both of us. Who knew that this is where we'd wind up? It blows my mind," he stares contemplatively down at his coffee, a wistful expression donning his stubble-covered face.

The shift in the air is swift, though it doesn't make me uncomfortable. We have a long history, and it's been only weeks since we signed the finality of it - literally. It's understandable that we're going to have awkward moments.

"I know what you mean," I smile, his eyes returning to mine. There's an unspoken understanding between us - a mutual respect, a friendship evolved from our many years together. No more anger. No more resentment.

"So, where is Mr. Hot Shot?" Liam asks, taking a sip of his coffee, my quirked brow at his reference to Alex making him laugh. "I mean, *Alexander*," he corrects himself, pronouncing Alex's name with a lazy drawl.

"*Alex*," I state, albeit dramatically, "…is at work."

"What, he got a *real* job?" he's purposely trying to egg me on.

I ignore his attempts to rile me. "Very funny. This from the man on an extended vacation?" I tease in return.

"Hey, don't shit on the temporary leave," he smiles knowingly. "But, seriously, where is he?"

"He's filming. We're only in L.A. for the duration of the shoot."

"Ahhh, yes. Well your digs certainly scream temporary," he sarcastically spans the gourmet kitchen with a head gesture, and I roll my eyes. The humor in his gaze glazes over with sincerity, "He's treating you well, Abs?" His tone reflects the slight shift from playful to serious.

"Yes, he is. I'm very happy," I smile. It's impossible to keep the overwhelming love from emanating in my voice, and despite our easy camaraderie, I note him flinch slightly at my admission.

The air around us stills in silence before he adjusts his position on the stool, as though mentally shaking off the momentary sentiment. "I have to say, it's weird seeing your picture in newspapers and magazines."

Not exactly the best change in topic. The painfully swift transition from my overwhelming love for Alex, to guilt at Liam's expense, then on to disgust of the media, makes for an interesting test of composure. I'm not sure my grimace goes unnoticed. "Tell me about it. I haven't quite wrapped my head around it myself. Most of the time, it's avoidable, but not always. It comes with the territory, I guess. Alex is really understanding about it, though. He tries hard to keep it to a minimum where I'm concerned."

Yet another moment of silence, laced with slight awkwardness this time.

"Will he be upset that I'm here?"

The question throws me. In fact, in my shock and excitement at seeing Liam, I hadn't even considered the ramifications of his visit, or how Alex would feel about it. He certainly wasn't too pleased the last time he showed up and Liam and I were together. Perhaps it's a preconditioned reaction from being subjected to Liam's jealousy for years, but I instantly feel a sense of dread. *How* will *Alex react?* Not only am I having a nice visit with my *ex*, but moreover, in *Alex's* home. *Well, it's* our *home*, I try to shake off the free-loader vibe.

"Ummm...he'll be fine," I reply with forced pep. "There's nothing for him to feel jealous about. We're friends," I mumble, trying hard to disguise my unease with an act of defensive bravado - though I'm a little irked by my use of the jealously thought aloud.

"Suuure," he drawls, taking a large gulp of his coffee, resting the empty cup on the counter. "I should go," he pushes up from the island to stand.

"No, don't. You just got here..." I stop short, my internal tantrum that *I'm allowed to have a visitor for Christ's sake* suddenly replaced with question, "How did you know where to find me?"

He hesitates, just for a second, but long enough for me to feel an uneasy chill as he sits back down. My eyes, however, signal he should just spit it out. "Your Mom," he purses his lips, clearly anticipating my reaction. He won't get one though - at least not verbally, since I'm speechless. "Abs, I didn't call her for it. She…"

My eyes bulge sarcastically with my head gesture for him to *please go on*.

"Well, she's called me a couple of times…to see how I am," he adds as though explaining for her.

"Oh," I nod, my lips sucked into a straight line, before taking a quick breath that in no way disguises my snarky contempt towards my mother at this moment. "Right, cause that's not weird…or inappropriate," I grab the recipe book, pretending to continue a perusal, flipping the pages too quickly to be focusing at all.

"Aby," he waits for me to look towards him, and I do with a sigh. "She's just being nice. There's nothing else behind it. No ulterior motives," he quotes the air, attempting to quell my familiar defensive reaction to my mother's actions.

Stop, drop and roll - my inner actress takes center stage, reminding me to hide what I know is damn well true. My mother may be smitten with Alex - his god-like looks, fame and wealth - but her keeping in touch with Liam tells me she thinks it won't last. My translation: I'm not worthy and Liam should be kept close for the eventual fall back. *Damn her.* No, damn me, for still tainting her actions with a lifetime of insecurity.

"Anyway," Liam interrupts my continued silence, "…on that double negative note, I should hit the road." I must look confused by his statement, though I'm not - I know he's referring back to what Alex will think about this visit - but he continues in explanation anyway, "If it were me, I wouldn't want to share you with anyone either - least especially another man that knows what it means to love you."

I'm frozen in place, though contrastingly burning from the sudden flush of embarrassed heat in my cheeks. I wouldn't know what to say to that even if I could find the courage to open my mouth. It both breaks my heart and fills me with dread…yes, this visit was too soon and Alex will not be happy about it.

Liam, however, shows no signs of verbal remorse. He simply offers a warm smile before pushing himself up from the island once more, turning in the direction of the front door.

I follow him, slightly annoyed that a pleasant visit that filled a homesick void turned so suddenly into the reality that it is - a visit from my very recent ex-husband in my boyfriend's home.

Turning back to me, Liam pulls me into his arms for a swift hug, placing a chaste kiss to my head. "Thanks for the coffee, Abs. It was good to see you," he finishes, opening the door.

I summon the strength to just enjoy our cordial farewell. I don't want this to be another goodbye with an awkward end. "You too. Take care, Liam. I really am glad you stopped by," I smile warmly, sincerity in my statement despite the potential disaster that will ensue once I fess up to Alex later.

Leaning on the frame, I watch Liam make his way across the walk before stopping to look back. "Oh, and Abs...Go easy on him. Take it from me, the fear of losing you inspires many different emotions," he finishes, waving goodbye one last time.

MUSIC...? CHECK. RECIPE and ingredients...? Check. Shield of ignorant bliss...? Check. Yup, my composure is well in place in the hour since Liam departed, the loud thundering of his Harley long evaporated from my sound memory bank. As a matter of fact, I feel great. Peppy even. Suffice it to say, Pharrell Williams' *Happy* blasting through the sound system is undoubtedly contributing to my chirpy demeanor - well, that *and* my refilled glass of wine. I can't resist bopping around the island to the happy-go-lucky beat, clad in my, now dry, bikini after an emotionally cleansing dip in the pool.

More than just its catchy uplifting tempo, the lyrics themselves ring true in my ears - I am *happy*. So very, very happy. I smile to myself, shimmying and swaying around my culinary efforts, turning and shaking my butt in absolute glee.

"Now that's a show I would pay to see at the end of every work day."

Jumping in surprise, I startle to find Alex leaning casually against the entryway to the kitchen, his eyes filled with both humor and equal parts desire.

I fumble a little, shyly embarrassed, before pulling down my mask of confidence. "How long have you been standing there, mister?" I ask with a playful smile.

"Long enough to absorb the sexy and incredibly adorable essence that is you, Miss Ryan. Well-captured for future reference," he taps his temple to signify the memory capsule.

The man is like a dip in a too hot bath - scorching the skin as your body gives way to the delicious heat enveloping it. He's simply a spectacular specimen. A shiver of delight runs through me as I take in the sheer masculinity he exudes. Add to that, the sudden erotic beat of the switched track and my recently donned mask seems to change to one of seductive bravery.

My skin prickles with desire as Beyonce's *Drunk in Love* blares through the speakers; the sensual beat, combined with Alex's sexy-as-shit stance, overtaking me. *How very fitting*, I note. I most certainly am *drunk in love*. So very drunk in love with this man. The lyrics, the wine, the unbound sexuality he's emanating, are all fuelling my building desire. A suddenly bold and naughty desire.

Slowing taking a sip of wine, I lay the glass down before flashing him a mischievous smile, my eyes burning with the sheer magnitude of my lust. Making my way around the island, I sway to the sensual beat, lip-syncing the words that so effectively encompass my actions, '*I get filthy when that liquor get into me*'. Sashaying my hips erotically from side to side, I move towards him in a sensual dance, '*Why can't I keep my fingers off it, baby? I want you...*" I finish, reaching him, sliding my fingers fleetingly along his hardening erection.

Watching his amused gaze metamorphose into a glaze of lust is intoxicating. Empowering. With a final teasing touch, I pull my hand away from his manhood, flashing him a tantalizing come-hither gesture as I back up towards the open French doors to the deck - my alluring beckoning enticed with a teasing lick of my lip before nipping it between my teeth.

With a sinful crooked pull of his lips, he follows without a word, igniting my passionate lure all the more. I'm on fire for him, wanting to simply rip his clothes off, yet my emboldened need for seduction overrules. Turning around, I continue my seductive swaying, sliding my hands along my body to the rhythm of the sexy song blaring from the deck speakers as I walk towards the pool. Its inviting misty fog of steam acts as my playful backdrop as I face him once more to tease with the lyrics, '*Baby, I want you, na na*'.

I caress my neck and chest, gliding my hands down to my ass, tempting him as I imagine his own touch. I'm enraptured by the sensual beat, my daring seductress stimulated by my consumed glass of wine, heightened even further by his evident building desire. It's a thrilling feeling to be incited by his wanting gaze.

Making my way towards him, I grip the hem of his shirt, pulling it up and off him, his arms raised in assistance. Tossing it behind him, I trail my fingertips down his deliciously sculpted chest, feeling the power from his husky intake of breath as my hips goad him in the rhythmic dance, '*Drunk in love*'.

Releasing a growl, he bends to capture my lips amid my persuading lyrical mimicking and I swiftly pull away, shaking my head 'no'.

I slowly tread the stairs into the pool, a teasing smile on my lips. The warmth of the water against the cool late afternoon chill is exhilarating. It burns through my electrified flesh as I remove my bikini top, giggling with the music, flinging it towards him.

His eyes are a pool of latent hunger, taking in my strip tease, his gaze tracing my bikini top's landing on the stone floor at his feet. At the wet drop of my bikini bottoms alongside my discarded top, his gaze darts back towards me, his lips parted beneath his burning sapphire-blue eyes. He looks ready to pounce.

I'm enraptured, spellbound by my affect on him, relishing in the warmth of the water cascading around my naked body as I continue swaying sensually to the music. I close my eyes, delighting in my body's movements, like a snake charmer hypnotizing her cobra. I'm lost in my soliciting euphoria, inspired solely by him. For him.

The feel of his naked body suddenly behind me is electrifying and I shudder against his muscular form. Wrapping his arms around my waist, he pulls me tight against him. I moan, torn between wanting to turn to face him and the sensation of his hardened erection tantalizing my behind. The pulsing in my core wins the struggle and I succumb, gyrating against him with the rhythm as his greedy hands explore my flesh.

The slosh of the water around us adds a cold-heat cocktail to my perked nipples, and I quiver as he slides his palms erotically across the pebbled peaks. I love that signature touch of his. The way he tantalizes my nipples with a circular tease of his palm. I'm on fire for him. *Desperate* for him.

I spread my legs slightly in my circular grind, pushing my ass into his hardness jutting between my legs. His cock teases my core, sluicing between the cheeks of my ass; his body melting into my rhythm, grinding into me with slow, seductive sweeps of his hips. It feels incredible, our bodies flowing weightlessly in the steamy pool, floating in sheer ecstasy, swaying against each other in the fluid waves, luxuriating in our erotic dance.

Moving my damp hair aside to lick and kiss along my neck, his breaths come harder, faster from behind me, his hands sliding along my slick flesh.

*Oh, how I want him...*I close my eyes, savoring the explosive effects of his tongue, lips, and hands on my skin.

Gripping my hips firmly, he wrenches me snuggly against him, grinding into me further, his forceful push and pull exaggerating the exhilarating position of his cock. The feel of his thickness brushing along my core, combined with the swills of water, releases our mutual moans.

I reach back for him, a silent signal of desperation. I need to get my hands on him, frantic to touch him, to feel him under my fingertips.

Turning me swiftly in his arms, I'm assailed with the incredible feel of his tongue brushing my lips, his sinfully erotic invasion of my mouth. It's an assault of the senses, fueling the fire within me as I grab and pull at his slickened flesh, moaning into his kiss.

My want for him is mirrored in his own touch, his hands devouring me, working their way over every slickened inch of my body. Our crazed ardor is fluidly controlled; our eagerness evident, though restrained, as we lose ourselves in the sexual lyrics, the sensual beat, silently grinding into one another amid the dance of our tongues and hands.

Playfully, I pull my lips away to continue my tempting mimic of the lyrics, '*Then ride with my surfboard...*' I sing to him, my eyes alight with seduction.

Releasing a growl, he walks us backwards, returning my playfulness with a teasing, lingering sweep of his lips against mine before taking me in another earth-shattering kiss.

I gasp into his mouth at the feel of the cool porcelain tiles against my back.

Pulling back, he offers his fuck-me grin before grabbing my ass to lift me against him, a husky groan leaving his parted lips as he settles tightly in the apex of my spread legs.

I'm captivated by his sensual gaze; instinctively wrapping my legs around his slick body, securing my arms around his neck.

Bracing me against the tiles, his devilish stare is molten. "Do you have any idea what you do to me?" he mutters through succulent kisses along my neck. "I should have come home even earlier," he growls, inhaling a slow deep breath as though luxuriating in my scent.

Earlier? The sudden remembrance of Liam's visit instantly hits me, my body instinctively tightening from the unwelcome intruding thought. It doesn't escape me that this amazing welcome home treat could have been either interrupted, or worse, nonexistent had Alex arrived just an hour earlier. Almost as depressing is the fact that I will actually have to *share* Liam's surprise visit with Alex. I can't exactly keep it from him. I've learned all too well that waiting is not exactly the best solution.

"Aby?" He leans back to look into my eyes, gently releasing his hold of me.

Damn. I hate that he can read me so well. I keep my arms draped around his neck, flexing my fingers through his damp curls. I don't even notice that I'm biting the corner of my lip until he reaches up and pulls at it with the pad of his thumb, that sexy eyebrow of his is urging me to start talking.

Double damn, I wasn't planning on talking anytime soon. Why am I so nervous to tell him about Liam's visit? So, a friend stopped by. No biggie. Right? *Ugh.* Maybe it's best to just spit it out. No. I should just ease into it. *Yes, that's a better idea.*

"Aby, you're ruining the mood here…Just tell me what's on your mind," his tone is clipped.

I don't do well with 'clipped' - it's a trigger for my verbal diarrhea. "Liam stopped by today…It was a lovely surprise vis-it," I quickly blurt, overemphasized and high pitched. *Ugh. Ugh!* I'm such a dumbass.

Alex's expression abruptly changes from playfulness to an-noyance in mere seconds, his eyes boring into mine. Seconds feel like minutes as he absorbs what I've said, and based on his body language, he's none too happy. Not surprisingly, he pulls my loose hold from around his neck, aimlessly tossing my arms down.

My hand darts directly to my mouth, fiddling nervously with my pursed lips as I await a reply. I cautiously watch him slowly, methodically, run his fingers through his damp hair, seemingly attempting to calm himself. Not sure if it's working for him, but it sure as hell isn't calming me. *This is not going to be good.*

He says nothing before reaching for the side of the pool, bracing his weight effortlessly to jump out.

Good God. It's ridiculous how incredibly sculpted this man is, every muscle bulging and flexing in his efforts, the water slid-ing down his perfect body. I'm momentarily lost in the delicious-ness of the visual, until he looks down at me briskly, turning to grab one of the conveniently folded towels set aside for periodic dips. The sternness with which he wraps it around his waist is the final little pinprick in *my* euphoric bubble, and I certainly didn't miss the deflation of *his* between his legs.

Begrudgingly, I wade towards the steps, slowly emerging from the pool.

Alex tosses me a towel, which I manage to catch before he turns to head back inside, leaving me standing, dripping. Not the best move on his part. Yeah, I get it. He's digesting the informa-tion about my surprise guest. But his flippant reaction is pushing a few of my own defensive buttons.

I purposely take my time drying off, refusing to run after him like some lovesick - and *guilty* - girlfriend. As I towel dry, I start weighing my options, gathering my defense, effectively getting a grip on my defensive leash.

Wait. My defense*? What the fuck?*

Defensive leash snapped.

Discarding the towel, I grab my cover-up off the sun chair, wrapping it around me swiftly as I march inside the doors Alex disappeared into moments ago. I bow the tie around my waist like I'm donning a karate gi, ready to kick some ass, shutting off the music with the remote as I pass.

And *ass* is exactly what I get, perfectly displayed as I enter the bedroom to find Alex bent over, stepping into his gym pants - sans boxers. Not surprisingly, I'm momentarily thrown off my game. *Damn that body of his.*

Adjusting the strings at the waist, he turns to face me. The look in his eyes is enough to sound the bell in a ring. Screw a quick kick, I'm ready to grab the proverbial gloves and go for a right hook. Unfortunately, he comes in with a left first.

"Did I tell you that Helena dropped by my trailer on the set today? It was a lovely surprise visit."

And, I'm down. Cheek to the floor, the Ref's countdown reverberating in my ears. *Who's* the Ref in my head? *Whore-a the Explorer* herself, Helena Adelaide, her slithering hand banging down on the mat as she smiles at me.

Well, this was no knock out. I'm not down for the count. I know exactly what point Alex is trying to make. And it's pathetically ridiculous. "Are you seriously suggesting that there is some similarity in a *hypothetical,*" I quote the air for dramatic effect, "…visit from your former phone-a-friend fuck-mate and a man that I spent over twelve years of my life with?"

"Do *you* realize your own statement justifies my point?" he spits back.

"What?" I screw up my face and shake my head. "Alex, Liam and I are *divorced,*" I slur the word for emphasis. "You know, D-I-V-O-R-C-E-D," I spell it out just to be clear, "…as in no longer together. Done. Finito. We are just friends."

"Yes, absolutely. As are Helena and I."

"Oh!" I fist my hands at my sides. "Really? Is that what you call your *relationship* with Helena? A friendship?" I can't help my huff of disgust. "Don't even get me started on the whole labeling of that…that…"

"*That*," he slings the word at me, "…is over. But it goes without saying that you would not appreciate her dropping by for a *lovely* little visit, now would you?"

"It's not the same thing!"

"The hell it's not."

"Nice camouflage, Alex." Now it's his turn to look pissed off and confused, so I continue on to help him out, "You're jealous of something - or should I say *someone* - that you have no reason to be jealous of."

His clenching jaw pulls my attention, right before I note his flared nostrils. If he wasn't pissed already, he certainly is now. "Don't I?"

"No. You have absolutely no reason to feel jealous when it comes to Liam," I throw back, my arms crossed in my defensive stance. *Obviously a visit from Liam is not anywhere near the same as one from Helena.*

He closes the gap between us in one long stride, grabbing my bent elbow to spin me around, pulling my back firmly up against him. "You think that a man that once kissed your neck like this," he brushes my hair over my shoulder, raining kisses down my neck, "…or touched you like this," he caresses my ass, reaching around to cup my breast, "…a man that loved you - that assuredly loves you still - spent a lovely, and quite *private*, little visit with you today, is no big deal? You don't think that warrants my jealousy?"

"No, it's…it's over with Liam" I manage, despite the distraction of his touch.

"Like it's over with Helena? Then you would be okay with her paying me a *little* visit?" his tone is condescending, refueling my defenses.

I try to pull away, but his grip around me tightens, holding me in place against him. "It's not the same thing," I mutter, feeling the heat from his hold.

He spins me around to face him, his grip firm on my arms. The fury in his eyes is both frightening and desirable at the same time. "The only difference is that I fucked her...he *made love* to you."

I gasp at the dominant harshness of his statement, but I'm not giving in just yet. "Well, that's just semantics, Alex," I bite. "And regarding any love involved, in case you didn't hear me the first time, I'll repeat it for you...that part of my history with Liam is *over*."

"It's over for you," he bends to whisper firmly in my ear, "That doesn't mean it's over for him." The brush of his breath against my neck is exhilarating. The words, however, are infuriating me further, more so because they echo my sentiments regarding his lame-ass use of Helena as some basis for a comparison.

"Thank you for proving my point, exactly," I jerk my arms from his hold.

"Your point?" he practically snarls. "Jesus, Aby," he turns from me, running his fingers through his damp hair, pacing back and forth, away from and towards me, in frustration.

"Yes! You're the one who threw Miss Adelaide into this argument. I'm merely reminding you that...that..." *Shit. I don't even remember my own point*, I grimace, undoubtedly pouting. Damn him and his sexy manipulation of the situation, touching me to prove *his* point, his damn seductive whispers. *Seductive... Temptress. Yes! That was my point...*"Liam and I ended a marriage. We transitioned from couple to friends. *Helena* was your... well, your whore - for lack of a better *label* - and she can easily attempt to renew that role at any time. It's. Not. The. Same. Thing."

Stopping, he glares at me, "If you weren't so goddamned stubborn, I'd..." he huffs, pacing once more.

"What? What, Mister Jealous? Or should I say, Master of denial of said jealousy - what would you do?"

He growls at me this time, stopping to look me straight in

the eye. "I certainly know what I'd like to do," he spits.

"Yeah, what's that?" I bite back.

"Fuck some sense into you. That's what."

Holy shit. I've never been one to imagine sex in a moment of anger. Never before felt the rage and lust cocktail. But right now, it's burning through me like moonshine in my veins.

For several seconds, minutes even, as though the earth has stopped on its axis, we stare at each other amid panting anger and craving. We're trapped beneath a ferocious tidal wave of desire; frozen, looming above us, around us, and we both know its about to come crashing down to drown us in its lustful fury.

I sense the moment Alex is about to pounce, the moment my eyes secretly, silently, whisper so much more than any words ever could. I want him *now*. As much as I know he wants me.

He reaches for me, his attack viciously laced with dominant desire, his wide grip spanning my waist to pull me into his arms. Our lips meet in a ravenous kiss, pent up anger fuelling our lustful want for each other as he grips the back of my thighs to lift me, my legs wrapping tightly around him.

Winding my fingers through is hair, I pull and tug in desperation, his hands mirroring my actions in my soaked tresses hanging down my back. I feel possessed, moaning into his mouth, sucking on his tongue. There's no concept of our surroundings as we ravage each other, completely engrossed in our deep, anger-fuelled need to fuck each other senseless.

Turning towards the dresser, Alex sashays his hand abruptly along the top with a fluid glide of his muscled arm, the articles crashing to the carpeted floor with a clatter as he secures me in his grip, his hand at my backside. The erotic display of dominance has me biting his lip in hunger, driving us higher.

Setting me atop, we struggle with needy hands and fingers, tugging and frantically pulling apart the bow of my robe, spreading the material to reveal my nakedness beneath. His hands engulf my slender waist as he pulls his lips from mine to attack my nipple, sucking it deep before swirling his tongue along the pebbled tip.

I can't resist the urge to hold his head in place, my legs shaking amid the pounding tempo of my clenching core. "Alex! Fuck me!" I cry out in a breathless pant.

He groans through a final nibble, his husky breaths slipping through parted lips as he lifts me off the dresser, making his way towards the bed. Dropping me to the mattress, I yelp, barely able to catch up as he swiftly shoves his gym pants down, his returned erection bobbing against his stomach.

Bending, his large frame looming over me, he spreads my legs with his strong hands, "Is that what you want, baby? You want me to fuck you? Maybe I should make you beg for it."

"Oh God…" I gasp, closing my eyes against the sheer decadence of his dominance.

"Is that a no? You don't think I should make you beg?" he questions, sliding his fingers along my soaked pussy, gliding with ease through the juices coating my folds.

"No!"

"Then tell me who you belong to," he orders, his tone firm and sexy as hell as he slides his fingers inside me, pressing deeply against my g-spot.

"You!" I scream in absolute frustration and need, gripping his wrist in an attempt to push his fingers deeper, my body bowing with desire. I am his. His, and his alone.

"You're fucking right, you are," he growls, pulling his fingers from my depths, kneeling down on the bed between my widespread legs to thrust his cock fluidly inside.

He owns me in this moment - in every ridge, every ripple I feel against my sensitive nerves, my pussy throbbing and pulsing around his thickness. God, I will never tire of the feel of him. Never stop wanting him. Never stop loving him.

"And I'm yours, sweetheart. Always yours," he whispers huskily, driving us to the brink.

"I'M SORRY, ABY," Alex whispers, gliding his fingers along my spine as I lay sprawled across his chest. "I shouldn't have gotten so angry about Liam's visit, it's just that…"

I lift my head to stare into his eyes, his expression showcasing a myriad of emotions as he trails off. Turning his striking blue gaze to me, a small, shy smile dons his face.

"It's just that, I don't want to lose you. After Julia…Ben… I-I just love you so damn much."

I'm torn between the sweetness of his words and the curdling sensation at the mention of…*them*. Ben. Julia. My insides shrink further as I reflect on the avid hurt Julia has caused Alex, the extensive damage her cheating did to his self-esteem. *That bitch*. Add to that, the fact that his best friend could betray him so utterly, so totally. I can completely understand his issues with trust, jealousy, however annoying, and unwarranted, they may be.

Anger, frustration, and rage towards them for the hurt they've caused wells inside me, fueled further as I remember Julia's avid denial that she slept with Ben. Although I didn't - and still don't - believe her denial for one second, I realize that I have yet to share that tidbit of information with Alex. *Ugh*.

"Alex, I get it. I don't like it, but I get it. But you have to trust me. I'm not her, and Liam isn't Ben," I relay, cupping his jaw lovingly in my hand. His returned, though sad, smile breaks my heart a little. "She denied it, you know," I finally confess the information I'd withheld - albeit, unintentionally. Not shockingly, I've tried my best to mentally block everything *Julia and Ben*-related since it all went down.

"Who denied what?" he asks, a bewildered look on his face.

"Julia. When she came to see me before I left London…she denied having cheated with Ben. Obviously, I didn't believe her for a second, and in fact, forgot all about it until this moment." I hold my breath slightly, awaiting his reply. Will he be mad? This could classify as an omission of sorts, regardless of how much I'm trying to downplay it. And God knows how Alex values omissions.

I can see the wheels spinning as he contemplates what I've just divulged, from curiosity to frustration to anger. "Why *would* you believe her? Everything she says is a lie," he spews in disgust, pushing to sit on the edge of the bed.

Hmmm. I certainly didn't expect *that* reaction. I thought he'd flip out, demand to know why I didn't tell him. Moreover, be thoroughly upset with how everything played out with Ben - the demise of their friendship. Not for one second did I think he'd brush if off as another lie. His adamant tone has me questioning the validity, "But what if she's telling the truth? What if your anger at Ben is misguided and he didn't betray you?"

"He betrayed me when he made a pass at you, Aby. That alone is betrayal enough. Besides, I don't fucking care *who* she was with," he states with vehemence. "You know what," he continues, standing to pull his sweat pants on, "...no more talk of Julia and Ben. Done. Over." His gaze softens on a breath of composure, "I'm sorry I let my past show itself in my present. My jealousy has no bearing on my trust in you, Aby. I promise, it won't happen again."

Standing motionless before me, his sincere smile effectively halts my need to talk more, to mull over the possibility that perhaps she *was* telling the truth. Clearly, he not only doesn't care, but also refuses to give it any credence whatsoever. That's fine. At least I've told him what I know, whether it's the truth or not. No more secrets.

The shrill ring of the phone breaks our silence, and I stand to get dressed as Alex reaches to grab it.

"Hello? Yes...What do you mean?"

Tugging my tank top into place over my yoga pants, I still at the shift in Alex's tone, his previous smile replaced with an expression of worry. Walking towards him, I sit at the edge of the bed, sliding my hand into his as he leans against the nightstand, clutching the phone to his ear.

"What about Ben?" his gaze darts to mine as the question falls from his lips.

What are the chances given the chat we just had?

"He's *WHAT*?" his eyes bulge in alarm, a flash of pain radiating from his pose, "...an *overdose*? I'm on my way," he finishes, abruptly returning the receiver to its casing. Turning to face me, I note the trepidation in his gaze, and my heart starts an erratic beat in my chest. "It's Ben. He's in the hospital."

CHAPTER
Twelve

"JESUS, HOW DID this happen?" Alex questions, pacing the hospital corridor, running his hands through his hair. He isn't asking anyone in particular. Nor does it appear he's looking for an answer. He's merely repeating the same question he's been consistently speculating aloud since we heard the news about Ben.

Finally stopping his incessant pacing, he leans his back against the wall, his fingers still in place in his unkempt curls, once again falling victim to the unresponsive silence.

I hate seeing him this way, his beautiful face baffled and etched with pain and concern. He's been like this since we received the call less than eighteen hours ago. Having not eaten a single thing during the twelve-hour flight to London from L.A., it's beginning to show, the lack of his usually healthy glow in his unshaven face darkening his boyish good looks.

Seated in the uncomfortable chairs along the wall, I feel helpless staring up at him. I want so badly to provide comfort, to hold him in my arms, but my previous attempts were all but dismissed. He doesn't need anything I have to offer him right now.

Julia is leaning against the wall opposite Alex, staring down at the floor, her arms folded. Not that I'm complaining - my disdain for her rearing its ugly head as I purposely avoid offering her a seat beside me. No, she can stand where she is - far away from me.

I haven't seen her since that fateful day she came to my flat; her incessant meanderings that I wasn't fit to live in Alex's world, wasn't good enough for him, rushing back like a second slap to the face. I wonder how she feels now, given my active presence in his life ever since, her words having held no weight whatsoever. Or maybe she's not thinking about me at all.

It's obvious she's trying hard to maintain her icy veneer, standing expressionless, slightly vacant eyes honed towards the tile floor. But it's clearer to me now that she's not just Ben's publicist, as well as Alex's, she's also a friend. Though even in this unfortunate circumstance, she's getting no empathy from me. As far as I'm concerned, she's still just a bitch. A cheating, lying bitch.

Of course, I now know that she wasn't lying about one thing - when she accidentally let it slip that Ben was 'dabbling' in drugs. *Dabbling*? Was that what she really thought? Was she really blind to the enormity of his habit? Or did she not give a shit? To look at her now, I would assume she really had no idea how bad it was. But, then again, it's Julia-*fucking*-Cox. I don't think it's safe to ever assume anything when it comes to this woman.

"Alex, it's so good to see you, darling," a well-dressed, older woman approaches. Though she's clearly been crying, her tear-stained cheeks and red eyes don't take from her attractive features. Her blonde hair is perfectly groomed in place, curled under at her shoulders, her attire screaming wealth and stature.

"Catherine," Alex leaves his place at the wall to embrace her. "I'm so sorry I wasn't here for Ben…" he trails off as she hugs him, rubbing his back in comfort.

"Shhh, Alex, don't blame yourself. My son is a big boy," she reaches up to take his face in her hands, looking into his eyes. "He will get through this. We were lucky," she says, her aristocratic British accent befitting her wealthy station.

"I-I just didn't know…" Alex stumbles on his words, trying to contain his emotion, his bewilderment seeping through.

"I know, darling, I know," she pulls him down to kiss his cheek before releasing him. "Have you been to see him yet?"

"No, we arrived not too long ago. The nurse said he's resting."

"Yes, he is, I just checked in on him. I know he will want to see you when he wakes, Alex. He's been asking for you."

Alex winces slightly at her words and my own guilt builds to a lump in my throat. He hasn't spoken to Ben since that night at the club, since their horrible fight. My God, the last contact they had was with their fists. And all because of me.

Closing my eyes, I cringe with remorse momentarily before defensive anger spikes its way through my veins. *No! It is* not *my fault that Ben hit on me. I* had *to tell Alex. I can't keep harboring guilt for* his *actions.*

Looking up, I catch a glimpse of Julia, still staring at the floor. Instantly my fury shoots towards her and her part in all of this. Though I feel a little better having been honest with Alex about her questionable claim that it wasn't Ben that she cheated with, I can't help but regret not mentioning her slip of the tongue about Ben using drugs. Particularly now, when that was clearly *not* one of her lies. *Damn her*. She's like a spider in a web of deceit, and I'm now a fly caught in her trap. Along with Alex. *And* Ben.

But it's Alex she has hurt the most. It's obvious that his feelings for her were, at one time, very strong. They *must* have been for him to keep her in his life after what she did. There's a friendship there that runs deep. And though I don't understand it, I can't help but feel for how her questionable behavior has affected him.

Flashing back to the look on his face when I told him that she'd denied it was Ben…He was so torn, so confused. How could I possibly question his refusal to discuss it further? But I *should* have pushed the issue. I also should have shared her comment about Ben using drugs. I clung so very easily to Alex's dismissal and refusal to talk about it - grabbed so very eagerly to the vine he inadvertently offered away from the ugly shade of truth. Not dealing with it didn't help anything, though. It merely added more regrets. And, clearly, things are just getting worse.

Looking towards him now, a boyish, sad demeanor as he stands with his best friend's mother, I take a deep breath and swallow back my venom. I'm not doing any good for Alex by giving in to my fury for Julia Cox.

"Is Harrold with you?" Alex questions Catherine.

"Oh," she seems to snap back from a hushed moment of escape, looking up to meet his gaze. "Yes, of course. He is gone in search of something edible, darling. I will join him after I let the nurse know where we will be." With a slow, gentle smile, she turns to walk towards the nurse's station, the fog of silence refilling the void of her momentary departure. "Would you like me to get you something, Alex?" she stops to inquire as she passes.

"No, thank you, Catherine," he smiles, though it seems as much as he can force. Brushing his cheek with her dainty, well-groomed fingers, she smiles back at him before continuing on down the corridor.

Alex remains standing in the middle of the hallway, gazing towards her long retreated form.

Pushing up from my seat, I walk to his side, taking his hand in mine, rubbing it gently as I take in his ashen face. For a moment he doesn't acknowledge my presence, despite my touch.

Finally looking towards me, he offers a pained, forced grin, "I'm sorry, I didn't introduce you. That was Catherine Arnold. Ben's mum."

"It's okay, I assumed," I smile. "Alex, if you won't eat anything, at least let me get you some coffee…something?" I wait for his answer, but he just takes a deep breath, looking down. I won't force the issue. Not yet. Though, it's killing me to see him like this.

The shifting of Julia's position against the other wall breaks the silence. Alex's gaze darts to her, his face contorted in frustration. Angered frustration. "Did you have any idea?" he asks her.

Though she finally looks up from the floor to meet his gaze, she says nothing, her blank expression still in tact.

"I asked you a question, Julia. A simple yes or no answer will suffice," he throws in annoyance.

"Alex, this is not the time, nor the place, to get into an argument," her tone is as bitchy as I remember.

"Who's looking for an argument? I asked you a simple question. Did you, or did you not, have any knowledge that Ben was using drugs?"

I can feel the tension racing through Alex's veins through my hold of his hand. *This is not going to be good.*

Julia straightens, taking a breath with a sniff as though preparing for war. *Oh shit.* Alex is not going to like her answer. Provided she answers truthfully, of course.

She opens her mouth to speak, but pauses momentarily to look towards me, a flash of *something* in her gaze that makes my heart stammer. Pulling her eyes back to Alex, she finally replies, "As I told Abigail last month, yes, I knew he was using," she pauses, flicking another glance my way.

You fucking bitch! My silent scream crashes through me, giving way to a sudden shaking dread. My heart lodges in my throat as Alex's hand flinches in mine enough to shake my light hold of it. *Oh God.*

"But I had no idea, that it was this serious," she finishes, her tone clear and firm, completely unrepentant of the shit storm she's potentially caused me with her admission.

"As you told Aby?" Alex asks, his brows twisted in confusion. "What are you talking about?"

The tension radiating off of him is suddenly heightened, and I can feel the penetrating shock waves towards me at his side. Standing motionless, I'm at a loss for what to say, what to do, shaken silent in avid denial that this is even happening.

"Abigail and I talked before she left for Canada," Julia continues, not skipping a beat. "It was after your fight with Ben." She sustains eye contact with Alex as I continue to stare shell-shocked towards her. "I was trying to clear the air, and I inadvertently let it slip. I'm sorry, Alex, I should have told you. I just didn't realize it was this serious." She catches my crazed gaze before continuing, "I'm actually a little surprised. I thought Abigail would have told you herself."

"Are you *kidding* me right now?" I blurt at her audacity, finally finding my voice, my breaths barely contained in my chest. *I can't believe this is happening. How does she always manage to fuck me?*

The look of evil triumph in her eyes as she glares back at me pushes me over the edge.

I make a step toward her before Alex grabs my arm, turning me swiftly to face him. "You knew?" he shakes his head in question.

I can't speak. I just stare at him, frozen in panic. All of my previous thoughts run through my head - the inner diatribes about what to do with the information the bitch had given me. *I thought she was lying. I thought she* could *have been lying.* I open my mouth to speak, but no words come out.

"Aby, answer me! Why didn't you tell me?"

"Alex, I…"

"Excuse me, Mr. Tate, Mr. Arnold is awake and is asking for you," the nurse's interruption doesn't shake his lock of my gaze.

His face is contorted in question, his eyes boring into mine. "Mr. Tate?"

I stare up into his beautiful, pained baby-blue eyes, my lips still parted in their disrupted position.

He shakes his head slightly, finally turning to acknowledge the nurse, releasing my arms as he composes himself. "Yes, my apologies," he turns, leaving me standing in place to follow the woman down the corridor.

I watch in shocked awe as he disappears around a corner at the end of the hall. Frozen in place. In panic. Until I suddenly remember *her*. "You bitch!" I scream, locking her in my sights.

Her smug smile is my undoing and I bridge the gap between us as though distance has no measure in time. I've never been in another woman's face filled with such venom and hatred. Yet she stands in place, arms folded, her arrogant smirk signaling she's ready for whatever I have to give. Damn her and her composure. It takes me aback, though it's probably for the best - in my momentary surge of rage I may have clawed her eyes out.

"What have I ever done to you? Why are you so intent on ruining my relationship with Alex?"

"I don't give a shit about your relationship with Alex," she retaliates, unflinching.

"Oh, so you just enjoy throwing me under the bus because…you hate *me*? Or just because you're a *bitch*?" Her eyes twinkle with amusement, forcing me to take a deep breath before continuing. "You *asked* me not to say anything about Ben using drugs, remember? Although I can't really say that I kept that secret for *you*. Let's be honest, I couldn't really be sure you weren't lying…it's hard to tell with bitches like you. One minute your agreeing to having slept with Ben, the next you're telling me you didn't. So many clichés come to mind…Liar, liar, pants on fire… The bitch that cried wolf."

"I lied about Ben to protect Alex. Why was it *you* lied to him?" she tilts her head mockingly to the side, "Oh, yes, to protect yourself," she smirks and I feel my nostrils flare with heightened breaths behind my tight-lipped stance. "I don't have to throw you under the bus, Abigail, you made your own bed and have to sleep in it. I feel awful for Alex, having to sleep in those cheap sheets with you."

"You really are something, aren't you? Cheating on Alex was the best thing you ever did for him, so that he could throw *your ass* out of his bed." I move in closer to add, "Oh, and I didn't lie to Alex about you and Ben. I told him all about your messed up and very questionable denial."

"Yes, of course you did," she laughs, pushing me out of her way. "You silly. Stupid. Selfish girl." Walking away from me, I grab her arm.

"Where the hell do you think you're going?" I ask bravely, holding her tall, piercing gaze.

She looks amusingly at my hold of her, "I have a feeling this is going to be a very interesting evening, Miss *Ryan*, and I, for one, need a little caffeine, if not a drink, before I witness you ruin Alex's career to protect yourself." Snatching her arm from my grip, she moves to continue on.

"The only one that lie was protecting is you!"

Turning swiftly on her heels, she leans in, her face aligned with mine, her lips grimaced in a stern line. "No, naïve, little girl. My lie was protecting Alex, remember, sweetie? What he doesn't know doesn't hurt him. But hurting him seems to be something *you* are very good at," she adds, silencing me before making her way down the hall and out of sight.

I'VE LOOKED AT my watch every five minutes for the past hour since Julia walked away. Alex is still visiting with Ben. I can only hope that it's going well for them. If he comes out smiling at least that will be a wonderful sign. If Julia was telling the truth about not sleeping with Ben, maybe they can begin to repair the damage, if only slightly, since it doesn't negate what he tried with me.

"Oh goodie, I didn't miss the show," Julia saunters up the hallway, resuming her position against the wall.

"Can the circus really start without the dancing bear?" I reply with sarcastic hatred.

"Oh, sweetie, you mean the elephant, don't you? And the elephant in the room is you, dear, Aby. I do enjoy seeing Alex torn to bits every time you cut his heart to pieces," she rolls her eyes, busying herself with her phone.

"I would never intentionally hurt Alex," I retort, despite the pang from the memory of running away from him. She snickers, but says nothing. "The question is, Julia, what are *you* planning on doing tonight to hurt him? Are you finally going to grab those balls you hide under your skirt and be honest with him? Because if that's the case, I think that would be a good thing, he deserves the truth for once."

"Well, look at you throwing stones from your little glass shack. You're going to learn a lesson tonight, princess. A lesson at the expense of Alex's pain." She hasn't even glanced up towards me; ignoring me, despite her words, as she flips through the phone in her hand. "I warned you. You don't have a clue what it takes to live in his world."

His world? Whore. "Right, of course..." *Ugh,* I spin away from her in frustration. I'm starting to realize that Julia-sucks-Cox is more fitting in a role as the Riddler than a porn star fluff. Or maybe both. *Oh, yes...* She could pull off a show. *'Tittle me this'.*

Shit. Pull yourself together, Aby. Sleep deprivation. Guilt. Fear. I'm a lethal combination of shit storms. I need to snap out of it, for Alex. He's going to need me when he comes out of that room. At least I pray that's what he's going to need...or want. Either way, continuing an excruciating bitch-banter with the Queen "B" is not going to help me get through this.

Taking a seat, I take a deep breath at the thought of what I'm about to witness, or aide in, as I notice Alex making his way up the hall towards us. He looks more than pissed. Either it didn't go well with Ben, or he's about to continue his questioning of me where he left off. *Shit.*

To my surprise, he walks directly to Julia. "You are one fucked up bitch. Why would you let me think it was Ben? Why the hell would you play out that charade?"

Pasting on the eerily warm smile of a Stepford Wife, Julia touches his arm gently, "Alex, are you sure this is something you want to know the answer to? Some things are better left alone."

Flinching at her touch, he jerks his arm away, the coldness of it blowing towards me like an arctic wind. "Enough fucking games," his tone is firm and much too elevated.

"Jesus Christ, Alex," she whispers, turning quickly towards the nurse's station, their avid gazes now upon us. "Is there somewhere we can go to talk privately?" she asks them, smiling.

Nodding, a nurse motions for us to follow her down the hall.

"After you," Alex sneers to Julia, grabbing my arm to pull me from the chair, dragging me along with him. I struggle to keep up.

"You have to understand," she begins as soon as we're behind the closed door of the empty room, "...this is not something I ever wanted to discuss, Alex. I need to ask, please, let this go."

"Do you have any fucking idea how much I want to let this go?" he snarls. "I honestly don't give a shit *who* you *fucked*, Julia. I don't relish the fucking sordid details of your cheating ass story. But to lie and say it was *Ben*? My best friend!"

I'm surprised to see Julia flinch - an eerily odd momentary blip of her stone demeanor.

"Don't you see? This is all on the table - the past pulled out for discussion - all because of her," she motions towards me as though I were a pile of garbage ready to be put out on the curb. "Ben never outright said he was with me, *she* made that assumption. And to that end, I too, never offered confirmation myself."

"Ben didn't deny it! And neither did you!" I argue in desperation. *I'm so fucked.*

Ignoring my presence completely, Alex continues as though I've said nothing. "I swear to God, Julia, if you don't stop dancing around this bullshit…"

"Yes!" she exclaims, interrupting him. "This *is* bullshit. Bullshit we've all moved past. Leave it there, Alex."

"Fuck you. We could have done just that the day I confronted you. You had the opportunity right then and there to correct the implication."

Julia's wall of composure instantly crumbles before our eyes, her gaze suddenly crazed with her own recognition, and I, too, see why. She's just realized that her split second decision to run with the Ben lie has now blown up in her face. Had she just denied it, told him outright that it wasn't Ben, that I'd been mistaken, Alex would never have asked her to delve further. He never wanted to know the details. Her rash choice led us down this path. It's a dead end, and there's no turning back. *Who has to lay in their own bed now, bitch?*

"I'm losing my patience, Julia," Alex growls at her lack of reply. "Why didn't you fucking deny it?"

She flinches at his harshness, her brave mask no longer a shield, her stone cold demeanor replaced with a contorted gaze of dread and panic. Though, when she looks towards me, I catch a glimpse of the underlying contempt. It's an eerie sight to see, to witness this woman fighting an obvious inner battle of strength against…compassion? At least that's what I *think* I see when she looks back to Alex.

"This is my career…*your* career. This should have stayed in the past," she looks towards me once more.

"God dammit, what are you talking about?" Alex grabs her arms to force her gaze. "*Why didn't you deny being with Ben?*" Staring into her eyes, his jaw clenches in the silence.

"I saw an opportunity and I took it," she finally mumbles, almost incoherently. "It was a chance to fill a gap in the story…"

"Just fucking tell me why you lied!" he spits, a slight shake of her in his hold.

"Because I didn't cheat on you!"

What?

Alex recoils, his body renouncing her proximity with a sudden release of her arms, a step backwards akin to the jolt of a magnetic rejection.

Julia's hand darts to her mouth as though the admission burned her lips.

What the hell is she saying? My gaze ricochets between them, torn between Alex's confused torture and Julia's twisted battle for composure. You can visibly see the wheels turning so palpably through her desperate mind. I don't understand it. The woman that warned me that *I* would be the one to learn a painful lesson if this all came out, is now burning in an agonizing fire of her own.

"I didn't mean…I…" she's grasping, frantically searching for her mask of control.

I barely recognize the woman standing before me. It's not the Julia I've come to know. She's suddenly fragile, her soft, almost caring tone foreign to my ears. And the way she's looking at Alex, there's suddenly something there that I've never seen before. And it scares me.

"You didn't cheat on me?"

I look towards Alex at his question; spoken with such bewildered calm it sends shivers down my spine.

"Why? Why, Julia? What are you saying?" his anger builds with every word released. "You told me yourself…you told me you cheated on me!"

"Alex, they knew…they knew you'd purchased an engagement ring," she looks down momentarily, before returning to his gaze. "They…"

"Who?" The word is thrown from his lips on a gutted breath.

"The agency. They said it wasn't good for your career…not the right time. I was ordered to put my job, your career, ahead of…us. They gave me no choice, Alex! I *had* to end it! I knew you wouldn't let me go…not unless I gave you reason. Not unless I-I broke your heart."

Alex stumbles a little, his eyes bulging beneath the enormous strain of his twisted brows. I can't pull my gaze from him, fighting to hold strength in my own legs against the dizzying pull of the air around me.

"You knew I was going to propose to you?" he asks her, the question slashing through me to reveal the pain she foretold.

"Once they told me, yes. They showed me the photographs of you at the jewelry boutique…"

"Photographs? How did they get…That wasn't released in the media."

"They have their own photographers, Alex. You pay them to look out for your career."

"My career, NOT my personal life!"

"Your image is your career," her statement is filled with pain. Her own pain. *Oh, God.* She still loves him. She never stopped loving him…

"And you? You ended it, left me…to save *your* career?"

"No! I did it for you! Alex, you have to understand…" she pleads, reaching out to him.

Turning away from her in disgust, he opens the door with enough force to shake it on its hinges, storming out into the hallway.

I bolt to follow him as Julia grabs my arm.

"Are you happy now?" she spews with a lethal cocktail of venom and pain.

Wrenching myself free from her grip, I run to catch up with him.

"Alex," I call out him as he slams the button for the elevator.

He says nothing as I reach his side, the doors opening in the ghostly silence of the empty vestibule. Stepping inside, he bangs the panel to take us to the ground floor.

Instinctively, I reach for his arm, his flinching shake of me sending a ripple of painful terror down my core. "I'm so sorry…"

"Don't," he barks, staring straight ahead. "My best friend

could have fucking died. And you," he turns his crazed gaze towards me, "...you are no different than her..." he trails off, battling with his emotions. I know he's lashing out at me in pain.

Closing my eyes, I try to fight my guilt. My fear. I'm trembling inside, knowing the role I've played in his hurt right now. Not telling him what Julia said about Ben using drugs, regardless if I thought she was lying, forcing Julia's hand with the cheating scandal. *My God.* I've reopened a wound. A wound so deep, its depth of pain so clearly shared between the two of them that I feel I'm falling into its black hole. She still loves him. *Does he still love her?*

The elevator doors are barely open before Alex bursts through, heading straight for the front entrance as I follow, my pace to keep up heavy and painful.

"There they are!"

"Alexander!" The camera flashes explode through the evening dusk in a blinding storm.

"Is it true that Benedict Arnold overdosed?"

"Mr. Tate! Mr. Tate! Was it an attempted suicide?"

Alex grabs my arm, forcefully ushering us through the throng of paparazzi to reach his car.

"Did you know that Mr. Arnold was an addict, Mr. Tate?"

Flinching at the question, Alex glares at me, his eyes screaming his unspoken answer, *No, I didn't know because you didn't fucking tell me.* He releases his hold of me with a slight shove; so slight it's masked to those around us, yet enough to slash through my heart.

"Does it have anything to do with your bar brawl last month?" the man in nearest proximity calls out.

Alex turns, slamming his fist at the camera. The damage is minimal, though stirs a cluster of reactive comments. He doesn't bother opening my door as he usually does, making his way around to the driver's side.

"Alex..." I begin in the privacy of the vehicle.

"Don't say another fucking word right now," he orders, not looking at me. The rage in his face is unfathomable. I've never seen him this angry. NEVER.

He screeches the tires pulling out into the road. I'm amazed we aren't pulled over by police, as he races through the streets. I'm almost afraid to ask where we're going before I realize he's heading in the direction of my flat.

After a whirlwind of Nascar-like maneuvers, amid dread-filled slow passing time, he pulls the car up at the curb. For moments, he sits calmly, and I open my mouth to speak, praying he'll at least talk to me…

"Get the fuck out, Aby," he orders with venomous spit, still withholding his gaze.

"What?"

I'm shocked at the anger in his eyes as he turns his head to face me. No longer baby blue, they're a stormy sapphire, burning with a rage I couldn't imagine he could emit. "I said, get the fuck out of my car."

"No!" I spurt mechanically, shaking my head, trying to understand what he's saying, scrambling to find more words of my own.

With an annoyed sigh, he abruptly removes his seatbelt to get out of the car before making his way to my door. Flinging it open, he reaches in swiftly to release my belt, aggressively pulling me out by the arm.

"Alex, you're hurting me," I attempt to twist from his grip to no avail as he pulls me aside to slam the door shut.

Grabbing my other arm, he pins me against the vehicle. "Hurting you?" he questions incredulously, his face nose-to-nose with mine, "I thought you liked a little alter-ego play?" Maneuvering quickly, he takes both of my wrists in his one large hand, his other free to grope my behind before sliding his way up to my neck.

How the hell can I be trembling in fear and lust in the same moment? I'm petrified. Yet so filled with love and sexual yearning, my head is spinning.

Grabbing my chin, he firmly turns my face to the side, his lips brushing my ear. "Your fucking lying is what hurt you. Not me," he whispers huskily. "And I'm not going to stick around to let you hurt *me* one more time."

I gasp as he releases me and pulls away, gravity suddenly pulling my entire being as I strain to remain upright.

Adrenaline kicks into gear as he makes his way back around to the driver's side, and I race after him. "Alex, wait! Don't do this. We need to talk!" I scream, reaching him.

"I don't have anything else to say. And I think you've had enough time to say anything and everything you should have," he opens the car door.

I frantically continue pleading, "Alex, please, let me explain…"

Slamming it once more with the palm of his hand, he turns towards me, "What is there to explain? You promised you would never lie to me again. Remember? Right after you promised you wouldn't leave me, but did anyway."

"Please, it's not that simple…I…You…We need to talk about what just happened. Please, just come inside."

"Aby? You're back." We look to find Andrew walking towards us. "Is everything okay?" he asks, clearly feeling the tension in the air.

Alex sniffs a laugh, "There you go, perfect timing. Now you can go inside and explain your *hurt* away to your good little friend." Opening the door once more, he climbs inside.

"Alex, don't go!" I scream as he revs the engine, pulling away from the curb before driving off.

CHAPTER
Thirteen

"**A**BY...I DON'T even know what to say."

"Well, that makes me feel better," I mumble, sarcastically. "Stacey Stevenson at a loss for words. It can't get any worse than this."

"Bitchy humor, good for you!" Stacey quips, obviously grasping at straws. "Oh, wait, me speechless and you being funny...Shit. I think this means the world has turned upside down."

"No," I sigh, "...just my world."

"That's not exactly true, my little ginger snap. I'm pretty sure Alex's world is pretty fucked right now. Even Julia Cox-sucker's...that...ugh...I'd call her a whore, but you and I both know nobody would ever pay for that shit."

I laugh through a lingering ball-your-eyes-out hiccup. "Thanks for trying to make me laugh, Stace."

"Oh, buttercup, I'd do anything for you. I'd pee on your jellyfish sting."

This time my laugh is half-hearted, my drained emotional lament reaching the pit of its spiral to twist its way back up again. I'm exhausted. Having cried off and on all night, I was a blubbering mess when Stacey returned my call this morning. It took several attempts of explaining and re-explaining for her to decipher my crazed detailing. Eventually, my emotional eruption simmered out, leaving me to wallow in the numbness of the lingering ashes. But as with any volcano, you never know when the lava will spill over, and I brace myself, feeling it bubbling once more. "She still loves him."

"Aby, don't do this to yourself."

"What if he still loves her? He was going to propose, Stacey," newly formed tears stream down my cheeks.

"That's in the past, Abs. It was years ago. Yes, it's something he has to deal with - a door reopened, but, sweetie, he will close it again. You're his present. He loves *you*," she pauses at the chime of my doorbell. "Are you expecting someone?"

"No." My heart lodges in my throat. *Oh, God.* "What if it's Alex?"

"Okay, listen to me. Stay calm. Go answer the door. Hear him out. Give him shit for the way he treated you - cause that's *not* cool, babe - and then hug him. Pull out your tits and flash him a smile, I think he needs it."

"I-I don't know what to say to him. What do I say, Stace?"

"Be, honest, and listen honestly. And, babe, try to dial down the defensive diarrhea mouth. Call me as soon as you can, okay? I love you!"

"I love you too, Stace." Ending the call, I swipe at my tear-stained cheeks, walking to the door, taking a deep breath as I open it.

"Hey," Andrew smiles bearing coffee, his smile full of concern. "You okay?"

Releasing the breath I didn't realize I'd been holding, I take the cup with a forced smile. "I've been better. Thanks," I mutter, still trying to decide if I'm relieved or disappointed to find Andrew instead of Alex.

"What can I do?" he asks, shrugging his shoulders slightly - a testament that he's well aware there is nothing he can really do, but he's offering anyway.

"Can you turn back time?" I ask, motioning for him to come on in, turning to make my way back to the sofa.

"I assure you, if I could, I would definitely include that on my business card." With a wry smile, he sits down beside me. "My shoulders are free, though, if you need one."

I grin slightly in return, remembering the last time I cried on his shoulder. "I'm not sure I have any tears left to fall. The well is a little dry at this point."

"Well, I promise I'm not going to ask you to tell me what happened. You kinda made it pretty clear last night that..."

"It's none of your business," I repeat the words I suddenly remember lashing towards him, covering my mouth with my hand at the horrible memory. "I'm so sorry," I manage.

"Don't be. You were right. It was none of my business. And it still isn't, but I needed to make sure you were okay. *Are* you okay?"

"To be honest, I'm not sure. I'm a little numb, actually."

"I'm sorry," he flashes a smile of pity.

"Why? It's not your fault."

"Are you sure about that?"

"I'm sure I don't know what you mean," I cock my head, confused.

"Well, it's just that Alex rushed off last night just when *I* showed up," he looks down awkwardly.

"No, no. Don't even think that. It was just bad timing...it had nothing to do with you."

"Well, that's a relief. I'd hate to think I made things worse for you."

Andrew's words float through my head, inadvertently setting off a replay all of the run-ins I've had with Alex as a result of Andrew - the many misunderstood situations that he's found Andrew and I in. *Of course Andrew's right.* His presence last night, potentially at the worst possible moment, probably *did* make it worse.

Perception is everything... Alex's words inflate my remorse, guilt seeping through my pores. Though my intent towards Andrew is innocent, I never stop to think about how it makes Alex feel. And even in this moment, when Andrew's presence here is one hundred percent friend-based, I know that if Alex were to show up right now, it would surely make matters ten times worse.

Suddenly, I need Andrew gone. "Ummm, yeah, I wouldn't worry about it, Andrew. But you know what, it's been a rough day so far and I'm exhausted. Thanks so much for the coffee, but do you think we could visit another time?" I question in the most innocent tone I can muster.

"Of course, I'll leave you to it. Just promise me that you'll let me know if there's anything I can do, okay?" he pushes himself up, making his way to the door.

"That's very sweet of you, but I'm pretty sure there is nothing you can do to help me with this one."

"Maybe not, but if there's anything you need, you know where to find me."

"That I do," I smile, following behind him. "Thanks."

"Anytime," he winks, pulling the door open to leave, revealing Alex, standing on the other side.

Shit, my heart drops in my chest. *Honestly, I have the worst fucking luck EVER.*

"Andrew," Alex's greeting is curt.

"I was just leaving," Andrew offers just as flatly.

"Hey, don't rush off on my account."

My eyes bulge at the razor edge in Alex's tone.

"I wouldn't," Andrew is equally clipped, meeting Alex's stance in some silent agreement of a showdown of brawn.

The testosterone bounces between them, ricocheting from chest to chest in an imaginary fight for alpha-pride.

Ugh. I turn on my heels, leaving them standing at the door. At this point, I don't have the strength of body or mind to deal with it.

Clearly, my departure initiated the end of the alpha-dance, as Alex makes his way in not long behind me. "Did he stay the night?"

"What?" I spin around in shock.

"I think you heard me."

"Oh, I heard you. I just can't believe you asked me that."

He says nothing as he stares at me, jaw clenched.

The display is incredibly sexy and I can't help myself from taking him all in, unable to resist devouring the length of his beautiful form. Every tense muscle is outlined in his white shirt, the sleeves pushed up to his elbows highlighting the strength of his arms, the hem partially tucked beneath the belt of his dark blue, perfectly hanging jeans. He looks sinfully delicious. He always does.

Damn him. Why can't he be just another pretty face? He's so much more…a truly wonderful man whose flaws, even in his anger, are so easily forgivable and insignificant when weighed against the pure core of the gentleman I've fallen in love with.

The gentleman Julia *fell in love with.* The idea that he may still love her turns in my stomach, and I feel the need to brace myself against the ripples of acidic fear building inside me. I need to be strong.

"Why are you here, Alex?" I ask, turning to casually take a seat. It's a move of self-preservation, and a poorly executed show of strength, my inner actress nowhere to be found, my inner dreamer still crying in the corner.

"I came to apologize."

Oh God. I swallow the vomit lining my throat. An image of him and Julia together, lost in the throws of reunited passion, twists my ailing heart to ice. "Where *did* you drive off to, Alex, when you left me standing on the curb last night? Did you go to *her*?"

"Her?" he spits.

"You know exactly who I'm talking about. Or are we playing games now?"

"This isn't a game, Aby, this is my life."

It's mine too! I want to scream, but bite my tongue. "You didn't answer my question."

"No. You know damn well I wouldn't do that."

"Do I? I'm not really sure of anything right now," I mutter the latter on a whisper, looking down.

"Nor am I," he replies.

My gaze whips back to his, "What are you saying?" My heart, so full of love for this man, is breaking apart. I need to know I'm not losing him. I need him to tell me he's choosing me, not her.

"I'm saying that yesterday was a lot to take in. I think I need some time," he says softly, avoiding my eyes. "And," he pauses to look at me directly, "…I'm saying I'm sorry."

Time for? "What are you sorry for?" I barely manage the words, my charade of strength crumbling and evident in the shaking timber of my voice. I want to curl into a ball, to close my eyes and wish this all away. *He can't leave me to go back to her.*

"I'm sorry for the way I treated you last night, Aby."

I say nothing, silent in my fear and self-doubt. *He can't leave me for her...He wouldn't.*

"And, I'm sorry that I need to take some time to sort through everything," his words drag me, mentally kicking and screaming away from my bubble of denial.

"What does that mean?" my thundering question shoots straight down my legs, bolting me upright to stand.

"I need time to figure everything out," his tone is laced with an underlying plea for understanding. "Remember when you needed time?"

I fall back in place on the sofa, reeling from the punch to my stomach, the additional stab to my chest.

"Aby..."

My mind is spinning, furiously trying to win the race against the pounding of my heart.

"Aby, look at me," he pleads.

Realizing my eyes are clamped shut, I open them to meet his gaze. The sight shatters me. He's broken, torn and ragged from the pulling of the seams of his reality. Everything he thought was real shredded to pieces in the blink of an eye.

"I need to return to L.A. today. They can't hold off the shoot any longer. I think..." his jaw clenches as he seems to recalculate his words. "I'm going back alone, Aby." He stares at me in the silence, waiting for me to say something. Anything.

But I don't. I can't speak.

"There will be a break in filming in two weeks. I just need this time."

I want to be strong for him, but I'm drowning in an ocean of uncertainty, the waves pulling me under, tearing him from my grasp.

"Aby, say something," his plea is so full, yet so empty as it reaches my ears.

"I don't know what to say, Alex," I whisper. "What do you want me to say?" My eyes are pleading, desperately begging for him to come to me.

He doesn't.

"I need you to say that you understand."

"Understand that you may leave me to go back to her?" my voice quivers as I swallow back my building tears.

"Aby…I…"

"Do you still love her?" A tear trickles down my cheek, the question cutting through me, slashing my heart.

"No…I don't know…Fuck," he runs his hands through his hair, "…it doesn't even matter, I…"

"It doesn't matter?" I stand in a burst of adrenaline. "It matters to me!"

"Don't you think I know that?" he flinches, closing his eyes, his jaw still clenched in pain. Finding my gaze, his words are cautiously soft, "This is about so much more than just Julia."

Her name on his tongue burns through me and my body fights against it to step closer to him. I need to be closer to him, to steal the strength he's holding, to use it as a shield for my breaking heart.

With each step closer, I realize I'm losing him. I may have lost him already. My dream world snatched away with the snap of her fingers, torn from me by the lies of their past. *Damn her!* I have to look away from him, desperate to hide the lash of contempt. *I HATE HER.*

I hate myself, too. I aided in the shattering of his reality that now echoes through the demise of my own. This is why I have to let him go. He needs this from me right now. I owe him that much.

"You're right," I begin, looking up to him, just feet apart, the surge of his will aiding my composure. "You should go alone," I falter slightly.

CHAPTER
Fourteen

*U*GH, LONDON WEATHER. It's officially pouring. And I mean *pouring*. Although, I will say, it's quite fittingly ironic. Mother nature seems to be mirroring my fallen tears since Alex left two days ago. Even if I wanted to venture outside - which I *do not* - her mocking cry fest is enough to keep me sheltered behind closed doors. Not that it matters. God knows I wouldn't subject anyone to my pathetic form. Except for Stacey, of course. She's flying here tomorrow night on the pretense of visiting Thomas, but I know that's bullshit. My best friend is coming to my rescue. That's what best friends do, I suppose. And, normally, I'd say it wasn't necessary, but in this case I absolutely need my BFF.

For now, though, I think I'll settle with pouring myself a glass of wine. *See, perfectly fitting*, I smile at my brilliance, grabbing a bottle of my favorite Shiraz.

Reaching for a wine glass, my cell phone signals a text and I freeze. Literally. I'm like a statue, my hand mid-air as I wrap my head around the idea that it could be Alex, my heart pounding loud enough to threaten shattering the glass at my fingertips. I've yet to hear from him, the trepidation building with every hour since he walked out the door. I'm dying to hear his voice, yet frightened to death about what he'll be reaching out to say.

Moving incredibly slow - a sloth comes to mind - I drop my hand at my side and turn around, leaning against the countertop to stare at my phone on the island. My heart screams *pick it up, you fool*, but my head is shaking *no*. Again, literally. Gripping the countertop behind me, I watch as the reminder alert sets my phone vibrating in place, eerily akin to a puddle, its still water blasted by the pouring rain. *How fitting*.

Are we done with the weather analogies? - my inner actress rolls her eyes. *Yup.* Sink or swim time, I reach for the phone, sighing when I realize it isn't even him.

Subject: Rain Day

Monopoly?

Andrew

Monopoly? Well, at least this time Andrew has good timing, I could use a distraction right now. Although, given the recent happenings, the initial thought of seeing him stings. But…Alex isn't here. He's in L.A. *And, I need a friend*. And that's just what Andrew is - despite what Alex thinks.

I quickly type a reply…

Subject: Love Monopoly

Come on over.

An afternoon of mindless games sounds perfect, I convince myself, making my way downstairs in time to hear Andrew knocking on the door. "Come on in," I yell, taking a seat on the sofa.

"Hey there," he smiles walking in, closing the door behind him. "What are you up to over here all by yourself?" he asks cautiously, though his natural playful charm seeps through.

"Ugh, being depressed," I confess on a sigh.

"Well, I figured. Thought you could use some company. And given the weather sucks, there's no better time like the present for a Monopoly-fest," he holds up the board game, the box beaten up and slightly dilapidated - quite the contrast to his brilliant white, toothy smile. That grin would make the saddest frown turn upside down.

"I admit I haven't played in years. And I mean *years*. You'll kick my ass," I smile half-heartedly.

"You can't be good at everything you do, Aby," he winks, joining me on the sofa, emptying the box of all contents on the coffee table.

I laugh - the realization that it's not a forced one easing up my initial wary discomfort. *I'm glad he came over.* "What can I get you? Soda? Beer?" I ask, pushing myself up.

"Beer would be great, if you've got it," he flashes that wide smile, arranging the blue, orange, yellow and pink money into neat little piles.

"Two brewskies coming up," I head for the stairs, feeling lighter and more human. "I'll grab some munchies too."

He eyes me cautiously on my return, doling out our allotted cash, as I lay down our snacks and sit cross-legged on the floor.

I can't help but chuckle at the neat piles of properties he's spread out, but when I look up to his face, I see he's still looking at me with an odd expression. "What?" I question.

"Nothing," he smiles, "I was just wondering how you're doing?"

"Ummm, I've had better days. But, so far it's looking up," I reach over, giving him a playful shove on the shoulder.

"Happy to be of service," he laughs, shoving me back as he moves to sit down on the floor across from me. "So, I'm the car," he states, pulling the silver pieces out of the bag.

"Hey! What if I wanted to be the car?" I question like a fifteen year old.

"No can do, beautiful. I'm *always* the car. Here, you can be the thimble," he dangles the piece that nobody wants.

"Fine," I laugh, "I'll be the man on the horse. You know, it won't matter what piece you use, I'll still beat your ass."

"That may very well be the case, but you'll always wonder if I let you win," his mock charming smile makes me laugh out loud.

"Thanks for coming over, Andrew. I really needed the company."

"Hey, what are friends for? But, you know, you can't stay holed up in here forever, Aby. You have to go out sometime."

On a sigh, I pick up the dice, needing the distraction from the serious turn of conversation. "Yeah, I know I do. I just…I don't know. Stacey will be here tomorrow. She's flying in from Toronto to stay with me for a while."

"That's great," he smiles, as I roll and take my respective moves. "When does she arrive?"

"Sadly, not until tomorrow night. Maybe I'll go into the office. That way I'm not 'holed up' in here," I drawl sarcastically. "*Reading Railroad*, buster. It's mine," I mutter with delight, handing him two hundred dollars.

"Oh, it's like that is it? You're a railroad hog."

"Yup, prepare to lose, car boy."

"In your dreams, horse." He takes his turn rolling the dice. "So…"

"So, what?"

"So, we're *not* talking about Alex? And by *we*," he adds quickly, "…I mean you?"

"Nope. You taking *Park Place*, racer?"

"Nah, too high a price to pay."

Well, isn't that a kick in the teeth, I try to hide a grimace at the eerie, though unintentional analogy. *Park Place* is the equivalent of Alex's world. Wealth, fame, and all the other expensive shit that comes along with it. And right now, *Park Place* can kiss my ass.

"ARE YOU SURE you really want to be here today?" Emily asks, her face giving away her recent membership in the *Poor Aby, Pity Party Club*. I'm really starting to hate that club.

"I think the office is the best place for me to be," I reply with a closed lip smile. "That is of course, unless you're going to look at me that way for the rest of the day."

"What way?"

"You know what way," I fold my arms, rolling my eyes.

"I'm not some fragile little bird that…you know," I flail my arms in search of the word fairy, "…lost her puppy or something."

"Aby, birds don't have puppies, love. What you have is called the blues," she offers the *Pity Party* forced smile salute.

Ugh.

"You still haven't heard from him, have you?"

"It's only been a few days," I feign indifference, thumbing through my files. I can't bring myself to admit to her that it's killing me. He outright left me. It's not all butterflies and rainbows anymore. And I know exactly how long it's been - day three, and it sucks - but I'm sure as hell not going to give a member of the sympathy club more pathetic ammunition.

The feel of her concerned stare burns a hole in the side of my head, and I exhale an annoyed sigh before turning to look at her.

"He said he needed time, Emily. And I don't doubt that," I shake my head at the thought of what he must be going through, despite what it's doing to me. "I have to respect what he needs right now." Although it *is* killing me that I haven't heard from him. *Doesn't he want to talk to me? Does he even miss me?*

"He isn't giving you much of a choice either way," she shrugs sympathetically, turning back to her work.

No, he isn't. I lean back in my chair, hugging the files to my chest. He did, however, take the time to explain it to me before he left. In so many words, at least. *That's a hell of a lot better than just leaving without any at all,* I close my eyes against the shameful memory. But at the end of the day, it's not *my* lack of choice that concerns me. It's his. And, more to the point of the dagger aimed at my heart, it's the fact that he has to make one at all. Julia…or me.

"Good morning, ladies."

I cringe at the sound of Helena Adelaide's silky, and rather cheery, voice. "That's quite the pep in your step for so early in the day," I offer without turning her way. *Why does she get under my skin so easily?* She's never really done anything to me, personally. So, she slept with my boyfriend on a whim, or a phone-a-friend whore-call, up until the point he met me. That doesn't exactly make her a threat. Or a whore, for that matter. Maybe it's her timing. Yeah, I'll go with that. She has whore-timing.

"Good morning, Helena," Emily shoots me a questioning glance.

"What a pleasure to see you at the office, Aby. I must say," Helena pauses to sit on the corner of my desk. "I was concerned to hear that Alex returned to Los Angeles without you. Is everything okay?"

And, there it is. My Ho-bra alarm going off again. She may be innocent as a mouse, but in my mind, she contorts into a snake that's actually chewing on one, its poor tail still sticking out of her slimy jaws. "You've got a little something right there," I brush my finger at the corner of my mouth with patronizing sarcasm.

Of course, it's lost on her; concern plaguing her gaze as she discreetly wipes her lip.

Oh well, I mentally shrug her off, pretending to look busy with my files, although I do feel a little guilty for being such a bitch. Just a pinch.

Ignoring her, however, isn't making her go away. *Ugh.* "Everything is fine," I lie, without looking up. I just want to get rid of her annoying gaze. I'm sure as hell not telling dial-a-goddess anything about Alex and I. "Our return to London was for personal reasons, a friend of Alex's is in the hospital."

She says nothing, and I look up to find an odd look in her eyes. That's all the information I plan on giving her. It's not my place to divulge anything further about Ben's situation. As far as I know she barely knows him, other than the introduction I gave her at the office that day Ben picked me up. That *fateful* day. A shiver runs down my spine, and I quickly shake it off hoping it goes unnoticed.

"Alex will be back in a couple of weeks, when he breaks from shooting," I add, hoping that will satisfy her and get her off my desk. *Two long painful weeks, during which I may, or may not, hear from him at this rate.*

The look on her face is just...*weird.*

"Is something else concerning you, Helena?"

"N-no," she finally replies, her mouth hanging agape as

though she's considering saying more, before closing it, suddenly avoiding my gaze. "Oh, it looks as though Thomas is ready to see me," she stands in an awkward rush, brushing the wrinkles from her perfectly fitted skirt. "It was nice chatting with you ladies. Perhaps we can meet for lunch one day this week," she smiles, making her way towards his office.

"Wow," Emily gushes. "*That* would be the woman to befriend."

I turn to look at her, taking in her bitten lip. *Really?*

"Aby, she is the lady with connections to the hottest men in London, remember, the perks of her job here. All those models and celebrities," she swoons, staring at Helena through the glass wall of Thomas's office, suddenly turning back to me. "Oh yeah, right, you *have* yourself one of those hot celebrities..." she stops suddenly, her face twisting in regret. "Sorry. It's not like you're actually broken up," she shrugs with an awkward grimace.

"It's okay," I shake it off with a forced smile. *I just died a little.*

"So you can't just hang me out to dry. You're the reason she is so friendly, she certainly never gave me the time of day before you came along. We're having lunch with her, right?" It's more an order than a question.

"Ummm...sure. I mean, we'll see," I attempt a smile, nipping the corner of my mouth. Her expression is killing me, and I quickly turn away, sorting through my files.

In my peripheral vision, I see Emily roll her eyes before looking back to her computer. Then I roll my own. *God*, could I get through a lunch with that woman? I mean, how exactly would that play out? In my mind, I imagine something like: *Would you mind passing me the cream, Abigail? Oh, that reminds me, isn't Alex the best creamer?*

Gross and completely messed up, right? But it's my prerogative to dislike someone who's probably creamed my boyfriend more times than the cow's been milked. That's my story and I'm sticking to it. Guilt be damned.

"Goddammit!" I toss the files on my desk, quickly stuffing my finger in my mouth to still the bleeding and quell the instant pain.

"Paper cuts are a bitch," Emily notes quietly.

More like karma, I grimace, swiveling my chair to face her, my digit still stuffed in my mouth.

"That's what happens when you're preoccupied," she pulls out her sympathy card for another stamp.

I ignore it, *and* my guilty conscience for the Helena-karma. I'm a pathetic mess. Maybe coming into the office wasn't the best idea. I hear wine calling. Wine and pajamas. Wine, pajamas, and a chick flick. I'll need tissues.

"Speaking of seeming preoccupied, have you noticed anything weird with Thomas lately?" she continues, jarring me from my momentary loss of focus.

"I'm sorry, what was that?" I struggle to keep up, still lost in thought.

"Thomas. Have you noticed he's been acting weird? He seems off."

Thankful for the change in topic, and somewhat intrigued by her question, my gaze instantly darts to his office. "Hmmm, I hadn't noticed." How could I notice? I'm selfishly absorbed in my own battered and broken heart, shattered dreams, and losing the man that I love more than life itself. *Shit, I hope it has nothing to do with Stacey.* "I haven't spoken to him much," I try to waylay my guilt for possibly being a super shitty friend. *Double shit.*

"Well, he's definitely been acting prickly. Yesterday he was just staring through that glass wall for, like, twenty minutes straight. Arms crossed, expressionless, just staring at *nothing*. I get staring off into space now and again, but for *twenty minutes*? And, at least sit down to do it, if you're so inclined to daydream. Standing up just seems silly. He's been uncharacteristically quiet lately, as well. Even at the board meeting this week, he barely said a word. No playful banter. No jokes. Nothing. Something is definitely amiss."

Humph. I'll have to feel him out when he's done with *Handy*-Helena.

Watching them through the glass wall, her hand brushing his arm as she leans over him at his desk, I can't help but want to slap her touchy tentacles away. On second thought, maybe I'll touch base with Stacey and feel her out first.

Grabbing my cell phone, I type a quick message.

Subject: Can't wait to see you!

Everything on schedule for your visit? I came into the office today. Thomas seems a little stressed. Is everything...

What a joke, I delete the last two lines. Passive-aggressive won't work with Stacey. If I'm concerned, I have to outright ask.

Subject: Can't wait to see you!

Everything on schedule for your visit? I came into the office today. Thomas is acting more than a little 'off' — please tell me I haven't been a shit friend, and that everything is okay with you two.

Aby xo

Hitting send, I turn back to my work, instantly relieved to get her quick reply.

Subject: Not as excited as I am!

Thomas and I are great! But he is a little stressed with work. He's all mine tonight, baby! I'll suck all his troubles away as soon as I land :) Gotta run, my flight is boarding.

Stace xo

Shaking my head on a smile, I attempt to blow off the visual I *did not* need, and toss my phone in my bag. *They're great. Good.* I'll have to remember to drink to that, right after I drink to my own broken heart. Yup, wine is calling.

POUR. IT'S MY word of the day - *word of the week, actually*. Pour myself into my work. Pour myself another glass of wine. Pour myself into the pursuit of distraction, while I watch the rain continue to pour down outside. What the hell else can I do? I need the diversion. I need to hide from the absolute pain that's been permanently imprinted on my heart.

It's been four days since I've seen, or even heard from... *Alex* - just the thought of his name triggers a sharp pang in my chest. Four days, six hours and thirty-two seconds since I last heard his voice...saw his face...felt his arms around me. I feel sick. I haven't eaten. I'm barely sleeping. I haven't even read. God knows I've tried. Food turns my stomach. Sleep brings a combination of beautiful dreams mixed with nightmares. And my beloved romance novels break my heart at the mere mention of any form of passion, love - each conjuring heart-wrenching thoughts of Alex and what I've lost. I miss him so much it physically hurts. The painfully excruciating days spent contemplating all the many scenarios of what he's doing, who's he's with, are haunting me.

No calls. No texts. Nothing. Our 'break' seems more like a *break-up*. I've come to realize that. And I'm dying as a result. It's been a hard pill to swallow to accept that it could be over. The salt in the wound being whom I may have lost him to - *Julia*.

I want to hate her. I want to despise everything she is and everything she's taken from me, but I can't. I never thought I'd say this, but I *understand*. It's been a shocking revelation in recent days - the bittersweet taste of rationality amongst my irrational heartbreak.

I truly can't imagine what it must have been like for her to be forced to give him up, to sit idly by while he dated others, knowing her love for him probably never waned. Sure, she *chose* to give him up; a conscious decision that she'll have to live with for the rest of her life. But, understandably, that doesn't lessen the hurt she's likely felt all these years - the absolute torture of watching the man you love move on with his life, secretly hating you for betraying him. Oh, I understand *exactly* how Julia must have felt. The thing that scares me the most, though, is the part I *can't* fathom an understanding of…*What is Alex feeling*?

The thought elicits another surge of bile, and I slide my hand to my throat, squeezing gently in hopes of pushing the vile sensation away. Abandoning the marketing campaign on my laptop, I push up from the kitchen island in desperate search of a much-needed alcohol refill.

"Aby? Are you here?"

"Yeah, I'm upstairs, Stace," I call out, immediately opening the fridge to grab the makings of a salad - I don't need another lecture from her about how I'm wasting away to nothing while I waft through my days like a zombie.

Discarding the lettuce, green peppers and tomatoes down on the island, I refill my wine, smiling slightly at Stacey's exuberant run up the stairs - my smile effectively kicking my buzz back into gear with the pending distraction of my best friend's quirkiness. *God, I've missed her.*

I chuckle as she rounds the stair rail with quick works, slightly out of breath. She never runs, so this should be interesting. "Is this a wine run, or are you being chased by someone?" I ask, alluding to her out of character display of energy, as I start chopping the lettuce. "Hungry? I'm about to make a salad."

"A salad? Ugh. In my state, that's about as inviting as going to a whore for a hug. Unless that's chocolate covered lettuce, I'll pass."

"Oh. Okay," I reply, purposely attending to the cutting.

"Dammit, Abs! Don't play coy with me. Clearly I'm distraught! And all you're offering is rabbit food?"

Laughing, I lay my knife down and give her my full attention. This must be *quite* the pickle she's dealing with given she hasn't commented on the fact that I'm actually preparing a meal.

"Okay, I'll bite. Why are you *distraught*?" I ask with teasing sarcasm, though I'm completely intrigued as to what's got her in such a huff.

Sighing, she flops herself dramatically on a stool at the island. "Thomas," she says his name as though it will explain everything.

Clearly she wants me to pull the information from her. "*Oookaay*, what about Thomas? Is he still stressed?"

"No, he's fine. The fucker is more than fine."

Of course he is, Stacey sucked all his troubles away. And, now I'm stuck with that visual again. *Great.* "So, what's wrong then?"

"Well, he's gone and ruined *everything*, that's what!" she pushes up from the island, pacing the kitchen and hallway. I watch, eyes wide, as she marches back towards me, only to turn for a repeat trudge around the tiny space. "Everything was perfect and he had to go and fuck it up!" she finally continues, flailing her arms. "Why he felt the need to change the rules of the game are beyond me!"

Her little tirade is clearly not detrimental - in a worrisome kind of way - so it's kinda fun to watch, though I have absolutely no clue what she's talking about. Obviously Thomas has pissed her off, but that's nothing new. They have this cat and mouse romance that typically results in ridiculous and petty arguments. I actually think it's adorable just how much he gets to her. No one 'gets' to Stacey. The fact that they've maintained a relationship this long - a long distance one at that - is shocking in and of itself. However, considering the off mood he's been in, according to Emily, it's not surprising that he's twisted Stacey's knickers into a knot.

"Stacey, calm down," I grab her arm, steering her to sit back down. "I'll pour you a glass of your favorite wine and you can tell me all about." Turning back to the fridge, I note the sudden silence. *Of course, the mention of wine was exactly what she needed,* I giggle to myself.

"Thomas proposed."

Her utterance is like a stun gun to the throat, and I knock the bottle of wine off another jar, the clinking glass reverberating in the silence.

"See, even *you're* shocked."

*Shocked...Stunned...*So many exasperated words come to mind. And I can feel the sting of all of them directly in my heart as my abandoned thoughts of Alex shoot right back to the forefront. *How selfish is that? How selfish am I?*

Well, if anything, this certainly explains Thomas's strange behavior. And now I have to quickly adjust my own. "Wow," I pull myself together, turning to face her with the mask of my inner actress. "That's incredible, Stace! What did you say?"

"After I fell on the floor and shit my pants? Well, I eventually said yes. Can you believe that? I said yes! *I'm* getting married! I mean this is crazy shit..." she trails off, finally catching my expression - which, from the way she's suddenly looking at me, suggests its recent contortion to her news. "Oh, God. Shit, Aby, I'm sorry."

"What?" I pull my inner actress up off the floor, along with my bottom lip. "What on earth do you have to be sorry for? This is wonderful news!"

"Are you sure, Abs? Are you okay with this? I wasn't going to say anything at all given what's going on with you and Alex, but...well, I couldn't help it."

"Don't be silly, Stace. I'm fine. Truly. I have to move on. The world doesn't stop revolving just because..."

"Yours has?" she questions, interrupting me with an understanding grin.

Yes! - my inner dreamer screams, the anguish burning my wounds. My world does feel as though it came to complete stop the moment Alex walked out the door. But this is not the time to give in to self-pity. This is Stacey's moment. And though the distraction is a double-edged sword, I have to stand up and fight the cutting reality. "Come here," I put my arms out for a hug, pasting on a big smile. "I'm so excited for you!"

"Don't be an unselfish whore," she whispers, squeezing me before pulling back to look into my eyes. "I would so slap you into next week if you pulled this shit on me," she winks with a laugh. "I love you, Abs, and you don't deserve to have to deal with my crisis right now."

"Stace, you are not in crisis. You're getting married!" I smile sincerely, finally feeling the excitement I should for my best friend.

"Isn't that the same thing?"

"No!" I laugh, giving her another hug. "We get to do wedding stuff! Go wedding dress shopping!" I add, selfishly looking forward to the distraction.

"Do you think I can pull off white?" she winks.

"Ummm, cream is nice," I shrug playfully, pursing my lips.

"You're a bitch," she laughs, shoving me. "Good thing I love you. Besides, what whore can get married without her special bitch for the day? Will you be my Maid of Honor, Abs?" Stacey chokes out the latter, tears welling in her eyes.

"Oh, Stace," I grab her again. "No one deserves a special day more than you. I wouldn't be any other place than by your side." I pull away to look into her eyes, "I love you."

"I love you too, pickle. Now enough of the mushy shit."

"Okaaay," I laugh. "But, when's the big day? We have lots of fun planning to do."

"Ummm, well...Thomas is adamant that we have a *quick* wedding. I think he's afraid I'll change my mind," she chuckles, seemingly trying to camouflage her reply.

"I can't say I blame him, but *how* quick exactly?" I ask cautiously.

"Less than two weeks," she flashes a cheesy nervous grin. "Well. More like ten days," she cringes.

"What?" my high-pitched squeal sends her grimacing playfully, and I have to roll my eyes. Leave it to Stacey to add dramatic madness to an already enormous life event. "Okay, then. Well...I guess we have a lot to do in a little amount of time. Totally doable," I smile, finally turning to pour her glass of wine and handing it to her. "Spicy Stacey has been tamed and has fallen in love. Cheers to that," I hold up my glass, saluting the next ten days of bittersweet distraction.

"Cheers to the fucker that made me fall in love with him,"

she adds as we take a drink.

"I always knew this would happen, you know. I could tell right from the start that Thomas was 'the one'."

"Was Alex *the one*?"

Stacey's continued stare and knowing gaze has me summoning every ounce of confidence I can muster, my strong shield avidly in place. "Ah, hello…this is still *your* time. Now sit your butt down, I want to hear every detail about the proposal.

CHAPTER
Fifteen

"**O**H MY GOD, Stacey! It's perfect. *You're* perfect! You look so beautiful," I beam through a well of tears.

"I *feel* beautiful!" she gushes, spinning around to take in her reflection. "Is it too much, though? I mean I get that Thomas wanted a traditional dress, I really do. But," she turns her head to look back at me conspiratorially, "...the sexy short one you and I chose *will* be making an appearance at the reception," she winks, looking back to the mirror. "I admit, I do love that he picked this out."

"He has amazing taste, and he certainly knows what suits your figure."

"Oh, he knows my body very well," she giggles. "And these puppies," she cups her voluptuous breasts, "...are framed perfectly for their daddy."

"I hate you and your big boobs," I tease with a laugh, stepping behind her to place the sparkling choker around her neck. "You know I'm going to be a bumbling fool at the wedding, right? I'll bawl through the entire thing."

"You and me both, sister. I'm just not sure it will be because I'm completely, utterly in love with Thomas - which I am, of course - or because his dick will be the last I'll ever suck," she mutters dramatically on a laugh. "Oh, and don't hate on the Humpty Dumplings - my boobs are my *thing*. Everybody has one. Or, in your case two, bitch - that hair of yours, for one. And don't get me started on your ass, which looks *amazing* in your dress. Alex won't know what hit…" she gasps, clasping her mouth, her eyes frozen on mine in our reflection. "Shit, Aby," she turns to face me. "Damn it," she unclasps the choker around her neck. "All this mushy shit, my brain is completely warped into lovey-dovey mode, and it just came out. I'm so sorry."

"It's okay, Stace," I take the necklace from her, moving to return it to its casing, grateful for the hidden breath of composure I sneak. "I'm doing fine."

"*Fine?*" she slurs the word to remind me that, to women, 'fine' means anything but.

"Really," I roll my eyes, "I'm doing great."

"Promise?"

"Promise. Now stop. This is supposed to be about you, re-member?"

"Honey, it's *always* about me," she winks. "Besides, I think we can make your 'great' into greater…Let's get out of here and hit that salon down the street for a mani/pedi. I heard they even serve *cocktails*."

"Sounds great. Wait…how do you drink them while you're getting your nails done?"

"Humph. Good question. You can ask for a straw, my little sugarplum, I'll order a tall dark and handsome drink holder."

"OH, GOOD LORD, this Cosmo is divine," Stacey moans, suck-ing the last sip through the straw. "I swear, sometimes I come up with ideas of epic proportions," she gleams her big green eyes at me, a charming smirk donning her face.

True enough, the mani/pedi idea combined with alcoholic beverages a-la-straw while we got our nails done *was* a fantastic idea. "Why do you think I've kept you around this long," I tease.

"Hardy-har-har, *sweet tits*," she sits up, testing the drying red polish on her nails. "I have a fantastic rebuke for that less than adequate assessment of our friendship's duration, but I'll withhold my sarcasm for the moment out of respect for those around us," she gleams at the other patrons sitting nearby, all smiling at our incessant back and forth banter. "But, for the record, I'm sarcastic because throat punching is frowned upon," she pauses to blow across her nails, eying me wickedly from behind her bent knuckles. "Keep that in mind when I tell you that holding my tongue physically pains me."

I literally bust out laughing, almost snorting, my hand darting to my mouth to shield my lingering giggles as the esthetician makes her way towards us.

"Follow me, ladies," she requests in her cockney British brogue, "Let's get those feet soaking."

"Mmmm, music to my ears," Stacey drawls as we follow behind her. "Hey, be honest," Stacey displays her perfectly manicured fingers, "…does this color make me look like a whore? If not, I have to pick another one."

"Shut up," I nudge her into the seat.

"Sweet heavenly Jesus," she sighs on a whisper, submerging her feet in the miniature hot tub, leaning back in the massage chair, eyes closed. "My ideas are epic, aren't they?"

"Almost always," I tease, smiling at my best friend.

Screw you, she mouths through a playful smirk, not bothering to open her eyes to look at me.

Laughing, I shake my head and reach for a magazine on the table. *Glamour UK*. My breath hitches on a painful sigh as I'm assailed with the memory of Alex's stunning face gracing the cover not so long ago. *World's Sexiest Man*. He's so much more than that very accurate designation. The thought of just how much more burns through my system until it reaches the tips of my fingers, singeing them at my hold of the memory-eliciting nuisance. I quickly drop it, its unopened pages flung from my hold like unwanted filth.

I'd managed to get through most of the day so far without giving in to the pain he's left in my heart, only to be reminded by something as innocent as a stupid magazine. *Well, I'm not perusing my nose through that particular one*, I grab another, sniffing back my heart's warning of impending tears. Although it doesn't matter what I do anyway, something always brings me back to him, leaving me reeling in the empty feeling that consumes me in his absence, as equally as he consumed me in his presence.

Time and distance is slowly chipping away at my heart, but more hurtfully is that he's yet to reach out to me. *Thirteen long days* - and that fact is seeping into the breaking cracks, threatening to shatter me. *He needs time…*his parting words are like razors in my stomach. I swallow hard, desperate to wash them away. How much time does he need?

Isn't this killing him as much as it's killing me? I purse my lips inwardly, rolling my shoulders to push off the sheath of fragility the thought of him has created. I need to be strong, no matter how much the words *I'm losing him* crash through my core.

Sitting up straight on a breath of composure, I flip through the pages of my second choice, *Hello* Magazine. I'm unfamiliar with many of the celebrities plastered throughout - not surprising, given it's the UK edition - but it doesn't matter. My aimless perusal is perfectly numbing as I catalogue their fashion choices and hairstyles, versus paying attention to who they are and what they're doing.

I stop to admire an attractive woman's hair, wondering if I need a change myself, before turning the page. My eyes widen, almost to the point of blurring as I take in Alex's stunning face, my lips parting on an unwelcome gasp.

"What is it?" Stacey asks in alarm, pulled from her semi-conscious relaxation.

I can't formulate a reply as my focus returns, absorbing the images. I'm completely tongue-tied, quickly flipping a glance at the issue date on the cover. *Current. No! It can't be*, I return to the inside pages, staring transfixed at Alex…and Julia.

Standing side by side at some sort of event, they look the epitome of the happy couple. Bile rises in my throat as I aimlessly turn the pages, the numerous pictures of them together returning my vision to a blur…Alex leaning into her, his arm wrapped around her waist as he whispers in her ear. Her smiling face cuts through me with a boomerang strike of anger. A combination of bone crushing hurt and rage that I can feel down to my toes.

"Aby? Is that Alex?" Stacey leans over, peering at the pages gripped in my trembling hands.

My mouth opens long before I manage to get the words out, "Alex…a-and Julia." I can't stop myself from staring at his perfect face leaned into her ear.

"What do you mean, Alex and *Julia*?" she mutters, tearing the magazine from my tight hold. "I don't understand…these photos were taken in L.A.. He's in L.A. with *her*?" she questions, shaking her head at the images as though looking for an answer that isn't there.

I'm going to be sick. The memories of his parting words lash me once more…*I'm going back alone, Aby.* He lied. He wasn't going alone. He was going with *her*. 'Alone' translation: without *me*. My worst fear when he left coming to fruition, smacking me dead in the face through the superfluous pages of a celebrity tabloid - Alex has reunited with Julia. *I've lost him.* He needed *time*, a 'break' from *us* to work everything out…a break that was merely a prelude to the breaking of my heart.

"Aby?" she pulls me back to the present. "These pictures don't mean anything…"

"Don't they?" I barely whisper, numbness seeping in, my body fighting to quell the ache consuming me. I stare straight ahead, my focus turned off, realizing why he hasn't called. His acting skills could never hide the truth from me. I would have heard it in his voice. *But, surely he would have known I could find out this way.*

"God, Abs, I'm so sorry. I can only imagine how you're feeling right now, but clearly you're in shock."

Turning to look into Stacey's watchful eyes, I shrug my shoulders slightly, my act of bravado an epic failure as my eyes well with tears. "I always knew it was a strong possibility. I'm not in shock. It's just…having it smack me in the face…" I trail off, unsure how to articulate my disdain at the moment for Alex's very public life, despite my many months having become accustomed and acceptant to it. At this very moment, I *hate* that he's a celebrity.

"Awe, babe," she reaches over to squeeze my hands. "I assure you, you're in shock. Otherwise, you'd be flipping right the fuck out. Or, maybe deep down you realize that you're making assumptions - assumptions that aren't worth making at the cost of the pain in your eyes right now."

"A picture is worth a thousand words, Stacey."

"Yeah, and there are times when all of those words are *whore*," she jabs her finger in Julia's face on the page. "But just because she's a ratchet whore, doesn't mean Alex…"

I look away, taking deep breaths through my nose to fight off angry, painful tears.

"Abs, listen to me. I know you've said you thought he'd go back to her, but let's face it, that's bullshit. *I* thought for sure that…well fuck…I don't know what I thought anymore. Yes, I agree, *this* looks bad. But you can't do this to yourself. Not without confirmation from Alex."

"Should I wait by the phone for his call?" I huff through my arched jaw, taking my lip in my mouth, biting down and closing my eyes. "I'm sure as hell not reaching out to him, especially not now…" I cringe, thinking of the very many times I stared at his number on my phone, wanting so much to connect. It killed me every time. My heart's slow painful death.

"Okay listen, this is what we're going to do…I'm going to call Thomas and tell him that dinner tonight can't happen, and you and I are going to get drunk. And I mean piss-eyed hammered. You can take out your anger, frustration - everything - on Captain Morgan, and within a few hours you'll have snapped out of your shock and moved on to drunken rationale. It's time for a ladies night, babe. You need it."

"Stacey, don't be crazy. You're having dinner to meet your future in-laws. I'm pretty sure it would be highly frowned upon for you to cancel. As much as I'd love a ladies night, I could *never* let you skip out on Thomas for that. I'll be fine."

"Abs…"

"Stacey, no. It's not happening. Go do your thing…meet your future family and show them how amazing you are. We can have our girls' night another night. My broken heart's not going anywhere." She grimaces in concern and I feel a pang of guilt.

She doesn't need my pain right now. "Actually, I believe some-one is due a bachelorette party," I add, forcing a smile, trying like hell to hide my brokenness behind the mask of my inner actress.

"A bachelorette party, hmmm?" Stacey quips, successfully distracted for the moment, or at least pretending to be for my benefit. "Okay, Hun, tomorrow night. We'll go out and have an impromptu shit-faced alcohol indulgence - which for the record is the natural progression through the seven steps of recovery from a broken heart. Although, *also* for the record, that heart of yours has no confirmation that it has actually been broken yet - just saying," she shrugs. "But, I'm all for jumping on the tequila train on the pretense of a bachelorette party - whatever you want to call it. So, no ifs, and or buts about it, we're going out. I think you need it. Deal?"

"Deal," I nod, hiding the squeezing pain from my *absolutely* broken heart.

"YOU KNOW WHAT? This is bullshit," I mumble to myself, pouring my fifth glass of wine. *I think it's my fifth.* I've lost count. But I'm pretty sure the ratio of wine-in-glass versus spillage on countertop is a clear indication that I've had *way* too many. Well, that and the now empty bottle.

"Ah, fuck it. I'm drunk. *And,* I'm talking to myself. It doesn't get any worse than this," I raise my glass in salute to my drunken-ass, moving to stand from the island. Sadly, my struggle to maneuver in my inebriated state is reminiscent of a baby cow trying out its new legs.

What a thought to have at this moment...a baby cow.

"You know who else is a fucking cow? *Julia-fucking-Cox.*"

No. Wait. Alexander Tate is coming off particularly cow-ish at the moment. Him and his *sweet nothings.* "So fuck you too, Alexander The Great!" I raise my glass once more, spill-free despite the shaky gesture, since most of my attempted refill is pooled on the island counter. *What a waste*, I turn towards the wine that *should* be in my glass, the notion a metaphoric stab to my heart. *Such a pathetic waste.*

I mean, I knew we were over - I knew it deep down in my gut. "But, *come on!*" To have reunited with *her* so damn quickly? And to be so friggin' cozy, you'd swear they'd never broken up? *What a whore. What an asshole.* "What a bunch of *whore-ass-holes!*"

I need to get them out of my head. Never think about them again. Somehow. I *have* to find away. Drowning my sorrows in Vino isn't working. *But...*I tap my finger on my chin, pensively. *A drinking buddy...that might be just the trick.* Pursing my lips, I turn haphazardly towards the stairs, grabbing hold of the railing with a death grip, taking each step with measured movements. It feels like a walk on a tightrope, my eyes peeled to my wine glass as I attempt to keep its half empty contents inside. I'm not wasting another drop. *I've wasted too much already.* I smile to myself, despite the painful analogy, successfully reaching the bottom and heading for the front door.

There's a funny thing about patience and wine...One doesn't work with the other. What does work, however, is knowledge of where your good neighbor hides a spare key when they take *forever* to answer the door. "Andrew? Are you here?" I question lightly, letting myself inside. "*Helloooo*? I'm looking for a drinking buddy..."

"Aby?"

My gaze darts in his direction. Emerging from the bathroom, he's wearing nothing but...a towel. He's wet. And naked. And wet. *Holy mother of pearl.*

Devouring him in my drunken stupor, I can't pull my gaze away - his smooth muscular chest, hint of abs and happy trail dusting along his lower tummy to creep below the fold of the towel down to a foreign place I *should not* be imagining. *Oh. My. God.*

"Abs, are you okay?" his jars me back to the present, my mind suddenly registering my lengthy, outright ogling.

"Ummm, yeah...fine. I-I just came over to drink."

Flashing me a quick smirk, he shakes his head, his eyes light with mischief. "You came over here to drink?" he makes his way towards me, unaffected by his partial nudity.

"Ahhh, yup. With you," I smile brightly, snapping back to the brilliance of my original plan - *Distraction 101.*

"Call me crazy, but I'm guessing you're way ahead of me," he chuckles lightly. "Am I wrong?"

His sudden proximity and slightly somber gaze locks with mine momentarily, my words lost in the fog of my inebriation as I trace the features of his handsome face. Bright blue puppy dog eyes, stubble-covered cheeks, and that brilliant, wide smile. *Jeez, my friendly neighbor really is quite the looker.* He's no Alexander Tate...*But, Alex Tate can kiss my...*

"Aby?"

I jerk slightly as he pulls me back to reality, quickly turning away in embarrassment from my obvious perusal. *Oh, good lord. Diversion. Think of a diversion!* This was supposed to be a distraction. Now I need a distraction from my distraction? *Shit.*

"Wine. I could definitely use more wine," I blurt, a little too exuberantly, raising my glass in the air, its contents sloshing and threatening to spill.

"Whoa, there," he reaches for it, the touch of his hand igniting a spark I wasn't prepared for. *What the hell was that?*

My breath hitches as I struggle to break his gaze. "Sorry," I laugh awkwardly, quickly turning towards the kitchen.

Laying my glass down on the island, the memory of the first time I was here hits me - that *other* awkward moment when his hand brushed mine as we cleaned up the spilt wine. *Humph. Was I drunk that night too?* I can't even remember.

"What is it with your place?" I try to brush it all off. "I have a habit of klutz-ing out in the wine department every time I'm here."

"Maybe I should serve you beer instead," he laughs. "Or, coffee wouldn't hurt at the moment," he shrugs his shoulders when I shoot him a teasing evil glare. "Hey," he raises his hands, laughing, "...I'm just saying."

"I came here to find a *drinking* buddy," I reply, opening the fridge to grab two bottles of beer. "You in?"

"I'm in," he smiles.

"Good. Heads up," I warn, tossing him a bottle - probably not the smartest move considering my current hand-eye coordination.

His quick reflexes kick into gear to catch it, the efforts showcased in every glistening, flexed muscle as he reaches up and to the right. Bad aim on my part, poor towel wrapping on his. My eyes trace the quickly falling towel, pooling at his feet on the floor. *Shit.*

Lifting my gaze to find his, I inadvertently catch a glimpse of what was, just moments ago, left to my imagination. *Double shit.* Wait. *Why is it...like that?* "Jesus, Andrew," I blurt, without thinking, my eyes glued to his *package*. "That's not exactly what I meant when I said heads up," I finally compel myself to find his eyes.

"Ah, humor," he nods his head, bending to retrieve the towel. "That's one way to handle an awkward situation."

"I wasn't trying to be funny."

He says nothing as he wraps the towel around his waist, though his gaze is locked on mine. His expression, however, is leaving me in the dark - which is a dangerous place to navigate under the influence of alcohol.

"Is *that* because of me?" I nod towards his now covered, though still evident, erection. "*Please* tell me there's someone in the bathroom."

"There's no one in the bathroom, Aby," he replies flatly, twisting off the beer cap to take a rather large swig. "Are you really implying surprise that I'm attracted to you?" he asks after seconds of silence.

"I...well, we're friends," I manage, reeling from the unexpected confrontation.

"Yes, we are." He walks towards me. "Our friendship is something I truly value. But can you really blame me for feeling more?" He searches my eyes for a moment despite the rhetorical sentiment. "And, since we're asking," he shrugs slightly with a small, warm smile, "If we'd met before you met Alex..."

"We didn't," I interrupt him curtly. I'm drunk, hurt, and suddenly a little torn and confused. The last name I need to hear is...

his. Not right now. He left me for *her*. Isn't that why I've drunk myself into this ridiculous stupor?

And, you know what - my inner actress steps into the spotlight, booting my sulky inner dreamer off stage - *maybe testing the waters with my handsome neighbor* isn't *such a ridiculous idea*. I've said it myself, Andrew is a wonderful guy. A great catch. Any girl would be lucky to have him. *And, if things* had *started differently…*

I meet his gaze, my eyes whispering what I'm thinking before he slowly bends his head towards me. It's a soft, slow brush of his lips against mine, just enough to set off that small spark that's been hiding in the shadows waiting for the right time, if and when it ever came. There's no reason to deny it. Nothing standing in the way of seeing where it can go. Nothing…*and, no one*.

He leans back, our gaze locked, my breaths labored as I absorb what's about to happen, what line we're about to cross.

Taking the bottle from my hand, he turns to lay it down beside his on the island, his eyes returning to search mine. It's a silent, gentlemanly request, awaiting my returned approval. And I give it, without a word.

"Are you sure?" he whispers, cupping my face in his hands, the pad of his thumb brushing along my lip.

My nod of certainty is quick.

His kiss…is slow.

Slow and sensual.

And though my body awakens to the spark of arousal at the hands of my inebriation, it quickly fizzles. My mind isn't in the game. Or maybe it's my heart.

His lips feel…soft…*foreign*. My head spins as I struggle to give in to the moment and the feelings it should be evoking. I shouldn't be thinking at all, but I can't ignore the words floating through my mind like cue cards in grad school study hall - the most prevalent in bold italics: ***Awkward***.

I gasp when he pulls away, though not from passionate despair at the loss of his lips. It's more a sigh of relief from somewhere deep in my gut.

Dropping his hands from my face, he takes a step back, his gaze taking in mine. His blue eyes reflect my inner battle of mind over need, and every part of me wants to beg him to form an alliance against the prevailing side of thought. I need to forget. I need to lose myself in mindless passion. Forced or otherwise.

Have you ever been so drunk in both wine and despair that you can't think straight? That's pretty much where I'm sitting. "Try it again," I mutter in a desperate plea to force something that doesn't seem to be there.

"I should get dressed," he replies in forfeit, but I convince myself I see a flicker of hope in his eyes as I reach to stop him from stepping away. "Aby, don't," his tone is gentle, understanding.

Ugh. He knows what I'm refusing to admit. "Come o-n-n-n…" I whine like a five year old, a smidge away from stomping my little feet. *Yup, I'm officially pathetic.* I want an escape. I'm desperate for one, even if it means trying to force a cube into the circle hole. *Try summoning a slutty grin, and bite your lip like a whore propositioning him at the curb* - my inner actress rolls her eyes at me from the corner. I purse my lips - it's an outward action that hides my inner flipping her the bird.

He says nothing to my childish plea.

It makes me feel foolish. Which ties in a whole bunch of other feelings that don't mix well with my consumed bottle of Vino. And together, the lot certainly doesn't sit well against my drunken, defensive wall. As a matter of fact, they shatter it. "I know you want this," I challenge him.

"Not like this, Aby," he shakes his head, and the pity I see in his eyes - whether I'm imagining it or not - makes me want to scream.

Instead I call bullshit, and reach for the towel around his waist, a quick tug sending it falling back to the floor. If I felt like a fool before, I now see one dancing between us, smiling and laughing at me as my unveiled trump card hangs its head in shame - Andrew's limp biscuit.

Oh God. "I'm so sorry," I turn around in embarrassment - no, it's full-fledged shame, with a capital "H" for humiliation. "I don't know what's wrong with me," I shake my head, wanting to disappear. What I really want is for everything that's happened in the last two weeks to disappear. I want time to turn back and transport me into Alex's arms, back in L.A., before the call came about Ben. Before everything fell apart. Before *she* told the truth and turned our worlds upside down. *My* world upside down.

"No, *I'm* sorry," Andrew pulls me back to reality, flicking a switch in my mind that returns a seething bitterness for allowing Alex back into my thoughts. "Aby, it was really shitty of me to take advantage of the situation."

"What situation?" I spin around defensively, noting the return of his towel around his waist yet again.

"The one where you're drunk. And heartbroken." His closed mouth smile of sympathy elicits an urge to vomit.

Literally.

I make it to the bathroom just in time.

"FEELING BETTER?" ANDREW asks when I finally have the courage to emerge. "I made you coffee," he holds up a steaming cup, cautiously walking towards me.

I feign a small smile of gratitude before the scent hits me, sending a nasty ripple through my emptied, though still churning stomach. It takes a moment of pause to wash away. "Maybe a water instead?"

"You got it," he winks, turning back to the kitchen.

I note his newly donned clothing, and wince as everything that just happened threatens to poke its finger down my throat. *Jesus.* Is there anything left in my stomach to come up? "I don't know why I was sick," I state aloud, though it was more a thought.

"Probably because you haven't been eating much," he calls over his shoulder, and I roll my eyes defiantly at his accurate assessment.

Every part of me wants to head straight for the door and leave this entire mortifying event behind. But I can't do that. I can't do that to Andrew. Especially when he turns, and I see that fun-loving smile - the one that belongs to my good friend. The friend I came here to see before it turned into a gong show. And, since I feel like the one that banged the gong, I should be the first to still its pounding reverberations.

"Andrew, I'm really sorry," I begin, taking the bottle of water with a humiliated bite of the corner of my mouth.

"Don't," he shakes his head. "Let's not do that. Aby, I took that kiss because your eyes said you were feeling it too. But it was selfish, because I knew you heart wasn't."

"How…" I pause, remembering that he said I was heartbroken, "How did you know that Alex and I are…" I can't even finish, looking away as another churning wave assaults my core.

"That fight…Then no sign of him in the last two weeks." I meet his eyes as he continues, "You've been crying a lot lately - those thin walls," he shrugs. "And when I saw the latest publicity pictures…"

My legs feel suddenly weak, and I rush to the sofa to sit down.

"I knew as soon as you showed up tonight that you had seen them too. That you drew your own conclusions about them."

"Them? You mean, Alex and *Julia*." *Ugh*, I close my eyes, regretting how much I've leaned on him for support in the past when Stacey's not around. *Drew my own conclusions?* "Are you suggesting I'm wrong? That those pictures don't scream that he chose *her*? It's obvious," I stand, unable to sit in one place, despite my body's disagreement.

"Nothing is obvious. It's just marketing, Aby. Perception is everything."

Alex's words spewed from Andrew's mouth stab at my heart, the serrated edge too much to take. "I know what those pictures mean, Andrew. I knew it the minute he walked out the door." Tears loom in the corners of my eyes, and the minute his face flashes sympathy at seeing their impending fall, I turn away.

I need to get out of here. I need to sleep. Just sleep. And not wake up until this all goes away. "I'm so sorry about…everything," I manage, making it to the door.

"Aby, don't go," I hear his concerned plea as I quickly reach my flat, no longer able to see him in the open doorway adjacent to my own.

"Please, just let me go," I whisper, unsure if he can even hear me, or if the words were even meant for him at all.

CHAPTER *Sixteen*

"HOW'S MY LITTLE buttercup?" Stacey quips. Her pity-pouted question reverberates through the phone line like an annoying stab to my pounding eyeballs. *How am I?* Well, let's break this down...One, I'm hung-over, the residual taste of puke lingering despite scrubbing my teeth four times. Two, the man that I love is fucking his ex-girlfriend - *brilliant*. Three, I practically groped my friendly neighbor like a drunken whore - *fucking brilliant.* "I'm fine."

"Well, that's a two-worded load of crap that I'll ignore. Are you ready to drown your very possibly unwarranted sorrows? I believe my bestie offered me a bachelorette party," she adds.

Fuck. Drinking? I just threw up in my mouth a little. *Unwarranted* sorrows my ass - my *seriously* dumb ass - for falling in love with a man that it seems was never really mine after all.

"Hellooo? Abster? Why do I sense hesitation? You know I know what's best for you babe...shit-faced alcohol indulgence, remember?"

"Ummm...about that, I kinda started without you. Last night."

"Okaaayyy. And...?"

"And, I puked."

"Okaaayyy."

"Andrew was naked."

"I'm sorry, come again? Did you just say that you were

drunk, you puked, and were in the presence of a naked Andrew? Back the fucking train up. I get the drinking, I get the puking, but how - and *WHY* - is Andrew naked in this story?"

"Well, it started innocently…"

"If you're about to tell me that you fucking had sex with Andrew, I'm going to have a stroke."

"Of course not!" Although it was nowhere near that, it *could* have been. "Do you want the story or not?"

"I'm *listening*…"

"We kissed. It was awkward. *Beyond* awkward. Long story short, I felt nothing. Not one iota of passion." *God, the look on his face when he pulled away.* "I think I hurt him, Stace. I don't want to hurt him."

"You don't want to hurt *Andrew*? What about Alex?"

"Well, I think that point is moot, since he's bumping f'ugly's with his whore of an ex-girlfriend."

"Well, one, that's speculation. And two, can we please get back to the *how was Andrew naked* part?"

"He was in a towel…bad aim…I saw his goods," *which I wish I hadn't,* "…and it went down hill from there. I shouldn't have gone there in the first place, I was drunk…lonely."

"So? What? You see random dicks and you're inspired to kiss people? I'm really worried about you, Aby. I will not allow you to turn into an almost as attractive version of me - no offence. You obviously should *not* be allowed to drink alone. We're going out tonight and doing it properly, no random dicks. Hair of the dog, as Thomas would say. But listen, babe, I'm just glad that it stopped at a kiss. That's all I'm going to say to your blind assumptions - a.k.a Alex and Julia."

Their names together like that sends geriatric shudders down my spine. "*Okaaay,*" I give in. It is Stacey's bachelorette after all - well, in lieu of my pity party. "But hear this, my whore-friend, those names are hereby stricken from tonight's conversation."

"What names? Alex and Julia?"

"You really are a whore."

"At least I'm a whore that can drink alone. And, about those names…"

"Don't!" I stop her.

"…Time starts now."

"SO…I TOLD him, if I'm still able to walk to the kitchen, you don't deserve dinner," Stacey fills us in, her tone completely serious.

I almost choke on my sip of beer with a laugh. "And at what point, exactly, are you actually going to admit to your poor fiancé that, if and when you ever do cook him dinner, he should expect a sandwich at most?"

"Listen bitch, I can summon a little Gordon Ramsay - Can you see the *fuck you* in my smile?"

"I hate to tell you ladies, but mad culinary skills amount to nothing more than a can of beans in the relationship department. Although," Emily pauses, "…perhaps it's just my department that's full of beans." She contemplates her statement a little. "Humph. I need another drink."

"Then let's get the woman another drink!" Stacey squeals with delight, flagging the attention of the waiter.

"You just haven't met the right one, Emily," I attempt to make her feel better, though my words put a bad taste in my mouth - which I decide to wash away with another swig of beer.

"I swear to God, if I go on one more blind date…" she trails off with a dramatic shiver.

"You just have to *feel* it with the right guy," I interject again. *Or the wrong guy. Fucker.* What the hell is wrong with me? Am I channeling Doctor Ruth or something?

"I don't know…I have mixed drinks about feelings," Emily purses her lips, clearly already feeling the alcohol.

"Are you *sure*?" Stacey asks conspiratorially, the waiter departing with her whispered order of drinks. "I do know a few good men," she winks.

"A few?" I laugh.

"Shut it," she glares at me playfully, looking back to Emily. "I would be honored to give you my little black book. *I* won't be needing it anymore," she adds with a giddy squeal.

Emily and I join in, paying homage to the bride-to-be in girly style, clinking glasses and dancing in our seats with rambunctious laughter.

"Hey, whatever happened to that Ken Doll neighbor of yours?" Emily asks, and I almost choke on my beer a second time. "Andrew? Is he still available?"

"Oh, he's available," Stacey mutters sarcastically.

My head darts towards her to return her recent glare, but much more harshly.

Pursing her lips, she shrugs.

It's so not funny. The last thing I need to think about right now is my run in with Andrew - and by run in, I mean his naked glistening body against mine…right before *that* kiss. How did I let that happen? *Oh, right, I was drunk.*

"Now, we're talking!" Stacey's attention is pulled towards the return of the waiter with a tray full of shots. "Let's get this party started, ladies!" she gushes, swaying sexily in her seat. "It's tequila time!"

Oh shit.

"OKAY, I ADMIFF it," Emily begins through a drunken hiccup, "…the shots are much better than my red wine. Cause you know, well, for one," she holds her finger up, trying to focus on it, "… my teeth aren't purple."

"Yup, that's always a good thing," I nod in agreement.

"And!" she continues, as though her next point is very important, "…wine always makes me…what's the word?"

"Drunk?" Stacey asks.

"Noooo," she replies like it's a dumb answer. "All needy and shit."

"Ahhh," Stacey replies, nodding her head. "Like, 'Give me wine, and tell me I'm pretty'", stupid shit?"

"Yes!" she shrieks at Stacey's apparent brilliance.

"As opposed to 'Give me tequila, and call me a whore'?" I

question, feeling rather witty. And horny. *Damn tequila.*

"You can always drunk text Alex," Emily nudges me, winking.

"Brilliant idea!" Stacey agrees.

"Okay," I smile, pulling my phone from my bag.

"I spy with my little eye…something HOT!" Emily suddenly stands, heading across the bar towards what's caught her eye.

"Abs, I was kidding," Stacey mutters as I fiddle with my phone.

"*I'm* not. I'm sooooo not. He needs to know what he gave up. What time is it in L.A. right now? Screw it," I start typing…

Subject: You suck, but I'm horny

If I sit on your face, will you tell me I'm pretty?

Aby

"Sent," I announce aloud on a cheeky smile, proud of my possibly dumbass rambling. *Wait, what did I type?*

"Give me that," Stacey grabs it from me. "*Ugh*," she replies, reading it. "If you're going to do it, it has to be done right. And that, my little slurring whore, is why it's good to have me around…"

Subject: Be still, my beating vagina

You gone long time…Confucius say, he who masturbate only screwing self.

Aby

We can't stop laughing, until my phone suddenly vibrates on the table.

"Oh. My. God," we utter simultaneously, staring at each other momentarily in shock before bursting into laughter once more.

"Well, what did the *amazing* Alexander Tate say," I ask, laced with a snarky edge.

"Ummm…Abs, he's asking where you are."

"What? *Now* he wants to know where I am? Why the fuck does he care - he's in L.A.?"

"Well, what do you want me to tell him?"

Grabbing the phone from her I begin commentating my reply as I type, *"Where am I? I'm at FUCK YOU,"* I hit send.

"Well, you certainly weren't ambiguous," Stacey laughs.

"He was an arse," Emily plops back down.

"Yes. He. Was," I add. I know damn well that Emily was referring to the guy she just walked away from, but the timing of her statement was perfect.

"What did I miss," she asks, clearly confused.

"Let me tell you what I *don't* miss," I quickly reply, "… Alexander-fucking-Tate."

"Ahhh, Aby? Did you know you have an old *unread* message from Alex?" Stacey asks, scrolling through my cell.

"I'm sorry, what? How old?" *How the hell did I miss that?*

"Like, this morning old," she replies, pausing to read it before looking at me, eyes squinted in confusion.

"Well? What did it say?"

"It says, 'I need to', and then…*jibberish*," Stacey reads it aloud.

"He needs to *jibberish*?" Emily questions as I stare at Stacey, holding my breath.

What? My gaze darts to Emily, "Is that some British thing? What does that mean?"

"No! I don't know," she replies, her drunken defense laced with *what the fuck*.

"You dummies. It means the text didn't come through. It was cut off in delivery, hence the bunch of weird symbols, a.k.a. *jibberish*. You fuck-tards," Stacey holds it up quickly for us to see, before pulling it away again in scrutiny.

"Humph," I snort, "…you never know, maybe he was drunk too. I could see how his *whore*-able replacement for me could drive him to drink. So, what, no subject line?" I ask, pulling down a drunken mask of bravery.

"The subject says, 'I'm so sorry for everything'," Stacey begrudgingly meets my gaze, pausing at whatever she sees flash across my face. "You don't know what his text said, Aby."

I stare at her for a moment, my broken heart begging my head to ignore what I know is true. It doesn't matter what it said. He's gone.

Gulping down the remains of my drink, I slam the empty glass down with a bang, standing to exit our little booth. I can't shake my anger at Alex, my frustration, and now Stacey's hopeful mixed messages on top of that. *Fuck him.* Not even losing myself in a drunken stupor is doing the trick - though I'm surprised I'm even standing at this point.

"Where are you going, Aby?" Stacey questions.

"That way," I point to the crowded dance floor.

"Go girl!" Emily calls after me, "Shake your bootay."

Forcing my way through the throng of sweaty patrons, I settle in the middle of the crowded space, closing my eyes to will thoughts of Alex and his message from my mind, my body giving in to the rhythm of the track. I just want to forget. I want to feel numb. Yet I can't seem to let go. *Damn you, Alex Tate.*

I love him.

I hate him. For what he's done. *Julia. How could he go back to her?*

Even in my drunken state, rationality answers that question - *He never stopped loving her.* The bitter poisonous bile builds in my throat and I reach to caress it away in the sensual beat, desperate to lose myself to the consumed alcohol, the erotic tempo of the song.

Swiping my hands through my hair, I pull it over my shoulder, the strands cascading along my chest as I sashay my hips in a slow rhythm. I startle at the feel of large hands circling my waist, fingers spread wide, engulfing me. I fight the urge to imagine they're Alex's. I know they're not. His are likely wrapped around *Julia Sucks-Cox. That fucking whore*.

The vile poison rushes through my veins, contorting my irritation and anger into a meaningless grind against the stranger behind me. I cover his hands with my own, leaning my head back to rest on his shoulder. I don't open my eyes. I don't want to. I have no desire to give in to reality. No care to know who's holding me, dancing with me, his hips mimicking my side-to-side gyrations. I just want him to make me feel numb.

"Yeah, baby…you like that?" the man asks, annoyingly pulling me from darkness.

I say nothing in return. I have nothing to say to him. I don't care who he is, or what he has to say. I just want him to dance with me. Help me forget for just a moment that the man I love is currently with another woman. *Just let me forget…*

The abrupt absence of his strong hands from around my waist jars my renewed escape into ignorant bliss, his large body no longer behind me. *Jeez…I guess I should have replied.*

Although I don't really care that he's gone, curiosity wins out and I open my eyes to turn around, no man in sight. *Fuck it.* I continue swaying to the music, arms raised, losing myself. *I don't need a man's arms around me.*

Sensing a penetrating gaze, my eyes dart in the direction of its pull.

The sight of Alex, standing at the edge of the dance floor, takes my breath away. Dressed in a light beige sweater, lightly tucked into loose fitted jeans, his hands in the pockets, his eyes bore into me. Alexander Tate, in the flesh, a glimmer of anger flashing in his eyes as he moves to make his way towards me.

I stare shell-shocked at his beautiful face, unable to formulate a word in my drunken haze. *Am I hallucinating?* I'm flooded with emotion, gawking at him, shaking through the beer goggles. I've missed him so damn much, his presence is like a knife twisting my broken heart.

"Having fun, sweetheart?" he spews sarcastically, his eyebrow arched.

What the fuck? My momentary forgotten anger instantly courses through my veins, returned full force. *Am I having fun? I was!* He has the gall to stand here and judge me dancing with another man when he's…he's…"Fuck you!" I blurt, pushing past him to march off the dance floor.

Escaping through the crowd, I mutter to myself at his audacity - *He shows up after two weeks and thinks I owe him some kind of explanation? How did he even know I was here?* The question pops from my bubble of inebriation, before it hits me - *Stacey*. I throw a dirty glare in the direction of our table - I can surely wager a guess that she's responsible. I head in the direction of the ladies room, deciding it's a viable hideout until *Mr. Uninvited* hits the road as quickly as he came.

"Aby, where are you going?" he calls from behind me.

Ugh. Go away! Screw the ladies room, I need to leave. *There has to be an exit back here somewhere...* "I'm leaving, that's where I'm going! Getting the hell away from you!" I yell back, my words slightly slurred as I blindly attempt to maneuver the darkened hallway, praying it harbors an escape.

"You're going the wrong way, sweetheart."

"Don't fucking call me sweetheart! I know where I'm going!" I lie, huffing as I scan for exit signage. *Ugh! Where the hell is the goddamn exit?*

Reaching a dead end, I'm trapped with no escape as Alex's large hand wraps around my arm. *God, don't...I'm done if you touch me.* Pulling away instinctively in self-preservation, I take a step back. "Don't touch me! You lost the right to touch me," my anger and hurt is seething through my every word, biting in its harness.

"Sweetheart, I *own* the right to touch you," he reminds me, that sexy as sin smirk donning his delicious face, his large muscular body taking over my proximity.

I gasp at his cocky, yet incredibly erotic words, evading him with a backward step, my back hitting the wall. *Holy shit.* Even madder than all get-out, he can still turn me on in an instant, take me prisoner of his desire with mere words.

I want so much to believe that he's still mine...to feel that he's still mine. But it's a lie. A lie I saw with my own eyes, and I lash against his imaginary binds, "Oh really? Am I branded somewhere?" I spew with sarcasm, searching up and down my body before looking back to him slyly. There's no need to willingly admit that my implication is a boldfaced lie - I *am* branded by him, deep down to my soul. Utterly ruined for any other man. Yet, I want to hurt him. I need to hurt him, as much and as deeply as he's hurt me. "Andrew didn't seem to think so," I mutter, my cruel tone unrecognizable to my own ears as I purposely launch the silly kiss in his face.

"What the fuck does that mean?" he snarls.

"Do you really need me to spell it out? It was really *good*," I spew, my venom and will to cause him pain in full effect with wicked ambiguity. I don't care that it was meaningless - a kiss that felt more like sucking face with my own brother than sparking any form of passion. Again, I'm utterly *ruined* by the man standing before me. What's worse is that he knows it, and I watch as slight recognition that I'm lying passes across his face.

"You're angry with me, I see that. And drunk."

"Don't flatter yourself, my actions have nothing to do with you," I inwardly cringe at my desperate attempts to carry on the charade.

His tilted head and knowing grin tell me he calls bullshit. Stepping towards me, he pins me against the wall with his masculine frame, his scent invading my psyche, sending me into a spiral, thickening my drunken haze. I reflexively brace my hands against him to maintain his distance.

My efforts to keep him at bay are for naught, as he pulls my hands from his chest, pinning them above my head on the wall, holding them securely in his large grip. My chest juts out, colliding with his, and I'm panting as his warm breath fans my cheek.

"How *good* was it?" he questions sardonically, gliding his tongue along my jaw.

On a stifled gasp, my fingers flex within his grip as he glides the palm of his free hand across my ribs and around my hips. His expert touch - the touch I've missed so much - is delicious torture, igniting my accelerated breaths. The stutter of my heartbeat in my chest is exaggerated in the echoed beat of the club.

His hand slides along the front of my belly to my aching nipples, the swipe along the puckered flesh beneath my silk top sending a wrack of desire along my spine.

"Did it feel like this?" he growls in my ear, nipping the lobe, his sensual tone and seductive work of my body stealing my gasp.

*Oh, God. No, it didn't…*And he knows it.

"We take a break and you think we're done…you're over

me?" his lips suck and lick along my neck, my pulse careening out of control beneath his magical tongue.

The alcohol burns through my veins, heating to a boiling point of lust. I'm drunk with desire, whimpering as his fevered hot kisses on my searing flesh instantly spike my need for him.

"*Are* you over me?" he whispers huskily, brushing past my lips with his to continue his teasing along my jaw, his hand slipping under my skirt to slide along my saturated core. "Were you this wet for him?" he growls with a harsh grope of my sex.

I moan at the touch, my pussy clenching in desperate need for him, pulsing uncontrollably at the claim of his hand before he abruptly pulls it away.

It's sudden absence jars my lust-filled haze as he places his hand on the wall, caging my gaze to his, locked onto his brilliant, angry, blue eyes. "You're *mine*, Aby. Do I need to help you remember?" his lips take mine, his tongue invading my mouth as he releases my hands to cup my face, tilting my head to give him better access.

I tremble in his grip, falling mercy to his attack. How easily I lose myself in him. I kiss him back with a vengeance, hungry and desperate to reclaim what's mine - the sudden need catapulting me back to reality. *He left me. He's with her now*. Why is he doing this? Playing with my broken heart with cruel implications that all of the torture and heartache was nothing more than a temporary time break. *Well, I know different!*

"Agh…stop," I mange to pull my lips from his, pushing him away with all my might. Quickly skirting around him, I run back towards our booth. *I need to get out of here. I need to get away from him.*

"Aby, wait," he calls after me, catching up as I reach the table to grab my clutch.

"I'm leaving, sorry about your night, Stace," I offer the rushed apology as she stands in alarm, her gaze ricocheting between Alex and I before I turn for the door.

"Aby…"

"Let her go, Alex," I hear Stacey interrupt him.

"The hell I will," he spews, quickly on my tail at the front doors. "Goddammit, Aby, stop."

"Leave me the hell alone," I slur, making my way to the curb to flag a taxi.

"Let me take you home."

"Are you serious?" I lash, spinning on my heels to face him dead on, the motion throwing my drunk-ass off kilter.

He reaches to steady me and I tear my arm from his supportive grip.

"Don't. Touch. Me," the order is firm, my eyes screaming a clear warning.

Raising his hands in a sign of surrender, he continues in a calm plea, "Just let me see you home."

"I have a better idea," I begin, waving down an oncoming taxi, "Since you really enjoy the view of my ass," I continue as it pulls to the curb, turning to look him straight in the eye, "...how about I let you watch me leave."

CHAPTER
Seventeen

FUMBLING FOR MY keys, the screeching tires of Alex's car jar me in a wave of rushed panic, sending them tumbling to the step. He's out and standing before me in the time it takes for me to scoop them up. *He fucking followed me home? Fuck!*

The view of the length of him as I straighten to stand is impossible to resist, and after two weeks without him, I struggle to hide his effect on me. Away from the crowded club, the distance between us at this moment allows me to take him in. The beauty of him is like the calm before a tidal wave, but even my drunken rationale tells me that if I give in I'll drown.

"Wow," I muster a surge of confident indifference, "...to what do I owe the pleasure of this quick second visit? And more importantly," I continue quickly, ignoring his sexy clenched jaw, "Are you having trouble hearing? I said LEAVE ME THE HELL ALONE."

"Aby, as much as your drunken little temper tantrum is trying my patience," he pauses for a second round of panty soaking jaw clenching, "...we need to talk."

"My *little temper tantrum*?" The need to slap him across the face flashes quickly through my mind - the fury merely adding to the well of lust flooding my system. It's an overload of primal ravage need, and I fight the urge by turning away to unlock the door. "Well," I begin, composed restraint returned as I step inside, preparing to close the door in his face, "...I guess whatever it is you think we need to talk about can wait, since I'm clearly not in *your* required state of mind. You've seen me home now, *sweetheart*, you can be on your merry way, back to wherever you came from."

"Aby..." he makes a move to halt the closing of the door.

"As a matter of fact," I interrupt him, "Where the hell *did* you come from? It was very sweet of you to suddenly show up out of the blue," my sarcasm is biting, a desperate shield against the gnawing desire to simply bite *him*, devour him.

"Out of the blue, Aby? I told you I would be back from L.A. in two weeks."

"Oh, has it been two weeks already? I hadn't even noticed," I lie with bitter contempt, cursing my sorry, drunken ass for possibly impeding my performance.

"No? So it was just a coincidence that I received your messages on my way home from the airport. I must say, they were rather...intriguing - for lack of a better description - and they certainly got my attention. Is that not that what you intended of them?"

"So sorry to disappoint, but there were no intentions behind my silly drunken texts - tequila is a chatty bitch. And, yes, it was absolutely a coincidence. Does that make you feel better? You and your guilty conscience can go home now," I slam the door quickly, leaning back against it, attempting to catch my breath from the adrenaline and alcohol cocktail I'm suddenly spinning in.

"Aby, open the door," his order is firm.

"I have nothing else to say to you," I manage, cursing the aphrodisiac effects of the damn tequila coursing through my veins.

"You can open the door, or *I* can - the choice is yours."

Are you kidding me? I spin around, pulling the door open to face his audacity head on, "You have some nerve threatening..."

My words are no match to the speed with which he wraps his arm around me, lifting me off my feet as he steps inside, closing the door behind us.

The feel of his evident arousal pinned against me is intoxicating. *Damn him* and *the alcohol.* "Let me go," I demand, hammering his chest, each pound of my small fists against the sculpted mass echoed in the clenching of my core.

"I couldn't do that if I tried," he whispers huskily, setting me down on my feet against the wall before grabbing my face in his hands. His kiss is paralyzing.

I ache to touch him, to feel him again, but I can't move. I'm lost in the dizzying, slow, erotic brushes of his tongue, the delicious taste of him. I want him. Need him.

Gravity twists at my spiraling haze as he pulls back to look into my eyes, his cradling of my forced gaze in his hands seemingly holding me upright. I brace my hands back against the wall in desperate search of support, afraid that if he let's me go I'll fall.

"God, I've missed you…" he grabs my hands, pinning them up in his hold, his lips crashing back to mine.

I moan into his kiss, my body arching against his, the erotic pull too strong for my will. I couldn't fight it if I tried.

Releasing my hands, he grips my thighs to lift me, groaning as I wrap my legs around him, his arousal brushing my core in the movement. "Fuck, Aby," he whispers, wrenching me against his erection with a repeated sensual, rolling grip of my ass.

"Oh, God," I moan. The absence of his lips is too much, and I grab his nape to force the return of his tongue as he carries me effortlessly to the sofa. I grind into him, our bodies unlinking as he lays me down. I can't get enough of him. My primal need to feel him inside me is savage at the hands of my drunken arousal. I'm drunk from the consumed alcohol. Drunk from the love I feel for this man.

My hands devour his strong back, reaching for the hem of his shirt, pulling it up in desperate need to feel his flesh. His assistance in leaning up to grab it from behind and pull it off gifts me with the delicious view of his incredible abs and chest, my fingers greedily consuming every ripple. The perfection of him is sinful.

I'm unable to contain my moans as he grinds into my core,

my legs gripping him, begging for more as he glides my shirt up, bending to lick along the exposed flesh. He palms my breast through the lace cup of my bra, massaging it in his grip as his lips find mine once more.

"I've been thinking about this for two long weeks," he mutters, moving to lick and nip along my neck, his words clipping the aura of my euphoric daze.

I'm suddenly falling, crashing down to earth, shattered reality rearing its ugly head. The image of him leaning into Julia's ear, the flirty smile his whispers evoked flash repeatedly behind my closed eyes, forcing them open to escape the nightmare of what I've lost, only to see it head-on laying over me. "Why are you doing this?" the question escapes in my desperate plea to understand.

Confused pain fills his gaze as I attempt to push him off of me.

Tugging my shirt down into place, I sit up, my hands reflexively crossing my chest in protection of my heart. "I know about Julia," the admission escapes on a whisper.

"What?" he pulls back to look into my eyes.

"I know you chose her."

"*Chose* her?" his body recoils as though stung by the words. "Aby, there wasn't a choice to make. You think that after everything that's happened, knowing how I feel about *you*, that I..."

"Don't..." I stand to distance myself from him. "I saw the pictures." I shiver from the visual, from the pain of knowing that even after the choice she made, I lost him to her anyway. "You were holding her closely at your side, smiling at each other..." I look away from him, the images in my mind morphing into the reality of his presence before me.

"You see a few photos of Julia and I, and you draw the conclusion that we're back together? Aby, that's ridiculous."

Ridiculous? The word slaps me, his use of it reigniting the heat of my alcohol infused blood. "Oh, it was a lovely collage that led to said *conclusion*, particularly the one of you leaning into her ear - the smile she wore from the *sweet nothings* you were whispering may have sealed the deal."

"And what is it that you think I was saying to her, exactly?" he asks, standing, gripping my arms gently to force my gaze.

"You left the door open for me to think anything my breaking heart wanted to. *Perception is everything*, right?" I bite.

"Jesus, Aby, how little do you think of me?" he searches my held gaze. "It was a peace offering - a negotiated agreement to save face with Julia and the agency before the announcement of my new publicist. Fuck," he releases me, turning away, running his fingers through his tousled curls before retrieving and donning his shirt.

Feeling suddenly lightheaded, I turn to make my way back to the sofa.

"You *were* with Andrew," his realization stops me in my tracks.

Oh, God.

My ambiguous exaggeration of the silly, meaningless kiss jolts through my hazed memory, and I brace myself to face him. "It wasn't like I made it out to be," I cringe at the image I portrayed at the club, my body wracking with an extra shiver at the realization that he didn't believe me at that moment - he would never believe I would do that to him.

"You thought I was with Julia, so you ran to *him*?" The pain in his gaze almost breaks me. "To get back at me?"

"No! It meant nothing."

"It means something to me," his body jerks as though I've stabbed him with the need to remind me. "Jesus, Aby, what the hell?" he turns to pace the room.

"I haven't heard from you in two weeks! What did you expect me to think? The photos, the lack of contact...Alex, you didn't even *try* to call me."

Guilt flinches in a ripple through his body before he replies, "I *should* have called. I was wrong not to, but I thought I was protecting you from all the shit I was dealing with."

"Protecting me?" I snicker. "From what? You making a choice between Julia and me? You know what? You're right, I wouldn't want to *deal with that shit* with you."

"I can't believe you even thought there was a choice to be

made, Aby! After everything we've been through, *now* there's a question of trust? I've never once made you question my love for you."

"You mean, up until the day you left me on the curb?" I question, seething despite his flinch of anger or pain - possibly both.

"Ironic, I know exactly how that feels," he pauses to take a calming breath. "The difference is, I came back."

"You're right, you did come back. However, I remember very clearly how you weren't able to confirm whether you did, or didn't still love Julia."

"Fuck, Aby. I didn't know what I was saying that day...I could barely think straight. I was emotionally battered. And do you think I couldn't see the hurt in your eyes? I was trying so hard not to pull you down with me. I was trying to protect you," he searches my eyes. "Clearly, I failed, and for that I'm sorry," he looks down, running his fingers through his hair. "My natural instinct was to protect...was yours to *hurt* when you went to Andrew?" his gaze rages a war between anger and pain.

"It wasn't like that. It just happened. It was a kiss, just a stupid silly kiss..." my words trail off as I witness the pained twist in his gaze at the hands of the visual I'm unintentionally painting.

He can't even look at me, his jaw clenching, his eyes closing on an intake of breath. "You have no fucking idea the hold you have on me. The last thing I ever thought, with all the shit that I was dealing with, was that you wouldn't be there at the end."

Oh my God. How did this get so twisted? "Alex, I..."

"I have to get out of here before I lose it," he turns to leave.

"Alex," I call, chasing after him. He doesn't turn to face me when I reach the door. "Please, try to understand, I thought we were over. I was hurting...there was alcohol involved," I mumble the latter, not sure this is the best time to include my current, identical state. "I don't know what else to say. It was a mistake. I thought..." I trail off. *What did he expect me to think?* "You left me, Alex..."

"You were always mine, Aby," he spins on his heals, shaking his head. "A short break in time to deal with my shit doesn't constitute leaving you."

"A *break*? This isn't a Goddamn sitcom. I thought I'd lost you!" I scream, my defenses taking over.

"Are you taking the piss right now?" he stares at me, the darkened blue hue of his irises permeating the anger in his eyes.

Having no idea what to say to that, I decide to hold my punches, folding my arms at my chest - undoubtedly pouting at the entire turn of events at the loose hand of lingering inebriation. My head is spinning. "How did all of this happen?" my thoughts come out on a whisper.

"Perception is everything right, Aby? You seem to like throwing that back in my face. And, since *you're* so good at seeing the *real* picture," his sarcasm is biting, "...allow me to enlighten you," he continues through his clenched jaw. "Those *sweet nothings* that I whispered to Julia were my avid warnings that if she ever comes within five feet of you or I in the future, I'll sue her ass faster than she can fucking blink."

"Alex..." his name slips out on a quiet, shocked murmur, my arms falling in defeat to my sides.

Grabbing my nape, he bends to my ear, "The irony is brilliant don't you think? If only I had known how little it would take for you to run to another man faster than *I* can fucking blink," he adds on a whisper, before walking out the door.

Fear twists into defensive anger, and I grab the closing door to yell, "Perception my ass! You-*You* were an ass to presume and assume."

He spins around at his car to face me in question, his jaw clenching.

"Two weeks without a word, Alex? Maybe you shouldn't preach about something you so easily take for granted yourself," I slam the door quickly, leaning against it, sliding to the floor.

"NEW BEGINNINGS ARE often disguised as painful endings."

"What?"

"Oh, shit. Wrong quote. What do you want from me? I'm

drunk, woman," Stacey, fumbles with her phone, searching for this quote she swears will make me feel better. "What is the point of pinning the damn thing, if I can't fucking find it when I need it! Ugh!" She tosses her phone down on the bed.

"How hard can it be?" I sit up to grab it. "You have so much shit in here. How many Pinterest Boards can one person have?"

"As many as I want. Oh! I have a quote for you, right off the top of my head! 'Stupid is as stupid does'," she shoves my cross-legged knee with her foot.

"Ha ha. What does that even mean, anyway? Wait…Are you referring to me, or Alex?"

"I'm thinking you're both wearing the same shoe, pumpkin. And if the shoe, fits," she shrugs.

"I thought you were looking for a quote to make me feel *better*?"

"The truth hurts, pookie, but it's good for you. Besides, add that to the tequila you just threw up, and you'll be feeling better any time now," she flashes a playful smirk. "Unless you start crying again. Please don't," she pleads playfully, "Or at least wash the rest of your mascara off first. You're starting to look like a Marilyn Manson video."

"You suck," I throw a pillow at her.

"Yes, and very well," she winks. "And on that note, did you happen to stub your camel toe on his dick before the shit hit the fan?"

I grimace, throwing her glaring daggers. The thought of how easily and close we came to losing ourselves in our familiar tropical storm of passion jabs instantly between my legs - right before ricocheting up for a stab to my heart.

Rolling her eyes, she shakes her head, "I just don't understand why you told him about Andrew."

"It wasn't me," I scowl. "It was our friend, tequila, remember?"

"Riiiigggt…Whatever, Abs. You wanted to hurt him the way he hurt you."

"The way I *thought* he hurt me," I correct her, feeling the well of tears threaten to build once more.

"Yeah, that too," she purses her lips.

"Why are you here, again?" I tease sardonically, attempting to waylay another cry-fest.

"Besides the fact that I'm getting married in less than two days?" her eyes bug out dramatically for effect. "Because you can't live without me, my little tulip," she blows me a kiss.

"Well," I sigh, lying down beside her, "I guess I'm going to have to learn to." I turn my head towards her, and we're practically nose-to-nose.

"Why on earth would that mean you have to live without me?" she takes my hand, and for a moment we're like kids again. All for one and one for all. *Wait a minute...*

"You!" I twist onto my side, plunging an accusing finger in her face, "You told Alex where we were. That's how he ended up at the club!"

"Get that thing outta my face," she swats my hand away. "You're damn right I did. He wouldn't have asked where you were if he didn't want to know - and I, for one, was more than curious as to why."

"Well, you could have at least warned me," I pout, turning onto my back, crossing my arms.

"How was I supposed to know he would fly over there faster than Superman? I thought I'd have a chance to tell you when you came back from dancing. I have to say, Abs, he looked pretty hot when he arrived looking for you. God, he looked like..."

"I know what he looked like!" I grab the pillow behind my head and plough her with it - right in the face.

Grabbing hers, she hits me back. "Don't start something you can't finish, cookie. Do I need to remind you of all the pillow fights you've lost?"

"No," I grumble, flinging my pillow behind my head, resuming my cross-armed pouting. "You only win because your boobs are like balloon armor. It's like trying to win a fight in a bouncy castle."

"Jealously is a sick disease. Feel better, bitch," she bounces on top of me, crushing me with her oversized cantaloupes, winking as she pushes up to sit on the side of the bed. "So, did you happen to get a chance to discuss my wedding in between your stupid ass bickering - as in will he be attending as your date?"

"Oh, yeah," I roll my eyes. "It was the most prominent topic of discussion. Ouch!" I yelp when she flicks my boob. "Seriously?"

"Did that hurt? Well, how do you think you're going to feel if he shows up at the wedding - on his own?"

"Maybe he won't."

"And, maybe he will. He received his own invitation from Thomas, Aby...and he *is* in town. Just sayin'."

"It doesn't matter how I'll feel. It's your special day. I'm not about to let my issues cast a shadow on that," I smile, gladly allowing my feelings of true happiness for my best friend to wash over my pitiful state. "Besides, I'll be too busy trying to keep you from running away from the best thing that's ever happened to you."

"Oh, running won't be an issue, sweet cheeks, there's nothing I want more in this world than to marry Thomas. However," she purses her lips, "...some Vicodin might help."

CHAPTER
Eighteen

"**Y**OU DO REALIZE that if I had known we would have to *walk* somewhere to get coffee this morning, I would have stayed at Thomas's," Stacey mutters, turning her head to get the attention of my gaze. "He has this great new invention at his place, it's called a *coffee machine*."

"The fresh air and exercise is good for you."

"Oh, honey, I get plenty of exercise," she winks. "And fresh air my ass - it's cold as fuck. Did you see it? I just farted the cutest little snowflake," she nudges me midstride, rolling her eyes.

"Shut up," I playfully shove her. "You didn't have to come, you know. I would have gladly gone myself, and would have brought your coffee back to you - despite the fact that you wouldn't deserve it."

She gasps dramatically, "I'm highly insulted. I'm getting married tomorrow - it's both the most wonderful and most terrifying event of my life - I *soooo* would have deserved it."

"You're so dramatic," I roll my eyes, laughing half-heartedly.

Reaching the flat, she turns me to face her, offering a loving, though slightly patronizing, head tilt. "Me thinks you're misplacing pent up frustration, love. Alex is the one you want to…Oh, *hello*," Stacey - no longer looking at, or talking to me - steps towards what's pulled her attention.

Turning, my breath hitches in an uncomfortable lump at the

sight of Andrew, locking up and turning from his door.

"I'm Stacey Stevenson," she's already in his face, "...and you must be *the* Andrew Davies I've heard so much about."

Ugh.

Andrew shakes her jabbed-out hand with a slightly uncomfortable smile. It's certainly not the wide, brilliant smile he usually dons, and when his eyes meet mine, I'm instantly assailed with why. *Shit.*

We haven't seen each other since the 'kiss'. And though I dreaded the next run-in a little myself, deep down I was hoping that it would be as though it never happened.

"*The* Stacey Stevenson I've heard so much about," he finally replies with a wink, and for a moment I think I see my fun, carefree friend again - but just for a moment. *Double Shit.* Oh, *yeah*...he's uncomfortable. He's *never* uncomfortable - *it's Andrew, for shit sake.* This entire situation sucks balls. *No.* It sucks donkey dicks. "It's very nice to meet you, Stacey," he adds, his gaze skirting my way for another dose of awkward vibrations.

Pursing my lips, I attempt to ride the uncomfortable wave, noting the eerie silence of it threatening to drown all three of us at once. "Stacey is getting married tomorrow," I blurt the obvious, my pitch high and absolutely edged with the impending shriek of swallowing a mouthful of water.

"Yes, that's right," Andrew jumps in, nodding off the tight line of his lips. "Congratulations, Stacey."

"Ummm...thank you," she replies, her gaze flickering between Andrew and I repeatedly in the seconds of silence. "We actually celebrated my bachelorette last night. Lot's of fun, dancing and tequila - we were drunk as whores. That was two nights in a row for you, wasn't it, Abs?" she adds, winning herself an inconspicuous pinch of the back of her arm from me.

"Yes," I manage through my clenched jaw, glaring at her through a grimaced smile, "It was fun watching Stacey offer up her little black book to the next willing slut of the centur..."

"Drink up, Abs," she cuts me off with a smile, directing her teasing attention to Andrew, "I had to drag her out for coffee - her double hangover lollipop is triple dipped in grumpy this morning."

"I'm not grumpy," I assure Andrew, shaking my head with a smile as though I have to explain myself. *What the hell is wrong with me?* Oh, right, this sucks donkey ass, and my best friend is an added teasing pain in its big fat cheeks. "We have a lot to do, though, Stace. Maybe we should head inside and get started on that list." Number one being slap my best friend in the head for making an awkward situation even worse with her *so not funny* shenanigans.

"Well, actually," her tone is familiarly conspiratorial, "…I do have to run inside and call my future hubby," she turns quickly, opening the door. "You two can catch up."

"Ahh…"

"It was super to finally meet you, Andrew," Stacey winks, dismissing my attempt to dispute her wicked plan to leave us alone.

"You too," he replies.

She flashes an over-wide smile, her gaze dancing in devilish delight, before rushing inside, closing the door quickly. *Damn her.*

"I should really head in too," I begin after painful, torturing seconds of silence. "I have a lot to do before the wedding," I add with a forced smile, turning away to reach for the doorknob.

"Aby, wait…"

My lips purse in a thin line as I close my eyes against the dreaded pull of his request. Sneaking a breath of composure, I spin on my heels to face him.

"We can't keep avoiding each other, can we?"

"*Are* we avoiding each other?" I retort, cautiously gauging how he truly feels about the whole thing.

He doesn't answer right away, allowing the panic to build within me. *Just great. Lose a boyfriend* and *a friend.* I look down to avoid letting him see it in my eyes, not wanting him to misconstrue my feelings. As much as it saddens me that my friendship with Andrew has taken a slippery turn, it pales in comparison to what losing Alex is doing to me.

The thought of him imagining what I did with Andrew tears

through me. Alex has to know that it was nothing. It meant nothing. And the first step is to make sure both Andrew and I are clear on that as well. No more pussy-footing around the unavoidable.

Looking up to face him, our eyes lock uncomfortably in the silence before we both attempt to speak, our words overlapping, swallowed by uncomfortable air. I look down momentarily once more, biting my lip before returning to his gaze.

His broad, white-toothy grin flashes a signal of welcome relief, and I smile as well, staying quiet to let him go first.

"It was a mistake," he begins. "That's all. Let's just chalk it up to a…*rather* awkward test of friendship. The key word being *friendship*, yeah?"

"Absolutely," I smile, more than relieved. I just want to forget that entire night ever happened - well, that's not exactly possible right now where Alex is concerned, but it's a more than welcome start on this end. And I'm jumping on the bandwagon with a serious giddy-up distraction, "*Speaking* of friendship," I can't keep the glimmer of plotting from flashing across my happily relaxed face, "…my good friend, Emily…"

"Uh oh," he laughs. "Are you about to set me up?"

"Only because I believe it's a *good* set up. Trust me."

"I do," his smile is genuine.

"Good."

"Are *we* good?"

"We're good," I mentally make a check off the bottom of my shit-storm list.

"Are *you* good?"

A loaded question. My insides scream no, but I can't ignore the sudden pull of my heart telling me that I *can* be. One simple phrase floats through my mind, echoing through every pore… *Fight for him.* And that's exactly what I intend to do. "You know what," I finally answer with a smile, "I think I will be."

*FIGHT FOR HIM…*You're damn right I will.

There's just one problem.

I'm T-minus twenty-four hours away from my best friend's wedding. A wedding that has been less than two weeks in the making. *Where, exactly, can I fit in this epiphany?* I scour over the items on the to-do list, the shit unchecked like a kick in the teeth.

"Abs, you look like your brain is about to explode. Should I be concerned?" Stacey asks, walking towards me from the stairs.

"Ahhh," I look up to meet her painfully twisted gaze. "No," the word is far too high-pitched and perky to pass for believable, so I offer a wide forced smile. "But, we do have a lot to do today, where would you like to start?" I look back to the list, preparing to make suggestions.

"Is this your way of avoiding telling me about how it went with your Ken Doll neighbor?"

"Actually no," I slap her arm, ignoring her over-exaggerated open-mouthed shock, her arm darting to rub it away, "But thanks for the reminder that you deserved that. Everything is fine with Andrew."

"Well, you're welcome, bitch. At least that's one thing off your dumbass plate. And you know what?" she grabs the list from me, "Maybe that quote wasn't the wrong one after all."

"What quote?" I look up, confused.

"The one I used last night. I think you should really think about it right now."

"And you think calling me stupid again today is going to help us get through that list how, exactly?"

"Not that quote, *stupid*," she grimaces sarcastically. "The one about painful endings being the start of new beginnings."

"Okay, Stace," I roll my eyes. "Even sober I don't have any idea what you're trying to say. And we don't have time for riddles and games," I stand from the sofa, snatching the list back, "We have too much to do."

"No, *you*," she points a finger in my face. "You need to pick up the damn phone and just call Alex already."

"And say what?" I shout, begging for the answers to make everything better. I'm dying, with every minute that passes since seeing him again, touching him again. I'm *dying*.

Looking down, I swallow the lump in my throat, attempting to seal the well of tears that are building. The sunlight flickers through an opening in the clouds outside, its unshielded rays hitting Stacey through the window, her beautiful engagement ring sparkling. My best friend is getting married tomorrow, and *I'm* the only thing she's worried about. After everything she's done to be there for me.

Shame and guilt seep into the cocktail that fills my broken heart. "Stace…"

"Please, Aby," she pleads. "Call him."

"I want to, I just don't know what to say…yet."

"It will come to you," she picks up my cell phone from coffee table, holding it towards me.

I just stare at it. My brain completely shut down, my broken heart suddenly racing at the thought of hearing his voice. An image of him hanging up on me stabs my chest.

"Fine," Stacey snaps, opening the contact list to find his name, hitting 'talk' before shoving the phone in my face. "You can say something, or hang up on him. You decide," she releases it just short of my grasp.

Shit! I struggle to right the phone, shaking as I draw it to my ear. Luckily it's still engaging, and with each ring, I gasp for air as my lungs seem to close in protection against the pounding thunder in my chest.

The ringing finally stops, signaling his missed call message is about to engage. *Voicemail*, I mouth to her, even more panicked.

She gestures in sarcastic silence, rolling her eyes, and before I know it his recorded voice slams me in to la-la land. His silky British accent melts through me, gliding over every sensitive nerve. His delicious voice could tame a tiger, leaving it purring like a kitten in his hands.

The sound of the beep slams me back to the present akin to the alarm of an atomic attack. My heart leaps from my chest realizing it's time to talk and I have no idea what I want, or need to say.

Completely lost to my panic, I hang up.

"What. The. Fuck. Was that?"

"What do you think it was?" I bite. "I…"

"You freaked out like a pimple-faced teenager calling the school jock about the fucking prom."

"Yeah, something like that," I scowl, folding my arms, flopping down on the sofa.

"So, would you like to discuss what you're going to say when he calls back?"

"What?" I gasp, struck by the panic gods yet again.

"Caller ID, dumbass."

"Humph-humph-humph," I moan-pout dramatically, bouncing in place like a frustrated child. "Why did you make me call him before I was ready?" I lay my sour, venomous gaze on her, "You're evil."

"Look at you, for shit sake, you're shaking like a candy crack-head in rehab. You have a disease, my little petal, and Alex's dick in your vajayjay is the only cure."

"One, I hate you, and, two, you're disgusting."

"You don't hate me, and you know what I'm really saying is that you're head over heels, madly, insanely in love with Alex Tate. The only cure, poodle, is to go get your man."

"Go get him? I couldn't even form words using the telephone. Stace, I'm going to need a little time."

"And therapy, my little drama queen, but that's neither here nor there," she winks. "Okay, let's make a deal…"

"I don't make deals with the devil," I retort sarcastically.

"Zip it. If he calls back, you can just deal with it your way. But," she puts a finger up, "…if you haven't heard from him by the time we're done our errands, we stop at his place so you can talk to him in person."

"Stace, the last thing you should be doing the day before your wedding is waiting who-knows-where while I beg my boyfriend to take me back."

"Nonsense. There's no place I'd rather be then supporting my best friend. But, if your little chat turns into _bow-chicca-bow-bow_, I'm outta there. Do we have a deal?"

Rolling my eyes, I wrap my pinkie around hers, outstretched.

"Deal."

"Good, now I'll go grab a shower and make a few calls while you finish your speech."

"My speech?"

"Are you kidding me? You haven't even started it? And here I am helping you turn your painful endings into new beginnings," she playfully gasps. "Get to it, slacker," she winks, heading for the stairs.

Shit.

"DID HE CALL yet?"

"No. Will you stop with the kid-on-the-family-trip repeated question. If you ask me one more time, I'll hurt you."

"I'm just saying, maybe you should check your phone. Is it on mute?"

I glare at her until she turns my way.

"Maybe he sent a text," she continues, ignoring my daggers.

"I. Will. Hurt. You," I repeat with a second load of darts in my gaze. "It's bad enough I'm still trying to survive your driving. Why on earth did Thomas let you use his car?"

"Let's just say I had a *head up* in the persuasion depart-ment," she winks, taking her eyes of the road for a millisecond - *Shit, she's as scared as I am.*

"I think we would have been both faster *and* safer riding the tube."

"I'll have you know, I passed the drivers test six months ago - mind you it was the third test, but whatever," she laughs it off.

"Oh, *nice*," I grab the upper support handle dramatically to tease her. "What made you do the drivers test, anyway? You were never here long enough to necessitate the use of a vehicle."

"Thomas, of course," she glances at me, rolling her eyes. "He was insistent that I learn to drive like a *proper* British citi-zen."

"Oh was he? Six months ago, hmmm? That's interesting. He did realize that you were still freelance in the playgirl department back then, right?"

"I wasn't," she almost whispers, not taking her eyes off the road.

"What?" I turn in my seat, staring at her in shock. *How did I not know this?* "You never said a word, Stace! *I* knew he was 'the one', even back then, but I had no idea that *you* knew. Why didn't you say something?"

"What, and ruin my perfectly good reputation?" she laughs, half-heartedly.

"Seriously, Stacey, why didn't you tell me?"

"Because I was scared shitless, that's why."

Oh my God. "You are the most unselfish person I know," I shake my head, guilt seeping through my pores at the idea that my best friend - who does so much for me - needed me herself, and I didn't even know. "I'm sorry, Stace. You deserve a better friend."

"Oh, shut it. You have no idea what having you in my life all these years has done for me," her gaze remains locked on the road ahead, though I sense it's to keep me from reading more in her eyes.

"Stace," I rest my hand on her leg in a loving gesture.

"I mean it, Abs, shut it," she smiles at me. "One nut job at a time, babe. We have to get you to your man. Those pretty manicured fingers of yours will look fab wrapped around his dick tonight," she adds quickly, signaling the conversation has clearly changed.

For now. I plan on making it up to her very soon though. I've clearly let the ball drop, lost in my own issues. And that guilt is suddenly, and dangerously, mixed with the dread I feel at seeing Alex shortly. My stomach is in knots, my heart pounding in my chest.

"Okay, pookie, this is it," Stacey flashes me a boosting smile, locking the gear into park. "Off you go," she scoots me out of the car, leaning over to catch my terrified gape before I close the door, "Rock that apology like a sorry whore on a big juicy dick. Oh! And don't forget," she pauses for me to bend down to her gaze once more, "…Alex, a.k.a the sorry *dick* in this dumbass equation, already apologized for his stupidly, but not enough - make him work for the metaphorical orgasm, babe. You may have kissed the neighbor frog, but he left you out on the lily pad without a boat."

Humph. I walk away shaking my head. Very well said, but somehow the butterflies in my stomach are still twisting into a swarm of bees, and I'm not sure I'm ready for the big sting.

Taking a deep breath, I knock on the door, waiting half a second before trying again. There's no answer and I look towards Stacey in the car.

What? she mouths through the closed window.

"No answer," I whisper, shaking my head at the ridiculousness of it - it's not like she can hear me.

She starts pointing frantically, and I have no idea what the hell she's trying to say. *What?* I mouth, putting my hands up, shrugging my shoulders.

See if it's open, she mouths, her finger jabbing towards me, poking the air. I'd laugh out loud at the intensity of her communication struggle if I weren't so out of sorts as it is.

Turning back to the entrance, I weigh the idea. *Okay.* I'll just try the knob, but this is silly. I reach for it and turn, *Alex never leaves it op...* "Oh. Humph," I whisper to myself, walking inside. "Alex?" I peek into the kitchen before making my way down the hall, looking into each empty room as I pass.

Footsteps from the floor above stop me in my tracks. I literally freeze, bracing myself for when he comes down the stairs. I still have no idea what to say first. *Shit.* Everything seems to go wrong with us lately. Can whatever pops out of my mouth be right for a change?

For a moment, I hear nothing, realizing he obviously doesn't know I'm here. Pursing my lips, I make my way towards the spiral staircase, pausing at the bottom for an extra breath of strength. *Time to fight for my man...*

With light steps, I make my way up, delicious visuals of what I might find at the top filling me with a renewed fluttering of butterflies. The bees have left the nest, leaving me anxious, but pleasantly, just for the sight of him. It's a giddy nervousness. Like we're back at the very beginning, when every breath is filled with tingly anticipation.

Dusk is setting in, chasing away the light in the upstairs hallway, and the glimmer from under the bathroom door catches my eye as it dances with the shadows on the floor in front of me. Stopping to listen, I hear the shower.

Oh, gawd, he's in the shower. My heart pounds faster, threatening to burst from my chest at the instant visual of a naked Alex on the other side of the door. That would certainly save me from having to think of what to say, since I know I would simply jump him on the spot.

The attacking echo of a woman's laughter stuns me in place, frozen in pained confusion with no time to recover as the bathroom door opens. My palm darts to my mouth to stifle a gasp at the sight of a naked Helena Adelaide emerging.

Giggling, her attention is drawn back inside before her gaze is suddenly locked on mine. Cold, sparkling eyes hold me hostage sending a shiver of horror slithering down my spine.

My hand drops to my side at the eerie curl of her lips, her killer glare enough to turn me to stone - my only salvation being the doleful cry of my heart that escapes on a silent gutted breath of defeat.

Pain-filled seconds of time pass in the blink of a snake-eye before she's pulled back inside, her returned giggle stabbing me over and over, shattering my hardened heart.

"THAT WAS FAST," Stacey mutters in surprise as soon as I open the car door.

"He wasn't there," I lie quickly, and flatly, fighting to disguise my trembling hands reaching for the seatbelt.

"He wasn't there? But the door was open?"

"I guess he's a dumbass *and* a prick for all those times he reminded me to lock *my* door," I bite, quickly realizing my sudden unshielded wrath. "There was no one home," I add, my inner actress returned in top form as I evade looking directly at Stacey.

No need to add to my slip of rage by letting her see the hurt and pain in my eyes.

"A *prick*? Aby, what's going…"

"Stace," I interrupt her firmly, but cautiously, turning to face her with every ounce of Oscar-worthy composure I can muster. "I held up my end of the deal," I smile, fighting the quiver in my lips, "…now it's time to get the Bride-to-be home. You're getting married tomorrow!" I add a little extra pep of excitement to my performance.

"And you're clearly upset that you didn't get to talk to Alex. I'm sorry, Abs. Maybe he'll call later tonight, or in the morning."

The look of empathy in her eyes is like a knife in my heart, and all I want to do it tear it out and slice every beautiful memory of Alexander Tate.

"ALEX," I MOAN, my eyes closed in the pleasure of his perfect kisses along my neck. No…why are you here? How could you run to her?

Turning around, I see him on the bed, his hands gliding along my trembling body, smiling, gliding his lips along my skin. I look so happy, but I feel…pain. Agonizing pain. My heart is breaking as I watch our tender, sensual embrace.

A bird chirps, my eyes closing at the sudden hum, before opening to the evil sneer of Helena Adelaide, held in Alex's arms. It's her flesh he's devouring, her body he's worshipping. "No. Why Alex? To get back at me…?"

My eyes flash open to darkness, my breaths coming in a pant, my heart aching with each beat. It was just a dream. *No.* Not a dream. Biting reality haunting me in my sleep. It's pain very, very real.

I jump at the chirp of my cell phone, its reminder alert of a recent message sending it vibrating along the top of the night-stand. Begrudgingly, I reach for it, the bright light burning my eyes as they adjust to the screen…A text from Alex. *Why? Why is he doing this?*

Subject: I'm trying

Please answer my calls. We need to talk about Andrew. About everything.

Everything? *No need to explain* everything, *Alex…I know what you did*. And I'm not ready yet to *talk* about it, let alone listen to him fill me in on something I already know. It's painful enough without his words. His guilt - if he even has any.

I've ignored his repeated calls, finally switching the phone to mute before falling into bed. Since I'm not ready to hear anything he has to say, it wasn't too difficult - painful with each ringing stab to my heart, yes, but the pain quickly recoiled into resentment. Resulting in rage-filled painful glances towards my phone with each unanswered call. Stupid me for leaving his contact settings for messages on over-ride.

What could he possibly have to say anyway? Would he even *tell* me that he was with her? Or would he leave that part out? If he did have the balls to admit it, would he tell me that he ran to her just to get back at me? Ironic since he questioned if that's why I kissed Andrew.

Screw him, I grimace a little at the harshness of the thought. Yes, my reasons for visiting Andrew that night *were* innocent, but I'd be lying if I said the question of why I crossed that line wasn't lingering at the hands of Alex's suggestion. Was I desperate for an escape? Or simply trying to hurt Alex in return? Maybe both.

Well, cheers to Alex for shining light on the double-edged sword - its razor edge now dripping with the blood of my broken heart.

CHAPTER Nineteen

"WHY DID I agree to get married in London again?" Stacey pouts dramatically, fluffing her mane of red tousled curls, cringing at her reflection. "Damn humidity in winter. I mean, what the hell, Abs?" she spins around holding up her mass of hair on either side. "If I'm going to look like the goddamn Lion King, I could *at least* be sitting on a beach getting drunk before I pledge an oath to the last man that will ever stick his tongue in my box."

"You mean the man you love dearly?" I smirk.

"Yeah, that too. I'm marrying him aren't I?" she shakes her head in exasperation, her expression screaming, *DUH.*

"Stace, your hair will be perfect. *You* will be perfect. You have a full staff, for heaven's sake, coming to transform you into the most beautiful bride Thomas has ever seen. Stop freaking out."

"I. Am. Not. Freaking. Out. I'm getting married. *I'm getting married*. Oh. My. God. I'm getting married," she's suddenly panting and gasping for air, stumbling to sit down.

"Okay, just breathe. *In…and…out*," I demonstrate for effect, as though that's going to make a difference.

"Fuck you, Aby. *You* breathe. I'm freaking out here!"

"You just said you weren't!" I glare at her in panic. Frantically turning towards the bar, I start opening and closing cupboards and drawers in search of something to help her.

"I lied!" she shouts. "What the hell are you doing? I need help here."

"I'm *trying* to help you. I'm looking for a paper bag or something, you're hyperventilating!"

"A paper-fucking-bag? Listen, bitch, unless there's a bottle of booze in it, you can stick the paper bag up your…"

"Stacey Stevenson! Bite your tongue."

Our gazes dart towards the voice to find Stacey's mother, Evelyn, standing in the entrance of the suite. She looks as beautiful as always, despite her customary low-maintenance appearance. Evelyn was never one to take the time to wear make-up or do anything special with her naturally stunning tresses, yet her natural beauty always shines through. She's the polar opposite of Stacey that way, though their striking resemblance is uncanny. They share the same brilliant emerald green eyes and figure, but Evelyn is taller with lighter, strawberry blonde hair, next to Stacey's bright copper tresses.

"Mommy!" Stacey jumps up, running to hug her.

I can't help but smile at their loving embrace. Evelyn is the only family Stacey has in this world. That I know of, anyway. It's been just the two of them since they moved to Toronto when we were in high school, neither having ever spoken of Stacey's father. And I've never crossed the line she suggestively drew to warn that the topic was off limits. Though I have to be honest, I've always wondered if it played a part in the obvious 'daddy' issues that plague Stacey.

"Why is my beautiful baby girl so upset on her wedding day?" Evelyn pulls back, looking into Stacey's eyes. "I don't know how you put up with her, Aby, sweetie," she winks at me, walking over to give me a hug. "It's so good to see you."

"You too, Mrs. Stevenson," I smile.

"Ahhh, *hello*? Bridezilla over here! Woman. In. *Crisis*…" Stacey displays her best damsel-bitch-in-distress neck crane with exaggerated eye popping for extra effect.

"Crisis?" Evelyn looks concerned, gazing back and forth between us. "What's happened? Is everything on schedule with the wedding?"

"Everything is fine. Perfect actually," I glower at Stacey, to which she rolls her eyes. "Stacey is just having a minor panic attack it seems."

"Baby," Evelyn puts her arm around Stacey, guiding her to sit down. "This isn't like you. You're the *queen* of control," she smiles encouragingly through her playfully loving sarcasm, cupping Stacey's face to look into her eyes. "What can I do to help?"

"You just did," Stacey smiles, hugging her mom. "I'm just so glad you're here. You always know exactly what to say," she adds, pulling back to look at her.

"I barely said anything at all," she laughs. "And where else would I be?" She kisses her cheek.

"It's not what you say, Mommy, it's what you *do*. But actually, where you *should* be is down in the spa. It's a gift from your soon-to-be son-in-law, Mom. You can't blow it off. Pamper yourself this one time, okay?"

"It's *your* day, Stacey," Evelyn's brows scrunch in gentle defiance. "I don't need..."

"Mom. This is non-negotiable. I want my mother to look and feel amazing on my wedding day. You already have the look part down pat. So for just *one* day, play with that and get all dolled up. For me? *Please*?" she pleads dramatically with an exaggerated wide smile.

"You're incorrigible, you know that don't you?" she shakes her head. "I suppose I should at least try to do justice to the incredible dress you picked out for me. Mascara and all?" she grimaces.

"And all," Stacey warns lovingly.

"Okay," she kisses Stacey's cheek again before standing. "I'll see you in a couple of hours. I would really like to be here when you put on your dress, okay?"

"Of course, Mom. Now go. Enjoy," Stacey scoots her towards the door. "I'll be fine, I promise. I've got Abs," she looks towards me with her tag-team grin.

"I've got her covered." My well plastered, forced smile falls the minute the door closes behind her. I'm sensing the impending return of Bridezilla any minute. "Ummm, you just brushed your

Mom off like a dusty rug. What was that?" I question as she turns to face me.

"That, my little gumdrop, was me getting rid of the only person I know that can passive-aggressively talk someone down off a ledge, while leaving them shaking their head as to exactly just how she did it."

"So…you're okay then?"

"Well, that's the catch. My mom rocks, but I don't want to burst her bubble by letting her know that her charms on me are short lived. My metaphorical ledge is as inviting as a male stripper waving his dick and a shot glass at me. I could jump back on at any moment."

"Great," I grimace playfully. "Then as long as you don't jump *off* it, we'll be fine."

"Ha ha, whore. So, what about you? Are *you* fine?"

"Of course I'm fine," I nonchalantly walk towards the armoire, fiddling with her wedding dress hung from the door.

"So, you're trying to tell me that though you have yet to speak to Alex, you're *fine*? I call bullshit, Abs."

"And I call *shut-it*," I turn to flash her a cautioning smirk, my inner actress quickly shifting gears to hide any signs of my instantly boiling blood. The past twenty minutes had been the first time since last night that I'd successfully silenced *their* giggles in the shower, or the constant replay of a naked Helena's little peepshow. Not to mention the way she looked at me - the evil glimmer in her eyes haunted me all night, yet, in the cold light of day, I can't help but wonder if I saw something more behind that eerie stare.

No doubt, Stacey's Bridezilla attack played a large role in my short-lived distraction. Yet with her mere question of concern, the disgusting events are now back in full force, poking me square in the head once again. *Ugh. How could he?* I quickly turn my attention back to the dress, squeezing my eyes closed against the tears threatening to emerge. *Was it his turn to get back at me?*

"How long have I known you?"

"Just let it go, Stace. Please."

"I can't, Abs. I've known you long enough to know when

you're hiding something - especially pain. Your acting skills are useless on me, Scarlett O'Hara. You're pining over your Rhett Butler, and you can't fool me that it's not bothering you."

"What was it that Rhett said to Scarlett? 'Frankly my dear, I don't give a damn'. Irony is a bitch," I whisper to myself. *A confusing bitch*. I know what I saw, but my heart is fighting to believe it.

"Stop mumbling. I *can* hear you, ya know. Alex certainly gives a damn. I know he's angry right now, Aby, but he's proven how much he cares."

I cringe at her words, fighting my body's urge to buckle to the floor and cry. Or throw up. *I thought he cared. I thought I trusted him.* I don't know what to think anymore.

"And," she continues, "…like me, he can see through you as well. Translation - he loves you as much as I do."

Oh, God. I exhale deeply, desperate to keep it together, bending to reposition her sparkly shoes for distraction. "Your theory is flawed," I retort - with no intention of offering the razor-sharp edge of truth that if Alex truly loved me, he wouldn't have been with Helena. "Liam never saw through me, and *he* loved me," I deflect instead, turning to face her, my resurfaced anger controlling the breaking of my heart.

"Liam was in denial, hun. And nice try. Deflection doesn't work with me either. Talk to me," the concern in her gaze kills me.

"Stace, it's your wedding day. Please let this go. It will still be here tomorrow." *And the next day…and the day after that…*

"Don't make me hurt you. Do you really want me to splatter the blood of my Maid of Honor all over my wedding dress? Come on," she takes my hand, leading me into the bedroom to sit on the bed. "I promise, dealing with your shit keeps me from losing *mine*," she smiles wide, teeth and all. It's a psychotic breakdown forewarning that I know she means.

Ugh, I close my eyes on a deep breath. "Last night…Alex *was* home, but he wasn't…alone."

"What? What the hell do you mean? Did you talk to him?"

"He didn't even know I was there." My attempts to avoid her

gaze are fruitless against the locked and mirroring movements of her head. "I heard laughter coming from the bathroom…from the shower."

"Go on," her jaw cocks at an eerie angle that matches the crazed look in her eyes.

"I heard the door opening, someone came out," I lose focus, staring into space, fighting to keep the visual from resurfacing.

"Who, Aby? Who came out?" she grabs my shoulders, forcing me to look at her.

"It was Helena," a tear slips down my cheek. "She was naked."

"What? Holy fucking shit!" Stacey bolts upright, pacing erratically before looking back to me. "Alex wouldn't do that to you. *Would* he?" she questions the air. "Oh, but that tramp would," she folds her arms, retracing her circle of steps. "I bet she was just waiting, like the slutty vulture she is, to swoop down and…Oh, shit, Abs," she rushes to sit down, taking my hands in hers. "I'm so sorry."

"I don't know what to believe anymore…She looked right at me, Stace. She knew I was there, and she didn't say a word," I give in to the overflowing emotion I've been holding inside as she hugs me. "So many things have gone wrong. Maybe we just weren't meant to be."

"Oh, bumblebee. I don't know why bad, stupid, painful shit happens to people, but I do know that you have to fight back. Don't let it win. Deal with it. Learn from it. And start over," she smiles. "Thomas taught me that."

"I'm so happy that you're happy. You deserve this, Stace."

"So do you, baby girl," she wipes my tears.

We sit in silence for a few moments, staring at nothing as if weighing the situation over and over in our heads. "Maybe he was drunk…" Stacey finally suggests.

"Would that excuse him from playing rubber ducky with Brothel Barbie?" I look down, fumbling at the fold of my jeans at my bent knee.

"Well, *you* were drunk when you went for a test drive with Ken Doll's tongue," she purses her lips.

"I was upset!" I stand to walk off my defensive outburst, swiping at my tear-stained cheeks.

"Alex was upset too. Just saying," she adds, re-pursing her lips with a head tilt when I turn to glare at her.

"I *kn-ow*," I release a defeated sigh, joining her back on the bed. "But, Stace, what happened with Andrew was just a kiss. I'm not sure Alex and I could get past..." I trail off, having to swallow back the vomit-laced words. "I'm just not sure I could ever forgive him."

"You will. Although, whether that means he's lost your heart forever is up to you. But you do have to forgive him. Forgiveness is a gift to yourself, pookie."

"Wow. That's deep."

"I know, right?" she laughs. "Thomas has invaded my psyche."

"He seems to have done more than that. I hate to break it to you, but you're beginning to portray him in the light of a knight in shining armor. Maybe one day you'll open up about why you would even need one?" I force her gaze, squeezing her hand.

"What, and open the dungeon floodgates?" she forces a pained laugh.

"To quote a wise and wonderful friend, 'do you know how much I love you'? You have been there for me for anything and everything, anytime. I'm waiting for the day when you'll let me return the favor."

"Well, lucky you! Today is that day," she smiles. "I want my bestie slash beautiful Maid of Honor to have a wonderful day by my side," she squeezes my hand. "Are you going to be okay?"

"Leading you up the aisle to the man of your dreams? You bet your cute ass I will. Let's go start getting ready."

"*My* cute ass? You must have me confused with this perfect-assed whore I know," she smiles with a wink, taking my hand as I lead her towards the bathroom.

"I love you, Stace."

"I love you too, bubble-ass," she playfully pinches my butt, stopping to give me a tight hug.

"THIS IS IT!" I mutter, practically bouncing in excitement. "You look so beautiful! I can't wait to see the look on Thomas's face when he sees you walking up the aisle."

Stacey's face, however, looks a little frozen in fear, her eyes glazed over, staring right through me.

"Stace? Are you okay?"

"What?" she seems to snap back to reality, shaking her head a little as she focuses on me. "Ummm, yeah…good to go. Just nervous."

"Stacey Stevenson nervous? Get outta here," I tease her, smoothing out her dress.

"There's a first time for everything," her grin is more fitting to that of a psych patient the moment before meltdown. "I'm more nervous than a whore in church, Abs."

"You are a whore in church," I laugh, trying to break through to her.

She smiles, and I'm elated to see it's real. "I hate you."

"No, you love me. And more importantly, you love Thomas. So, let's go make you Mrs. Stacey Fines."

"Mrs. Stacey *Stevenson*-Fines."

"That works too," I wink, just as the processional begins to play. "Are you ready for this?"

"As ready as I'll ever be," she takes a deep breath, reaching for my arm as the usher prepares to open the doors. "I'm madly in love with him, Aby."

"I know," I squeeze back impending tears, turning to give her a quick hug. "I'll see you at the altar?"

"We'll see," she smiles again, its edges laced with a returned nervous twitch. "Hey, Abs," she pauses for me to look back at her, "…don't trip."

"I hate you," I tease, blowing her a kiss before nodding to the usher.

The doors open fully to reveal the church full of standing guests, all turned in their pews to witness the impending bride.

My breath hitches instantly at the thought that Alex could very well be here among the crowd, his eyes on me, watching my every move.

A quick scan through the smiling faces sends my pulse racing, and I immediately stop looking. Meeting Alex's gaze would be the death of me. I couldn't bare the look I imagine would be on his face, not to mention the stab to my heart if I found him sitting with *her*. *Would he really come with her?* I squeeze the stem of my bouquet with every small breath of composure through my shaky steps, measured in time with the beat of the bass of Canon in D. Each stroke of the chord echoes in the pounding of my heart as I turn my full attention towards the destination ahead.

Thomas looks the epitome of poise, radiating a love and excitement that would make any woman weak in the knees. His warm smile and sweet wink instantly transforms my forced performance into genuine calm as I reach my place, turning to join in to welcome the bride.

The traditional bridal march precedes momentary gasps and elated whispers as Stacey comes into view at the end of the isle.

I glance quickly towards Thomas, a quick gasp myself, tears threatening to form at the sight. He's mesmerized, his awe apparent as he swallows a well of loving emotion through a jubilant smile. The love emanating from his gaze is breathtaking as he watches Stacey walk slowly up the aisle, beaming radiantly in her stunning gown, her direct focus locked in place on his.

I've never seen her more beautiful - her stunning red tresses styled to perfection, the curls cascading over her bare shoulders, a sparkling diamond necklace peeking through. The sweetheart neckline of her strapless wedding gown hugs her curves beautifully amid a jewel-beaded sash at the waist, the ruched chiffon flaring out slighting just below her hips into a simple A-line to the floor, her shimmery Jimmy Choo heels peeking out from underneath. The dress is simple, yet elegant, a classic look reminiscent of a nineteen fifties glamour wedding.

Reaching for Thomas's hand, Stacey exudes happiness, love. So much so, that I feel a jealous pang in my chest. Guilt seeps into my pores as I witness the commencement of their union, plagued by my own broken heart. It takes everything in my power to refrain from peering into the crowd. For him. The man I wish desperately was standing up at this altar with me in their place. I'm a fool. A foolish, lovesick fool. I've lost him. Yet here I stand, at my best friend's wedding thinking about him. *And, clearly, he's not thinking about you* - my inner actress snaps me back to the present just in time to catch the pastor's call for objection.

"May you speak now or forever hold your peace."

The momentary opening gives me the perfect opportunity to sneak a glance through the seated guests, and I shamefully take it, to no avail. I don't even spot Helena, though I may have missed them both in the quick scan before turning back to the bride and groom.

No, I close my eyes at the realization. I didn't miss him. I *know* he's not here. I know that if he were, I would be drawn to him. It's a painful reality I can't deny.

"IS IT RUDE to throw a breath mint in someone's mouth while they're talking?" Stacey whispers at my side.

"Stop it," I laugh. It's funny, but such a good question. One more kiss to my cheek and I may turn into a toad. It'll be a whole new kind of fairytale.

"I'm dead serious. I think that last dude brushed his teeth with moth balls," she adds, shielding her mouth inconspicuously in time to greet another guest with a smile. "I know I won the battle for my quaint little wedding, but, Jesus, did you see the guest list for this reception? Look at all of these people. Thomas knows the whole fucking city."

"Yes, it seems he does. And, on that note, perhaps his bride should dial down the *wearing-say* a little."

"What? Speak fucking English, Abs."

I roll my eyes. "The swearing, Stace. Dial it down a notch."

"*Oh, sure*. Anything for you, sweet-tits," she rolls her eyes, and I pinch her underarm. "Ouch," she drawls dramatically, shooting me an *I can't believe you just did that* glare.

"There's my beautiful bride," Thomas greets us from behind, folding Stacey in his arms before she has time to turn. "Have I told you today how lucky I am?" he kisses her cheek.

She leans back into him, beaming. "Tell me again. Or better yet," she turns in his embrace to face him, "…show me."

"Gladly, Mrs. Stevenson-Fines," he stares lovingly into her eyes before cupping her cheeks, bending to take her in a sweet kiss. "Today, tomorrow…forever."

I feel like a voyeur standing next to them, completely absorbed in their moment of bliss. Yet I can't turn away, each second I stare pulling me into a bubble of fantasy as they morph into a visual of Alex and I. It's Alex's face I see as he kisses her a second time, *my* lips he's kissing; the tingle created there so real it draws the pull of my hand to my mouth, suddenly breaking the spell. Shaking it off, I turn away and close my eyes against the aching pain in my heart.

The hurt doesn't keep the torturing memories at bay, however, as I'm thrown back in time to our island retreat. All of the beautifully romantic ways Alex showed me his love, *proved* his love, before even saying the words. His love was perfection, whispered so perfectly in his every touch, every glance, every kiss.

Too good to be true - my inner actress bites, pinching the arm of my inner dreamer. I grimace from the sting of reality, taking a deep breath of composure, its bitter aftertaste begging to be washed down with a large gulp of Champagne as I reach for my glass.

"I'm sorry to see Alex absent from your side, Aby. Filming obligations?" Thomas questions innocently.

I notice Stacey purse her lips as I take another large sip of Champagne. Of course she hasn't had a chance to fill Thomas in on the latest drama. *Humph.* My love life can now be summed up in theatrical highlights. Irony really is a bitch. *Well, take a bow, Cupid. You deserve it, you chubby-faced whore*, I take another drink.

"We're not…exactly sure if Alex will be able to make it,"

Stacey chimes in with an awkward smile.

"Oh, well, it's a shame he missed dinner, but perhaps he will arrive in time to sweep you onto the dance floor," Thomas winks.

"Perhaps," I raise my flute in cheers to my pathetic lie, emptying its contents in time for a refill from the lovely young waiter with impeccable timing. Maybe I can get drunk and stumble my way through the rest of the evening. *Yes, that sounds like a perfect plan*, I smile to myself on sip as another guest greets Stacey and Thomas.

"You look lovely this evening, Abigail."

I spin on my heels at the slithering sound of the voice - Helena Adelaide, in all her sickeningly, beautiful glory, smiling radiantly at me. I can't help peering over her shoulder wondering if Alex lingers not far behind. Instant hatred burns through me, exploding through my veins before hardening my bitter heart. I never had any real reason to hate her before, at least not before last night. But now, as I'm assaulted with the visual of her naked body emerging from Alex's bathroom, her evil sneer, I realize *hate* isn't a strong enough word. My hands tremble noticeably from the onslaught, spilling my glass of Champagne.

"Are you all right, darling? You look as though you've seen a ghost."

No, whore-dusa, actually. For a moment in my mind, she contorts into the whorish reptile that she is, bulging in the center from devouring her latest victim. *Well, I'll be damned if she thinks that's going to be me.* "Let me guess," I lay the flute down, picking up a napkin to wipe my hand, "…you're dying to brag about your little conquest? Maybe rub my nose in it a little?" I bend to whisper the latter in her ear with patronizing composure - a silent salute to my inner actress.

"Not at all" she slithers coyly.

Her performance of indifference makes me want to slap her. I refrain, though the idea may have twisted my smirk into a looming snarl.

"You know," she pauses slightly, "…I've always wondered if Alex told you about us. I had my suspicions, of course, based on your behavior."

Really? Ugh, I roll my eyes, tuning her out. I don't see any penises in the general vicinity, so why does she keep opening her mouth? "Oh, put the coy card away. Does it really matter that I knew about your slut status, Helena?"

She flashes me a closed-lip smile that screams condescending. "So, I assumed correctly. Alex *did* tell you," her smile twists into a smug grin.

Are you kidding me? I want to punch her in the throat. I can't take my eyes off her little swan neck. *Alex didn't have to tell me you're a whore. That information,* sweetheart, *seeps through your pores.* Though my inner sarcasm is keeping my calmed demeanor intact, the unconscious use of Alex's term of endearment almost puts me over the edge.

Her eyes sparkle with glee, peering at me over the rim of her glass of Champagne as she takes a sip, patiently waiting for me to say something. How Alex could have anything to do with this woman is beyond me. *Oh, right...Perception is everything.* And she plays the game so *very* well.

Well, I'm tired of playing games. "What is it, *exactly*, that you want, Helena?" I pull the indifference card from her deck, picking up my Champagne.

"I simply wanted to apologize for leaving you in the dark last night," she shifts her weight to one perfectly toned leg, running her palm along the pearls around her stupid swan neck - the motion holding my attention to her gullet. I'm not sure how much longer I can refrain from grabbing it.

"Oh, did you need confirmation that I saw you? Surprise!" my brows rise, screaming *ta-da,* "It certainly was for me," I mumble the latter into my flute, taking a sip, looking for an escape before I really do hurt this woman.

A couple seated at a table in the corner catch my eye, the dark haired man leaning in to whisper in the woman's ear as she smiles - a smile full of love. Happiness. She glances my way, our eyes meeting in an instant before she finds the gaze of the man at her side - a gaze full of trust. Devotion. *I love you, too,* she whispers, the words shooting across the room like an arrow of clarity to my heart.

Try to look past what appears on the surface...try to see what is real beneath, before allowing perception to come into play, Alex's words rush through my mind, *I love you, Aby.* He proved his love long before he ever shared the words. He made sure I saw it. Felt it. Trusted in it. And I doubted him once. Am I really going to do it again?

"Is everything okay here?" Stacey's alarm jars me back to the present, her concerned gaze flickering from mine to Helena's and back again.

I'm not going to doubt him again..."I have to go," the words fall from my lips as reality of my love and trust in Alex smacks me in the face. I can't explain why that whore was there last night, but I do know I can't believe for one more second that he would do anything to hurt me. I choose to trust him.

I move to sidetrack Helena but Stacey stops me with a soft pull on my arm. "The MC would like to start the toasts," she says softly, her gaze unwavering between the two of us.

"I have to find Alex," I mutter, leaning over the table to grab my clutch.

"What? Aby, what's going on?" Stacey grabs my arm again.

Glancing quickly towards her, I gently pull from her hold, catching a glimpse of Helena's amused gaze before scanning the crowded ballroom. "I have to find him," I repeat on a whisper, grabbing my dress to avoid tripping.

Helena steps in front of me, halting my retreat, and I glare at her, "I don't know what happened last night, but I do know one thing, I trust Alex."

Smiling, she steps aside. "Clever girl," I hear her whisper as I pass.

"Excuse me?" I turn to face her.

"I knew you saw me last night, Abigail, but what I needed to know was what you would conclude," Helena's smile is surprisingly warm. "A man that loves you as much as Alex does deserves your trust, I'm glad to see he has it."

"He does. But how sweet of you to decide to test it," I motion to leave.

"It was Ben, Abigail. I was there with Ben," her words halt

my departure. "But Alex is important to me - as a *friend*. And I look out for my friends."

Pausing for a second, I continue on, making my way quickly through the crowd. I need to find Alex. Every cell of my being screams run…run to him. And I know I'd run to the ends of the earth if it meant finding him there.

The crowded room blurs around me, inundating me with grins from guests as I pass. They could all be wearing the same blank mask for all I know, since the only smile I'm hoping to find is on the face of Alexander Tate - the man of my dreams. The man I love more than anything in this world. The man nothing is going to stop me from getting back, regardless of all my stupid mistakes. *Our* stupid mistakes.

Reaching the center of the room once more, I stand and turn in an unconscious spin, a lost soul amid a sea of faces. The laughter and smiles dance eerily around me, hauntingly echoing through my panic. *He's not here.*

I spy Stacey, now seated at the head table, the MC bending down to her in conversation. I'm running out of time. Frantically, I search for the nearest exit, grabbing my dress to run for the double side doors. I fumble for my phone in my clutch, dialing his number the minute I walk through.

"No, no, no…" I utter, frantically, disengaging the call when his voice mail kicks in before opening the text app. The MC's call for attention reverberates from inside the reception and my fingers shake as I prepare to type. I have so much that I need to say, and I'm out of time. *I've wasted so much time.*

Struggling to hold back the sudden build of tears threatening to fall, I realize there's only one thing I need to say. It screams from within me, stronger than anything I've ever felt before…

Subject:

I love you

CHAPTER
Twenty

MY HEAD IS spinning, my pulse pounding in my chest as I make my way back inside the reception hall, the attention of the room on the MC at the podium. Timing has not been my friend lately. *Nor has trust and common sense*, I grimace at the painful self-inflicted stab to my naïve heart, contemplating the most inconspicuous route back to the head table.

Deciding to go around the long way, I scoot along the far wall in hopes of avoiding attention. The only notice I seem to steal is that of Stacey, eyeing me with equal parts concern and Bridezilla-frustration as I reach my place to sit down. I mouth *I'm sorry* and try to summon a grin of some kind in return to her momentary loving gaze - very momentary, as in an instant her face contorts back into crazy bride. Jabbing her finger towards the wedding agenda on the table in front of her, I realize she thinks I should have a look at mine.

Great, I'm up next. As a matter of fact, with the exception of the MC reading the regrets and loving messages of those absent right at this moment, I'm the *only* one making a speech. It was decided that since Evelyn is Stacey's only family present, I would speak for both the bride and the groom. My mission statement: Don't focus on either as I say something nice about love and marriage to toast the celebration of their union.

Any other time, that would be lovely. Right now, I just want to find Alex and beg for a reunion of my own. *How am I going to get through this?* I slide my cell phone partially from my clutch, desperate to see a reply from him. Any reply. I would take 'fuck you' even, since that would at least give me the chance to reply with 'Oh, God, yes…please'." I just need to know that he saw my message. That he knows I love him. At least from there, I can begin to prove just how much.

But there's no reply. And I can't help but look up, attempting to take in the crowded room, scanning every face in hopes of finding his. I don't. I choke back a sudden need to cry, trying to brace myself for the task at hand. But I'm failing. My heart rate picks up speed as I realize he may not come at all.

What must he be thinking since I've ignored his calls and messages since late last evening? Thank God he doesn't know what *I* was thinking - what I almost let myself believe. I pull my fingers to my lips, swallowing back a mixture of regret and fear as a sob I've been trying to quell builds in my throat. He would have no way of knowing what I walked in on. And, therefore, no idea why I've avoided him. *Oh God, I feel sick that he thinks I was ignoring him.* The threatened sob chokes me as the MC calls my name.

"NEW BEGINNINGS ARE often disguised as painful endings," I pause to look up with a half-hearted smile, my hands trembling, gripped tightly to the edges of the podium. "I know what you're thinking…what an inappropriately *odd* start to a wedding speech. Well, an amazing woman once shared this quote of advice with me, and at the time, I too, thought *she* was rather odd - just one of her many adorable quirks," I glance at Stacey, the love I see in her eyes giving me the strength to hold back my looming tears, though my voice is quivering from emotion. "It took a long time for me to find the beautifully hidden message in its meaning, or at least, to find my *own* interpretation of that message, so in light of saving you time - *and* the rest of the evening discussing the crazy ramblings of the Maid of Honor - I'll get to the point and share it with you."

"The dictionary coins beginnings as an act - the point at which something begins. And every love story is full of so many beginnings, all of which we capture and record into pretty memory capsules." Pausing, I brace myself against the barrage of memories assailing me, picture perfect memories of Alex and I that I don't want to let go. "The first time you meet. The first glance. First date. That first *kiss*," I pretend to swoon, and the guests giggle, easing my inner turmoil slightly. But as I glance down at my speech, I'm thrown back into the sights of the emotional hurricane…"The first *I love you*." I have to pause as it blasts through me along with a vision of Alex's perfect face. "These, and so many more, are all the beautiful beginnings of love."

"But love isn't *always* pretty. It's full of acts that don't make it into the pretty memory capsules, for when they end, they're discarded in their painful ugliness. The first fight," I cock my head, pursing my lips playfully, earning another round of quiet laughter, despite feeling as though they can see right through me. "The first 'I'm sorry'. And even the first heartbreak. We've all had at least a few of those," I brave another small smile. "We've actually had many of all of the above, and in most cases with the same person. Welcome to love and marriage," I tease a wink at Stacey and Thomas, the quick glance affording me another little shot of strength from the loving gaze of my best friend.

Looking back to the seated guests I fight the urge to look for him, the thought of finding his blue eyes staring back at me sending a stutter of hope through my heart. It takes a moment to catch my breath and my focus back in place on the paper before me.

"Yes love, ugly *or* pretty, is full of repeated beginnings and endings. And it comes with this amazing gift at the end of every single day - the gift of knowing that when you wake up in the morning, you have the chance to start them all over again." Looking down for a moment, I close my eyes in hopes of squeezing back the tears that I can no longer fight. "That's the message that spoke to me from that *odd* quote. That true love is trusting in the magic of starting over - new beginnings from what may sometimes feel like painful endings. Because with the start of every new act comes an end, and with that, another beautiful new beginning."

Picking up my glass, my hand trembling a little, I feign a smile at Stacey before turning back to the crowd. "Please raise your glasses with me in celebration of Thomas and Stacey, and their love. May they always trust in the magic of starting over, and wake up every day together to experience a lifetime of beautiful new beginnings."

Taking a sip of my Champagne, I turn to lay it down as Stacey catches me in a bone-crushing hug amid the claps and cheers of the crowd. Instantly an escaped tear slips down my face. "I love you, Stacey, but I have to go," I whisper, pulling from her hold.

"Aby...?" she questions, a gentle grab of my arm halting my process.

"I just need some air," I plead, wiping the tear from my cheek as I welcome her understanding gaze.

"Okay..." is all I allow her to get in before I turn and step down from the podium, lifting my dress in preparation to run.

My aim is on the quickest retreat - the side doors - however, I don't make it past the first row of tables; an isle full of smiling guests all waiting to say something nice as I pass. Their kind comments about my 'beautiful words', and my 'witty' and 'well written' speech are all a blur with each forced smile and empty 'thank you' I offer, my focus dominated by my desperate need to escape.

Flashing a final appreciative smile to the 'you make a lovely Maid of Honor' from the last table, I turn my attention back to my destination, the wide gap of bare floor the only thing separating me from the exit doors I crave. Doors now blocked by the one thing I crave more...Alex Tate.

Alex, I tremble, his name echoing through my mind, his presence stopping me dead in my tracks. He takes my breath away as I devour him, dressed to perfection in a black tux, his hands stuffed into the front pockets of his pants. For a moment I wonder if he's a figment of my imagination, so desperate to find him that I've actually conjured him from fantasy. He certainly looks as though he just stepped out of one. But when I meet his gaze, his penetrating stare, the reality of him hits me harder than a bolt of lightning. It's an overwhelming blast that shatters me into a million thankful pieces.

He's really here, I gasp for air, swallowing hard against my suddenly dry throat. Every part of me screams run. Run to him. Yet I don't. I walk slowly. As though time is in slow motion, and if I rush, if I move too quickly, it will speed up again and whisk him away.

I reach him in an envelope of silence, lost only to his eyes. Eyes that never left mine, wrapping me in a cocoon of calm, pulling me to stand before him to say the only thing I need him to hear, "I love you."

He says nothing as he stares into my soul, and that's okay, because I feel safe having him there. And in his silence, I'm grateful for this chance to say more. "I'm so sorry," I search his eyes, needing to see my hope reflected there.

His returned gaze glistens in its penetration, almost as though he's capturing a moment for himself, before he reaches up to wipe a slow falling tear from my cheek.

A breathless whisper escapes my lips at the touch, our stare broken as he looks down momentarily, almost bashfully, before returning his gaze to mine. His eyes ensnare me, holding me hostage as I painstakingly await his reply, frightened to death that he'll say nothing in return.

"Hi," he finally speaks, his eyes flashing a brilliant blue, "I'm Alex Tate," he takes my hand, lifting it to his lips. "It's a pleasure to meet you."

I lose myself in his perfect smile, adrift in a haze as I try to understand.

"That was a beautiful speech. I particularly liked the part about starting over," his sweet words explain everything.

Oh, thank God! "I thought…there's so much I need to explain," I manage as my emotional dam breaks.

"Shhh," he whispers, brushing away more tears. "Not tonight, Miss Ryan. Tonight is about new beginnings."

I stare at him in wonder, desperate to try to understand what we've done to deserve so many chances. And thankful that we're so willing to take them, despite how we've allowed them to be so carelessly thrown away. This *is* our new beginning. We couldn't fight what we feel for each other if we tried.

"Will you do me the honor of dancing with me?" he holds out his hand.

It's only then that the world around me comes into focus - the music pulling me back into reality - though as I take his hand, I can't help but feel the warmth of our loving fantasy.

I realize as we turn that guests have joined Thomas and Stacey on the dance floor. *I missed their first dance*, I grimace with guilt and awe at how long we were lost frozen in time.

Taking our place among the crowd, Alex wraps his arm around my waist, securing his hand in mine, swaying us in time to the rhythm. We're lost to each other, our gazes locked, our eyes silently conveying thoughts of regret and mistakes, forgiveness and fresh starts…love and never letting go.

He pulls me closer, releasing my hand to secure both of his around my waist, tightening his hold as I snake my arms around his shoulders, his cheek brushing mine in the motion of our desperate embrace.

I run my fingers through his tousled curls, a new tear escaping my fresh well of relief. Leaning against his shoulder, I relish him - the feel of the warm flesh of his nape under my palms, his perfect scent as I inhale deeply, the way he makes me feel when I'm in his arms. I don't ever want to lose this feeling again. And though I'm so grateful for his plea to leave our regrets unspoken tonight, I can't ignore the nagging reminder that he was never able to forgive Julia her indiscretion - fictitious or otherwise. Does he really forgive *me* for kissing Andrew?

Whether or not it meant something to me doesn't matter when it's his heart that has to swallow the reality of my lips against another man's. I tense at the thought, and he squeezes me tighter. "Don't," he whispers. "Don't think about anything right now…nothing matters except where you are. In my arms, where you belong."

His perfect words remind me that he can see through me, sense what I'm thinking, and always know what I need to hear.

But as much as I want to be able to let it go, I can't. *My* heart is begging in fear for reassurance that what I did won't mean losing his.

Pulling back marginally, I look into his eyes, pleading for an answer before finally speaking the question, "But…what about the kiss?"

He halts his lead, releasing me to cup my face in his hands, the look in his gaze taking my breath away. The kiss he takes me is so deep and sensual, I feel it down to my toes. He tastes divine. Perfect. Heavenly. It's the type of kiss that sets off fireworks, explosions of shooting stars illuminating us in the light of our love. And that's just what I find when he finally pulls his beautiful lips away, as we stand under the glistening spotlight, surrounded by the crowd, all clapping and cheering.

"You mean *that* kiss?" he whispers. "Because that kiss is the one I'll remember forever," he pulls me against him, lifting me, my feet dangling above the floor.

Looking down into his eyes, I thank the lucky stars above for gifting me this wonderful man.

"And," he adds, placing me back on my feet, "…just so you know, Aby Ryan, I love you, too."

"WHERE HAVE YOU been all my life," Alex asks playfully, spinning me around, dipping me to steal a kiss.

"I'm not sure," I tease in return. "If I had known you were such a good dancer, I would have stolen you for myself a long time ago."

He wrenches me tight against him, his gaze devouring mine with its heat. "You stole my heart the moment I looked into your eyes."

It takes a moment to reclaim my stolen breath, lost to the inferno of his burning stare and heart-melting declaration. "I just can't believe that you're here," I add, overwhelmed that he's come for me a second time. That he loves me that much.

"I couldn't fight my pull to you if I tried, Aby," the sincerity of his promise for a night of starting over oozes from his loving gaze.

"Alex, I love that you're here, and that you're sweeping me off my feet as though nothing has happened, but…" I pause, trying to find the right words.

"Not 'nothing', Aby. *Everything*. Everything that's happened - as painful and avoidable as it all could have been - lead us to where we stand right now," he searches my gaze, cupping my jaw, brushing his thumb lovingly along my cheek. "The mistakes we've made, the wrong choices, both of us wanting to protect the other, while at the same time avoiding our own fears. The guilt can be equally distributed. I'm not pretending that none of it happened, baby. I'm fighting for the reality that despite all of it, I simply can't live without you."

A single tear slips down my cheek, wiped away with the pad of his thumb before he leans in to brush his lips against mine. "I love you, Aby. That's why I'm here," he kisses me again. "That's all that will ever matter to me." And yet another kiss. "And that's why I will *never* give up on us." His final kiss tears through me, shattering every regret, every fear, and every doubt. It's almost painful in it's cleansing. A beautiful beginning from a painful ending.

"I love you, too," I gasp against his perfect mouth.

"I love you more." I feel his smirk at my lips, and I can't help but smile in return.

His playful love feels delicious, and hits me down to my core. His words, his touch, everything about him ignites me. Owns me. And above all else, drives me wild with want. A desire for him, and only him. *It will always be him.*

Grabbing his curls, I pull him to reignite our kiss, deepening it with my forceful hold of his nape, his hands dropping to fold me in his arms.

He wrenches me tight against his perfect, sculpted form, and it takes everything in me to hold back a desperate moan. It feels like a lifetime ago since we lost ourselves to the passion that consumes us. It's been much too long since he's owned me in the way I need him right now.

"Get a room, you two. What have I told you about displays of public affection?" Stacey mutters, dancing beside us with Thomas. "Although I have to say, that *earlier* kiss was pretty stellar, Mr. Tate. Just so you know, you have my approval."

"I don't think he asked for it, love," Thomas teases her.

"Congratulations, Thomas, my friend," Alex releases me to shake his hand. "Congratulations to you both," he bends to kiss Stacey's cheek, before flashing her his perfect smile. I can't help but light up seeing it. "And, on the contrary, I highly respect the opinion of anyone who loves Aby as much as I do," he looks back into my eyes, his gaze glistening with his devotion.

"Well, in that case, my opinion is that you two need to get out of here and hit this great place I've heard about - it's called *A Bed Near You*," she winks. "Unless, of course, you can break away from each other long enough to let me get in some dance grooves with my bestie for a bit first. What do you think, Abs? Is it time to get this party-a-started?" she gives us a little shake preview.

Smiling, I look to Alex, taking in his sweet grin and nod to signal he's willing to let me go, despite knowing that he really doesn't want to. "It's your party, you can shake-it if you want to. And I'm in," I reply.

"Yes!" Stacey double-fist pumps with a sexy, playful purse of her lips. "See you in a bit, boys. We're going to have a chat with the DJ," she adds, wrapping her arm in mine to pull me away.

I can't help but look back to Alex, biting my lip at the delicious sight of him staring at me with equal love and desire. Though this night is sure to be fun, it's going to be a tortuously long one, filled with needy glances and the occasional stolen touch.

"So," Stacey begins the minute we're out of earshot, "When are you going to tell me about...oh, you know...what the fuck, Aby?" she stops to stare me down for an explanation.

"You mean about the part where I walked in on Helena and *Ben* last night, not Alex?" I bite my lip harder; lust trampled by the herd of elephants that is Stacey's oncoming lecture. Once again, I don't think I need it - I seem to do just fine punishing myself for my stupid mistakes - but that won't stop her, so why bother trying to avoid it.

"Okay," she nods her head, seemingly walking the thin line of composure mimicked in her pursed lips, continuing on to our destination.

I catch up with a sigh, knowing she's not done just yet.

"You know how we're taught that if you don't have any-thing nice to say, don't say anything at all? Well, it's moments like this, my little twat waffle, that make that a very large pill to swallow. Like enormous," her hands demonstrate her point with a sweeping outlining of something imaginary, and really big. "H-U-G-E," she adds as we reach the DJ, now shaking her head. "Seriously, Abs…Ugh."

"You're not telling me anything I don't already know," I stand firm, my defenses always lurking despite my resistance.

She turns towards me, searching my gaze. "Oh yeah? Cause I'm having a moment of deja poo, myself - an overwhelming feeling that I've heard this shit before." Taking a breath of com-posure, she continues, "You know what?" I'm not going to say anything more. The torture you put yourself through this past twenty four hours is enough punishment for your gigantic, naïve, stupidity."

"Nice. I thought you weren't going to say anything more?" I try not to roll my eyes, but fail. "Alex and I have both made our share of mistakes…"

She jumps in with patronizing shock, "*Noooo.*"

"You know that high horse you're riding is going to be a bitch of a fall."

'Ohhh," she flashes a sincere, beaming smile, "Look at you, talking all *Stace-i-fied.* I'm so proud. Besides, I know I have flaws too, but my boobs usually distract people from them."

I continue, ignoring her, "Alex and I came with our own baggage…Issues with trust, insecurity, bad communication…"

"Assumptions," she adds. "Although that being said, I too would have made the same assumption you made last night. But the difference between you and I, princess, is that I wouldn't have left without seeing what was behind door number one. Just saying."

"Thanks for the clarification. My point *is* Alex and I have to learn to deal with our issues. There's no other alternative. He loves me as much as I love him, Stace."

"I know he does, poodle. You're like two peas in a fucked up pod. AND," she blurts to hush me, "...that's okay. We all are. You can take the easy road and walk away, or you stay and fight for what you have - if it's worth fighting for."

"It's *so* worth fighting for."

"Then I couldn't be more happy for you, Abs."

"Thanks, Stace," I take her hand, giving it a loving squeeze.

"So are we, like, at the intermission of your drama now? Cause I have to pee."

Laughing, I shake my head, "You're awful, my sarcastic trucker-mouth, pain in the ass, best friend."

"Hey, I may be a pain in the ass, but I bring a lot to the table - and I'll make no exception tonight, sista. Once I change into sexy dress number two, I'll be dancing *on* the table," her devious smile makes me laugh. "Come on," she pulls my held hand, "It's time to fulfill the most important duty of the Maid of Honor - holding my dress while I pee."

"Wouldn't it be easier to pee once you get out of the dress to change?" I question the obvious as she drags me along.

"Oh absolutely, but where's the fun in that? We're making memories, toilet duty and all."

"SO, TRADITIONALLY, THE man that catches the garter has the privilege of adorning it on the beautiful leg of the woman that catches the bouquet?" Alex asks from over my shoulder, wrapping me in his arms as we watch a loving Thomas bent before his seated bride.

"That's how it works," I mutter through a wide smile, leaning back into his delicious hold.

"Should we make a game plan?" he kisses my neck, his lips

a shock of sensual therapy.

"You do realize that, *traditionally*, the man and woman that do the catching are said to be bitten by the wedding bug in return, don't you?" I bite my lip at the thought. "Although that doesn't necessarily mean to *each other*," I add quickly, feeling suddenly nervous at the idea of Alex sliding the garter up another woman's leg.

"Semantics," he objects, kissing my bare shoulder. Stacey's choice of a strapless dress for me was brilliant, and Alex has been taking advantage of the exposed flesh all evening. "That garter is *mine*," he adds in a husky whisper.

Oh God, I close my eyes, my body's building and impending eruption to the constant attention of his words and touch reaching a point of no return. Combined with our evening-long consumption of alcoholic aphrodisiacs and suggestive glances, I'm not sure how much longer I can resist before imploding.

"We don't have to participate…" I trail off in a haze of lust. I need to get my hands on him. Soon.

"What? And miss being bitten by that wedding bug?" his words are inviting in their suggestiveness.

The entire idea of the ritual highlighting a path to our possible future is incredibly tempting. But at the same time, I want to experience our journey uninfluenced by wedding folktales. And more prominently, at this very moment, I want to experience *him*. Alone. Every perfect inch.

"Well, we could just bail on the games and go for the gold upstairs," I offer suggestively, unable to resist the urge to grind my ass back against him inconspicuously.

The hint of the arousal of his erection at my behind erupts my desperate needy core. Squeezing the want away before I attack him right here, I fumble in my clutch for the key card to my room, spinning in his hold to dangle it invitingly. "Stacey and Thomas thought it would be safer for some of the guests to have a room to retreat to."

Momentarily eyeing the access card, his molten stare darts back to mine. The desire that hits me in the motion of his sinful gaze is enough to blow the roof off my impending orgasm right here among the crowd. *Holy Shit.*

Grabbing my hand, he tugs me in the direction of the exit doors. My head spins as we rush through the lobby in our tornado of desire, his tongue taking ownership in lustful warning of what's to come before the closing of the elevator doors.

CHAPTER
Twenty-one

"BABY, I NEED you to hurry," Alex groans against the back of my neck.

He's driving me crazy with want, his finger grazing along my bare shoulder sending bolts of heat along my core. I need him. Now.

"Oh god, Alex...I can't..." I manage in needy frustration, my hands shaking uncontrollably in anticipation.

Chuckling, he reaches around to pull the keycard from my grip, seamlessly unlocking the door before pushing it open and dragging me inside.

Our lips crash feverishly as he pulls me into his arms, the door slamming closed behind us barely a pinprick in the lustful hazed silence, filled only by our restless moans.

Desperate to feel him, I slide my fingers inside the lapels of his suit jacket, pushing it off his shoulders and down his arms until it falls to the floor. I reach for the buttons of his shirt without hesitation, blindly releasing them one by one until his heated skin is at the mercy of my greedy fingertips.

"Alex..." I moan into his kiss, running my hands along his chest, clawing my nails through his chest hair as I slide his shirt off his shoulders. A whimper of pleasure escapes my lips as it falls to the floor, his perfect body bared to my touch. I can barely breath I'm so overcome, my need for him so great, I could combust from its heat, if not melt to the floor in a puddle of lust first.

"Mmmm, I know, baby," he murmurs, brushing his lips along my jaw, his hands splayed along my back, wrenching me flush against his strong body. "God, I need you too," he admits with a husky groan, squeezing me tight. "You're mine, Aby. *Mine...*"

"Ye-es, Alex. Yours. Always…" my breathless whisper escapes as my head falls back in absolute abandon, his fingers gliding seductively through my hair, securing the tresses firmly in his grip.

"There was no stopping what we started, Aby…" he trails off, tugging my hair to angle my neck to his lips and tongue, the onslaught singeing my sensitive flesh.

Mumbling incoherently in agreement, my hands devour his back, my fingers begging for him. My breasts are swollen and heaving, my nipples puckering, pushing against the constricting tightness of my dress - my body's affirmation of his ownership. He's owned me from the beginning; I could never stop loving him, never stop wanting him.

"What do you need, baby? Tell me."

"You. I just need you, Alex. I want you all over me. Do anything you want with me…" I plead, desperate for him. Needy. Crazed. Madly and irrevocably in love.

"Sweetheart, I'll give you *everything* you need," he growls. "I want you dripping wet, baby. I want the taste of you all over me."

I gasp as he lifts me in his arms, grateful for the speed with which he makes his way to the bed. *God, I've missed him…*I lick and nip along his corded neck, my arms wrapped tightly around his strong shoulders as I luxuriate in his masculine scent.

Setting me on my feet, he turns me, brushing aside my hair to reach for the zipper of my dress. Moans of need escape my lips as his heated breath dances across my flesh, eliciting delicious shivers as pulsing spikes of lust shoot along my core, my pussy throbbing in desperation. My body is aching for him, and as my dress sashays to the floor, I tremble in the anticipation of his touch and gaze.

Turning to face him, I'm stunned by the sheer desire flashing in his baby-blue eyes - eyes filled with animalistic hunger, devouring me in his stare, his fists clenched at his sides as though he's trying to restrain the beast inside.

"Make love to me, Alex," I whisper, cupping his jaw. "Don't hold back. It's what I need…" I sigh seductively, reaching back to undo my bra, aimlessly discarding it to the floor.

His jaw clenches in his show of restraint as he swallows me with his gaze, drowning me in his desire.

It's my undoing - his fight for control releasing mine as I reach for his pants to quickly unfasten his belt. Taking measures into my own hands, I tug on the button and zipper, pushing his pants and boxers down his legs. I'm desperate to feel him, to have his cock in my hand…my mouth…my pussy. Desperate to have him lose control, to take me. Make me his again.

I lose myself in the glorious sight of him, biting my lip as my needy stare caresses his arousal. His perfection is mouth wateringly inviting, and I can't help stealing a sensual stroke of his shaft.

Growling, he grabs my waist, stepping out of his pants, walking me back towards the bed.

I gasp as he pushes me down on the mattress, it's a breathless thrill as he steals control, and I love it. Crave it.

Wrapping his arm around my hips, he shifts me upwards, coming over top of me, his sheer size taking dominant ownership atop my fragile form. "Fuck, I've missed you, baby."

"Show me," I sigh, spreading my legs wide, feeling his hardness where I need it most.

"I can't wait, baby. I need to be inside you. Now."

"God, yes!" my fingernails abrade his sculpted back, his cock tantalizing my saturated core through a whisper of lace.

Frantically gripping my thong, he tugs hard, tearing it from my trembling body. He groans, grabbing my thigh, wrenching me back into position with nothing between our explosive heat but a desperate sexual burning fire.

"Now, Alex!"

"Fuck, baby…" his husky growl shatters me, his cock sluicing along my wetness, lining up to slide the tip inside.

Oh, God, I moan, quivering as each succulent inch takes me, fills me, deeper and deeper until I'm his. Only his. Always his.

My body bows, arching in the sensation of fullness, completion; my eyes closing in abandon as I settle around his depth. He feels incredible, and my pussy squeezes in hunger for more, desperate for his pounding thrusts.

His patient pause through wanton breaths lures my returned gaze to his; a look of love and longing reflected in his lingering sparkling blue stare. "Alex?"

"I just need to look at you, baby…just let me look at you," he whispers, gliding his fingers along my jaw, brushing his thumb across my lips. "You are so fucking beautiful," his gaze, words lost to me as I'm held hostage in the depth and intensity of his blue eyes, entrances me.

Overcome with happiness to have him in my arms again, inside me again, tears threaten to fall. I feel whole after what feels like a lifetime without him. All of our mistakes - my mistakes, his mistakes - begging to drift away into oblivion. I'm reeling amid the slowly passing storm of regret, desperate to welcome renewed thankfulness. "Alex, I can't…I-I'm so sorry…"

"Shhh, baby. No more words. No regrets," he lulls me, his sweet hushes carrying me through the tempest, attune to my every thought and need. "Let it go, sweetheart. Let it all go," he brushes a wandering tear from my eye, enveloping me in his loving smile. "Nothing will ever tear us apart again." His vow grabs me in its vehemence, and I watch his expression morph into one of sheer will, pulling me in its strong hold.

I believe him. I know without a doubt that everything up to this point has been the culmination of our future, only strengthening our bond, our ability to survive the darkest of storms. I surrender to it all, my breath releasing on a whispered sigh of relief, closing my eyes once more in submission. I'm a slave to my love for him.

Delicious shivers wash through me as he slowly slides his cock out, every hard ridge tantalizing my delicate, sensitive nerves. Moans of pleasure fall from my lips at the sheer decadence of the sensation, before he plunges deeply back inside, eliciting my breathless gasp.

"I love you, Aby. I love you so damn much," he releases on a groan, his thrusts quickening. His plunges are imperious in their ownership, harder and deeper until we're gasping for air. Leaning forward, his perfect lips devour my neck, his succulent kisses setting me ablaze as he reiterates his devotion over and over again, "I love you...I love you..."

"Oh god! I love you!" I scream, careening towards a completion I know will be the biggest, most earth shattering orgasm of my life.

"Come for me, sweetheart. Let me feel you," he whispers, recapturing my gaze, cradling my head in his hands.

I plummet, falling into a heavenly abyss as he watches, bound tightly in the love and serenity of knowing that he's mine. That he'll always be mine. Forever.

"That's it, baby," he murmurs against my lips as I gasp his name, my orgasm rushing through me, my body tensing, riding the wave of pleasure.

His thrusts quicken further, driving deeper and harder as I convulse around him, my pussy hugging his cock, holding it tight in its pulsing grip. Groaning into my neck, he stills, shuddering above me, filling me with his cum; our sweat slickened bodies cradling each other firmly, basking in the glow of our coming together again.

"ANY IDEA WHERE Thomas is whisking you off to yet?" I question Stacey, spreading a dollop of clotted cream over my scone.

"I have plenty of ideas," she mutters over the rim of her coffee cup. "He's been dropping hints like flies, but they're about as subtle as a crafty wench. Which pretty much narrows our destination down to...anywhere. Hence, *lots* of ideas."

"Well, wherever he's taking you, I'm sure it will be dreamy. He's quite the hopeless romantic, isn't he?"

"If by hopeless, you mean incredibly fucking sexy as shit

with rose petals and Barry White. Oh. Yes. He's the God damn pussy whisperer on cupid crack," she bites her lip, eying him across the dining room chatting with Alex.

"He looks good on you," I smile at her loving, captured gaze of him.

"You have *no* idea," she shakes her head, seemingly snapping herself back from some exotic fantasy. "I have many a video that screams, *hell yes*, he does. And I look even better on *him*," she winks.

"Ugh, gross, Stace. TMI. Can you be serious for one minute, *ever*?" I roll my eyes when she shrugs. "I'm really happy for you. You're glowing."

"I should be, he lit me up like a bonfire last…"

"Stop," I raise my hand in protest. "You don't need to hide behind your humor all the time, you know. You're perfect on your own accord, and I love you Mrs. Stevenson-Fines."

Her proud smile is a delight to witness. She truly is happy. We all are. I look towards Alex, feeling my own renewed glow. Last night was incredible. Unbelievable. A brand new beginning for everyone.

"It's too bad you ducked out before catching my bouquet, bitch. You had that in the bag - I was totally gonna throw it your way."

"I know, I'm sorry we didn't let you know before we left, it was just…"

"Clitty Clitty Bang Bang time with his magical dick?"

"Ummm, I hate you."

"You just said you loved me, whore," she shoves me playfully, looking suddenly serious. "I'm happy for you too, Abs," she pauses. "But if you fuck this up one more time, either of you, I will kick your perfect bubble-asses."

"That's a warning I'll take with heed," our gazes dart to Alex, having returned to the table.

"You better," Stacey smirks at him in playful warning. "You're here to take her away now, aren't you?" she adds, taking in his warm affirmative smile before pulling me into a tight hug. "Thank you for everything, baby doll. I have the bestest bestie in the world."

"Are you kidding me," I squeeze her back. "I'm the lucky one. Thank you for having brunch with us," I add, pulling back to look at her.

"I had to," she quips. "For all I know, I'll be eating with the animals, dressed in safari yellow this time tomorrow."

"Quite the Curious George, isn't she," Thomas chimes in, sitting down beside her.

"I look horrible in yellow," she pouts at him. "Just tell me… *please*…" her dramatic plea is laughable.

"You could wear anything, my beautiful queen," he leans in to kiss her, avoiding her desperation to bid farewell to Alex and I. "So good to see you, mate. Let's not leave it too long before getting together again."

"Absolutely," Alex smiles, bending to kiss Stacey's cheek before holding out his hand to me.

Taking it, I stand and give quick kisses of goodbye as he leads me to his side. "Have a wonderful honeymoon," I beam, before turning to walk away with Alex, looking back to add, "I'll talk to you soon," with a blown kiss.

Stacey's warm smile pulls my own, and I exit with a belly full of both delicious breakfast and loving confidence that everything is as it should be. Everyone is happy.

Actually, I'm more than happy. I'm elated. And by the time Alex assists me into the passenger seat of his Aston Martin, my blissful smile is starting to hurt my cheeks. "What's the plan," I turn my ridiculous grin towards him as he sits down beside me.

"Well, I was thinking we could hit my place first, pack up, and then head to yours?"

"Sounds great," my widely curled lips are beginning to feel clownish, and I turn away, pursing them inwards.

"Were you dipping into Mimosas on the side during brunch?" he questions, chuckling.

"Why? Are you hoping to steal my panties and hide them in your pocket all day?" I flirt shamelessly.

"That sounds incredibly inviting," he reaches to pull my lip from its bite. "However, I was merely commenting on your state of mind," he winks.

"I'm just insanely happy."

"Any particular reason for your elation?" his knowing muse makes my smiling lips tingle in delight of memories. He said that very thing so long ago. In the beginning. And the way I feel now, feels just as it did then.

I can't help but close my eyes, leaning my head back into the headrest at the fluttering of my heart, lost to the beautiful idea that with Alex, it may always be this way. The way it's supposed to me. "You're my *more*," I reply on a whisper, enveloped in the perfection of his love.

He takes my hand in his, whisking it to his lips for a kiss, before holding it in place in his lap. "That was quite the tall bill you had, Miss Ryan," he shoots me a glance of his sinful smile. "I'm honored to have finally filled it. Making you happy is the most important thing to me," his tone is suddenly somber, sending a nervous twinge down my spine.

Turning to gauge his expression, I find him glancing back at me thoughtfully, before retuning his gaze to the road. "You're worried about something, what is it?"

"I'm not worried, as much as I am cautiously concerned," his tone echoes the sentiment.

"Semantics, Tate. Spill it."

He takes a deep breath through his nose, his jaw clenching a little before he finally speaks. "How do you feel about seeing Ben?"

"What?" my eyes bug a little, and I shift in my seat to angle a better vantage of him. "What do you mean?"

"Well, I don't believe I've had the chance to tell you," he glances towards me quickly before looking back to the road. "Ben has been released from the rehabilitation facility."

"Yes," I reply taking a breath, "…I know."

"You do?" he glances my way again, his sexy brow arched.

Yeah, I walked in on him and your ex-playmate, but you don't know that yet…"Has he been staying at your flat?" I ask, my stomach sinking as his brow shifts higher.

He doesn't answer right away, and I have to wonder what

he's thinking.

"He *has* been staying with me, since I returned. We've been doing a lot of talking," his eyes remain on the road. "He is still there now," he turns to take in my reaction, though I'm more concerned with his. Wary caution colors his blue eyes, his thumb brushing along my held hand. "How did you know he was released?" he asks between glances to the road, his tone more than curious. He wants answers to a question I stupidly put on the table.

"Well, we haven't talked about why I was ignoring your calls and messages the other night," I look down at my lap, fiddling with my scarf. I feel every glimpse he steals as he concentrates on the road ahead. They're frequent, and I don't need to see them to sense their urge for my continuance. "I stopped by your place the night before the wedding. To talk to you…It was my turn to apologize," I pause, meeting his quick glance, his eyes filled with remorse of his own.

"Baby…"

"I'm sorry, Alex," I interrupt him, needing him to hear the words, to hear their truth. "Everything that happened with Julia…with Andrew. I was wrong…"

"We both were," he lifts my hand to his lips once more, flashing me his loving gaze. "New beginnings," his sweet smile melts me. "I'm sorry I wasn't home when you stopped by. Did you see Ben?" his quick look of compunction breaks my heart, "Is that why you were so upset?"

"Well, not exactly," I purse my lips. "When no one answered the door, I let myself in," I nip at the corner of my mouth. "I heard someone upstairs…a woman's giggles coming from the washroom."

His gaze darts towards me, before shaking his head, looking back to the road, "Ben had company…Well, that would certainly make me head back out the door," he huffs a laugh.

"It didn't," I pause awkwardly, his eyes returning to mine, his stare so long I wonder if we should pull over, "…I assumed it was you."

"*That's* why you were upset?" he throws me an exasperated

grimace. "You thought I was there...with someone else, Aby?"

"Not just someone," I blurt, a little defensively. "*She* came out. Helena came out. Naked."

"*Helena*?" her name spits off his tongue, the car suddenly swerving, shrieking to a halt.

Braced in my seat, I realize we've reached his flat. Thank God for perfect timing. *Or not*, I look towards the front door, remembering Ben just beyond it.

"Ben is sleeping with *Helena*?" it's more of a bewildered statement than a question.

I'm not sure if I'm relieved, or not, that his shock has temporarily washed away my assumption that it was him in the bathroom with Helena. I'm going to go with relieved. I certainly understand his baffled reaction to the awkward situation...Alex, his ex-phone-for-sex friend, and his best friend - former druggie slash girlfriend-hitter-on'er gone straight. It's messed up shit.

Staring at his hands on the wheel, he blows out a mouthful of air before looking towards me, "How do you feel about seeing him? I'm only asking because he wants to apologize. But, sweetheart, if you don't want to hear it, you don't have to. I can go in and make sure he stays out of our way."

I'm not sure what to say. Do I want to see Ben? I'm still lost in what just happened. Where's the gap in his reaction? Where's the frustration that I doubted him? "Alex, I..." my mouth clamps shut, lost for words.

"I get it," he angles in the seat to face me. "If I saw Liam, or Andrew," pausing slightly, his jaw clenches, "...in the same circumstance, I would have thought the worst as well. I think anyone would have, under the circumstances," he shrugs.

"I'm still sorry. I doubted you, Alex. Even though my heart was fighting it, questioning it, I let myself think..." I trail off. *Who am I kidding?* I doubted *myself* for twelve years. Do I really expect to be cured over night? "In the end, I just knew you would never..."

"I know, baby," he cups my cheek, brushing his thumb lovingly along my jaw.

"I told you, I'm a work in progress," I attempt a half-hearted laugh, though it misses the mark.

"*We're* a work in progress remember?" his perfect smile washes everything away once more.

No more looking back. We're starting over.

"You know what? I think I should hear what Ben has to say," I cover Alex's hand at my cheek, leaning in to his caress. Who am I to pass judgment on mistakes, when we're moving past our own?

Flashing me an approving grin, he leans in for a chaste kiss, before getting out to open my door.

The sight of both Ben and Helena when we enter throws me a little off kilter. It's more than awkward. Standing in the foyer, they look towards us with equal surprise. Yup. Awkward.

"I was just leaving," Helena smiles.

"Don't leave on our account," the look Alex gives her is a mixture of intrigue and discomfort. It must feel strange for him with this odd grouping.

"I'm not," she smiles warmly. "I do have to run," she explains, stepping on her tiptoes to give Alex her trademark kiss to both cheeks. "I'm sure you and Ben have some talking to do," her smile is aimed at both Alex and I, though there's a little unease when she looks into my eyes.

"Hey, buddy," Ben smiles at Alex, as Helena passes us to reach for the door.

He and Alex motion towards the sitting room, when I feel the pull to talk to Helena. It doesn't feel right to let her leave, not after I left things up in the air at the reception. I have a few things I need to say. "Ummm…I'll be right back," I smile as Alex turns, his brow arched slightly as I move to follow Helena outside. "Helena, wait," I call after her, closing the door behind me.

She turns with an anxious smile, but stops to meet me half way.

"I just thought I would let you know that I didn't throw you under the bus with Alex."

"I appreciate that, Abigail," she smiles warmly. "I do apologize for my method, but I won't apologize for looking out for my friend - and like I said, that's all Alex is to me…my friend."

"Duly noted. But, as his friend, you should know that Alex abhors people trying to control his life. This is your one get out of jail free card."

"Duly noted," a flash of guilt passes through her soft gaze.

"That being said, I feel I owe you an apology, myself. I said some pretty harsh things, not to mention I was wrong to judge you from the very beginning..."

"You judged me?" she interrupts in surprise. "I'd just assumed you considered me a threat from Alex's past."

His past? Their affair ended the night he met me. I hardly call that the past...*Ugh*. This is not the time to argue over semantics. I think there's enough on the table with my suggestive admission that I considered her a whore - *and* an evil, conniving snake. But let's just leave it at the implied whore part. "Yes, I judged you, wrongfully. I allowed petty jealously and insecurity to taint my opinion of you. And that's truly awful. Please accept my apology."

"How can I not, when you are being so open and honest with me? Thank you, Abigail." Her smile is warm, as always, and I realize there was never any ulterior motive behind it. Nor was there any meaning behind her touchy tentacles - she's reaching out and brushing my arm as we speak. She really is just the touchy feely type.

"Please, call me Aby."

Her smile widens, and she pulls me into a soft hug, kissing both cheeks as she pulls away. "I really do have to run, I'm sorry." She turns away, before glancing back, "Thank you, Aby. Perhaps we can all get together for dinner some time soon, the four of us." And with that she's gone.

I can only assume she means Ben, Alex and I in her total of four. Not exactly a visual I can wrap my head around just yet. Or possibly anytime. That's a *time will have to tell* kinda thing. I shiver a little trying to picture it, shaking it off and heading back inside.

"I don't know if I'd be standing here today if it weren't for Helena, man," I hear Ben from inside the sitting room as I enter.

Closing the door quietly behind me, I can't help but overhear more. I weigh the option of just walking in, but I have the feeling I should let them finish.

"So it's some savior complex? You feel you owe her?"

"No, Jesus, give me a little credit. I care for her, man. I did high, and I do sober. The fact that she was the one that stood by my side though the bitch of a transition just sweetens the pot. No pun intended, man, I swear."

I can almost visualize Ben's playful, dimpled smile, and it pulls at my own. Very interesting since the last time I saw him, he felt more akin to the devil, evoking feelings I never want to experience again.

"Well, then I'm happy for you, Ben. Honestly, man. If you have no problem with my history with Helena, I certainly won't," Alex sounds sincere. "But absolutely no sharing fucking crib notes, shithead."

My hand darts to my lips to squish away a threatening burst of laughter that probably would have been lost in the sounds of their own. It's funny, but so very inappropriately gross.

"So, when *was* it you two met?" Alex asks, his tone suggesting his sorting of the pieces to the puzzle.

Ah, yes, that would have been *that* night. The night Ben took me home. The night it all went to shit for Alex and his best mate. Ben and I had encountered Helena in the lobby of Ashley Fines. "I introduced them," I walk into the room, their attention turning towards me.

"Aby…" Ben begins, but I cut him off.

"It was the night Ben drove me home."

Alex looks up, taking a deep breath through his nose, his jaw clenching as he composes himself in the awkward moment. He and Ben are clearly on a path towards reconciling their friendship, but I'm not surprised to see Alex's inner struggle with getting past this. Under the influence of drugs or not, Ben crossed a serious line.

Ben bites the corner of his mouth, yet surprisingly he appears completely calm and in control. It's almost as though he allowing Alex and I the moment to absorb the reflux. He's had time to do that himself, isn't it part of his recovery?

I move to Alex's side, taking his hand before looking back to Ben, my eyes signaling in silence for him to go ahead.

"Aby," he begins again. "What I did to you, to Alex…no words can excuse it. I abused your trust, and I put you in a position you did not deserve to be in. I was in a bad place - no excuse, I know. I'm truly, truly sorry," he pauses, his gaze flickering between ours, before he continues, "I'm working really hard at starting over. And though I can't lose *this* ass," he gestures towards Alex, his dimples smiling lightly, "…he's not the reason I'm asking for your forgiveness. I'm asking because you deserve my apology. Whether you choose to accept it, or not, will be respected. But either way, Aby, I promise you, I will never ever make you feel the way I made you feel that night."

I don't speak right away, his words working their way through my system, their sincerity felt, though cautiously seeping into my psyche. The one thing I am sure of, though, is how I feel in his presence at this moment. I feel safe. And it's not because I'm sure Ben is no longer a threat. It's not even because I feel protected by Alex. It's because I finally feel like I can trust in myself. See things through clear and confident eyes. As I did just moments ago with Helena.

"You're like a brother to me, man," Ben continues in my silence, bridging the gap between us to hug Alex. It's one of those loving, though uber-masculine man hugs, with backslapping and grunts to swallow emotion. It warms my heart.

When they finally break apart, Ben looks down bashfully, before braving a look into my eyes at Alex's side.

"Alex and I are celebrating new beginnings," I offer a small smile, honest warmth in my gaze, "…I think it would be really nice to include you, shithead."

Breaking out in a huge, dimply grin, his eyes beam as he moves to hug me, almost lifting me off the floor. Releasing me quickly, he stands back with his palms held high in surrender, "Shit, sorry. I got carried away."

"It's okay, I could tell it was a brotherly type hug," I reassure him.

"If it wasn't, I would have kicked his ass," Alex chuckles.

"Yeah, and now we all now that he *can*," Ben mutters, and we all laugh.

CHAPTER
Twenty-two

"HI, HANDSOME."

"Mmmm…there's the voice that's been whispering through my mind all day," the sexy timbre of Alex's accent vibrates down my core.

I juggle to secure my cell phone in the crook of my neck as the sensual attack of his phone call halts me in the middle of the parking lot. "Do tell me, Mr. Tate, what have I been whispering?" I urge him, ironically on a whisper since his words stole my breath.

"How much you're looking forward to me bending you over the minute I walk in the door," he offers in a rough hush.

Oh God. "And," I pause to steal a breath, "…what do *you* say to my day long whisperings?"

"I want you all over me."

Holy mother of pearl. I'm unable to formulate a word, my mouth hanging open, chest heaving. I'm almost panting, over-exerted from my struggle with the overloaded grocery cart, my pulse skyrocketing at the hands of this man's sinful ramblings.

"Sweetheart?" he chuckles, the husky timbre lingering. "What are you doing?"

"Oh, you know, this and that," I finally manage through the barrage of lascivious thoughts burning through me, the cool December breeze blowing my hair like a welcome fan of relief. "Just running errands." *And, apparently, I've been running through his mind all day,* I bite my lip, suddenly startled by a car horn. Looking up, I realize I'm standing in the way of their attempt to park. I offer an apologetic smile, and push my loaded cart ahead towards my spot. "I'm just leaving Ralph's. I've picked up an enough food for an army, by the way," I chuckle, teasing him about his more than healthy appetite in recent weeks.

"Are you implying that *I* eat enough to feed an army?" his playful tone implies bewildered shock.

"Very funny. You know very well that you've been eating us out of house and home."

Since our return to L.A., Alex's astronomical food consumption and workout regime have been off the charts; a necessity for the final scenes he's filming for the movie. Not that I'm complaining. His incredible body was my kryptonite from the very beginning, now, however, he's a mass of steel and mouthwatering sculpted bulk. I've found myself unable to control my urges to constantly touch him, to run my hands over his ever-growing bulging muscles. A fact I've noticed he thoroughly enjoys. "You've eaten more food in the past month than I have in the past six. I can't keep up with your insatiable appetite."

"*You're* the only thing I'm insatiable for, beautiful. Always."

His words - so very, very true - send instant shudders of desire between my legs. "I'm equally insatiable for you, Mr. Tate," I whisper, the memories of this morning's sexual escapade floating absently through my mind - waking up at dawn to his large body curled behind me, his lips nipping and kissing along my shoulder, my moans reverberating through the tranquil silence, the ecstasy as he lifted my leg and slid deep inside, pumping until we succumbed to completion together. *Yes, insatiable.* Always.

In fact, he wasn't the only one filled with sensual thoughts today. "I actually picked up a special *something* today I believe you'll enjoy. I *do* know you love the color red," I tease.

"An early Christmas present, perhaps?" I can sense the sinful smirk behind the husky rasp of his peaked curiosity.

"Mmhmm. A very *sexy* one."

"I'm not the only one with an *alter ego,* my little vixen," he growls through the line, making me wish I could see those sexy curled lips of his. "If I didn't have to finish the day here…" the torture in his voice pulls my own devilish smirk. "You better be wearing it when I get home, baby."

"Oh? And, if I'm not?" I purposely egg him on, dying for a quick taste of *his* alter ego.

"Well, sweetheart, perhaps I'll have to tie you down and show you what happens to vixens that tease."

My grip of the shopping cart tightens at the mental image, desire pulsing through my sex, my thighs squeezing involuntarily to assuage the fire he's created. He can so effectively render me speechless, breathless, with his sexy British brogue, and equally sexy words. I'm a bundle of needy lust as I reach my Land Rover, eyes closed, hands braced on the cart.

"You there, baby?" he chuckles, absolutely hip to what his words do to me.

"Ummm, yes I'm here." *Barely*.

His charming laugh melts me. "I have to get back, sweetheart. Until later?"

"I'll be waiting with bated breaths, " I attempt to tease - though it's absolutely true, and clearly evident in my breathless pants. I disconnect the call at the sound of his continued laughter. *God, what that man does to me.*

PLACING THE LAST of the Christmas presents for Alex under our stunning tree, I sit back and admire the scene; the red and gold ornaments sparkling beneath the sashes of cream and gold ribbon and twinkling lights, a dozen or so gifts wrapped in complementary paper underneath. I've always loved Christmas, anxious to get all my shopping done, wrapped and ready to go; my family's gifts already en route to Canada in time to arrive for the holidays. But I'm particularly elated about the gift I've been waiting weeks for and was able to pick up today - a TAG Heuer Carrera watch, the inside engraving reading '*To my Alexander the Great*'. I just know he'll love it.

"What's all this?"

I startle at Alex having just walked into the living area. Turning on my knees, I flash him a brilliant smile, sighing slightly at his beautiful form. "Hi! You're home early."

"Well, a certain *someone* taunted me with red lingerie. Sadly, I see she's not wearing it," he offers a mock frown.

"Sorry, big guy, I wasn't expecting you yet, and I had gifts to wrap," I display my hand Vana White-style along the many shiny red packages.

"I see that. Hmmm, you've been busy," he kneels down beside me.

"Yes, sir. Very busy," I grin. "How did you manage to sneak away early today?"

"We wrapped up the final scene. Returning tomorrow for a few reshoots, so they called it a day."

"Well, aren't I lucky."

"Hmmm, looks like I'm the lucky one," he looks towards the gifts with teasing curiosity. Reaching for one, I slap his hand away.

"No touching until Christmas, Alex. I mean it."

I laugh as he flashes me his puppy dog eyes and pouty lips. "You realize that will be two whole weeks of torture, having these on full display, taunting me every day to take a peek."

"Yup," I smile conspiratorially.

His playful grin fades after a moment, his beautiful blue eyes lost in thought, and I cock my head in concern. "I feel terrible, I haven't had much time for Christmas shopping," he explains.

"Don't," I shake my head, reassuring him with a smile. "You've been busy trying to wrap up the film. And you can thank me later," I pause, a gleam in my eyes, my smile widening, "...I've already shipped the gifts for your Mom and Dad, Anna and Gerard."

"I love you," he cups my jaw in his hand. The adoration radiating from his gaze takes my breath away. *It always will.*

"I love you too," I whisper, my good deed humbled in the contrasting brilliance of his. I would do anything for him, big or small, simply out of my love for him. But his bashful gratitude is always an unexpected reward that moves me beyond words.

My smitten heart skips a beat as he leans forward to place a gentle kiss on my lips. I sigh in contentment as he pulls away, a charming boyish smile donning his face.

"Thank you," his gaze flickers between my eyes. "For believing in me...for believing in *us*," he says on a wistful breath, his gaze thoughtful.

"Where did that come from?" I'm intrigued by his change from playful to serious about a subject we've seemingly moved past over the last month.

His slow, shy smile pulls my gaze as he rubs his thumb along my jaw. "Must be the sentiment of the season...the holidays," he shrugs, radiating his boyish charm. "If you weren't in my life, I would be alone this Christmas...as I have been many times before."

My heart breaks for the lonely actor in him. He's spoken many times about how isolating his career can be. Most often away from family and life-long friends as he moves from one role to the next, making acquaintances, forming new relationships that drift apart naturally through passing time, new films, new locations.

"I'm just so thankful that you're here, with me," he reaches up to brush a loose strand of hair from my ponytail off my forehead, the pulse in his jaw alluding to his deep thought, before he looks into my eyes. "I've been thinking about all we've been through. The times we almost lost each other. I know you were scared, and I know I've done and said a lot of stupid things..."

"We both have."

He nods, somewhat reluctantly, wanting to take the blame for both of us. A gentleman to the bitter end. "We've had to endure and muddle through a lot of things. But you're *it* for me, Aby. I hope you know that."

I draw in a breath at his words, emotion welling in my eyes as the accuracy of them hit home. He's right. We could have lost each other. When I left. When he left. Our pull, our connection never letting us go, despite the struggles we were facing. And for that I'm so grateful.

Forcing the tears to remain at bay, I run my fingers along

the curve of his jaw, along his lips, "I do know that, Alex. And we *have* been through a lot, you're right. But I do believe it's made us stronger. We can get through anything. You're my tall bill come true, remember?"

He flashes a smile that I'm delighted to see, its corners quickly twisting into his sexy smirk as he reaches to pull me into his arms. "I *do* so very much enjoy those prerequisites of yours, Miss Ryan. Prepare to be *worshipped*, sweetheart. Right. Now," he whispers in my ear, taking me in a ferocious kiss that metaphorically brings me to my knees.

"DOES THIS LOOK okay?" I turn from the mirror to face Alex, adjusting the grey sash around the waist of my light grey peplum-style dress.

"*Okay*? You're stunning. And those heels," he simpers, walking towards me. Reaching me, his hands admire the curves the dress exaggerates. "I'm not sure I want to share you this evening," his husky whisper is sinful. "For some reason I have the hardest time wrapping my head around leaving the house," he leans down to kiss my neck.

"Mmmm…yes," I manage through his teasing onslaught, "I seem to remember the last event we attended started in a similar fashion."

"Will it *end* in a similar fashion?" I can feel his smirk against my flesh.

"Alex," I bite my lip, the visual of riding him in his ostentatious car squeezing through my core. "Don't we actually have to *start* the evening before we discuss how it may or may not end? *Behave*," I swat him away.

He flashes a playful, though ridiculously sexy pout.

"Alex, be serious."

"Oh, I'm very serious," he wiggles his brow.

Shaking my head, I try to stifle a laugh. "*Seriously*, I wasn't sure what attire was appropriate for a wrap-up party. Am I overdressed?"

Laughing, he gives my bottom a light slap, "You're perfect, sweetheart. You look exquisite. I'll have to keep my eye on you all damn night, I'll be beating the men away."

"Funny guy," I push against his chest. "I'm just not used to these types of events yet. They still make me nervous," I admit shyly, turning back to the mirror for one final look.

Gently running his hands up and down along my bare arms, his gaze finds mine in our reflection. "I know, baby, but you'll do great. You always do," he reassures me, bringing a smile to my lips. "You're so tall in these heels. *Damn*," he drawls, swiping my hair to the side to kiss along my shoulder.

"Alex, you need to stop. You made us late for the last publicity event. It's *not* happening again, buster."

Growling, he turns to make his way to his closet, returning in a white dress shirt, still hanging open. *Damn him.* Whether he's purposely playing me with this delicious teasing visual or not, I can't resist taking in the show. I relish in the simple task of the fastening of each button, kicking my inner actress to life in hopes of hiding the pout threatening to emerge as his glorious chest, defined abs, and mouthwatering happy trail disappear. He smiles at me playfully, tucking his shirt into his dark blue jeans.

He looks simply divine. Sex on a stick, in fact...*With the face of an angel.*

"See something you like, sweetheart?" his lips curl into that sexy smirk. "Perhaps it's *you* who'd like to delay our departure this time. I can undress again if you'd like," he motions to unbutton his shirt.

I rush towards him, halting the workings of his fingers. "Don't you dare, Alex," I laugh at his teasing, wrapping my arms around his waist. "You're an insatiable devil, Mr. Tate."

"And *you* are my angel."

THE EVENING HAS been...interesting, to say the least. I've had a good time, no question, but I haven't really seen Alex in ages. As a matter of fact, the last time I spotted him, a couple of leggy blondes were giving new meaning to the party's theme as they *wrapped* him up in their attention, their eyes devouring him amid flirty giggles. I stayed calm and shot imaginary daggers their way, feeling almost sympathetic towards Alex - *almost*. He handles the unwanted attention so well that I'd be absolutely lying if I said the ugly shame of self-doubt didn't rear her big, fat head. I'm human. Those two blondes, however…I'm thinking they hail from *Paradise Island*, perhaps. They're not human. They're Wonder Whores.

It's not like Alex to leave me to fend for myself for such a lengthy period of time. But I get it. This isn't like the publicity event, where he dangled me on his arm making the polite rounds. This is a party. A party full of co-stars and film crew celebrating months of hard work. He's enjoying himself, and he doesn't need me at his side for every minute of it.

He could be in any one of the many rooms full of guests, all mingling on the first floor of the directors stunning, supersized home. And that's okay, I'm doing fine on my own. Yes, I *was* slightly star-struck when we first arrived, the mass of celebrities present enough to give anyone heart palpitations, but it faded quickly. They're all just 'regular' people enjoying a night of 'normal' fun.

"Are you enjoying yourself, Aby?" Tracy Lynn, Alex's love interest in the film, jars me from my avid searching through the crowd.

"Ummm, I am, thank you," I smile. "Have you seen Alex?"

"I think he's…" she quickly scans the room, trying to place where she saw him last. "Oh, no, he's not there anymore. He's a popular man," she nudges me. "The *star* and all," she winks playfully, her striking espresso brown eyes glistening. She truly is a beautiful woman, and I secretly simper at the thought of Alex having to kiss her, even if it was only make-believe. But she's simply too nice to fake-hate for swapping spit with my incredibly amazing boyfriend. She's down-to-earth, sweet, and fun.

"Did you know that Alex has a small shrine for you in his trailer? Or should I say, *had*," she screws her face up in jest, "The movie's wrapped, no more trailer," she shrugs on a silly laugh.

Yes, she's adorably sweet, but my mind kind of exploded at 'small shrine'. *What?*

She laughs, and I quickly pick my lip up off the floor, though no words are formulating to give her a response. I'm gob smacked, trying to imagine what pictures he would have had on display.

"The crew nicknamed him 'Mr. Smitten'," she winks, her playful smirk progressing into a sweet smile. "You two are obviously very much in love. Lucky you," she holds my arm, the warm gesture making me like her even more. "My hubby is very well aware that I think Alex is one of the most beautiful men I've ever seen, so you'll have to forgive me the numerous interviews I've given in which I blabber on about that endlessly. He's so pretty, it's sinful."

Oh, you have no idea - my inner dreamer swoons.

"Anyway, he had a picture of you in his trailer - a stunning picture, by the way - and when we saw that he added a few more, the crew clipped out media shots of the two of you - anything they could find - and taped them up with the others in his trailer. Oh, my," she swoons, "…the way he would blush with affection," she squeezes my arm. "Mr. Smitten."

Holy crow. "I…" I don't even know what to say, my mouth opening and closing like a guppy.

Tracy laughs again, her gaze suddenly leaving mine, flashing over my shoulder.

"Ladies," Alex's sexy British brogue wafts deliciously from behind me, his hand absently sliding along my waist. My mind goes blank for a moment, the sound of his voice opening a cage of lusty butterflies in my stomach.

"Hey, Mr. Smitten," Tracy winks at me, giggling.

"Oh, no," Alex's laughter is divine.

I can't help turning my head to take in the heart melting moment, his head tilting back, his beautiful wide grin pulling mine in equal measure. A jovial Alex could pull a smile from the devil.

"Yup, I've spilled the beans, Tate," Tracy smiles like a giddy cheerleader.

"What other gibberish have you been spilling to my beautiful girl here," he smiles down at me.

It doesn't escape me that I've yet to manage a word in the past several minutes, but those baby-blues staring down at me just stole my voice once more.

"*Mrs.* Smitten," Tracy laughs, nudging me, my gaze darting towards her at the sentiment. My heart skips a beat at the entire notion of the title. "Oh and there's *my* guy," Tracy adds, noting her husband across the room. "I'll catch you two later," she pauses to squeeze my hand with a friendly smile, heading off as we say goodbye.

"She is *so* nice," I share aloud, watching her walk away.

Alex wraps my waist in his arms, squeezing me back against him. "She's very sweet, and a wonderful actress," he agrees genuinely, leaning into my ear, slight preoccupation in his tone, "I especially liked the sound of something she mentioned."

"Oh? What's that?" I can finally speak, though it's barely a whisper. *What comment,* exactly*, is he referring to?* I bite my lip, my inner dreamer shaking her pom poms, chanting, "M. R. S."

"Alex, my man."

Our heads turn to find John, the director, approaching, cupping Alex's shoulder in a friendly, masculine gesture.

"Can I borrow him for a moment, Aby? There's someone I have to introduce you to, Alex, one of my buddies from Toronto. Hey, you're from Toronto, aren't you Aby?" I smile and nod as he quickly continues, "I'll bring him right back to you, I promise." He moves to lead Alex away, Alex turning to flash me an apologetic, though brilliant smile.

I stare at his long retreated form, basking in the awe of him. *He had pictures of me in his trailer?* How sweet is that? My heart does a summersault and the pulse it uncontrollably sends down my core jars me back to the present. *Well. What now?* I look around, puckering my lips before I spy a waiter across the room holding a tray of hor d'oeurves. *Food works.*

I make my way towards him, grabbing a new glass of wine from another waiter as I pass. I've lost count of how many I've had, but the fact that I'm wondering may mean I should sip this one slowly. The combination of the effect on my inhibitions at

the hands of my consumption, mixed with *Mr. Smitten* himself…
Very, very, dangerous.

Popping the little treat into my mouth, I moan at the delicious taste, sucking the residue from my fingertip before licking my lip. I have no idea what it was, but *damn* is it yummy. *Shoot, he's gone*, I glance around for the same waiter, pouting before giving up and taking a sip of wine. Tucking my clutch under my arm, I clasp my hand across my chest, scouting the room for what to do next. I'm trying to look casual, without looking like a dumbass in the corner. Whether it's working, I have no idea.

Feeling a little vibration from my purse, I tilt my head towards it, catching the very faint chirp of my cell from inside. Juggling my wine glass, I fumble to get it out. It's a text…from *Alex*? *What?*

> Subject: Now
>
> Meet me in the hall off the kitchen. Turn right as you pass the media room. If you suck your finger into that pretty mouth of yours one more time, I may just have to take you right here.

My head darts up, searching the room for him. *Oh God*. I look back to my phone, taking in his closing…

Mr. VERY Smitten

Oh good God, my chest heaves with pants of instant desire. Where the hell is the kitchen?

I make my way to the next room, through yet another, and another, before finally reaching the large gourmet kitchen at the back of the ridiculously large house. It's empty, the island cluttered with empty food trays. One end of the room opens to what must be a family room - *or media room*? I don't know where the hell I'm going. Moving past the large leather sectional, I gasp as someone grabs my hand, yanking me into a hallway.

"Mmmm, there you are," Alex murmurs, leaning casually against the wall, pure lust exploding from his sparkling blue eyes. He looks absolutely sinful standing there watching me, his finger leaving my hand to trail deliciously up my bare arm. My mind couldn't find a word if I tried. "Come," he licks his bottom lip, taking a step back, and opening a door behind us.

In a trance, I follow him into...*the powder room*? It's bigger and incredibly more elaborate than any I've ever seen. Catching our reflection in the mirror, the sight of his gaze working it's way up my body sends the inhibitions that were lying in wait rocketing to life.

"Did you intend to take advantage of me in this ostentatious bathroom, Mr. Tate?" I inquire suggestively, turning slightly to rest my thigh along the large granite countertop, purposely exposing a bit of flesh from beneath the skirt of my dress.

"Perhaps I did," he smiles, taking a predatory step towards me. "Any reservations?" He reaches for me, lifting me further onto the counter before sliding his hands up my thighs to raise my dress, stepping between the widening spread of my legs.

"None," I manage on a moan, his hardness brushing my core, his lips placing succulent kisses along my neck that send shivers down my spine.

"Good answer," he whispers at my ear, taking my hand in his, placing it at his manhood, his clear indication that he wants me to take control.

This Adonis of a man is *mine*. The lusty power that reminder scores through me is carnal. It unleashes me.

I waste no time undoing his pants, his needy stare burning into mine as I slide my hand inside, gripping his smooth cock in my palm, giving it a gentle pull. His guttural groan through parted lips lights my ardor as I reveal his impressive hardness to my gaze, the glistening pre cum donning the tip.

Gripping my thighs firmly, he lifts my ass, shoving the restricting skirt of my dress out of the way.

God, I moan in anticipation, leaning back, desperate to feel him inside me, resting my hands on the cold granite - an eager, wanting participant in our erotic escapade.

Swiping his fingers along my core through my soaked thong, his eyes take possession of mine. The unadulterated sensuality is his gaze has me sucking in air. "Alex," I manage on a whisper of need, arching my pelvis towards him.

"Is this what you want, baby," he takes his cock in hand, rubbing it along my core. "You want me inside you?"

"God, yes," I moan, my head falling back against the mirror, eyes closed in abandon.

My body shudders as he slides my thong to the side, his hardness sluicing through my wetness before slowly, so very slowly, inching inside me. I can feel every ripple, every hardened edge hitting my sensitive nerves, my legs quivering in anticipation of his fill.

He grabs my legs, plunging deep, hitting the very edge of me. I release a small scream at the fullness, the sheer decadence of having him inside me. Here. Now. It feels naughty.

Holding my legs in the crook of his arms, he leans forward, placing a gentle kiss on my lips. "Shhh, sweetheart. You need to keep quiet," he whispers against my mouth.

"Oh, God, Alex…I can't," I manage, my body undulating towards his steady thrusts.

"You can, and you will," he leans back with a sinful smile, placing his hand over my mouth, shielding my cries of pleasure.

His thrusts quicken, plunging deep inside my pulsing core over and over again until my head starts spinning, iridescent spots of color invading my psyche. My orgasm looms, threatening to throw me head first over the edge of ultimate pleasure. I bite my lip to hold back my mewls.

"Open your eyes, Aby," Alex's voice barrels through my euphoria.

Lifting my head, my eyes open to his blue gaze, heavy with lust, his perfect full lips parted, breaths coming in quick pants through his pounding thrusts.

"I love you," he mutters, his steel blue eyes holding me hostage, my eyes echoing his words as I fall, plummeting into oblivion.

CHAPTER
Twenty-three

"WHERE ARE YOU taking me?" I giggle, grabbing a tighter hold of Alex's arm, fighting the urge to reach up and pull the blindfold away.

"We're almost there." There's a cute excitement in his voice that sends butterflies shooting through my tummy, exhilaration coursing through my veins. "I've got you," he reassures me as I stumble, a small squeak escaping my lips. Instinctively, I reach out, clasping his fingers tightly in my grip. "You're okay," he chuckles, securing his arm around my waist to guide me.

My heels don't seem to agree with the sudden change in the ground texture. It's uneven, and full of some kind of debris, and I maneuver with measured steps. Taking a deep breath, I inhale the air around me, my senses heightened by my restricted vision, the scent of the outdoors permeating my psyche.

Finally coming to a stop, he releases my death grip, slowly turning me in place. I feel like a mannequin in the movement, excited, but stiff as a board - a rather unpliable combination. "I'm going to sit you down," he warns, guiding me.

My body responds just as awkwardly, following his lead with caution. It's not easy moving to a sitting position when it feels as though you're bending to place your bum down on air. Only it's not air, it's a cushion. A very soft, plush cushion.

"Okay," I hear him say, feeling him sit beside me, "…you can remove the blindfold now."

I'm more than eager to comply. Pulling it off swiftly, I look straight ahead, my eyes adjusting, slowly taking in the scenery around us. I gasp as the beautiful scene comes into focus, bright twinkling lights illuminating the night sky above and before us. Tears build instantly, threatening to blur my already hazy gaze.

Alex says nothing, sitting idly by as I absorb our surroundings. The trail he just walked me up - its floor lined with mulch and twigs that contributed to its shaky journey - is draped from either side with more strings of lights than I've ever seen. *No, that's not true*...I've seen the likes of this magical fairytale image before - in the picture on my childhood vision board. My breath lodges in my throat, realizing my silly picture pales in comparison to the magnificence before me. The reality of it is simply stunning.

His perfect smile pulls my gaze, and I turn to look at him, my mouth agape. "How did you do this?" I whisper in awe.

"I have a few friends in the staging department," he squeezes my hand, and it's only then that I remember we're seated.

Looking down, I'm taken aback by the quirky loveseat in stripes of brown and tan. A floor lamp you would swear came right from the set of *Friends* stands to the right of the settee, its dim light but a whisper among the twinkling glow above us, trailing all the way down the magical path ahead. It's truly breathtaking.

"Alex, this is…" words escape me as my gaze takes it all in, returning to his with tears in my eyes. "It's beautiful," I sigh.

"Not as beautiful as you," he takes my face in his hands, his perfect words dancing across my lips as he takes me in a soft, sensual kiss.

"No one has ever done anything like this for me," I mumble, breathless against the warmth of his lingering lips, my hands curling around his neck to hug him.

His strong arms embrace me in return, and I lose myself in this amazing man before opening my eyes once more to bask in the beautifully lit scenery, secured in his loving hold.

Softly lit candles burn in glass votives gathered in a cluster on the ground beside the loveseat. My gaze follows the line of candles, momentarily cataloguing their placement. Adjusting in his arms, I turn, finding them on the other side as well, lining the floor around the base of the lamp, leading a new trail behind us.

I can't help but shake my head at how far he's gone to pull off the most romantic night of my life. "You thought of everything," I look back into his stunning blue eyes, before turning to look behind us, the trail of votive candles leading my gaze to a sight that steals the remaining air from my lungs.

"I was going for *iconic*," his humble whisper blasts through the silence of my gasp, as I stare, frozen in place, at the sign to which he's referring.

Every individual letter is lit from within its casing, a perfect replica of the Hollywood insignia. The only difference being its staggering phrase…MARRY ME?

Oh my God. My breaths return in a desperate pant, struggling to refill my lungs, my heart pounding through an explosion of excitement and shock.

"The first time I saw you, my heart whispered *she's the one*," his words pull my euphoric gaze to find him on his knee before me, my hand still held in his. "I knew from the very beginning that I wanted to be the man that makes you fall to your knees by whispering in your ear, the man you build a life with. I wanted to be the one that worships you, makes you feel desired…leaves you trembling in yearning."

My mouth drops open on a gasping breath at the realization of what's happening.

"You are more than just everything I need in this moment," he reaches for the inside pocket of his suit jacket, pulling out a velvet box, his beautiful blue eyes never leaving mine. "You are everything I have ever wanted…all I could ever dream of. You are *my* more, Abigail Dawn Ryan," he releases my hand to open the delicate jewelry box, revealing a sparkling pear shaped yellow diamond, the size of which I've never seen.

My hand darts to my trembling lips, tears streaking down my cheeks, my lips parted in awe as I struggle to breathe. Looking back into his eyes, the love I see reflected there shatters me.

"You are my beginning, my end, my everything. And I want

to spend forever enjoying all that will come in between. It's always been you, Aby. It will always *be* you." Removing the ring, he lays the box down to hold my left hand in his, his gaze worshipping me with his love, leaving me trembling in yearning as he whispers, "Will you do me the honor of marrying me?"

The words leave my lips without thought or hesitation, "Yes, yes I'll marry you." My hand trembles as he slips the beautiful ring on my finger.

Taking his perfect face in my hands, I lean down to kiss his equally perfect lips, feeling his smile against my mouth. I'm so overcome with elation, surprise, love, I can't slow my thoughts down, replaying over and over our journey, this moment, our futures. It's an overwhelming, yet incredibly decadent thought. *My future with Alex.* It's in that moment that I realize that everything I've done, everything I am, has led me to him.

"I love you, Aby," he whispers against my lips.

Pulling back, his face cupped in my palms, I stare back at him in awe. Awe that he's mine. That he'll forever be mine. "I love you so much," I manage through tears of joy, swiping my thumb along his plump bottom lip as he kisses the tip. "You *are* my tall bill, Alex. My *more*. I never thought I'd actually find you…that you even existed. I'm not sure how I got so lucky," I smile, rewarded by his humble, shy grin in return.

"And I don't know why I was the lucky guy that caught you that night," he flashes his charming smile, taking my hands in his lap. "I usually don't give much credence to fate, but finding you certainly makes me question its existence. What I *do* know, though, is that whether or not meeting you was destiny, falling in love with you was beyond my control," he leans in, lingering at my lips for just a moment before claiming them.

"We found *each other*," I smile against his lips. "And in this journey that led me to you, I also found myself," I pull back to look into his eyes. "I needed to do that. I had to be mine, before I could be anyone else's."

"And I promise to never let you forget who you are."

IT'S MID-MORNING ON a beautiful Friday in January, our fifth day back in London, and I feel…as though life couldn't get any better.

It's hard to imagine that I virtually walked into my ultimate fantasy - all on a whim of living my dream. An unfathomable desire for something *more*.

And Alexander Tate is *my more*.

Throughout the past six months, my mad and irrevocable love for Alex has been a prominent emotion that regularly incapacitates my days. I wake up every morning not from a dream, but *to* a dream - feeling blessed that he's mine. Feeling loved, and loving wholeheartedly in return.

Feigning a smile against the warm breeze from the large open windows of The Little Square - my favorite café - I continue to admire the sense of individuality the setting exudes - a trait I've recently uncovered within myself, and have made great strides in order to achieve…my *own* individuality.

The warm summer breeze caresses my face as I sit back and relax, awaiting my much-loved coffee. Staring out onto Shepherd Market, filled with passersby, I feel a sense of peace knowing that the many months spent dissecting and reflecting on my life altering changes have long washed away.

And now I'm getting married, having fallen in love with the man of my dreams - who *truly* does exist, by the way. *Thank God for dreams* - my inner dreamer stands up and takes a bow.

I used to question my dreams for *more* - feeling selfish in my desire for the perfect life, never quite understanding why I was so unsatisfied with the one I had. But I've come to learn that it was never a *perfect* life that I wanted, craved. It was a happy one. I've learned many things along the way. I've learned that the grass isn't always greener, but it's not about that. It's about making it work when it's the right fit. A perfect love is just two imperfect people who refuse to give up on each other.

I realize that most people would say I'm crazy - crazy for

our whirlwind romance, seemingly right out of a dreamy novel. But I no longer question my own sanity. The only thing crazy is how I feel about the man I'm going to spend the rest of my life with.

So here I sit, thirty years old, carefree and…perfectly happy, *madly* in love - a world away from my past, looking forward to walking head first into my future.

Pulled from my wayward thoughts, I notice an older couple sitting at a nearby table, all smiles and laughter, the occasional shared heated look. I smile inwardly, realizing that's exactly what I was searching for. What I've *found*. The one person who gives me tingles with just one look. The man I've always dreamed I'd end up with. The man with whom I can finally be *me*. The real me. No more pretending.

I pick up my double-double coffee and give myself a private salute.

A salute to dreams.

A salute to romance and inspiration and excitement.

A salute to endless love.

I vow to enjoy the present, look forward to the future, and live this new life to the fullest. It took me a long time to find it, it'd be a shame to waste even one second.

With that, my cell phone chimes, signaling a text from Stacey.

Subject: House hunting SUCKS

Have I told you today how much I HATE our real estate agent? I'm no gynecologist, but I sure know a cunt when I see one. If she shows me one more shoebox that needs "loving care" I'm gonna have a stroke. Call you tonight, my little twat waffle.

Stace xx

I can't help but smile at the changes we've all been through… though some things never change. Like my feisty friend's trucker-mouth theatrics. *I love my best friend*, I shake my head on a laugh.

"I'll never tire of seeing that beautiful smile on your face."

Looking up, I find Alex staring at me from the doorway, instant butterflies fluttering at the sight of him, as always. *I love the idea that he'll always make me feel this way.*

"Are you just going to stand there and ogle, or are you going to come over here and kiss me," I ask cheekily.

"As you wish," he smiles, it's perfection something *I* will never tire of it either.

I stand to meet him, though it was an unconscious move, possibly my body's eager need to be claimed in his kiss. His perfect kiss. *How does he always make it feel like the first?*

"Ready?" he pulls back to look into my eyes.

"That depends," I bat my lashes, "…where are you taking me?"

"Anywhere…Everywhere," he smiles. "You in?"

For you, Mr. Tate? Always, I nod, taking his hand with a beaming smile. A smile brighter than the sun…sweeter than fiction.

EPILOGUE

Alex

"LISTEN, SHIT HEAD, stop your damn pacing or I'll make you," Ben spews from his place in front of the mirror, absently styling his already styled hair.

"Fuck off," I reply, fiddling with my tie, aimlessly pacing back and forth, wearing thin the Persian rug-covered floors of the church chamber room.

Time is dragging, every minute passing painfully slower and slower. *Fuck*, I gnaw at the corner of my mouth. Aby Ryan is *mine*, and it's killing me to have to wait to slip that ring on her perfect little finger, sealing the deal for all time. That symbol that represents everything she means to me - everything I am for her, because of her - is so much more than the chunk of gold it was created from - is worth so much more in my heart than the diamonds adorning it.

"You do have the ring, right?" panic bites through my words, my feet frozen in place waiting for the relief of his reply.

"What ring?" Ben smirks.

"You're an asshole," I clench my jaw, continuing my restless jaunt around the room, her perfect smile, beautiful lips calling to me…to make her mine. To finally call her my wife. *My wife*. The thought sends intense emotions coursing through my veins. Elation. Possession. Completion. Love.

"Seriously, man, you need to calm the fuck down," he calls over his shoulder, returned to his reflection, adjusting his tie.

"You getting cold feet, fucknuts?" he turns to face me, his typical sarcastic expression contorting to genuine concern. *Misguided concern.*

"Don't be daft, dick. I'm dying here. The wait is killing me. I want to marry Aby. Right. Now."

"Fuck," Ben chuckles. "That's a relief. I hadn't anticipated having to break you out of here. I wouldn't know where to start," he adds, looking around for some kind of inconspicuous escape.

"Very funny." I make my way to the settee in the corner. "What time is it?" I ask, despite staring at my watch - the watch Aby gave me. *To my Alexander the Great*…If she only knew how much having her in my life made me feel just that.

"It's about quarter past my ass," he snickers. "Dude, I'm going to need reinforcements if you don't snap the fuck out of it."

I can't resist my long, drawn out sigh of frustration. Fifteen more agonizing minutes. *What's fifteen more minutes when I've waited a lifetime for her?* I've managed to make it through a full year since bending before her on my knee. Twelve long months since the day I proposed - Aby's adamancy that we prove 'them all wrong' with a lengthy engagement merely solidifying our love for each other, the rightness of *us*. *I can get through another fifteen minutes, right?*

Fuck me, I ring the back of my neck, pulling and stretching to work the kinks out.

"Wow, buddy, you've got it bad," Ben chuckles, jarring me back to real time - where moments slow further.

"If by that you mean I'm madly in love with her, then hell yes. She's my whole fucking world and everything in it."

"I'm happy for you, man, I really am. But all this gooey romance shit you're sprouting is pinching my last manly nerve. You're hooked, shithead. She has you fucking hooked. Wrapped around her little finger."

Bound to her…"Admittedly," the reminder pulls my smile, "And I love every minute of it."

"Knock, knock," Mo enters, closing the door behind him. "Almost ready?"

"Almost?" Ben quips, his sarcastic tone of old returned full force. "The man is damn near out of his mind ready."

Smiling down at me, Mo winks, reaching into in his pocket to pull out three cigars. "Perhaps a stogy will calm you down, my friend."

"Brilliant idea," Ben mutters, quickly making his way to join Mo at the door.

"Not now, Ben," I halt his process, eliciting his annoyed stare. "I don't want to smell like a cigar when I kiss my bride. But thank you for the thought," I smile at Mo.

"My pleasure, buddy. You ready for this?" he asks, sitting down beside me.

"More than you know. I feel like I've been ready forever - waited forever - for Aby."

"It was fate. Cupid's arrow," Ben swoons dramatically, dangling his hand through the air. "Cupid's arrow, my ass," he snorts, "more like your dick licking her ass when she fell into your lap."

My best friend is a dorky dickhead, I lean my elbows on my wide spread knees, looking down to the floor, shaking my head.

"That wasn't fate, brother, he made that shit happen," Mo pulls my gaze to his knowing grin.

"He didn't make her fall into his lap, *dick*," Ben retorts, his face twisted as though he's actually weighing the thought.

"No, but the minute she did, I knew I had to make her mine." Our connection was instant, and I can't help but smile remembering her nervous ramblings that night. So confident about she wanted, yet so real with naïve self-doubt. *Real*. My perfect reality.

"She's a good girl, Alex, my man. And it was clear from the first time I met her that she has it equally bad for you. That night at the Imagine Dragons' concert, the way she was looking at you…Man," he shakes his head. "I'm elated for you both," he slaps my knee, moving to stand.

"Come *on-n*! Don't encourage him. He's turning into a fucking chick - a blubbering, ass-whooped Romeo."

"You're one to talk," Mo pipes in, "I'm fairly certain I heard you babbling sonnets for the lovely Helena earlier."

Flipping us the bird amid our laughter at his expense, Ben

resumes my previous pacing of the room, Mo giving him a play-ful shove.

This feels good, I take in my two best friends, our incessant meanderings never waning, regardless of the venue and monu-mental event about to take place. Life doesn't get much better than this.

"Okay boys, time to make our way out," Mo warns, looking at his watch.

Hell yeah. "Let's do this," I rub my eager hands together, joining them at the door, the word *mine* carrying me through each step.

SHIT, MY HEART is threatening to burst through my chest at the introduction of the bridal march, my eyes glued to the double doors at the end of the aisle. It isn't nerves, it's fucking excite-ment. *Yearning.* And when she comes into view, it threatens to burn me alive.

Stunning doesn't begin to describe Aby in this moment. There are no words.

Her gorgeous brown curls are piled high atop her head, loose tendrils sweeping beneath the angelic veil draping down her back. I could never have prepared myself for the vision of her - her blue-gray eyes glistening, holding me hostage, her beautiful smile meant only for me. She takes my breath away.

She pauses there, in the doorway on her father's arm, her love radiating in her gaze towards me in the distance between us. My perfect love, calling to me in it's unspoken depth, every cell of my being fighting to run towards it, to claim it - knowing it's walking my way, the only thing holding me in place.

The need to devour the length of her pulls my gaze, my eyes begging to take her all in as she walks on the arm of her father up the aisle. Her dress is mind-blowing, the strapless lace top framing her chest in the shape of a heart - romantic, fitting and incredibly sexy. The full, flowing skirt accents her tiny waist to perfection. She looks like a fucking angel. *My angel.*

Reaching me, she steals my breath once more, a loose curl hanging along her perfect neck triggering an itch to just lean down and place a gentle kiss on the soft flesh. Time stands still as I lose myself in her beautiful face, the world around us melting away to nothing but my undying love.

She smiles wide as I take her hand, gently squeezing it as we turn to face the altar - in body only, since I can't tear my eyes away from the angel at my side.

Words blur - heard, though fleeting in comparison to her strong hold of my heart - before her vows steal, capture, what I will remember for all time, "…to honor and respect you, to laugh with you and cry with you, and to cherish you for as long as we both shall live."

I hang on her every word, overcome with emotion from the sincere purity of her love - love that steels the composure of my own overwhelming, recital of our vows. Every word, every promise I return, meaning more than I ever thought possible as I stare down into the face of the woman I love more than life itself.

I love you, I mouth, wiping a fallen tear from her cheek.

Anything and everything around us is nothing but a hushed whisper - the only thing that matters standing before me, her gentle smile, her eyes gleaming with so much elation it leaves me bewildered that she's mine.

Mine…even before I hear the words of declaration, "I now pronounce you man and wife. You may kiss your bride."

He doesn't need to tell me twice.

Cupping Aby's perfect face in my palms, I lean down placing the most heartfelt of kisses to her lips, trying my damnedest to convey the sheer magnitude of my love and devotion to her among the whispered cheers of the crowd. I feel the pull of her beautiful smile against my lips as the kiss extends a little longer than it should.

"I love you," she whispers as I pull away.

"I love you more."

"HOW DO YOU feel, Mrs. Tate?" I brace my hand on the back wall of the elevator, pinning my beautiful bride, stealing a caress of her cheek.

"Mmmm, perfect," her breathless reply slithers down my groin, my dick twitching at the perfection of her.

"*You're* perfect, sweetheart," I reply, meaning every word.

She laughs and the sound sends a second strike to my raging erection. I've waited hours to get her alone - hours to make love to my *wife* - each agonizing minute closer to *taking* her sending my ardor careening higher. I feel like a randy fifteen year old, unable to keep his dick in his pants from the excitement of using it for the first time. That's how she makes me feel. How she's *always* made me feel. I can't get enough of her.

"Fuck, I love you," the words escape amid my attack of her perfect mouth.

The memory of our first kiss - the intense rush of need to make her mine right there in the elevator of this very hotel - floats through the euphoric dance of our lips and tongues. It was in that moment, my lips touching hers for the first time, that I finally knew the taste of happiness. I *felt* it. And my need for her now - right here, in *this* moment - supersedes my wildest dreams. She makes me feel like tomorrow is more than just another day. And each and every day, I fall further and further under her spell.

Coming to a stop on our floor, the elevator signals the opening of its doors, our kiss unbroken as I pull her out into the hallway. The only thing allowing the pull of my lips from hers is my dire, desperate need to get her to the suite. Our *honeymoon* suite. The entire notion hits me hard with longing, possession…love.

Quick, needy strides lead us down the hallway, our hands linked eagerly with anticipation. Stopping at the door, I wrap her in my arms, pulling her flush against me, leaning my back on the wall.

Mesmerized, I watch her lips part on a breathless gasp, her cheeks instantly blushing, hands gliding up my chest to rest on my shoulders. She loves it when I lose control, showcasing my desire for her, my *need* for her.

Her blue-gray eyes stare back at me, the ever-raging fire and passion we can't seem to distinguish pouring from her gaze.

"It's indescribable how breathtaking you are, Aby," I whisper, swiping my finger along her delicate jaw. "I need you *now*," I lean down to kiss her lips, "…forever. Always," I continue amid swipes of my tongue, her avid surrender swelling my male pride.

Opening the door, I pull her inside, our lips crashing before the closing of the door behind us. She gasps as I release her, spinning her in place to unfasten her beautiful dress, my eyes begging the quickening of my measures, desperate to see her, my hands desperate to feel every bare inch.

She turns to face me, her perfect bottom lip bitten between her teeth as she allows the strapless gown to fall to the floor, pooling at her feet. *Fuck*. The visual is jaw dropping. And I take my time devouring her from the bottom up.

The sexiest white stiletto heels, long, mouthwatering legs wrapped in stockings, held sinfully by the clips of her garter… my dick threatens to explode from the confines of my pants at the sight. Her perfect bellybutton teases my tongue, peeking from her bare midriff below the white strapless bustier, her deliciously perfect breasts cupped in its lace. If I didn't know better, I'd think I was drooling, possibly frothing at the mouth.

"Like what you see?" she asks, devilish desire oozing from her angel face, her lips parted with fucking, sexy need.

Oh you have no idea, I shake my head, staring down at her. *Mine*.

"Yours," she whispers in response to my unspoken decree, as I bend to lift her in my arms.

~

TURN THE PAGE FOR AN EXCITING AND SEXY SNEAK
PEEK OF C.J. WELLS' UPCOMING RELEASE

Coming Summer 2015

~

"**Y**OU'RE AN ASSHOLE! A *fucking* asshole, actually," she spits, and I roll my eyes; I've heard it all before. "There's not even a word to accurately describe you…you're a…a…DICK!"

Sighing, I finish fastening my jeans and grab my shirt from the floor. "That's mighty feisty attitude coming from a chick that just *sucked* my dick." Flashing her a wink with my notorious smirk, I pull my T-shirt over my head, noting her open-mouthed gape as I make my way towards the door.

"Lose my number, asshole," she slurs.

Turning to her from the open doorway, I offer a final pull of my lips before filling her in, "Sweetheart, I didn't bother to note it." I just manage to close the door before the item she threw towards me smashes against the other side. From the sound of the breaking glass, I assume it was a picture frame? Maybe a lamp? Who knows?

Why women feel the need to throw things is beyond me. It's fucked up. So, you're pissed. Is fucking breaking something going to make you feel better? Maybe rethink the decision to throw yourself at the guy before turning on him for taking what you were offering. Or, maybe add your disclaimer before you wrap your lips around my cock - you know, the one that tells me you want more; the one that will tip me off to keep walking before I dip my dick in your happily-ever-after-wanting pussy.

And then they call *me* an asshole. Is it my fault if a woman approaches me at a bar? And just to be clear, by *approaches*, I'm referring to obvious 'I want your dick in my mouth' innuendos. Not assumed. *Obvious*. I never act on assumption. That *would* make me an asshole. Right? Wrong. I'm an asshole anyway, for excusing myself once I opt out of the non-disclosed figurative leash they try to collar me with afterwards.

I don't do happily-ever-after. It's bullshit. *Fucking* bullshit. I learned that lesson a long time ago. Four years ago, to be exact. When *she* left. She taught me that *that* bullshit doesn't exist. Maybe I should thank her for that. Maybe I could…if her last words weren't so fucking torturing…"*You're my always, baby, always mine.*" Maybe I could…if I could even fucking find her.

Maybe one day I'll stop looking.

ACKNOWLEDGEMENTS

We have so many wonderful people to thank…family, friends - new and old, many met along this amazing journey. Much love!

To our WONDERFUL readers, thank you for embracing The Perfect Plans Series! Thank you for picking up that book, and giving us newbies a chance. Thank you for taking the time to leave a review, for spreading the word, and for stopping by with your loving words of praise and encouragement. Without you, our stories would not be heard.

To the INCREDIBLE Book Bloggers, thank you, thank you, thank you! What you do for Indie Authors is so greatly appreciated. You give your time tirelessly, to promote, encourage, and support. #BloggersRock

Thank you to our Beta readers. Without you, our books would have been *sooooo* close, but no cigar ;) You helped keep the cherry on top. Your honesty and time is so much appreciated. #Gratitude

To our AMAZING Author friends, you 'get' us, and we love you for that. Being a part of such a wonderful support system is incredibly rewarding. #AuthorsSupportingAuthors

Team Uni…what can we say? Thank goodness for rainbows, unicorns, and pixie farts. We love you dearly. #TeamUni

To our Editor, C.P., thank you for giving Alex head, and for setting ours straight.

To our loving husbands, there are not enough words to convey our love and gratitude. Thank you for your constant encouragement, your endless patience, and your understanding. Thank you for your cuddles when we would crawl into bed late at night. We love you.

To our family/children, you are loved more than you could ever know. To quote Alexander Tate, "Trust me when I say, the few hours I get to spend with you are worth a thousand hours I spend without you."

ABOUT THE AUTHORS

Co-Authors, and sisters, **Christa Gibbs and Jill Syed** reside in London, Ontario, Canada. Born and raised on da'Rock [a.k.a. St. John's, Newfoundland], their laid-back personalities and eclectic sense of humor is indicative of their native roots. Although fluent in Newfinese, both are quite eloquently spoken, showing no remnants of an accent unless alcohol is involved.

Fluent in air-guitar [she trained in Europe], Christa, by day, transforms into her Executive role in the Property Management World. This wonderful position lends credence to her altruistic life experiences lived vicariously through the many residents within her keep. This translates beautifully to her evening endeavors, which include creating lovable characters and interesting storylines [when she's not catering to her loving 'Oooge' - a.k.a. biker hubby]. An avid reader of erotic romance [upwards of two to three novels per week], Christa decided to give her own incessant fairytale sex-capade fantasies a voice.

When she is not behind the camera in her Photography Studio, Jill spends portions of her days mentally cataloging all the reasons why she shouldn't become an indulgent drinker at the helm of her three young children during the absences of her Pilot husband [though you will hear her undying love and devotion for them often: "blessed"]. Passionately creative, Jill spent many years capturing life moments on film, canvas and even paper. Having dabbled in the writing of many children's books, all of which ended up covered in dust and never carried through, clarity hit once she collaborated with her sister: "Ohhh, the steamy sex was the missing ingredient."